AF243883

Loading The Stone

LOADING THE STONE

Harley Elliott

WOODLEY MEMORIAL PRESS

Acknowledgements

My deepest gratitude to Duane F. Johnson, who started this journey of conjecture by introducing me to flint, and to Steven Hind, who shared his understanding of the Flint Hills.

Too many people to call by name encouraged and enriched my fascination with flint and the people who used it; to these farmers, artists, scientists, companions in walking and conversation, thank you.

Thanks to Denise Low, who moved this forward, and Bill Sheldon, who gave it form.

Thanks to the editors of the following publications, in which some of this work first appeared: *Hanging Loose, Indian Artifact Magazine, The Land Report, New: American & Canadian Poetry, New Letters, Northeast, The Pegasus Review.*

The passage on the part-title 3 page is from *The Rock Book*, Carrol Lane Fenton and Mildred Adams Fenton, Dover Publications, Inc., Mineola, NY, 2002. Used with permission of Dover Publications, Inc.

Black and white cover photograph by Terry Evans.

Arrowpoints courtesy of the following:

Cover and Title page—Fungus the Dolly Site
Part-title 1 page—Rocking Deer Site
Part-title 2 page—Bluff Site
Part-title 3 page—Hummingbird Site

Published by Woodley Press
Washburn University
Topeka, Kansas 66621

Printed in the United States of America

First Edition

ISBN 0-939391-40-6

for
Darío and Elaine

Contents

3.

1

The land shall not be sold in perpetuity
for the land is mine; for you are strangers
and sojourners with me.

The Lord
Lev. 25:23

"Long, long ago, on a dark misty
prairie, there was a puddle of water
with two tiny creatures in it. And those
creatures grew. And they grew and did
things, and made things and ate an
apple. Pretty soon there was different
kinds of blood and they made things
and had wars, and made things out of
flint and that's the main thing I'm
talking about, stupid."

> --Young Walker's Version
>   (hacking a chunk of flint by campfire light)

The Story of Humans and Flint
Through the Names of the People

No Stone
Stone
Flint
Jasper
Red Stone
Crystal Stone
White Rock
Green Stone
Black Rock
Yellow Rock
Grey Streak of the Rock
Mountain of Rocks
Round Stone
Hard Stone
Stone Man
In the Rocks
Rocky Boy
Stone Forehead
Stone Teeth
Rock in the Mouth
Stone Eater
Stone Necklace
Walking Stone
Sitting Stone
Turning Stone
Split Rocks
Little Rock
Sharp Stone
Brave Rock
Image Stone
Medicine Rock
Drinks the Juice of the Stone
Yellow Stone Knife
Standing Stone
Arrow Point
Point Maker
Point that Remains Forever

Mind of Walking

The Bluff was where walking seduced him. Towering sheer above the river, it was for many generations a village of farmers, hunters, and potters; in Walker's youth it was a field prepared for spring wheat. Plowed, rained on, it revealed the splinters of its past: shards of pottery, bits of deer and bison bone, shell, charcoal, countless chips, flakes and cores of flint, most of it blue-gray flint from the ocean of canyons two days' hard walk to the east. Among the debris turned up by the plow, exposed by the rain, were flint tools lost, broken, discarded, ruined in the making, forgotten roughly eight hundred years before Walker first set foot to the remains of the village.

The first few times the old man had taken him along, Walker's boyish impatience had kept his pockets empty, while Old Man Walker had customarily found two or three flint hide scrapers, a small arrowpoint or two. On the second trip, Walker had found the broken base of a notched arrowpoint and had complained in the car heading back to town; Old Man Walker had found a whole point, pinkish-gray flint, carefully worked.

"Well, son," Old Man Walker had said, "I could give you this point"—tapping the pocket of his jacket—"but..."

Two miles passed. They went over the place the boy liked, where yellow-gray dirt road turned abruptly to red-brown dirt road. He remembered Old Man Walker's explanation.

"Iron."

He looked at the palm of his hand where the base of the arrowpoint lay mottled gray, thin, delicately notched and broken diagonally across the blade. Momentarily he hated the clumsy maker or hunter who had broken this, Walker's intended first perfect arrowhead. Sure, sure, having one given to him wouldn't be the same. He wouldn't have the thrill of finding it himself. He was eleven. He knew all that, but when was it going to happen?

They pulled onto the highway. Still looking idly at the fragment in his hand, Walker saw that the surface of the fracture was much shinier than the rest of the stone. It had not been exposed as long as the remaining original surface; the point had been broken relatively recently. Walker shifted his anger from the hunter to the driver of the tractor. There it was: automatic civilization, steel plow dispassionately breaking ancient stone tools in the path of a cold imposed order. He was irritated that chance had run this fine arrowpoint athwart a plow and then allowed him to find half of it. He was irritated that, as usual, Old Man Walker had found a whole arrowpoint. He was irritated at being irritated. He was pissed at history. He was eleven and he was, he would realize years later, full of crap. It would probably take him thirty or forty years just to find a shovel. Learning something from the fragment he'd found had been small comfort; despite Old Man Walker's suggestion that every piece of flint there told something, Walker lusted to find that first whole arrowpoint. *Then* the search could begin.

He rationalized his lust: if he were searching for liniment bottles or can openers, he'd hope to find whole ones. It was natural. His impatience, had he known it, could have been blamed on the classical Greeks, who had started the whole system of beliefs he'd been born into. He thought this way in spite of the fact that he'd already read the words of Sitting Bull trying to explain the property consciousness of the whites to his own people—"the love of things is like a disease with them"—and felt something vital there he didn't understand. But he suspected the irony of his impatience, which made him even more miserable.

He remembered Old Man Walker calling him across the field. As he walked over, Walker searched the ground near the old man's boots. There it lay, perfect and whole, and Walker began to reach down.

"Whoa," said the old man softly. He bent and lifted the point.

"Believe me, when you find one, you're going to want to be the one to pick it up." And so Old Man Walker had found a whole arrowhead and Walker had slumped in the car driving back, sunk in a graceless silence.

It took another three weeks of walking and grumbling on Walker's part before his path intersected with a complete arrowhead. Ecstatic rush, seeing it there suddenly, reaching down and picking it up, an arrowpoint the size of his smallest fingernail in banded dark and light gray flint. Then he saw the shallow tentative chipping around the edges, the barely indicated side notches; what he had found was a triangular flake rudely chipped into a gawky travesty of an aerodynamic stone point. His world was ashes. For an instant, he considered dropping it, pushing it into the dirt with his finger and starting over. There was some mistake, this junky piece of crap could not be the first whole arrowhead of his entire life.

"I mean, come on," he said to the field, the relentless sun. He had walked, he had sweated.

When he and Old Man Walker converged in the field, he held out the point with a weary sarcasm.

"Found this."

The old man glanced at the point and then at the sullen face. It was necessary for him to remind himself that the boy was eleven. Old Man Walker could have said:

"Son, take a guy about like you, squatting here in the heat, bothered by mosquitoes and peter gnats, trying to make an arrowhead, and he knows how to chip flakes off an edge by striking it, and he knows how to flake by holding an edge against a hard surface and twisting it, but he doesn't know fine flaking, putting pressure on an exact spot on the edge and coaxing a long paper-thin flake to pop free from the surface, from edge to edge, and again all down the length of the point on both sides until none of the original flake surface remains and the stone is truly sculpted for flight. Nope, can't do it. He can only do what you have in your hand and he's probably bent about it. How long do you think the emptiness in his belly will allow him to sulk before he sets himself to learn the finer technique? To eat, to kill the animal, to make the arrow fly, to make the arrow, to make the stone point of the arrow—all this has to wait until he works through his impatience, frustration, importance. Now, your task is different—you're learning to walk and look, and with no worry about a meal at the end of the day. Let's hope that guy shoveled his load aside, blah, blah, blah...." Sermon in the Field. But the old man restrained himself since, as he well knew, he too was full of crap.

"Well, I haven't found a damn thing," said Old Man Walker instead.

It was a full month before Walker found another complete point, so he had many evenings to open the cigar box where he kept the few fragments of tools he'd found, and slide open the matchbox there and come to know the little crude gray-banded point. He had noted the slight curve in the flake: it would never fly true. Maybe the maker had chosen the flake for its pattern of warm gray bands, but beauty had failed to overcome the impractical shape, the clumsy sculpting.

There were other thunderstorms to wash flint to the surface and they went many times again to the Bluff and its old footprints, softened and flattened by rain. Walker found his second arrowpoint, his third and fourth, as well as three carefully made thumb-sized flint hide scrapers, before snow and cold shut them out of the field. The other points he'd found had been made with more care than the first one, but the old man had been right: there was an attachment to the first. He had struggled along with the eight-hundred year old ghost who had made it.

He was eleven. He could not talk knowledgeably about cars. He did not play team sports. He did not know how to bring himself to the attention of girls, though his body and imagination continually reminded him it would be a good thing to do. He could hold a stone and throw his mind backward. He could walk, meandering feet, stalking eyes, for the pleasure of the walk itself, the charge of discovery, rush of sharing mind with the past. Now that he had found a few whole implements, he had quit hurrying to see. Wherever he was in his life, whatever turns his way took, he would continue to walk.

In the flush times he walked to enjoy his harmony, in down times to drain the thought and self-pity out through his shoes. He had accepted that he was full of crap. He *had* found a shovel once, lost it, found another, lost it, found a crutch posing as a shovel, lost it, kept looking. He walked through many old villages and camps, through a marriage, the birth of his children, a divorce, endless jobs, the loss of his old man, good friendships and bad, walking on the trail of people so forgotten they were part of the dust going up his nose.

The Bluff had given him that: walking was his best, most constant, shovel. He walked now with his own son who, since the age of six, had shared his interest in walking, seeing, finding, with considerably more maturity than Walker had at the age of eleven.

The Bluff had given more—old stories, a fingerprint fired in a piece of clay and, at least once, the work of an artist: Walker saw the fine tip of worked rosy gray flint sticking up out of the mud, grasped it and slowly drew forth a long, narrow point with two notches on each side of the base and one at the end. It had lain clasped in the ground for centuries. He held it up in the wind it was made for.

This high bluff towering over the river, where he could look down on the rustling cottonwoods on the other side, was his learning ground. Old Man Walker had taken him here so many times because it was clearly a favorite place for the old man, though he would never say why. But it was all history now, and Walker no longer went there. Most of the surface had been scraped together into a large flat-topped mound. It supported a long trailer house with a wooden deck and a gray pit bull. Where Walker had found the five-notched arrowpoint was now a cement-floored metal machine shed. The village becomes a modern homestead, the rest of the field going to weeds and farm scrap.

Things change, said the pit bull. I do the walking around here now.

Things change, says Walker, though often in a field he will still scan his eyes along a distant tree-line and think he sees the toes of the old man's boots pointing up in the shade where the old man lies calmed by the sound of the trees, drifting, where he was then and where he is now, beyond speculation.

Old Man Finds the Spot

Iron red country road
turns to yellow clay

right angles of wheat
and the dusty car closed up
our boots stop

on a bluff above the river.
Old Man finds the spot
where they first leaped
in to each other
and in the twisting

heart of the moment
two buffalo nickels slipped
away into the grass.

When he woke up the
sky smelled like her
and he breathed
in and out

turning to watch
this river come around
the bend at him again.

The Walking Circle

That part of the long prairie between the Rocky Mountains and the Mississippi river called Kansas had seen the comings and goings of many peoples. Walker lived near the center of the state at the junction of three rivers. His walking ground extended roughly fifty miles in any direction, though he favored the south and the peoples of the hunt and garden. The old man had led him to there and, farther southwest, the tattooed ones of Quivira.

Within and across the circle of his search, many had walked or ridden. The earliest ones Walker knew only through the names science had given their flint weapon points:

Clovis	c. 12,000 B.C.
Scottsbluff	c. 8,000 B.C.
Folsom	c. 8,000 B.C.
Eden	c. 5,000 B.C.

with the understanding that these dates would inevitably be revised backward in time.

Stone tools of these archaic bison hunters had been picked up on river gravel bars or in erosion gullies, but not by Walker.

The conjecture of overlap and influence between these peoples had kept the children of many scientists clothed and fed. The culture that followed, loosely designated as the Plains Woodland peoples, would support at least two more generations of conjecture. Walker knew of three campsites of these hunters and gatherers and had found some of their tools. Later, when gardening supplemented hunting, peoples settled along all three of the rivers in Walker's circle, taming plants, using storage pits, growing villages. In response to the situation came plains raiders. And more plains raiders, some with recognizable names—Sioux, Cheyenne, Arapaho, Kiowa. Finally, Europeans appeared and continued to appear. He later thought of this version of events as Walker's Pinhead View of History.

The few fields he walked and all he found there were a pinhead's worth of the whole story, yet they posed enough questions to keep him monitoring the late weather, trying to figure out which fields might get rained on that night. In winter, he looked at the things he'd found the past summer, then placed them with things found at the same place and looked at them again. He believed that, at one time or another, an artist had lived on each of these fields, regardless of degree of settlement or wandering, and across all bands of time.

The names of the artists, along with the names of the early peoples, were gone. *Amerind* had gone out of style as a way to speak of the early peoples and their descendants; *Native American* was currently the fashion. Walker continued to think of them as simply the early peoples. The all-encompassing "Indian" was popular, but it was a word he avoided. It called up the posturing equestrian, the feathered headdress, raw nobility.

Supposedly born of a misapprehension by Christopher Columbus, the word had no relationship to the people he encountered or the land they inhabited, or to the many generations preceding them, hunters of the big, antique bison and the mammoth. Nor did the word have any relationship to the generations to follow. It was a word that robbed identity, culture, and personality at once, too thin to cover the many varieties of humans it was assigned to describe. Walker grew up on the Hollywood version. It had taken him many years to uproot the word and its dumb tommyhawk reality. He knew it was too late, the word would not be retired, but he took comfort in one of the few authentic bits of wisdom television had given him:

> *A wise man knows the only true causes are the ones already lost;*
> *all others are just hype.*
>
> *--Dr. Johnny Fever*

Crawling into Enchantment

Walker didn't usually stray more than fifty miles from home base, but he spent a year crawling the foothills of the Sangre de Cristos in northern New Mexico. He had crawled the banks and dry stony bed of the Pecos River, the tops of mesas, canyon floors, hillsides crowded with boulders. Walking didn't work in that country; the land wasn't plowed. If a searcher wanted to see, it was necessary to go on hands and knees, with the eyes right down on the short, tough grass and mosaic of gravel.

The sky of New Mexico, the richest of blues, rang Walker's heart like a bell. The Kansas sky could be bright and beautifully blue, but never suffused, never pregnant with blue. It had a touch of white to its blueness. The same held true for flint. Kansas flint seemed generally to be a tint of a color, rather than a strong, pure color. Crawling at the feet of the Sangre de Cristos, Walker found bright flint—egg yolk yellow, dark red, orange, shiny mint green, purple, maroon, marbled milk white, translucent waxy quartzite, amber—both smoky and yellow—and the clear black volcanic glass called obsidian.

Excellence of material can inspire better work, but whether or not the rich variety of flint, jasper, chalcedony, chrysocolla, agate, quartzite, obsidian, and petrified wood had anything to do with it, the New Mexico flintworkers seemed to take more time or have finer skill at stone-flaking than the flintworkers of Kansas. That year in New Mexico had given Walker thirty-four arrowpoints and countless broken ones, and most of them were symmetrical and finely worked. The workers had belonged to a people that built small pueblos on river banks and foothills any time from around 1,000 A.D. to the first sight of a Spanish blade in the distance. Clunky attempts, either through resistance of stone or clumsiness of the maker, were much more prevalent among their contemporaries living in houses of wood, earth, and grass in what is now central Kansas, as were arrowpoints made to do the job but showing no particular attention to beauty of stone or symmetry of form and flaking.

Like all generalizations, this one had holes: the best flintworkers of Quivira, that multi-village population of growers and hunters in Kansas, were as good at what they did as their Pueblan counterparts, but the best flintworkers, in Quivira, were a minority. Among the Pueblans, they were the usual. More of them seemed, by the stones they left behind, to have taken the time or had the touch.

The question of why this seemed to be was one of the many that lived with Walker over the years, and one he'd discussed with his young son as they sat before the arrowpoints on the living room rug at least one summer night each year. To Young Walker, the answers could only be in the stones. Each of the arrowpoints was small enough to lie comfortably on his father's thumbnail, which made them smaller than the average size of the arrowpoints made by the Kansas workers of the same time.

In Young Walker's mind, on a hot, froggy August night, the question grows tentacles: is the smallness because of the stone, the arrowshaft, the bow, the hunter? Now he has something to think about over the years. The stones also tell him that flatness was either not valued or not achieved by the Pueblan flintworkers. The Quivira flintworkers labored after flatness in their arrowpoints, while those the Pueblans made didn't lie thin and flat between thumb and finger, but were slightly rounded, swollen. Young Walker thought of them as inhale points because they felt like they were holding their breath, and the thin Kansas points as exhale points. Again, discovery spawned questions. Were the Pueblan points slightly plump because the Pueblans thought it looked better, flew better, struck better, or was it a characteristic dictated by the stones?

There was no single moment in those years of summer nights when Walker and his son had made a strict decision, but the cumulative observation of their eyes and fingertips first led them to the feeling that it was the stones themselves, not human desire, that accounted for the plumpness. Many of the New Mexico stones were denser, finer grained—what the experts call cryptocrystalline—than the typical flints of Kansas.

"It's like the molecules of silica don't have as many molecules of air and water between them," Walker said.

"And the stuff we find around home here—it has a lot more air and water molecules?"

"There it is."

Young Walker thought of butter and whipped butter. Maybe the heavy density of the New Mexico stones didn't encourage thinning.

But another summer would come and they would remember pictures they'd seen of projectile points of much earlier people in New Mexico, the hunters of the giant bison and the elephant hunters before them, points made of the same dense stones and many of them flaked thin.

The issue of plumpness was revived. Did the Pueblans just like a little more body in their arrowpoints? Were the arrowshafts generally lighter, heavier, shorter, longer than those used in Kansas? And since the point of the arrow is in partnership with the base, did a heavier point express more feathers or less at the other end? If answers to these questions, and all the others, were all that mattered, they could have found them. For any subject they wondered about, a dissertation probably existed somewhere, but more and more of their time would have to be spent tracking literature instead of walking the fields and staring at the discovered stones.

Of far more interest to them was the conversation between landscape, searcher, and stone—and by extension, the hands and minds that had transformed the stone into a tool—so they seldom got around to scholarship. It was unprofessional and unscientific of them not to hit the paper trail more seriously, but since the greater pleasure was in the generation of questions, and since they had nothing to prove, they could afford to indulge their desires. It wasn't the lack of love of reading, at least not on Walker's part, that had kept them from pursuing the questions in libraries, but the presence of what Walker had come to recognize as tradition. He remembered sitting in his own boyhood on summer nights with his own father, as he and Old Man Walker handled and discussed the many stone tools his father had found and the few he himself had begun to gather. Walker hadn't understood, until his own adulthood, the importance of those summer nights.

Because his parents were divorced, Walker had seen the old man only during the summers, and—he knew it later—the stones had been a bridge between them. Because his relationship with his own father had only been seasonal, Walker had sworn he would not make the same mistake when it came his time to marry and have children, yet in spite of all his intentions, he had taken the same turn. Divorced, living alone, he looked forward to his son's visit every summer, knowing that as the fat little boy turned into a young man, the visits would shorten and finally end. So the moments of sitting on the fake oriental rug with his son, sipping iced cola and musing over stones while the frogs and insects sang, brought him a pleasure beyond the moments themselves.

Sometimes their summer night speculation seemed to arrive at a kind of sense. Along with the thirty-four New Mexico arrowpoints, Walker had found nine flint tools made for scraping fat from hides. All of them were crudely made. In Kansas they were more plentiful; for every arrowpoint he found, Walker would find five or six hide scrapers, many of them beautifully made. Why should the flintworkers in Kansas make so many more hide scrapers, and make them consistently better, than the Pueblan flintworkers? Father and son decided that because of the proximity of the great bison herds, the villagers of Kansas were more hunters than farmers, and for the Pueblans, the reverse was true.

It would be expected, then, that manos—stones for grinding corn and other seeds—would be much more plentiful in the Pueblan lands than in the remains of the river villages of Kansas, and so they were. In a year of crawling on New Mexico, Walker had found numerous manos, though he would find one in Kansas only occasionally. The stones had indicated that one culture knew corn as the bringer of life, while for the other culture, life grew from the buffalo.

Yet if the stones of New Mexico in themselves would do much to generate wonder and reveal possible answers, Walker had more. He had the memories of finding them, the landscape, the other objects lying on the same piece of ground, and these circumstances he would share with his son because the boy had not been there to crawl with him. Weaving a context around each of the Pueblan arrowpoints was a pleasure to Young Walker for the information he got from it, and a pleasure to Walker because he got an excuse to return to the moment. When Young Walker was a little boy, these moments were among his bedtime stories.

The little khaki-brown, notched arrowpoint with the serrations running down one side like the blade of a saw, expanded to include the banks of a wide, dry riverbed near Tecolote, the anthills where, along with millions of bits of flint and gravel, ants had carried bone beads, the scattering on both banks and in the dry river bed itself, of pottery shards painted with black lines, and two Mexican cowboys with chaps, scabbard rifles and ropes, who appeared on horseback one warm afternoon, threading through the mesquite, and sat without comment, wrists crossed on saddlehorns, to watch Walker crawling in the sun, and then still without speaking turned away to disappear again.

"Was that the day you found this point?"

"No, that was another day. I was all alone." One look at the point and he recalled walking away from the Little Owl site, knees weary with crawling, and passing a heap of dirt thrown up by a potholer. From where he stood to Tierra Del Fuego, old settlements were pocked with the holes of people who dug for commerce. It had rained since the potholer had been there and the mound of dirt had been washed smooth; bits of charred bone and flint stuck out of its surface. The point with one serrated edge had been lying right on top of the pile of discarded dirt and when Walker picked it up, its print remained.

"And the green one?"

"Oh, I found that arrowhead because of a carload of drunks." There he was, back in Dr. Whatsisname's living room, because the vacationing professor had turned his rural house over to a group of students for Thanksgiving, and Walker was one of them. They had made a big meal and eaten it. To walk off his turkey, Walker had taken a stroll, and Mary Jane had come with him. Down the dirt road they met a man and his young son coming toward them. The man jerked his head down the way he'd come.

"There are a number of young men around the curve, sitting on a car, extremely drunk," he said in a precise and almost accusatory tone. Walker recognized him as a professor of something. His gaze seemed to say that Walker, a callow student of art, would be tempting fate to continue down the road. Walker silently agreed. Even had he been alone, Walker would have agreed, but in the company of a young woman—and a woman who was, he remembered, half Pueblo—beside his pink, turkey-fed self, well...

"Was she your girlfriend, Dad?"

"No, son, this was the 'Sixties,' so we were all into brother and sister-hood and all that stuff." That was another, much longer story. "We were just friends out for a walk, with a carload of drunks around the bend." Young Walker accepted this with a small twist of his lips. Clearly he would have preferred a chivalrous roadside battle.

On the west side of the road was a weedy field, a small creek backed with a rocky bluff. Walker gestured in that direction, and Mary Jane, who was a student of physics and had probably already arrived at the same con-clusion, nodded. They cut through the weeds, across the thread of a creek, and up the modest bluff. From where they finally sat on the top, they could hear but not see the car covered with drunks. Both recognized the language as *Dineh*, the name Navajo called themselves. Mary Jane took a nap in the sun and Walker began to crawl. He hadn't crawled far before he found a chip of dark red jasper, the kind of thin chip that is struck free in the flintworking process. By the time they were ready to go back and punish more turkey, Walker had a handful of such chips and knew the bluff had been the site of a small settlement.

"The point, Dad, the point."

"Oh, that green one? I found it there later that fall." The creek over-hang, which he called the Jasper site, was the place he'd crawled most fre-quently, since it was only a couple of miles from town, and he could walk there, crawl, and walk back in one afternoon.

"It's a stone called chrysocolla. If you touch it to the tip of your tongue, when you pull it away, it'll act like it wants to stick. That's how you know it's chrysocolla."

Young Walker tested it, as well as three other points not made of chrysocolla.

"Cool."

Many artists had lived on the Jasper site—the maker of the seafoam green point, the maker of an obsidian point with a base in the form of a rounded cross, the maker of an elegant beer-colored point of clear chalce-dony, tiny notches near the end of the base, the maker of a glossy black tri-angle that seemed to swell with energy.

"Son, do you think one guy made all these different shapes, or did each hunter make his own?"

"Well, Dad, if you were King of the Flintworkers, why would every-body like *your* points so much?"

"Uh...because they worked?"

"Right. Well, to work the same, wouldn't they have to *be* the same?"

Well, yes, thought Walker. I would figure out which shape worked best aerodynamically, and that would be the shape I would go with. In which case, all the points I made would have my individual style, the same form.

"Unless..."

"Unless what?"

"Unless the King of the Flintworkers doesn't get to decide what the points look like. What if the differences in hunters and their bows, shafts, feathers, and the way they used them—what if these differences were so great that one guy would say he wanted the flintworker to make him short, broad ones, like the green point..."

"And another guy wants two dozen long with little notches high up. So the flintworker would have to be able to..."

"Make them all. Yeah."

"He'd have to be good."

"He'd have to be really good."

This artist they had created carried them off into silence. To Walker, the artist as squarehead, perceiving the Ideal arrowpoint and manufacturing it without variation, was not very appealing. That Ideal form would have been arrived at because it worked for most hunters most times. Hunters outside that category would have to adjust their tools and methods to the majority mode of hunting in order to take advantage of the Ideal arrowpoint. He thought the other kind of artist would have more fun, making various forms to suit the needs of various customers.

Another summer night, another year, they might decide the idea of a specialized flintworker was absurd. What if he fell and broke his hands? No, every hunter had to know how to make his own arrowpoints. It would be a part of learning to be a hunter. Some would be better at it than others, maybe good enough to gain a reputation and make points for others in exchange for food, skins, firewood, or services. Division of labor would be good for a small group, but specialization would not.

That each hunter was responsible for his own flint work seemed to be borne out by the only quarry Walker found in New Mexico, a slope capped with a mantle of variegated jasper, purple marbled with white, oxblood mixed with golden yellow. The ledge had been attacked along its length, by many hands over many years, the slope below covered with the shattered leavings. Groups of people had been knocking chunks of jasper from the ledge for generations.

On the south slope of the hill was a thick tumble of boulders where people had pecked images—serpents, turtles, spirals, hands—and down on the flats among petrified logs, the bits of pottery and flint chips showed where the camp had been. The gathering of this attractive jasper seemed to have been a communal affair. At least one artist had been in the crowd. Walker had found a small arrowpoint in the dust, with wide rounded notches running all the way down both sides. The stone was a clean, white sugar quartz, and the design was beyond function. The curved notches did nothing for the arrowpoint in practical terms, but they were the perfect form if someone wanted to make a flint piece look like rattlesnake rattles. Walker held rattlesnakes in intimate regard—he'd had many encounters with them—but even if that hadn't been the case, he would have picked up this stone rattlesnake charm. Not even sure he knew what it was, he knew it had been his day to find it, and left tobacco in its place.

"Dad?"

"Yeah, Son?"

"What happened to the drunks?"

"Oh, the drunks. Well, I expect some of them are dead by now..."

"Very funny, Dad. You know what I mean."

"I don't remember—can you believe it? Maybe they were gone by the time Mary Jane and I came down the bluff, or else we just avoided them. All I really cared about was this place we'd stumbled on. We went back, ate, somebody found some old Marlene Deitrich albums, the sun was going down—great Thanksgiving."

"Dad, did you ever think like all these arrowpoints were laying there that first time, and you didn't see them?"

"Oh sure, and the ones I never did see, that're laying there still unless the place is patios and swimming pools. But I did go back to that place a lot. I logged about fifty miles of crawling before it was all over."

He had seen New Mexico mostly from the viewpoint of his hands and knees, but even there, crawling below the mountains like a very slow dog, he knew the notion of enchantment was not just something the state's boosters had created in a vacuum. Starting with the pungent blue that breathed warm on the back of his neck, New Mexico was always a moment ripe for magic.

If Walker ever doubted that magic was a reason for artistry, he only had to look at the arrowpoints he'd found in New Mexico. The land itself was magic, catching his eye, luring him to the top of a small mesa where, hours later, pockets full of shark teeth, he stood at the edge of the mesa giving his knees a break. He could see a highway, small glinting cars, a distant man-made lake and the white scratches made by boats, the quick, tumbling rise of mountains, and he could see on the rim of the mesa, two strides away, a purple crocus. What leaped into Walker's eye was a bright, coral orange bit of stone standing up against the green stem of the crocus. It stood on its base, notched deeply, slender neck, long curving barbs, sides rushing inward and up to a delicate point. These conspiracies of circumstance, flashes of luck in the crawling chaos, were among the times he had to just throw his arms up and shout thanks at the moment.

When he wasn't crawling into enchantment, Walker was studying art and attempting to make some. How fine it would have been then if he had made the necessary connection and painted what he saw before him, wiry grass and colorful chips of stone, but he had been slow to see, so looking for finely crafted flint tools was in one drawer of his mind, and the process of making art was in another. That was back when Walker still mistakenly thought his mind had drawers and before he had a son to refresh his tired ways.

Atlatl People

Old Man Walker had been crawling in a soybean field at high noon. The rows of tall bean plants formed canopied tunnels he could crawl down on his elbows and knees, picking flint from the ground around the beanstalks, ignoring the itch of bean leaves and the sweat creeping into his eyes. He had the search fever bad, bad enough that he had badgered his friends into driving him out to a site and dumping him. If he had to crawl through bean plant tunnels to search, that would be fine.

He had been crawling those dim, hot tunnels, back and forth across the field, when he saw the thing through the bean stalks, two rows over and slightly ahead—an alien, featureless black pile that gave the impression of being alive. An ancestral chimp leaped up in his mind and told him it was death, his, though his civilized mind hurried to find reasons why that could not be. The hairs on his arms stood out and he froze, to keep from springing straight up through the canopy of leaves.

He'd begun to crawl slowly backward when a head rose from the black mound and turned in his direction. The malevolent, black specter became a coonhound, hiding from the sun. Still frightened, he'd backed out and abandoned the field. Good boy, he said, good boy, good boy.

This story, and others like it, had been Walker's bedtime stories when he was young, though the old man saved until later the stories of how he and his friends, men and women, had gone swimming naked in the Chariton River and spooked a couple of fishing farmers, who threw their gear into the back of a pickup and roared away when they spotted the band of naked people wading down the shallow river. Old Man Walker did a good imitation of a man sitting on an upturned bucket, jaw hanging open, speechless.

Walker's search away from home had concentrated on New Mexico; the old man's away place had been northern Missouri, where friends who shared his interest lived.

Walker had never bothered to count the points, scrapers, and other objects his father had found on those long-ago visits to Missouri, and the pieces themselves were now in parts unknown, but he remembered most of them. The flints had been grainier, more porous than those used by the peoples in Walker's Kansas circle, and where the colors of the flints of New Mexico were deep and rich, and the colors of the Kansas flints all seemed to have a touch of white in the mixture, the flints of Missouri were whiter still, so much so that it was natural to think of them as variations of white—yellowish white, grayish white, pinkish white. When the old man laid out his Missouri pieces, the objects that were less white stood out.

Walker, after he'd grown, had identified from memory an orange, gray, and nougat-yellow flint with a bulls-eye pattern of bands as Flint Ridge material from Ohio. The brown flints used in Kansas didn't show up in the old man's Missouri finds. There had been two pieces of black flint with threads of pale blue, and Walker was still on the alert for their source. The old man had found no obsidian, no petrified wood or colorful jasper. He had found plentiful use of a hard, heavy stone called hematite, "bloodlike stone," because it could be found in all the nuances of color between red and black. Its heaviness and color came from iron. The old peoples of northern Missouri had scraped it for red dust to make paint, had ground it into shapes and perforated it for ornamentation and chipped it like flint to make things like the round, maroon hematite gouge Old Man Walker lifted from the ground. Not especially beautiful, it had still been favored by its user with a long working life. Looked at edge-on, it swelled in the center, tapering to a bit on the business end, and there the hematite was worn smooth and shiny, polished from a lifetime of chopping earth, or wood, or meat. At the opposite end, it was thinned by a channel down the middle, suggesting that it was probably hafted. The old man had thought it was the business part of a hoe, lashed to wood, chopping the hard earth. Walker, remembering over the years how it looked and felt in his hand, was inclined to see it as a woodworking tool with a stout, curved antler handle.

On the nights Old Man Walker had laid out the Missouri tools, Walker had always reached first for the hematite gouge. Hand-friendly, it was to most of the other stones as dog is to wolf. It had served humans and been cared for by humans. Others of the tools and weapons showed little of their lives as tools, never gave up their strong identity as stone, but the worn hematite gouge made it clear at first glance: it had been there.

"Yeah, I remember that piece," the old man had said, "the Knoll site, above a creek, Silver Creek. This little number was down near the bottom of the field. Another five years and it woulda been in the creek. I remember that day because when we got back, we boiled up a mess of shrimp and beer at the farm and played volleyball naked till dark."

Walker doubted that part of the story but managed not to challenge it. The old man naked and larking in the river, possibly, but the old man naked and playing volleyball, never. It was hard to imagine him playing any kind of sport, even with his clothes on. Walker would appraise his father while pretending to look at a dart point made a thousand years ago. The beard, the absent-minded scowl, the old, sprung eyeglasses sliding down his nose—the old man was a complete stranger to glamour, and the boy could imagine no one but the glamorous getting a buzz on and playing naked volleyball. Well-trained by Hollywood, he assumed the natural conclusion to such a scene would be a group lovefest in the dusty grass, and it was even more difficult to shoehorn his old man into that scene. Walking the fields, hunched and squinting at the wind, the old man belonged, but he was just not good orgy material.

As he grew older and microscopically wiser, Walker wondered how many things the old man had not told him. Maybe the old man had been an orgymaster of the first water. Maybe the old man had visited his Missouri friends in the company of leggy redheads, smoldering brunettes. No, the only visions of the old man in Missouri that made sense were him walking the dirt between rows of young beans, corn, and tobacco. The old man's only passions that Walker could be sure of were the stone tools and the process of finding them. They were the passions he'd passed on to his son, but Walker had shifted them in another direction. The old man's regard had been for the objects themselves. He recognized degrees of quality, calling this point a beauty and that one so-so, but the quality or lack of it were attributes of the objects, not the thoughts and desires that had formed them. Walker did love the objects, but his attention had roamed through them to the makers.

The single most memorable aspect of the Missouri tools had been their largeness. "You're gonna have to change your eyes," Old Man Walker's friends had told him on his first visit. "They didn't make little points and thumb scrapers here." So, of course, at the first field they'd taken him to, he'd found a small, pinkish-white arrowpoint. The old man had said it was just Missouri's way of easing him in; from that moment on, all the points he found in Missouri were large, longer than a man's thumb and broad in the blade. Studying those giant points laid out on a towel on the old man's living room table, Walker's boy mind had gone from imagining what size sticks would have to be used to support those arrowheads, and then an enormous bow to shoot them with enough force and, it followed, great big people to pull those bows. Something told him it couldn't be—if there'd been Goliaths on the land, wouldn't somebody have mentioned it in school? He'd dithered it for a while until curiosity overwhelmed his fear of being stupid.

"Were they giants?"

The old man had caught the drift right away. To his credit, he smiled but didn't laugh.

"Well, you'd think so from the size of these things." He'd gone on to introduce Walker to the atlatl and in doing so, let slip one of his secret dreams.

"These big points"—he picked one up between thumb and forefinger—"went on a pretty good sized stick, as I understand it, really a kind of short spear. But an arm can only throw one of those so far and so hard. How about handing me that walking stick."

Holding the stick by one end, he cocked his arm until his hand was even with his ear, the stick pointing straight behind him.

"This is too long, really, but you get the idea. You got a groove." He indicated an invisible groove along the top length of the stick. "The spear, well, I've heard it called a dart, too, or a javelin, take your pick, lays in that groove. Your stick's got a hook at the far end that the butt of the spear rests against. You've got it like this, the spear is pointing forward, resting on your knuckles, so when you throw"—which he did in slow motion—"this spear flinger gives your arm extra length, and you can really whip some torque on that throw."

Walker had been staggered by news of this innovation, it seemed so outlandishly right. He wanted to spend some time thinking about how they thought of making this thing, but the old man dismissed the spear thrower, man and tool, as a prelude. "They call them atlatls, but here's the good part—if you tied a stone near the end of the thrower, or drilled a hole in the stone so that it could be fitted right on the end of the thrower, you'd get a lot more weight, punch, on the throw. Now these atlatl weights, they ended up being called bannerstones..." And the old man had gone from the why of the stone to a rapturous listing of what the stones were: granite, slate, quartz, in many colors, solid, speckled, splotched, banded, or swirled. Shaped by pecking and grinding with stone, grit, sand, a tedious sculpting of form around a drilled hole, "about dime-size, little smaller."

The old man had picked up a deck of cards and held it in his palm. "Our stone would be about this big, we'd have the hole drilled here"—he indicated the center point along the side of the deck. "Drill a hole right through, out the other side. Get this, using a hollow, woody stalk, dip the end in wet grit and rotate it against the stone. Eventually you make a circular groove. Keep going. It gets deeper, until you go all the way through. Now, we could slide it on the throwing stick"—he made as if to poke his finger through the long side of the deck—"and it would work, but maybe it'd be too heavy because they almost always took off more stone. See, you got a central axis, here, the hole, and the stone on either side of the hole, they call those the wings. You're gonna grind those wings down on all four sides"—he touched the top of the deck and the bottom—"so that the wings taper toward the edge. Some of them would go further, so you got the hole, a ring of stone around it, and on both sides of the circle a real thin, flat wing. If you were looking into the hole, it could look like this"—he picked up a pencil and drew the symbol for an eye on the tabletop–"or..." He drew a circle with a single line radiating out from midpoint on either side.

"All that work."

"Yeah, and that's not all. These wings, some of them would just be left rectangular, but they'd make some of them flare toward the bit like the blades of old-fashioned battle-axes, some them even made the wings circular."

"Man."

"Oh yeah. In fact..." the old man went to a stack of books and came back with a slim, oversize paperback. "I could've saved a lot of wind, there's all kinds of varieties right here. Oh, man," he said with sudden fervor, "I *really* want to find one." Walker caught the longing in his old man's voice.

"Will you?"

"Could be, could be." The old man went to his bedroom and came back with a King Edward cigar box filled with broken objects from Missouri. He stirred his finger through the flint pieces, making them clink together, and drew out a small, smooth, flat piece of salt-and-pepper granite, handing it to his son.

"This here's a piece of one, a piece out of a wing. That's all I've got so far. Now, one of my buddies in Missouri"—he couldn't keep a faint tremor of envy out of his voice—"he found one."

"Oh wow, were you there?"

"No, but I've seen it. It's kind of greeny black, rectangular, the wings taper away from the hole, about like this"—he tapped the symbolic eye drawing he'd made earlier. "They were walking a real muddy site, and he picked up this stone all covered with mud. It's no big deal to find a lot of different kinds of rocks in the fields there, it's not like here. He figured it was just a rock and was about to drop it when his thumb felt the depression of the hole through the mud. Man, I know he about crapped. There it was, a damn bannerstone. It's not gonna win any beauty contests, but it's a whole bannerstone. And along the edge of one wing, there's four or five shallow lines notched into it. He thinks it's a way of keeping score of something, maybe kills, or kills that were special somehow."

"Like kills with one shot."

"Like that." He took the fragment of bannerstone from his son's fingers and turned it over in his own. "This would've been, oh, I hate to even think about it."

"Can we go to Missouri?"

"Well, my friends moved down to Georgia—hell, I bet they'll find them down there—and they were the ones knew all the fields and all the owners. I guess we could still go, but we'd need more money and a damn sight better car than we've got now. But for now, I'm just gonna have to plan on finding one in Kansas. I think those atlatl users came this way once in a while, there's big points on the Rocking Deer, plenty other places around here we haven't found yet. Now I've never *heard* of one being found around here, but I've got this feeling. That's what I really want to find—a bannerstone, a really kickass bannerstone."

The discovery that his father lusted after some *thing* had been a bit of a surprise to the boy—he'd heard his father rail against materialism as the death of the human spirit more than once, usually in defense of whatever junker he happened to be driving at the time. He decided then if he ever found a bannerstone, he'd give it to the old man. Better yet, he'd pretend not to see it and let the old man find it. He was mildly pleased that the old man, just like everybody else, had the weakness of lust.

In years to come, whenever he'd thought of bannerstones, Walker would smile, automatically reminded of his father's desire to *have*. Learning about bannerstones, he began also to learn that his father was an ordinary human being, equally noble and weak. And it was bannerstones that first alerted him to the presence of magic in the lives of early peoples. That the old man could've talked so much about bannerstones without mentioning magic had puzzled the boy for two summers, until he figured out that Old Man Walker's interest was basically in the objects themselves—he searched for the beautiful ones without becoming obsessed about why they were that way.

Walker, looking through the bannerstone book that long-ago evening, had first been overwhelmed by the imaginative splendor of the objects. The names described the variety of wing shapes—butterfly, half-moon, bowtie—some, called bar bannerstones, had been drilled through the long axis. The fanciful symmetrical shapes had been complemented by choice of stones—flowing banded slates, splotched granite, translucent quartz with skeins and swirls of red trapped deep in the stone. All of them seemed to have been polished to a gleam, some to a glassy sheen.

His second overwhelming was the thought of the massive amount of time involved in turning a stone into a bannerstone, even if it had begun with a flat, oval stream cobble, a handy blank. If the bannerstone's job was to provide weight, why put all that time into the way it looked?

The old man had watched television through the weather report and then gone to bed.

"Good night, Son—hit the lights, eh?"

"Good night."

He'd studied the bannerstone book that night and learned that some people, in trying to understand what these strange things were, had theorized that they were emblems of rank, carried on poles in front of leaders, like a badge or banner of that person's authority—so the name *bannerstone*. Modern theory, the book continued, favored the idea that these things were atlatl weights.

Walker had gone to the wobbly bookcase and water-warped encyclopedias and learned the tongue-bucking word *atlatl* came from the Aztecs, and that the tool had been popular all over the Americas, with or without stone weights. Walker looked at the Missouri pieces again, the big dart points now part of a larger picture in his imagination. Almost all had lost a corner tip or a barb. This was the very reason they'd been cut free of the shaft and thrown aside—they could no longer be hafted properly—but

Walker wouldn't make the connection until he was a grown man. That night he was too stunned with the discovery of the atlatl and the artful, laborious stones designed to give it extra muscle. He remembered to turn out the lights and then paused, looking across the dark living room at the table, the white bath towel, the gray shapes of the dart points.

Decades later he could recall that moment clearly, when his mind had been at once full open and crawling to capacity with unborn question. Those dinged and battered dart points were now beyond his reach, the towel, the table, the dark room, the house had long since become a parking lot. He'd never found a bannerstone, and didn't expect to, and, as far as he knew, the old man never did either.

What Walker had found were words to fit the unknown questions of that distant moment, and he grew to look at the stone tools he found in more than one way—how they were now, how they were in the act of being made, how they were in the mind of the maker. The stories were sometimes hazy, but the stones could tell him of how they were meant to perform, where the hand of the maker had hesitated and why, the aerodynamic savvy of the hunter, and in the few instances where someone had worked his will in extraordinary ways upon hard matter, the persistence of magic.

A Tight Fit

Any area of any arrowpoint—tip, blade shoulders, barbs, notches, base—asked many questions and gave few answers, and as Walker's interest migrated from the hide scraper to the hand that held it, from the arrowpoint to the maker who intended its flight through space, each object became more and more a clue to matters beyond itself. One of the first aspects to grow in his thoughts from curiosity to obsession had been the appearance and nature of notches. He imagined a collective, inquiring mind that crossed lines of generation and tribal identity, telescoping invention and innovation that must have taken hundreds of years, addressing the question of how to wed two things, a stone and a stick, so successfully that they became an undeniable One, an arrow.

That imagined mind had been at work even before notching was perceived as an improvement. The very old hunters of elephant and big straighthorn bison, using points like narrow leaves, had already been in pursuit of that tight fit between projectile point and shaft. It had to have become clear that simply wedging a blade into a split in the end of a stick was not a successful union, no matter how extensively they were lashed together. The nature of a split is to continue, so the point, on impact, became a wedge driven deeper into the split.

The first innovation might have been not in the stone, but in the shaft, the engineering of a slot instead of a split, with a squared-away bottom to seat the base of the point against, a flat meeting place that wouldn't encourage splitting on impact. The narrow stone points were also given qualities to help the union. The maker had put his flaking tool to the base of the point and popped free a long flake of flint, leaving a wide, shallow channel down the face of the blade. Turned it over. Did the same to the other side. Sometimes the channels were short, sometimes they ran almost to the tip of the point. Some scholars had argued that these channels existed to promote blood flow from the wound, weakening the prey, shortening the chase, but Walker voted with those who saw a point that had been thinned for hafting. The elephant hunters had explored the channel strategy, but it had been the bison hunters who had seized on it and developed it as a form. And some bright hunters had developed the habit of grinding dull the edges of the point base so it would not easily cut the binding that helped hold it to the shaft.

From the tip, the edges of these kinds of points flared outward, turned, and continued straight back to the base; they were narrow and straight-sided. Walker always imagined it had been bad weather for hunting when a great mind, stuck in camp, went over his weapon inventory, idly contemplating how to correct a spear with a chronically loose head. This same mind, ranging through time, would also develop the foreshaft, a short piece of bone or antler with a square notch at one end to grasp the point, a deep socket at the other to hold the stick, a device that would unite stone and stick by coming between them, but this time the mind was listening to the sound of ugly weather and considering the X-pattern of lashings that held the stone to its shaft. If the sides of the point, instead of being straight, were to take a slight dip in the lashing area, to accommodate the binding, then the binding would gain tighter purchase on the stone from these valleys in the contour and, instead of being right out on the contour of the stone, they would sink in toward the axis, more protected from the friction and impact of the stone striking home. Such ideas came easily to this great mind Walker had dreamed. In similar moods, it had looked at the straight base of a projectile point and decided that the line of the base should be concave, creating two barbed points on the end of the base. Once inside the animal, these two backward-projecting spurs would help keep the point from working out of the wound; if it went anywhere, it would go forward.

Walker knew how much science loved a straight line. How clear and satisfying it would be if that collective spark of genius had made itself known every hundred years, surfacing each time in a hunter musing over a dysfunctional weapon. The straight-sided point would give way to the diagonal-sided point, each side dropping in a slant from the base, converging to a point, a fat triangle of stone that widened the area of contact, left a bigger wound. One hundred years later, the next creative genius would add a deep, narrow notch to each side of the base so that the point could be bound tighter. Another century, the flash of insight would reappear, and a notch would be added to the center of the base so that the point could be snugged more securely into the shaft slot. One hundred years later, another set of notches would be added to the sides, below the first set, for a more elaborate, tighter system of binding. These events would be evenly-spaced blips on the timeline, and any scientist looking at a point with two notches on each side and one in the base could say, "Yes, this is a recent point, the culmination of point technology, made no earlier than 1200 A.D."

But such thoughts were the dreams of the deluded. Nothing was that simple. Notching appeared in some cultures; others seemed to prefer the flat, unnotched triangle. Some points were notched at the sides of the point, some at the corners. Some cultures flaked the corners away entirely and left a tongue of flint standing out from the center of the base so they could haft the point in a socket instead of a slot. And these innovations appeared and disappeared all along the timeline at seemingly random points in both time and space. Homogenized, sequential invention was only the wishful thinking of a mind seeking order.

One night, as the air conditioner labored to falsify temperature, Walker's son had wondered about the history of notches, and Walker had run all the possibilities by him.

"So what did they use for string, Dad? Rawhide?"

"Yeah. I'll bet so."

"What's rawhide anyway? Leather?"

"Say it like two words."

"Oh. Yeah."

"And they could've used sinews, gut, twisted plant fiber, you know, the inner bark of trees, that stringy kind. And they had glue too. There were probably some plants they could make glue from."

"Like okra?"

"Well, kind of like that. And that resin that oozes out of evergreen trees, and they made it out of hooves, and buffalo wangers."

"What?"

"Buffalo wangers. They boiled them to make glue."

"Gah." The thought, clearly beyond his imagination, had got Young Walker by the vitals. "How'd they ever think of *that*? Is this a joke, Dad?"

"Hey, I wouldn't lie about a thing like that."

"Dad, that's gross, but when they went to making those triangle-shaped arrowheads? They might make a bigger wound, but they wouldn't go in as deep as narrow straight ones, would they? Wouldn't they, like, get hung up in the ribs more?"

"Well, yeah...yeah..."

"And maybe those points in the foreshafts? Maybe they weren't tied at all. Maybe they were just wedged into the slot and the foreshaft was, like, glued," he winced, "to the handle. Then when it hit the buffalo, if he took off, the point would come loose and stay in there and the handle would drop out, so if he got away, you'd only be out a point. But if it was tied on, you'd lose the point *and* the foreshaft."

"Well, yeah...you know, you're right. I better do some more thinking." And Walker would drift in time, hoping that dreamed creative tinkerer, sitting before the fire deliberating on technology, would untangle contradictions. But the fire, the inventor, the shaft, the bindings, were dust in the wind. Only the stone points remained, and, inevitably, whatever the question, Walker would have to abandon his romantic scenarios and come back to the stones.

Raining in Camp

Constant rain became a language after three days. Its voice had made Young Walker and the son of the Guide slightly crazy. They chased one another through the drumming water, they rolled in muddy weeds while Walker and the Guide watched a gray sun seep into darkness. When they thumped in and out of the leaky tent, the Guide said, "Boys, don't track mud where we're going to sleep."

To the sons, the expedition meant strange rivers to fish, but Walker had come to these hills, the Guide's home ground, to get blue-gray flint. He laid a few twigs on the heap of coals to keep the small flames alive. Water falling through the trees, rain striking hot coals, snakes of steam darted up in the flames.

In all his walking, he had come across other campfires, some days old, some cold for generations. Generations from now, when Walker would be dust, all anyone would know of a man who walked and thought by his fire in the rain would be through what he lost or left behind. Those distant people might guess why he was here, they might even guess he was a walker, but little of his thoughts and dreams would be revealed. Unless he lost his black luck stone, which would reveal they were on the traces of a man of superstition, possibly a fool.

"You boys are getting mud all over everything."

"You boys must be planning to sleep in the mud tonight."

The boys found this thought hilarious and attractive. The Guide, smiling, stood up, ignoring the water running down his face. The tallgrass hill was bloated, the trees soaked black.

"I think we better move to the river camp."

"In this mess? In the dark?" But Walker had no choice; he wasn't guiding this expedition.

Having broken camp, then having moved, set up new camp, and coaxed fire into a small hill of coals, all in the rain, they sat again huddled under the dripping shelter, even the sons breathing hard, everyone muddied and numb to the babble of water.

The Guide stepped out and snugged a coffeepot into the coals. A thin cold line of water spilled over the lip of the canvas tent awning and down the side of Walker's neck. The sons were struggling to see who could enter the tent first.

"Dad, our sleeping bags are kind of wet."

"So they are. And muddy, too."

The bedding was dried by the fire, but rained on in the process. The change of camp did not bend the rain or stop it. The sons were scraped and hugged and put away from the night in smoky sleeping bags.

Walker could have asked earlier, and the Guide would've told him: they'd moved to the river camp for the safety of its good gravel roads, but in fact, he was too sodden to care. It had taken three days, but Walker had finally gotten angry at the rain. Too much of it melts the world momentarily and slows everything, including Walker's plan to get up into the hills and find a flint quarry. Now he was bogged against the tree line of a weedy green river.

"Wet spring," allowed the Guide, over coffee. Modern adventurers, they did not have a well-built coffeepot. Such a pot was an investment in time and made coffee that hit the guts with a thud. Building the pot, for them, consisted in not throwing out the fraction of yellowish water in the bottom of the cup before adding more crystals and boiling water. Walker cheerfully sacrificed quality for convenience, shaking the flavored crystals-- of amber? clay? plywood? he didn't care—into the cup, heating the water on the handy fire. Idly, Walker cut the cards in the rain. Five of clubs. It meant he was a lazy swine. He deserved the world of the once-removed: margarine and imitation margarine, and dairy spread, and for his coffee, whitener and sweetener.

This unhappy man hunched in the rain, who could just as well be called Hard to Camp With, is saved from his misery by a screech from the black sky not far above his head. Frightened out of his misery, in fact.

"Green Heron," says the Guide.

With reality reduced to a Green Heron in an elm tree, Walker's neck hairs relax, though the monkey in his brain knows that names are thin magic against the night and, listening to the continuing shrieks, which are becoming increasingly comic, he forgets to be angry with the rain. If he were less of a fool, he would do more than merely resign himself. But he is only intelligent, not wise, and it's a source of comfort to him that he can finally, the last in camp to get the point, accept this running water, vast whisper, ordinary as breath.

From the tent, Young Walker calls out to the Guide.

"Uh, your son has to blow his nose."

"Well..." the Guide thinks. Another crisis in camp, but the Guide is wise. He stops listening to the rain for a moment and calls over his shoulder.

"Tell him..."

He listens to the rain.

"Yes?"

"Tell him to go blow his nose."

Heavy Thumbs, Slow Head

In the faces of limestone hills cut through for roads, the flint lies in wavy, horizontal bands and scattered nodules. Sometimes the finer flint, lustrous to sight and touch, appears in the middle of the band, gradually changing above and below into a rougher grain, duller finish, and whiter color, like an aerated version of the finer, denser flint. This coarse material, which merges with the surrounding limestone, can be worked but resists fine flaking, producing a rough zigzag cutting edge. Walker had seen many large crude chopping tools and gouges made from this, but fine microchip flaking called for the finer flint. Taken fresh from the hill, it has a living quickness and can be worked easily and with precision. Once in the air, it begins a slow process of hardening, becoming brittle, stubborn and tough in the hands.

It all seems very orderly on the graph of the mind: a sliced hill of alternating bands of flint and limestone, comfortably and symmetrically metamorphosing one into the other, over and over, through the relentless yawn of time. But as Walker traced his finger down the face of a sliced hill, he was apt to discover the next vein of flint was an abrupt transition from limestone to glossy, fine-grained flint, with just a thin line of coarse chert separating the two, as if a foam floated long ago atop a shallow lake of rich, cooling flint. Contradiction was in the nature of the stone—variety, change, and ultimate mystery.

Some geologists had admitted to being vexed by the problem of origin. They knew that silica is one of the basic glues of the planet and that it expresses itself in certain systematic forms, just as do other elements, such as carbon. One of the forms expressed by carbon was Walker. By a surge of imagination or ignorance, it was possible for him to surmise a sophisticated evolution of silica forms, co-existent with the evolution of carbon forms, but occurring within a different matrix, infinitely slower in cycle. If he could trace a silica molecule throughout existence, in how many mountains, ocean floors, deserts, beaches, volcanoes would it exist?

Those silica molecules, which happen to be presently in the form of flint, had each bonded with two molecules of the element oxygen, forming silicon dioxide. Scientists are united in this conclusion, and so they know that they know it. How it came to be is the question that vexes.

Cataclysmic thinkers may say flint was formed into its hard state fairly rapidly, geologically speaking. Gradualist thinkers say to the contrary. They believe in time and pressure as the formative combination, flint an intrusion into limestone matrix, chemicals and minerals deposited by eroding water. Some members of the flint family, such as agate and petrified wood, seem to support this; the process replacing a carbon form, cell for cell, with a silica one.

Those who might reject this long union of water, silica, and time prefer the formative powers of contrast. At any given time in the history of the planet, silica has run hot, in channels, spreading into pools, branching networks, and the form of nodules, bubbles turned to stone. Add an ocean, and intense heat meets intense cold. Out of such contrasts come rapid transitions. Cataclysm tyros know that a nuclear explosion over a desert of silica crystals will yield a fused glassy substance, much like volcanic obsidian, the clearest, sharpest, most elegant member of the family.

Whichever category Walker prefers, and he varies from day to day, science gives him further options of subdivision and specialization. Concerning the arrival of flint to the ocean floor, he may imagine the silica entering the ocean from the surface. Visions of rivers of volcanic silica sliding into the ocean and gobbets of it blown into the sky, arcing down into the water like colossal buckshot satisfied, at least, his sense of drama, and when he looked at a vein of nodular flint, Walker could see it happening that way.

Or he might suppose silica entering the ocean from below, still satisfactorily explosive, with plenty of subterranean magma. When he looked at the edge of a shallow lake of flint in a sliced hillside, Walker could see it.

The longer, more sedate view would see the forces of existence as relentless rather than violent, the enormous stalactite as the trail of drops of water. Confronted with a shard of Flint Hills flint, the gradual-minded theorist knows it is over two hundred million years old. Since academic duels are fought daily over the truth of these ancient circumstances, Walker felt at liberty to roam the peripheries of each camp, coming away, like all good scavengers, with a bit here, a piece there, since the truth was not rushing, after all these years, to reveal itself. To any of the theories—of silica, water, pressure, heat and time—he felt it appropriate to add at least a decimal place of factor X, that which we do not know. With X factored in, flint could very well be the blood of submarine dragons, or a slurry of pre-memory civilizations, or petrified beds of mountain seed. But science, knowing better, had decided flint was the child of minerals left by water percolating through rock.

Geologically, flint is a paragraph in the chapter of limestone, but the diggers of science have found it to be a stone of limitless variety in texture, color, and pattern. The Flint Hills yield milky light blue, gray, and cement-gray, brownish gray, deep brown, red-brown, tan to white, reddish pink, smooth single colors or mottled together in earthy combination.

Within a two hundred mile radius of where Walker and the Guide stand will be found flint carried in from other sources: the red and white streaked alibates, native to Texas, brown and yellow jasper from northern

Kansas, marbled, whirling purples, reds, golden yellows, whites, and pinks from New Mexico and Arizona, light, grainy pinks, grays, and whites from the Ozarks. Agate, petrified wood, and obsidian carried in from the Southwest, and down from the Dakotas, dark molasses chalcedony.

Of these varieties of flint, traded across time and distance from people to people, the dead ocean Walker and the Guide stare across is, and was to many, the source of one prized for its fine compact grain and the cool bluish cast of its color, a stone that suggested the sky.

"Oil drilling all through these hills. I think that scrape is their work." The Guide indicates a slashed bare portion of hillside just below where they stand.

"Getting flint gravel for the roads."

It looks too level and regular to be made by anything but machines, but the machine operator may have taken advantage of an area already somewhat cleared by primitive quarriers, so Walker decides to search the area, while the Guide wanders downslope.

Walker finds it easy to be alone here, slow, eyes down, sun hot on his neck. Drops of water still cling to shadows in the wild, curly grass. Fragments of flint and limestone are everywhere, but they are the normal random bits of a hill breaking down. He is looking for flakes that have been fractured by a hard, direct blow, and flakes with the regular chipping along edges, which signals the work of a hand.

Settling with a suitable chunk of flint, the early quarrier struck large flakes from it with a hammerstone of granite, quartz, or a tough-skinned cobble of flint itself. A smart worker would spend some moments studying the grain of the particular mass of stone he held and try to direct his strikes at points natural to the flow. One way or another, flint is the daughter of water, and the flow of the stone's formation is evident in its banding, striation, and mottling. By knowing the grain, he could knock free long flakes of a desired thickness, peeling the stone until he arrived at a core too small to yield an adequate flake. A stupid or impatient worker would get few appropriate flakes; he would batter the stone with directionless force, and the pattern of rippling shock that traveled through would cross and tangle, the flint shattering crazily.

The Guide whistles and beckons from near the base of the hill. He is standing on a flat place not much larger than a bed. At the point where the flat space meets the rise of the hill the exposed limestone has been gouged, hammered, and scattered. Chips and flakes of flint are abundant. The Guide, taking his title seriously, has found a quarry site. It is not the gigantic room of space cut into a towering cliff of flint which the word "quarry" suggests to the imagination, but a small, naturally bald spot, taken advantage of by the flint seekers. Walker picks up and drops flakes until he finds one which has, at its narrow end, the bruised swelling called the bulb of percussion, which occurs at the fracture when a piece of flint is struck with force. In the debris he finds other flakes with the swollen clue.

For how many generations people carried cumbersome chunks of raw flint on their journeys home from the hills before someone got smart is a statistic known only to the stones, but at some point someone saw the virtue of doing the early stage of tool manufacture at the quarry, the flakes chipped roughly into oval shapes, blanks from which projectile points, knives, and hide scrapers could be made at leisure back home around the fire. Bringing back five pounds of preformed blanks, ready for refinement, was a better investment of energy than bringing back five pounds of raw flint.

The Guide wanders uphill while Walker stands on the quarry shelf and attempts to think like a flintworker. If he had broken flint loose from the limestone, he would sit down and begin knocking off blanks. Walker searched the little quarry thoroughly, but the process only seemed to go so far: flint had been dug out, cracked, shattered, thrown aside, but not worked.

The Guide, three quarters of the way up the hill, whistles again. Walker is reluctant to walk all the way up the hill in hot sun to see an unknown when the quarry is right at hand. But a guide is a guide. He starts up the slope. Flint is thick in the grass.

The Guide is squatting by a spill of light blue-gray flint chips, all obviously knocked from the same piece of stone. Walker sits and looks down to the foot of the hill at the quarry area. He sees a vision of himself sitting down there in the heat, hacking on a piece of flint. It is much cooler up here, the ground is more comfortable, and he would be able to see his enemies coming, if they came, or animals he might want to chase or avoid.

"What's this?" The Guide steps to one side and picks up a piece of flint, a medium gray, rounded, butt-end fragment of a worked blank form.

"Here's another one." He fishes up a broken base worked from a mottled, dark gray flint. Bends down again—another base of a yellowish gray blank, carefully worked, broken at the middle. He also finds a small, crude chopping tool of bluish white chert, fat in the center and rudely worked around the perimeter. All this within five steps of the chips of flint debris. Of the blanks made by the man who sat here, at least three were broken, and their base ends were tossed to one side. Because the Guide has not found the pointed ends of the broken blanks, Walker assumes they were not tossed aside; a use can always be found for a sharp point. If the man who sat here on an old afternoon had not had heavy thumbs and broken some of his work, the Guide would not have found him. How long would he have worked here and how many finished, unbroken blanks would he have made?

If Walker had been here in that past time, he would still not know the answers to these questions. Easily distracted by details and not prone to the long view, he would have been way down the hill on hot, jagged rocks, breezeless, trying to work with sweat running into his eyes, ignorant of any prairie grizzlies that might wander by, a person to whom insight did not come easily.

Insects whirr and crackle. The meadowlarks sing, even in July. It is time to go back to camp, where the son of the Guide has taken Young Walker for a day on the river, swearing they will all eat fish. A voice calls out to Walker's sweaty ghost down in the quarry.

"Hey, Slow Head, throw us up a couple more chunks."

Silence at the Wrong Time

The sons of Walker and the Guide are eleven years old this time around the Flint Hills fire. Even as the four had pitched camp that afternoon, a fat channel catfish had been feeding on young crawdads and over-ripe mulberries rolling in the river mud. That fish now was grease around their lips. While the fish bones glow and curl in the flames, the son of the Guide slaps unsuccessfully at flies which enter the firelight to bite his arms. With a sigh he wants to know: do flies ever get struck by lightning? No one can answer.

Talk goes from lightning to thunder, UFOs, fossils droning in the earth, and Walker, watching his son's calm fire gaze, thinks of one of his own boyhood campfires, shared by his old man and others, and they had all been telling stories about speaking at the wrong time, and he dozed and nodded awake until it was only his old man across the fire from him, and his old man's friend, the trapper who'd heard and seen a beaver fart, and Trapper was telling a story about one time he knew of that he'd kept silent at the wrong time:

This friend and I went to northeastern Colorado to visit a friend of his. It was like a lark, we had nothing special to do, and well... Never mind, there we were. This guy had his own farm, had restored the farmhouse and was actually making money off alfalfa. So he turns out to be a likeable guy, and later that afternoon, we climb up in his tall pickup so he can drive us around his boundaries. Very much the proud farmer.

Now it had rained earlier but was cleared off nearing sunset. Everything was bright. You could get light-headed, you know, on the smell of clover. So we're grinding up a not very muddy red road with that kind of armored-vehicle disregard those high-step pickups have, heading west, purple mountains over the crest of the hill. I'm riding shotgun, sucking up the clover and daydreaming on the blue puddles in the road. We come over the hill in this pretty light, and way down the road looks like some sort of animals gathered together in the middle.

Dogs, says the driver. Dogs it is. The cluster breaks up as we get nearer, four dogs standing around one laying in the road, which raises its head and looks toward the sound of the truck. The four standing dogs run up the road a ways and stop beside the ditch, one sits, three keep standing, and they watch us as we pull up to the dog left in the middle of the road.

The driver leans out the window and looks down. He goes, "Aw, shit, hit by a car."

My friend goes, "Hurt bad?"

He goes, "Oh man, the worst. She's laying on her guts."

"Oh shit, what's she doing?"

"She's just looking up here at me. Damn," he goes. "I should have brought the rifle."

And my friend says, "Got a tire iron? A jack?" He doesn't have anything.

About now, over on the other side of the pickup, I'm beginning to get their drift, and I get this sinking feeling because I've been watching the other four dogs, and from their...it was like a concerned attention... I got the feeling they were waiting for us to move along so they could get back to their companion, and their attitude gave me the impression that they assumed we would leave. I remembered the way the dog in the road looked up as we'd driven up, a small, shorthaired terrier mongrel, small skull, large bat ears, big eyes, laying there in your basic odalisque curve, braced on her forelegs, the way a dog will lay in the sun. It was too bad. Like I said, the light was golden, big drops of bright water were still dripping off the barbed wire fences. The rain had shaken this sweet aroma loose from the clover, and this poor dog, so calm now, probably in shock, had been dying in a fine sunset with its buddies grouped around it when we showed up.

"Well, hell," goes the driver, and he shifts gear, and it was right in the front of my brain then to say, "Right, let's go," thinking the dogs have everything under control, but since I figured the driver and my friend were resigned to moving on too, I didn't say anything. Instead, leaning way out the window, the driver cramps the wheel, backs the truck up a bit and inches it forward. All four of the other dogs are watching this with real intense interest, the one that sat down has stood up. Part of what kept me from speaking then was the stranger-in-a-strange-land feeling—his land, his fields, his truck, his road, his dying dog, but I knew even then that was bullshit. What kept my mouth shut was realizing that, to my friend and the driver, this was the only possible thing to do, right-thinking humans always went ahead and put creatures out of their misery.

The driver pulled his head back in the window, shifted into low, popped the clutch and floorboarded it. When the tires spun and the gravel flew, we shot forward. There was a high, piercing yipe from the body of the dog in the road. The four watching dogs had been standing absolutely still. When the engine roared, their ears pulled forward, and when the truck peeled out and there was that one clear yelp, their faces changed. Snap! Just like that. And the only way I can think of to say it is, for all four at once, it was an expression of astonished betrayal. Just that quick, their faces changed to pure rage, and as we barreled up the road, they leaped toward us, all frenzied up, barking so loud and hard they were choking and strangling. I pulled my elbow in the window. They ran alongside and jumped against the doors, and I looked into the teeth and eyes of one who had some furry German Shepherd in his mix. He wanted to tear my throat out. We sped up then, and they chased us over the next hill before we left them behind. They never stopped barking.

We rode back to the farm, nobody said nothing. We were low in spirit for the rest of the evening. For the other guys, they'd done the right thing as they saw it, but had been forced to do it clumsily with the only tool fate allowed them at that moment, a pickup truck. I was down from being silent and allowing a dog to be cheated out of its own death.

This ugly story, heard in that muzzy drift between sleep and wakefulness around the fire, gave Trapper new dimension in the mind of the boy Walker; instead of just being the friend of his old man who had heard a beaver fart, he was now also the man who thought dogs had their own world.

When Walker grew, this story helped form his relationship to other animals. He'd come to it the hard way. His first act of homage to wild creatures had been to shoot several of them, of various species. He then took to catching them, examining them intently, and letting them go. Then followed a phase of just photographing them. Then the need for mastery or evidence dwindled altogether, and he was content to note animals in passing and do his best not to meddle in their lives. He stopped his old habits. To stop the car beside a turtle crossing the road and to get out and carry the turtle across to the opposite ditch was, after all, a selfish gesture, done for the glow of some ephemeral merit badge awarded by the mind. The turtle, whose world had just been momentarily ruptured, might just as easily crawl out of the ditch back onto the road.

Some part of the culture beyond the campfire shot cats in the head in order to study damaged brains, another group shot dogs in order to study damaged bullets, and playing Big Brother to other species resulted in miserable scenarios where humans rubbed out mountain lions in order to preserve deer and were then surprised when the over-populated deer herds died of hunger.

Around this particular campfire, where the bright orange fish bones curled in the flame, Trapper was gone, the four betrayed dogs were certainly gone. Walker knew he couldn't say across the fire into the eleven year old face of his son, "Son, never be an engineer for or a missionary to other species."

That kind of talk would only get the look it deserved, and he had, in any case, his own path to keep clean. He suspected already that his son would not grow up to shoot animals in the head for the sake of knowledge.

Old Man Walking Stick

When he saw the silver maple
growing out over water
the walking stick pulled the eye
and the eye pulled the hand.
Then he praised the tree going up

came down with the branch.
In the cream colored wood
dark grain swirls
a bird narrows into sight

so while wrestling with a knife
splashed with the sweat of his nose
a man will think
of the birds in his life.

The end to know the ground
is claimed by snakes;
scales and feathers spiral down
to cross his hand with sky
and walk him through

beneath these clouds
a momentary rush of fields.

Son

Old Man Walker, though he used the *Book of Changes* and other guides to keep from thinking himself into what he considered the hell of a linear world, was a hopeless maker of lists.

Year of the Snake
The following fragments found

26 fragments of flint knives
80 broken flint hide scrapers
 4 broken flint drills
29 fragments flint dart points
74 fragments flint arrow points
 5 pottery lip fragments
 2 pieces pipestone pipe bowl
 4 flakes obsidian, one worked
 1 flake polished petrified wood
 1 colorful piece alibates, worked on one side
 1 flake exotic flint, golden yellow, maroon flecks

Walker supposed the old man had probably made branching lists concerning this group of objects—how many of the projectile fragments were butts and how many tips, how many objects made of this kind of flint, how many of that kind, and so on into a diminishing trail of paper. The old man often cursed his addiction to lists, but accepted it as a necessary superstition, like going out onto the front porch to greet the first moment of the new year banging on an iron skillet with a big metal spoon, not so much in the belief that the demons could be bluffed or cowed as that the new year should be met with magic, crude exuberance.

In these lucid moments, the old man saw he was a slave to the concept of evidence, but the lists continued anyway. If the old man had not been such a packrat of written evidence, he never would have produced the Rocking Deer journal, the only thing Walker had, the only thing his father had made sure to leave him. On some of the days discussed in the journal, Walker had been with the old man, but he hadn't known the journal existed until he received it in the mail.

Old Man Walker had been neither a frequent letter-writer nor a very good one. Walker had received a letter from him about three times a year, invariably two-thirds of a page in length, with the writing becoming more expansive near the end, as if his father's hand had realized how little he had to say and had attempted to fill more of the page visually. The salutation was always the same lone word—"*Son.*" The old man would begin by asking after Walker's health and go on to mention the summer just past and his anticipation for the one to come. An update followed on which sites were plowed and which were not, which would be in corn, which in wheat or alfalfa or left unplowed. If the old man had been out walking, he would mention it and briefly describe anything he'd found. The last sentence would begin with the word "Well" and guess it was time to eat or sleep or run a necessary errand. No closing, just "Your Dad."

That the letters were infrequent, short, and emotionally thin, didn't bother Walker. As a young boy he had wanted the hugs that never came, the unspoken words, but by the time he reached his early teens, the desire for touch and word had subsided. Over the summers Walker had come to understand that the joke, wink, smile, quick clasp of the shoulder, were declarations, and he accepted that this was as far as the old man could go. His last act of love had been to send Walker the journal he'd kept of his activities at the Rocking Deer.

Son,

How are you? You always liked this place
so thought you might like to have this. Hold
on to it for me. I'll be moving around for a
while but will write.

Your Dad

A postcard of a buffalo in Laramie, Wyoming six months later spoke of weather and scenery. As that summer of his seventeenth year approached, Walker came to know the buffalo well, a shaggy, broadside old bull, shot in the late afternoon to bring out the red in his hair, gazing at something just above the tufted yellow grass. That, and the journal, was the last he would hear of the old man.

51

The Rocking Deer Journal

Sept. 27
afternoon

ZIP and turn to face a deer twenty-five feet away, looking as if she's just noticed me there. Prancing, eyes wide, white tail up, she turns in a circle without taking her gaze off me. I begin to whistle, bend over and hobble-dance. I do this for a while. When I look up, she's disappeared.

This was a different deer than one I'd seen feeding when I came into the field. I saw them together when I left the field.

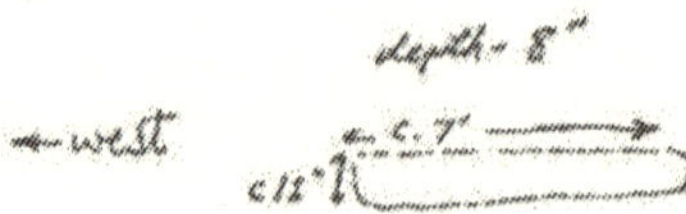

a few flint flakes
some charcoal streaking
in sample hole at 12"

Numerous fragments of split bison/deer
   bone
Fragment of animal tooth
5 small-to-medium cobble fragments
Flint flakes
Fragment of rose quartz hammerstone
1 small piece reddish sandstone
1 hand-size piece brown sandstone
Soil yellowish-black marbled, some
   slight charcoal streaking, red from
   granular sandstone
Most items found within 12" circumference at between 10–14 " depth

FLINT

1.   Large cobble fragment – smoky translucent w/ black mottling – agate?
    surface the same
2.   Large cobble fragment – butterscotch/red streaked – surface rough,
    grey-brown – cobble end
3.   Medium cobble frag. – earth yellow, coarse – surface same cobble
    end
4.   Med. cobble frag. – yellowish-grey mottled – fine grain – surface
    rough black

5. Med. cobble end – same as above – found together & fit along lines of fracture
6. Med. flake – med. grey, white specks
7. Med. cobble flake – rosy-red orange, fine grain – surface on one side rough black
8. Small frag. – pinkish to brown mottled, superfine – 1 surface cobble, rough dark brown
9. small flake – 2 tone banded grey – fine
10. sm. flake – grey - fine
11. sm. frag. – pinkish mottled – fine – 1 surface cobble – rough brown grey
12. Sm. flake – dark grey – med. grain
13. Sm. flake – med. grey – white flecks – med. grain
14. Sm. flake – very dark grey – med. grain
15. Sm. flake – yellowish white – med.
16. Sm. flake – butterscotch/brown mottled – fine
17. Sm. flake – mottled greys – coarse
18. Sm. flake – med. grey – med. grain

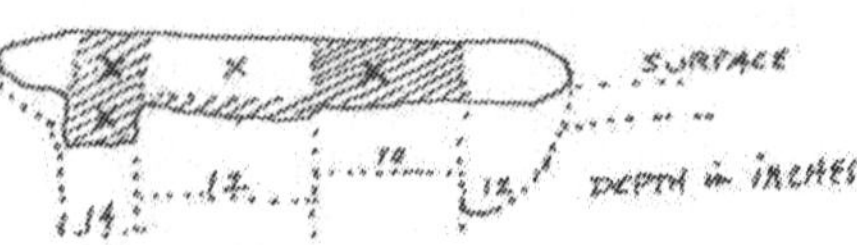

Had to shovel out water.
A Marsh Hawk hunts here.
Numerous bone sherds
Tooth fragment – deer?
2 bits calcified bone
4 small red sandstone
1 small brown sandstone
2 cobble slivers
7 flint flakes
x = bones found
More bones less flint. Concentration
seems to go to the north.

FLINT

1. Med. cobble fragment - same cobble as nos. 4 & 5 last time
2. Med. flake – butterscotch – fine
3. Med. flake – white to yellow-greys – med.
4. Small flake – yellow-brown – fine
5. Sm. flake – mottled greys – med.
6. Sm. flake – mottled creams – med.
7. Sm. cobble fragment – yellow-grey – exterior dark grey-brown, possible w/ nos. 1 and 4, 5 previous time
8. Sm. flake – yellow-grey – fine
9. Sm. flake – grey-brown – med.

Oct. 5
full day

2 deer
Red-Tail
Marsh Hawk
Baying Bluetick Hound
30–40 Bluejays flying west

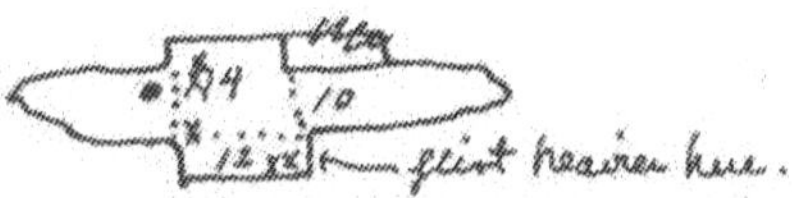

False horizon at 8–9"
most objects found at 9–12"
Fragments of bison/deer bone
Tooth (deer?)
Calcified bone bits
1 piece burnt hard bone
Bits of red burned sandstone

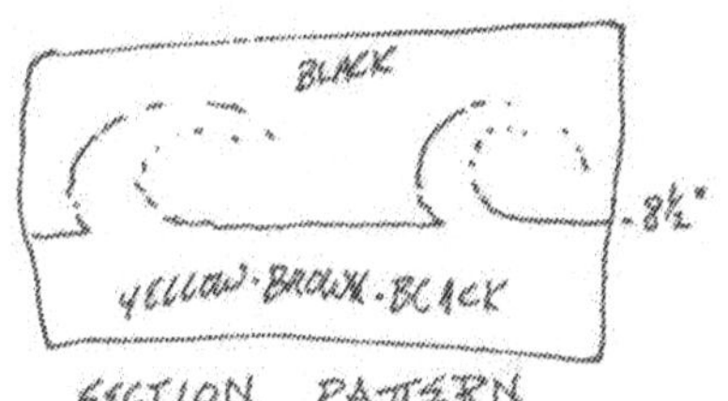

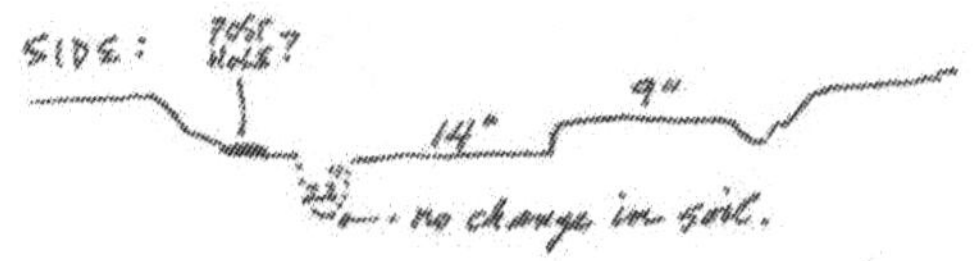

small test square here
to 9"—4 flint flakes

FLINT
Cobble

1. med. frag – looks related to #1 of visit 1. Found 7" to south of other piece – percussion bulb
2. sm frag – grey – cobble skin grey – med grain
3. sm frag – yellow-grey smoky – skin dark grey/black – fine grain
4. sm frag – yellow-grey – skin black – fine
5. sm frag – yellowish – skin black – fine

Flakes

6. sm light grey/brown – med grain
7. sm earth greys – med. glitter
8. sm light grey – med.
9. sm shaded greys – med.
10. sm yellow-brown – fine
11. sm brown – fine
12. sm dark brown – fine
13. sm light grey – fine
14. sm pinkish-grey – fine
15. sm brown – fine
16. sm yellowish – med – glitter
17. sm reddish pink – fine
18. sm med. grey – med.
19. sm mottled grey – med.
20. sm yellow-grey – fine
21. sm yellow-grey –fine
22. sm med. grey – med.

Oct. 6.
All Day

Red Tailed Hawk
Marsh Hawk

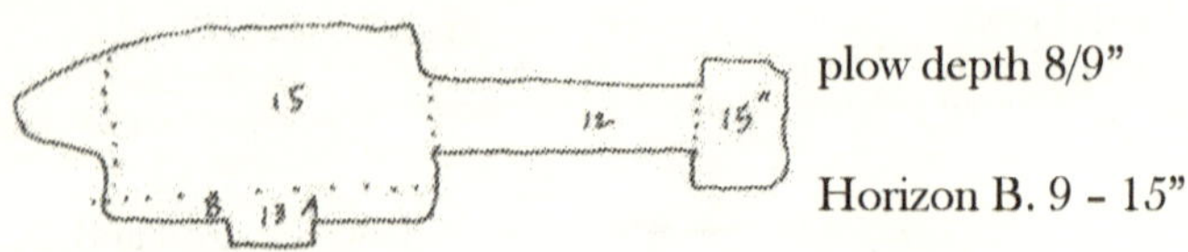

plow depth 8/9"

Horizon B. 9 – 15"

Point A – 3 split unburned long bones piled w/ fragments, 13–15"
Point B – Many burned bone fragments together, 13–15"
Charcoal spots at both points.

Excavated east end square today, and south wall. Flint chips and calcified
  bone in square.
South wall: split, unburned bone, burned bone, calcified bone, flint chips.
Greater incidence moving south of smaller bone fragments, burned bone,

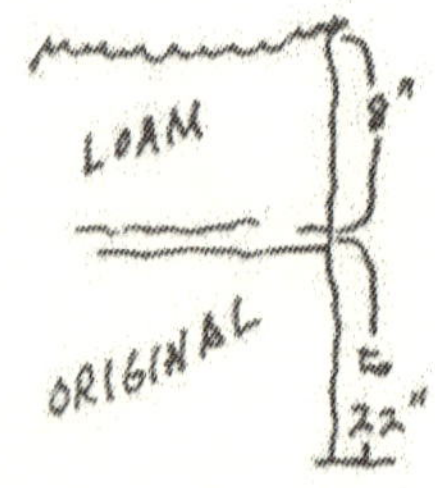

Sandstone throughout
Calcified bone fragments mostly in loam.
Flint: Surface to 13"
Bone fragments: 10–12" (top at orig.
  horizon)
Burnt bone fragments 12–15" depth

FLINT: all chips, small
  1. Yellow-brown, cobble flake,
       dark skin, found 13" lying flat.
  2. med grey mottled – med grain
  3–7. same
  8. dark grey – med grain
  9–10. same
  11. black, with limestone
  12. pinkish grey, med
  13. grey brown, fine
  14. browns, fine
  15. pinks and browns, fine
  16. mottled grey, med.
  17. light grey-brown, med
  18. pale yellow, coarse
  19. grey-brown, fine
  20. mottled grey, med.
  21. light grey, fine
  22–23. yellow-brown, fine
  24. pinkish – med.
  25. yellowish-grey – fine

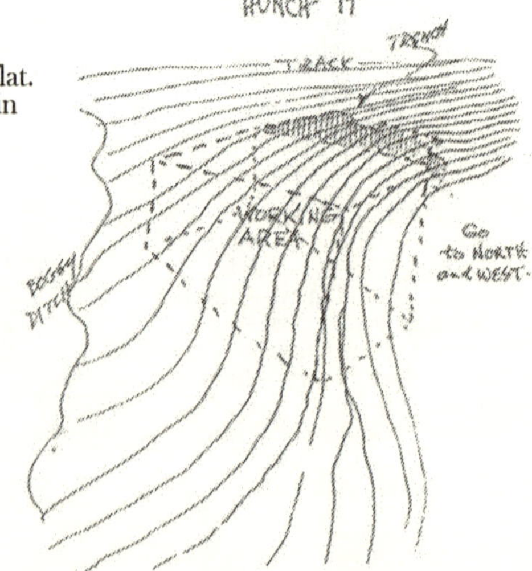

Oct. 12/13

Two bright quiet October days. Excavated
area between and slightly to north of two
trenches. Clearing the surface of old chaff,
I find a year-old Blue Racer. He's slow and
I take him to the bottom of the slope.
Sunday morning, just before starting to work
I hear a rhythmic breathing sound. A flight
of geese passes over close. The sound of
their steady wing beats swells and dwindles
with them, until they are a distant shifting
line on the southern sky. They weren't
calling and looked straight ahead.

BONE

Less than previous times. Few small broken fragments of raw bone, much
tiny calcified bone. Bits of 2 animal teeth.

FLINT

150 pieces. Much higher flint ratio, compared to bone, than before.
Just as most flint was found on the north edge of east trench, most flint
  here was in the northeast three quarters of the shape.
2 bits of broken quartz cobble
1 large cobble fragment – mottled greys, black skin, fine.
9 large flakes (8 of which are cobble fragments)TWO showing some
  further work along one edge
All others medium to small to tiny flakes – mixture of cobble flint and
Flint Hills blue-grey family of flint. Some cobble flint is beautiful, often
translucent and opaque designs in the grain of the stone. Given the beauty
of the flint, the people must have crafted some fine objects.
Handful of sandstone pebbles – brown, red, and softer yellowish variety.
Fist-sized brown sandstone rock on surface at Northern edge of shape.
The placement of 2 high density flint areas, and another possible posthole
mold, plus the sheer amount of flint found in this shape, make me think
the hunch is right. Big surmise based on the 2 probable post holes, flint
density, and surface indications:

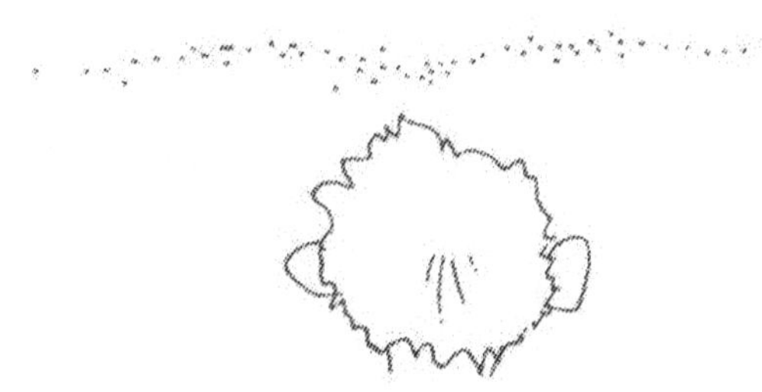

Watching geese go

F = flint
B = bone
CB = carbonized bone cluster

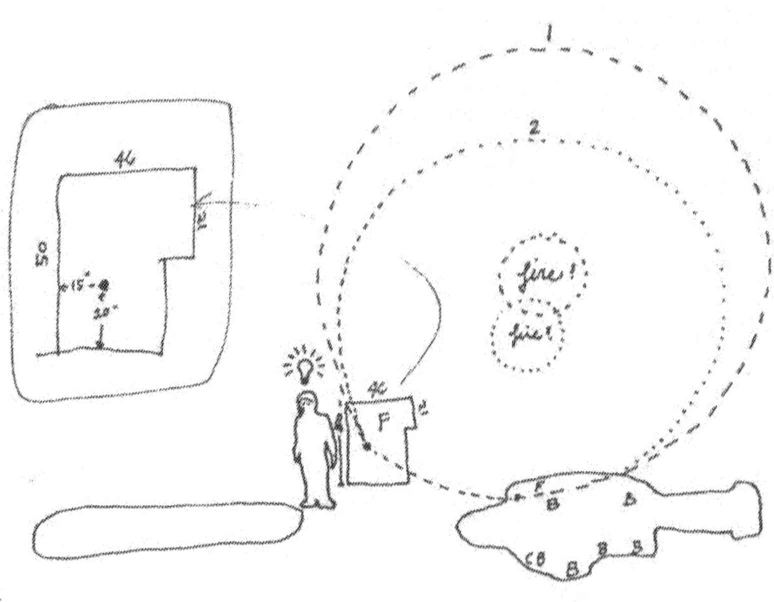

BIG SURMISE—projecting perimeters of lodge.
Starting at the northeast corner of shape just dug – measure in 36" in line with the 2nd post hole axis. Using that point as the northeast corner, dig a 36" square shape.
Concentration of flint – most trash would be pushed to the back edges of the lodge? Flint pieces are indicative of all stages of flint-knapping process, from cobble fragments to fine retouch flakes.
How many people would live in lodge? This looks like 3-5 people's worth of space.
No pottery found yet. No shell.
Artifacts should include arrowheads, hide scrapers, knives, and drills.
Possibility of pecked and ground objects – axes? celt? bannerstone?
Size of surface finds indicate thrown darts rather than bows and arrows.
Where in the lodge did the people sleep?
Where keep their tools?
Assume a small fire: "White man builds a big fire, stands back and sweats; Red man builds a small fire, sits close and keeps warm."

Flint-knapping done close to the fire, especially in winter.

Oct 16.
afternoon

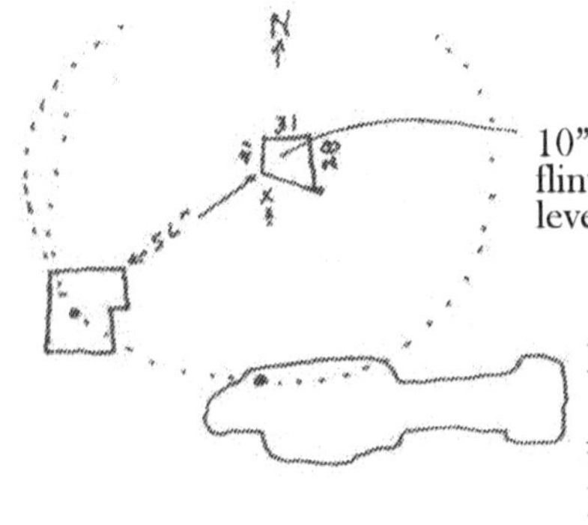

10" depth (rich earth yellow cobble flint occurs again and again at this level on all occasions).

BONE

As previous times, bits of white bone throughout – increase of larger BITS blue bone. Few small fragments of raw bone and black bone.

STONE

As previous time, sandstone bits, few medium to small brown sandstone pebbles. Few bits yellow soft stone, one navy-bean size, flat, smooth paint-stone bit. Two bits of quartz pebbles or cobbles – one brown-red sugar quartz, one conglomerate w/ 2 knuckle-size white quartz imbedded in granitic rock, original surface shows both types of rock abraded smooth – glaciated?
Clue to source of cobble flint – check glacial maps.

FLINT

80 pieces. 2 being med, cobble fragments – rich, earth yellow-brownish-grey – both fine.
All other flint, medium/small/bits of Flint Hills and Cobble equally. Cobble flint gorgeous in color/design/grain, as usual. 1 small flake appears to be a channel flake, thin, narrow, curved, small percussion pressure swelling at one end.
Small, thumb-scraper like flake, ridged head, seems to have been worked further. Functional as a small thumb-scraper but very little body – thins at tail. Pinkish-yellow flint, fine grain, size of a thumbnail.
Area today about ½ area done last time. Appears to be of the same nature in bone/stone ratio and amount of flint. Less large and medium cobble flakes – which would be expected as a person got further toward the center of the lodge. Larger more uncomfortable flakes would get kicked back to the perimeter of the living area. Also appears I have over-estimated circumference of the lodge and am now digging north of center. Hippie Knowhow overshoots the mark once more.

Nose in the dirt. Saw no wildlife. Sound of gulls (did see them), bluejays, and the kingfisher who has called every day I've been here. My approach is too expectant. I want to know everything immediately about the site. Fall back on the 6 directions, place yourself.

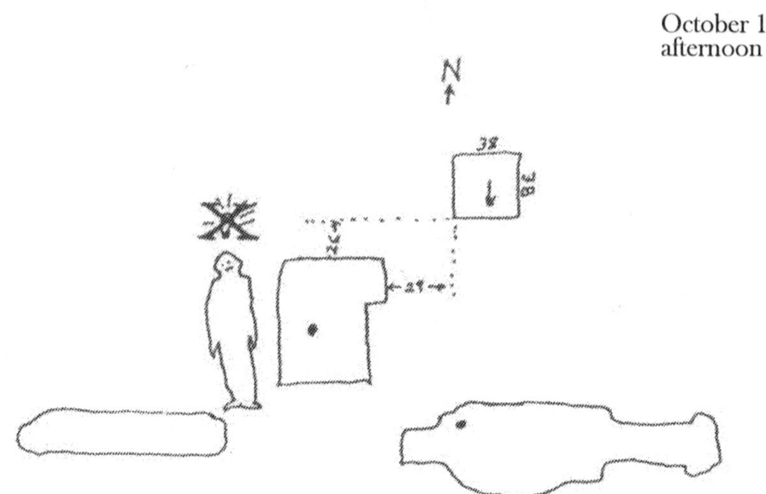

BONE – as previous time.
STONE – Sandstone pebbles, as previous time.
FLINT – 85 pieces. Two small cobble fragments, all the rest medium to
  small flakes.

Over years of looking at the surface, I've always considered this area to be
a dump. Most sites have a similar trash area, usually on a slope. This area
has always had bits of bone on the surface and small chips of flint. Have
never found surface artifacts here—those have been up on the level
ground, to the south and west. If this is a dump site, it's as good a place to
start as any.

Would a portion of lodge, exposed by erosion, show the same nature?
The plot thickens.

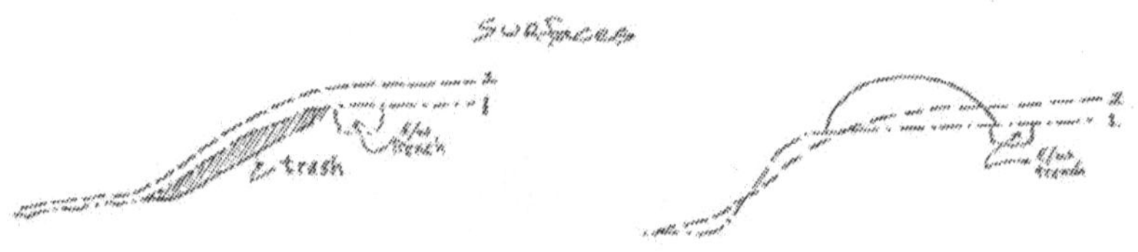

continuing in 38" x 38" shape,
moving south—character of finds
should remain the same until
connection with E/W shape.

continuing south in 38" x 38"
shape should result in
discovery of a hearth

Obvious solution is to profile the 2 supposed postholes.

October 20
afternoon

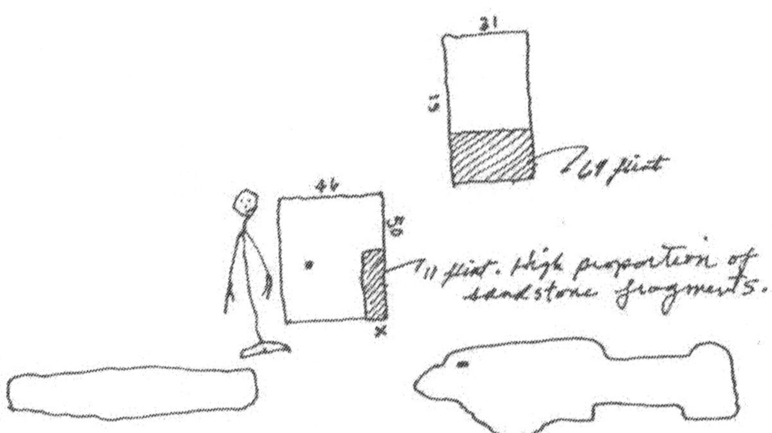

As before, bits & pieces of white, blue, and raw bone.

FLINT – Flakes from all stages of flintworking process. Cobble and Flint
Hills equally.

Flint thins nearing point X. I immediately begin fitting this fact to the
"supposed" lodge. Conclusion: thinking too much.

October 25
all day

All blue sky – 0 clouds
Just as I seat myself to work, a wedge of Canada geese flies over,
going north. Good sign? Only the ancient Etruscans know for sure.

R=fist-sized fragments of
sandstone
?=postholes?
x=fireplace, 10" diameter

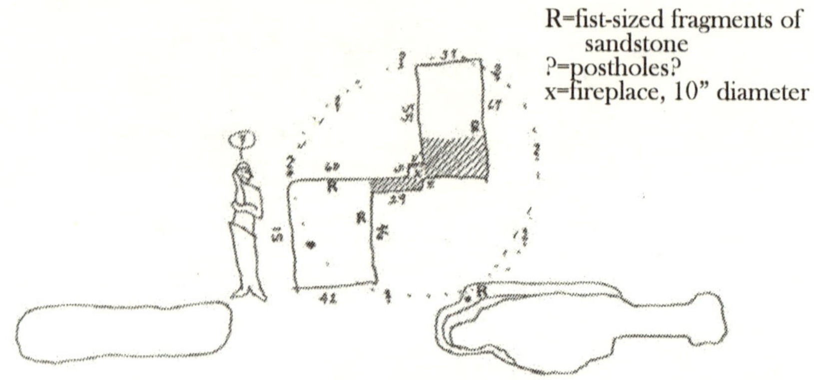

BONE – Burnt fragments, blue & white fragments, pieces of raw bone
including two large leg pieces of bison or deer. Bits of animal teeth.
Deer.

SANDSTONE – Small pebbles and bits – brown, yellow, and red, some
bits burned.

QUARTZ – 1 large long flake dark grey sugar quartz, 1 flake lavender
sugar quartz, 1 flake pink-white.

FLINT – 154 pieces. 2 large cobble fragments – rich golden yellow flint,
often marbled with browns. In quality, this stone is like jasper, smooth
and lustrous. Flakes range in size from large to tiny. Equal Flint Hills/
Cobble representation.

Most artifacts will obviously be made of Flint Hills flint, since it can be
obtained in large blocks with natural edges for hammering. A cobble
must first have the ends knocked off to provide a strike-platform. By
that time, the chance of getting flakes large enough, and of the right
shape, is diminished. There are more potential blanks in an angular
chunk of flint than there are in a cobble.

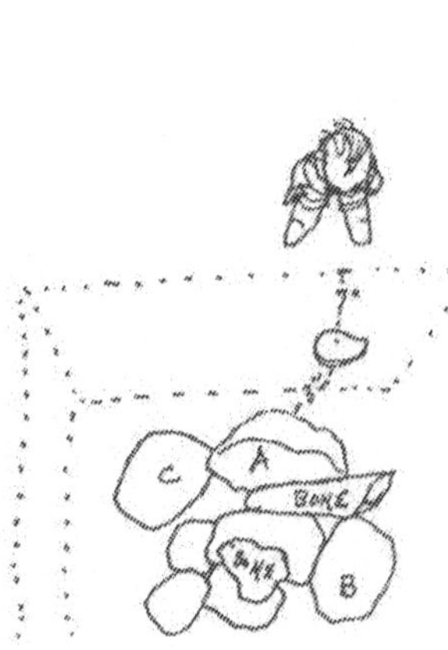

Fireplace – shallow. Bottom layer – light tan, rounded sandstone, fist sized.

A = Dark brown sandstone, jagged edges, set on edge.
B = Border rock of light and round sandstone.
C = Same as above.

All others either dark brown or light tan – one fragment sandstone burned red. Mixed throughout – bits of raw bone, burned bone. 2 large fragments of raw bone were partly covered by rock. The fire is layered roughly with burned matter and rock. Top of feature – 10" from surface. Bottom, 14".

This seems to be the tip of the hearth hollow – all that's left after extensive plowing. Most bone and rock has been dispersed. See location of large pieces sandstone from previous time. Whatever was left in this lodge has scattered over an area 5' around the lodge perimeter. Center of posthole to center of fire – 65" – diameter of lodge roughly 10 ½ feet.

First artifact is found. Large, thick, curving flake of Flint Hills flint – light grey streaked with white-black flecks and fossils, worked into a scraper. Grain: medium. Flake gone from side of the tail – either lost during the original striking of the flake, or knocked off by the plow. If the plow, this little fragment should show up during excavation.

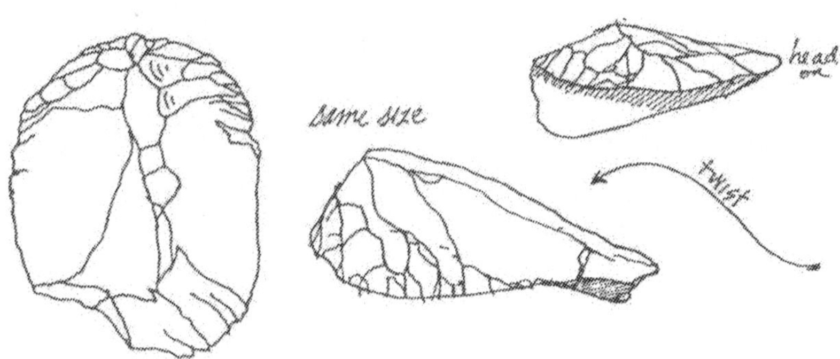

October 26
short day

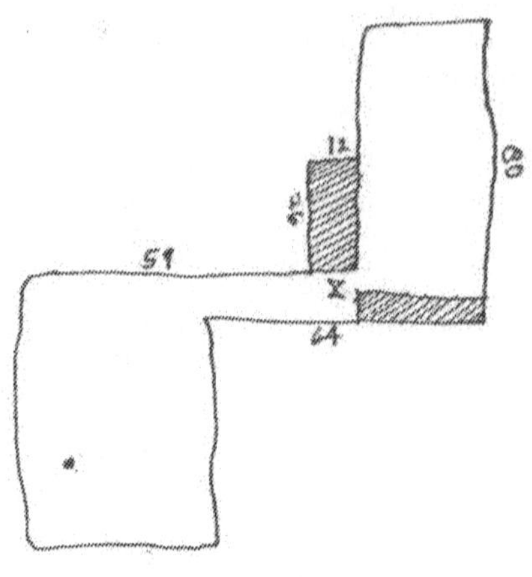

Again as I sit down to work, a noisy flight of geese heading North. Fighter jets have been doing bombing maneuvers—or is it strafing?—south of here both yesterday and today. Two sounds—something like scraping the sky, hard. And the sound of exploding charges. To the geese, it must be some strange warp in their flyway. Detour.

BONE – Fragments and bits, blue, white, raw bone.

SANDSTONE – Typical palmful of small pebbles. Dark brown, soft yellow, bits of red, often disintegrating into sand.

1 small fragment sugar quartz – pink-white
1 small fragment grey granite rock – no sign of polish

FLINT – 88 pieces

3 med/small cobble fragments. 2 milky grey with rough brownish rind. One rich golden yellow/brown (color pattern is visible on rind).

Medium to tiny flakes – 50/50. Besides the yellow/brown jasper cobbles – a smoky clear chalcedony with dark organic matter forming patterns is fairly common.

Red cobbles are represented by deep coral pink and a rich brick red, both fine-grained and lustrous.

Disturbed a colony of earthworms. Knife blade shaving at one end of the dirt, worms squirming out at the other end. When they first coil out into the light, their bodies are iridescent.
There were also tiny worms, like a short single strand of the finest white thread, smaller than lint.

November 2
all day

The Redtail, at his usual perch on top of a young cottonwood, watches me approach and takes off when I enter the field. Below the trees there is a blur and flash of white as a doe wheels and highsteps into the trees of the creek. She doubles right back up, takes another look at me, and darts away again.

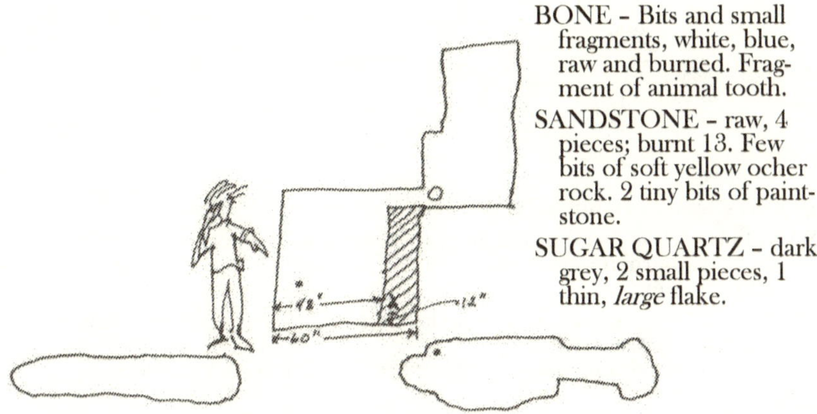

BONE – Bits and small fragments, white, blue, raw and burned. Fragment of animal tooth.

SANDSTONE – raw, 4 pieces; burnt 13. Few bits of soft yellow ocher rock. 2 tiny bits of paintstone.

SUGAR QUARTZ – dark grey, 2 small pieces, 1 thin, *large* flake.

FLINT – 139 pieces, including:
      3 small to medium chunks of a coarse light red flint. Flakes and fragments of all sizes and representing all areas of flintworking process, from shatter to retouching. 1 strip flake of medium grey flint with white specks has had one end lightly worked, making a very minimal flake scraper. One of these also occurred a few times back, the modified rosy orange flint.

At the point marked X, 2" down from the surface, the base of a projectile point appeared, lying flat. Material is yellowish-brown mottled cobble flint, slightly coarse-grained due to silica inclusion, which gives rough fracture lines. In cross section, the point was thick-bodied.

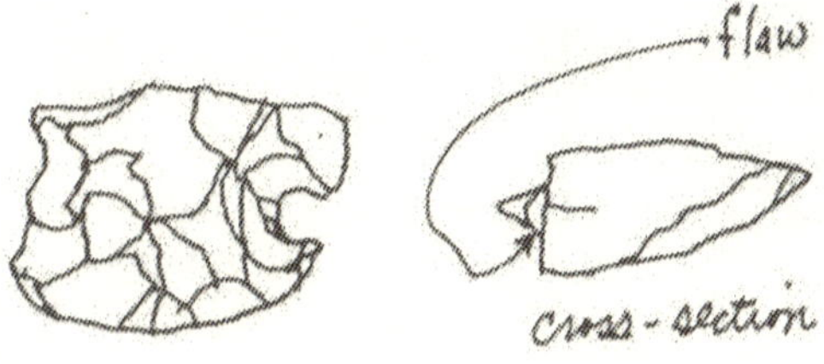

Surface of break not different than other surfaces. Granular flaw in stone at the point of the lost notch – suggests the point was broken in manufacture.

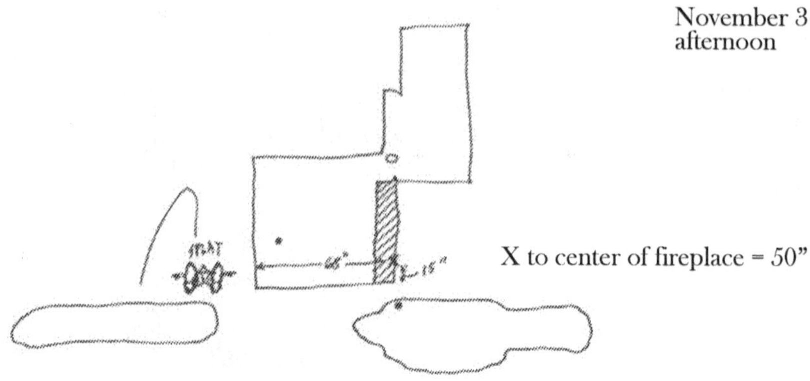

BONE – Small handful of bits – white, blue, burned and raw.

SANDSTONE – Bits, burned and raw. Two small and one medium-sized nuggets, burned purple-red. 5 bits soft yellow ocher stone. 1 knuckle of paintstone.

FLINT – 64 pieces, including long flakes, 2 bits of coarse reddish flint, as found on previous time.
10 medium flakes, all others small. + 1 artifact = 65 pieces.

This area lies directly south of the fireplace and has heavy flint concentration.

Depth from surface – 8"

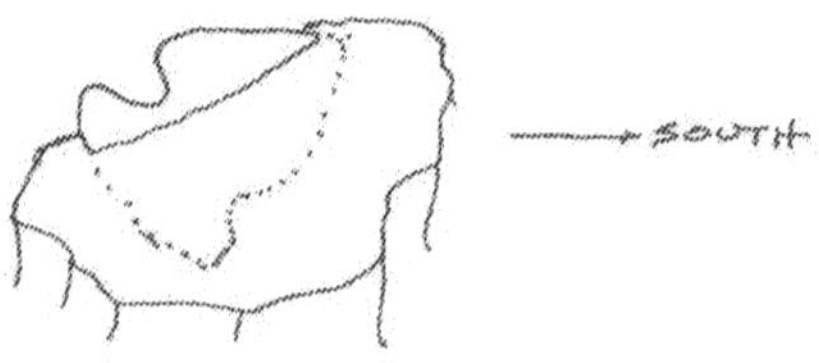

A smoky white translucent cobble chalcedony. Fine-grained. Held to the light, the stone shows an opaque pale yellow center surrounded by smoky clear quartzite. Flaking work is fine.

The shortness of the point may be due to its being made from a cobble.

Point end shows impact scars, suggesting this point was well used.

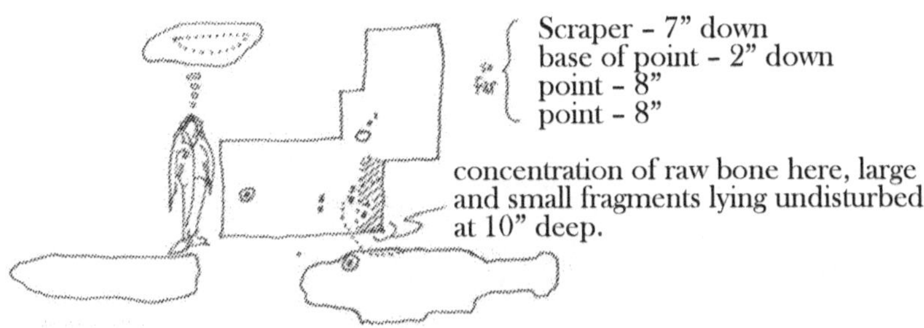

concentration of raw bone here, large and small fragments lying undisturbed at 10" deep.

BONE – Higher percentage of raw bone – fragment size is relatively large. Some burnt bone, blue, black, white, in small fragments, typically in plow zone. 2 tooth fragments

STONE – 1 large sandstone nugget, typical of fireplace stone, but not noticeably burned. Small to tiny nuggets of sandstone, raw, burned red, burned purple.
4 small yellow ocher stone nuggets.
1 small fragment of very bright red paintstone.
1 small fragment of rose quartz pebble.
1 small fragment limestone nodule.
1 medium flake dark grey sugar quartz, same as found earlier

FLINT –41 pieces. One medium cobble fragment – fine grain yellow-grey, brown-black skin.
Others medium to small flakes. All stages.
1 medium blue-grey flake has been worked slighty – 3 long wide flakes (shallow) have been taken off one edge. 1 large cobble flake lightly worked.
1 projectile point – medium grain pinkish-yellow. Light in color. Small and squat, with wide shallow side notches. Noticeable is the large amount of total area taken up by the base of the point as was the case with the earlier stubby point, suggesting they both may be re-workings of broken points.

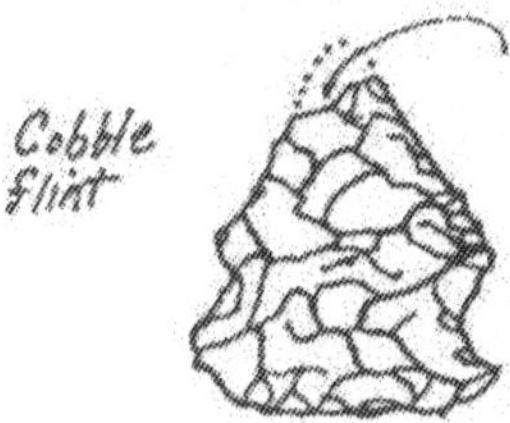

crystal flaw in flint here

Broken in manufacture & abandoned?

THEORY B – This cat was into stubby, wonky points.

Proximity of other point and presence of raw bone fragment at 10" level suggest the presence of a shallow pit. The very first digging would have tapped into the southern edge of the pit, and the stuff found then seems to make this a good guess.

November 8
all day

A small trash area is uncovered at the south edge of the lodge. Bone fragments, raw, seemingly sections of leg bone of bison or deer, some small burned fragments. Since the hole slopes down as it nears the border wall of the lodge(?) it would seem to indicate a garbage disposal pit. Flint found at the bottom is of same types found elsewhere on original surface and scattered throughout the plow zone.

BONE – Very much, mostly raw bone, small to medium fragments.
　　　Other types of bone throughout. Virtually all bone from pit is raw or burned – no blue or white bone.

STONE – Typical sandstone nuggets – some burned.
　　　2 small nuggets paintstone
　　　3 small nuggets soft yellow ocher stone
　　　1 medium nugget limestone
　　　1 small flat piece of limestone, soft, yellow
　　　2 flakes coarse light red opaque quartz
　　　2 medium flakes dark grey sugar quartz

FLINT – 71 pieces – 5 of which are medium cobble fragments. Type and colors of flint evenly represented. 1 flake dark grey flint shows pinkish-red tinge, possibly indicating heat treatment of flint cobbles and slabs. In that respect – some flakes of cobble flint, very much the same character as the golden yellow cobble flint, are bright red. Possible effect of heat? (Yes. A flake of golden yellow, boiled in water for 15 minutes, turned red. The cobble skin remained dark brownish black.)

November 17
all day
post mold #3 today?

Clear blue day.
Two Marsh Hawks hunting

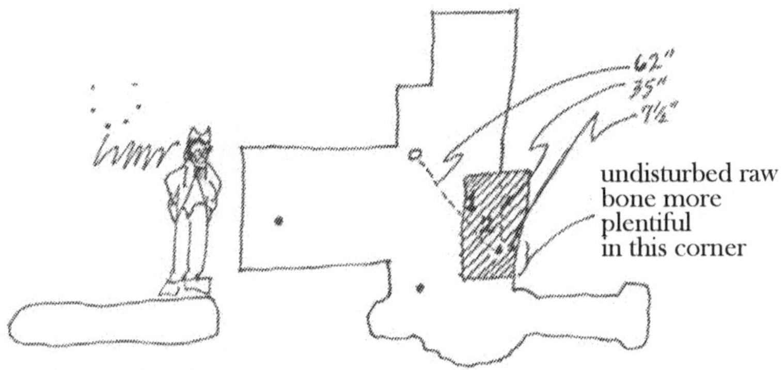

BONE – Considerable fragments of raw bone from SE corner – outside
   lodge perimeter. Otherwise normal amount and variety of bone. One
   tooth, molar, from a deer possibly. Not bison.

STONE – 3 medium to small fragments dark grey sugar quartz.
   1 flake lavender sugar quartz
   3 flakes coarse brick red quartz. Plus usual collection of sandstone
   nuggets.

FLINT—87 pieces, including 5 medium cobble flakes. All sizes and kinds
   of flint, 2 broken projectile points.

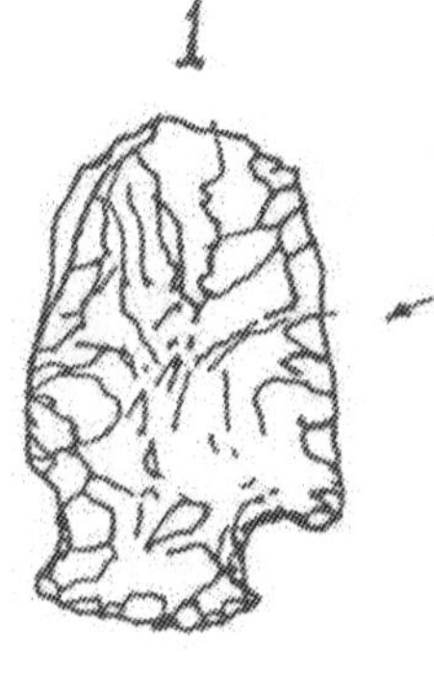

Creamy pink-orange cobble
flint fine grain, fine flintwork.
Fracture at point end seems
smooth and old. Fracture along
side seems crisp and new. 3 or
4 flakes of this flint found today
also. A very finely worked,
symmetrical, and flat point. 1"
down from surface.

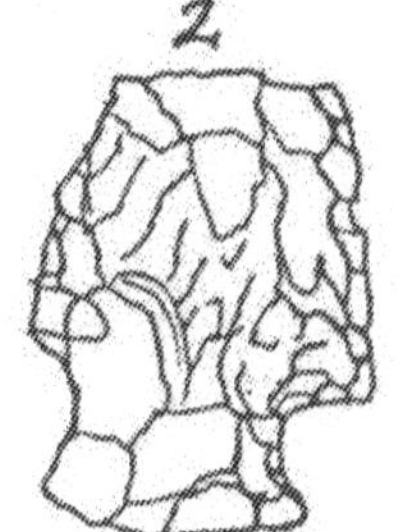

Flint Hills flint, medium grey
with pinkish marbling. Fracture
seems new. Finely worked,
body thick in cross section. 7"
down from surface.

Very rust eaten piece of
metal—nail? 7" down.

November 18
afternoon

mighty cold day
but the jets are zooming.

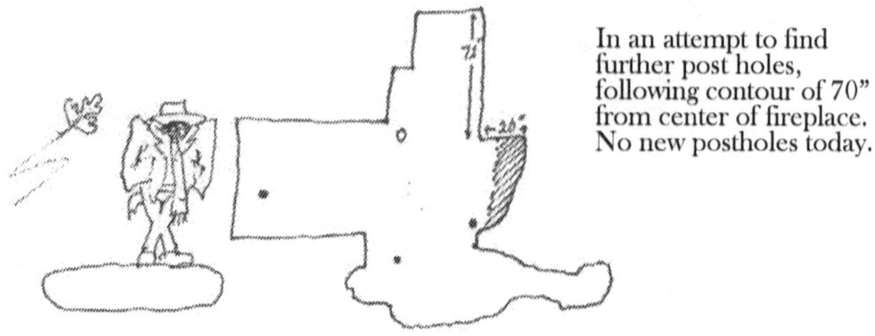

In an attempt to find
further post holes,
following contour of 70"
from center of fireplace.
No new postholes today.

BONE – Handful of small bits and pieces, raw, white, blue, and black. Undisturbed raw bone predominate outside lodge perimeter at 8-10" depth.

STONE – Small nuggets burnt limestone, raw sandstone, surface to 10" depth.

FLINT – 33 pieces – one large cobble fragment, yellowish brown – four medium flakes, all others small to tiny flakes of flint.

Evidence so far seems to indicate absence of : (1.) pottery, (2.) the bow and arrow, (3.) any farming and grinding tools. To the north, east, and south of this lodge are other areas which seem to have been inhabited at the same time. To the north, a couple of fragments of cord-roughened pottery have been found. To the east, similar pottery, but scarce, and a small waxy-white thumb scraper of fine design. To the south, fragments of *arrow* points, small, notched in from the corners of the base. All these are examples of the Quivira people and the Smoky Hills people of 5 to 8 hundred years ago, suggesting that some of the old campsites have been camped on by at least two different peoples, separated by hundreds of years. The Rocking Deer site has so far shown evidence of only the older people.

January 2
afternoon

West wind fifty miles an hour

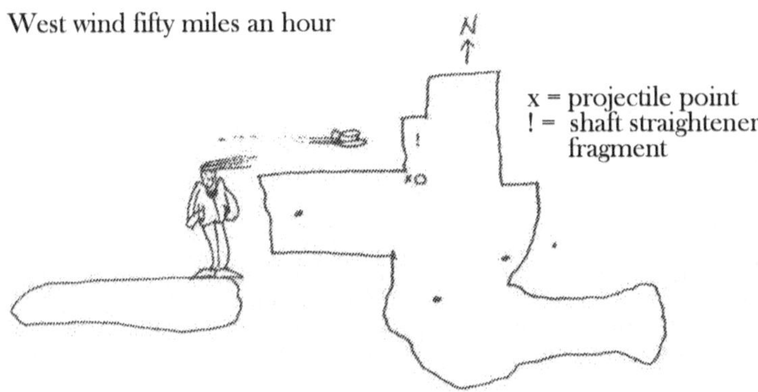

Snowfall and frost action have caved in most of the edges. Cleaned up the east edge, north edge, and around west edge to fireplace. Spent rest of time digging north from fireplace. Ground partly frozen – hard carving.

BONE – Small amount of fragments, raw and white bone. One outer fragment bison tooth.

STONE – Few small bits sandstone and yellow ocher stone
One large fragment whitish quartzite
One large fragment Sioux quartz – lavender
½ large rounded brown quartz cobble

FLINT – One small cobble core, fire-shattered and battered, reddish-white – many mineral inclusion.
56 pieces of flint – all varieties and sizes.

Artifact No. 7

Base of projectile point. Found in caved-in dirt just west of fireplace.

Cobble flint – brownish-grey streaked with dull white. Fine grain.

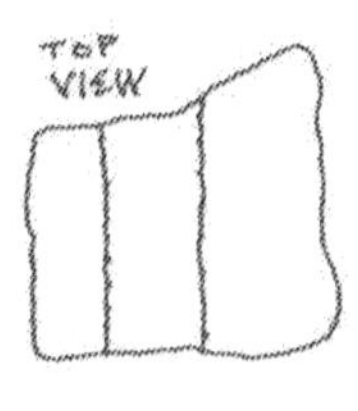

Artifact No. 8

Fragment of sandstone with groove. Part of a sander, straightener, for projectile shafts. 18" north of fireplace, 3" down from surface.

First ½" of surfaces are aerated, soft and fluffy dirt – below that, frozen earth. By working sides and top down to freeze level, then changing position to do the same in Area B, another ½" of Area A having thawed in the meantime. Working down from the surface and in from the sides at the same time.

BONE – Small fragments, raw, white, bluish. One deer tooth fragment.

STONE -- 1 piece paintstone. Small nuggets sandstone
      1 flake limestone
      1 small fragment rose quartz cobble
      1 piece sandstone, tabular, seems to have shaped side on
          three edges.

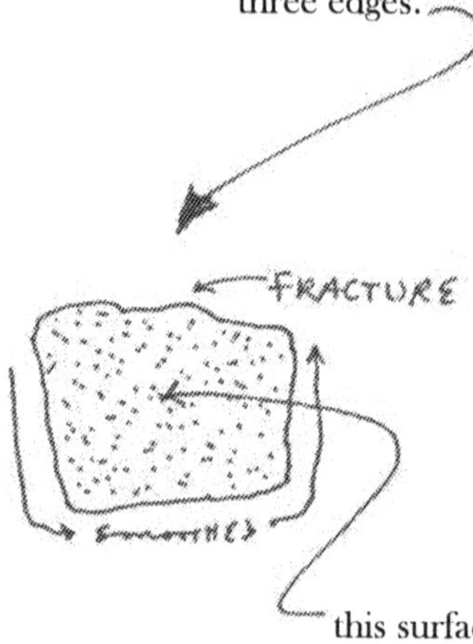

this surface flat;
opposite side unworked.

FLINT – 75 pieces, mostly medium to small flakes
    2 strip-flakes of rich golden yellow
    cobble flint.

LUNCH – 1 peanutbutter and apple jelly
    sandwich on wheat, kitchen-made
    with plenty of raisins.
    1 miniature chocolate bar.
    1 Coke.
    Best lunch all year.

January 10
most of day

Balmy Spring day: Kansas in January.
Red-Tailed Hawk and jet fighter planes.
Same lunch as last time,
doubles of everything.

Continued working areas
A and B, alternately, as
they thawed. Also worked
on Wall C.
Squared away Area D.

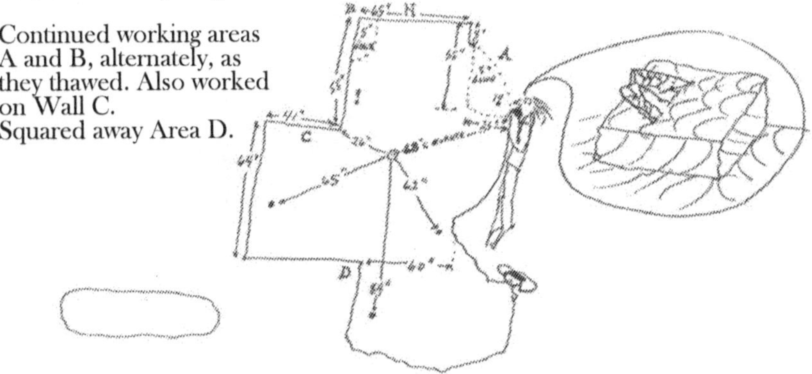

BONE – Typical mixture, all fragments. 1 bit outer enamel of deer or
bison tooth.

STONE – Double handful sandstone nuggets. One small fragment granite
cobblestone.

FLINT – 96 pieces: 6 large cobble flakes, 1 large Flint Hills flake. Other
flakes medium to tiny.
Two artifacts.

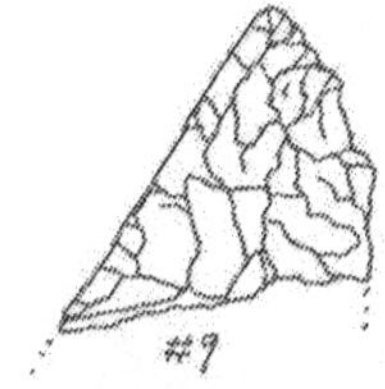

30" N of fire center
18" West
7" down
Flint Hills flint, dark mottled
grey, to pinkish grey at tip. End
fragment of projectile point?
Thick bodied, flint work
ordinary

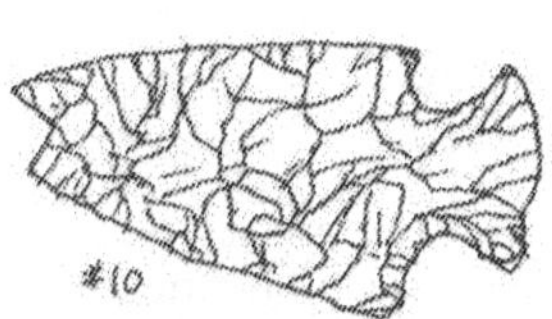

24" N of fire center
65" East
4" down
Brown-grey smoky quartz
from a cobble. Translucent.
Held to sun: amber-colored
with rich brown; clear edges.
Nice flat projectile point.
Very fine flaking – artist at
work?

January 14
afternoon

Red-Tailed Hawk.
Dirt is thawing
and swelling
with air.

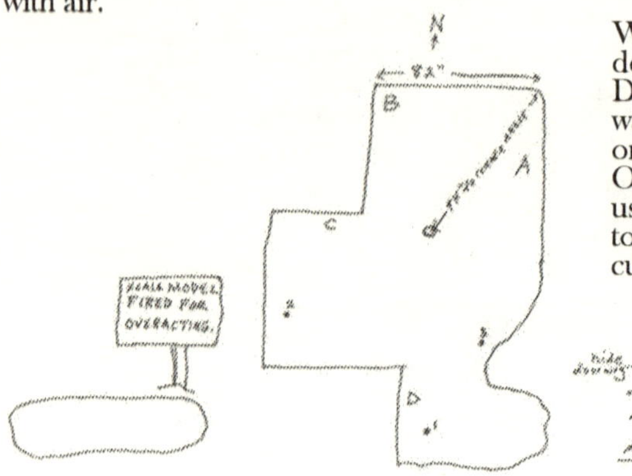

Worked Areas A & B
down. Squared up Area
D. Took a layer off the
wall of Area C. Waiting
on post holes to appear.
One kind of lodge could
use a snail shell doorway
to keep the wind out, a
curving hallway.

BONE – Usual quantity and types. Two tooth fragments.

STONE – Small amount sandstone nuggets, bits of yellow ocher stone.

FLINT – 100 pieces, including one medium chip grey sugar quartz.
Two large cobble fragments. Yellowish-grey with dark brown blotches,
black cobble skin.

At least half the flint is cobble flint. Translucent chips are about one-third
of the total number, in clear yellows, browns and blotched. Two exceptional flakes of cobble flint. A medium flake, fine-grained, black with very
dark red web patterning. Another deep purplish-red with swirls of dark
oranges, yellows, and browns – comparable to the finest jaspers, very fine-
grained. Either natural marbled jasper or the result of heat-treating a less
colorful cobble flint. Another flake which has the same coloring, turns the
deep yellow color at one end. Black cobble skin. Will vote for the rich
dark red marbling to be the result of firing the flint, until I turn up a piece
of obsidian. That would be a trade item and a surprise, and would mean
jasper could have been traded too.

January 15
afternoon

Have not seen the 2 does since deer season opened, though
I've seen fresh tracks. Bow season still open till end of month.
Deer go slow, old man no see.

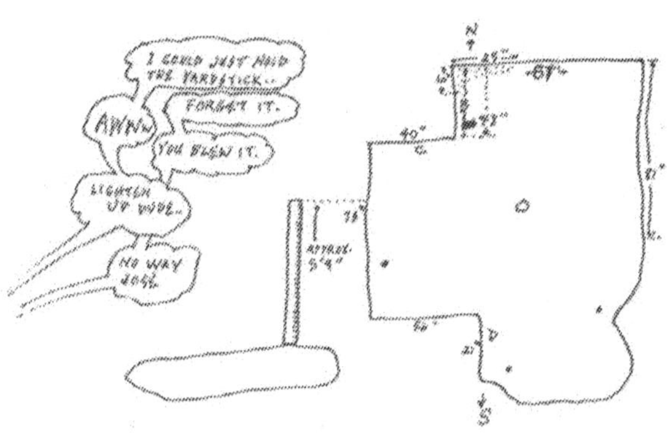

Worked on walls B, C, & D. Dotted area in corner of B = orange sub-soil, bits of granular charcoal, small fragment or two of burnt bone. Indicates an intense fire on the ground. Large raw bone fragments have been occurring *outside* the lodge perimeter. For example, the south end of wall D. Absence of any large fragments supports the idea this burned patch is in the lodge.

OR: Trash pit
OR: Top of fireplace of earlier people.

BONE – Two large raw fragments, south end of wall D. Elsewhere typical
    mix of "in-lodge" bone material – small bits, raw, white and blue-white.
    Small fragments burned bone in NW corner of wall B.

STONE – 1 large flake dense grey sugar quartz, tan skin.
    1 medium chunk coarse pinkish-red quartz.
    1 large chunk cobble – skin dark browns mottled with chalky white –
    inside translucent brown quartz, very fine grain, but shot through with
    veins of white chalky and crystalline rock, weakening the flint. Strike
    marks show crazy fractures and show little hope for long, large flakes
    of flint without crystalline or chalky faults.

FLINT – 87 pieces, mostly medium to small. Two large flakes, one a flat,
    broad flake of pale grey Flint Hills flint; one a cobble fragment of
    coarse, sugary flint, earth yellows, greenish browns.
    No worked pieces.

March 28
afternoon

Out of the field for two months.
The deer have investigated the lodge floor and pawed
down a section of one wall. A coyote has taken a crap
on the fill dirt.
Warm day. I work the northwest corner. An iridescent
bug comes by – half as long as my thumb, thorax
brilliant turquoise, abdomen brilliant orange. Looks like
a beetle, moves like a wasp.

BONE – Bits of raw, blue and white. No undisturbed bone at 10-12" level.
I am still within the lodge. 2 bits of animal tooth, one from bison, one
more conical.

STONE – Bits of sandstone, raw and burnt, soft yellow stone, one bit red
paintstone. One knuckle fragment of pink-white quartz pebble. 1 small
waterworn flat piece of flint.

FLINT – 116 pieces, predominately small. 6 medium to large flakes and
chunks, two of them showing work marks along an edge.
2 fragments of projectile points.

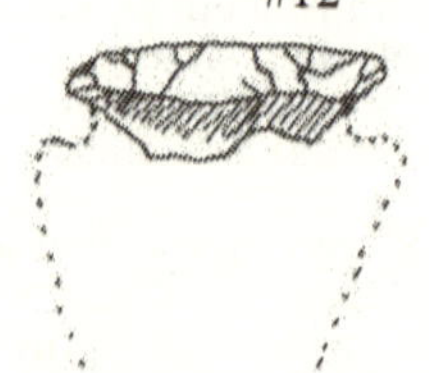

#11	#12
24" from N wall	55" from N wall
6" from W wall	33" from FAR W wall
9" from surface	7" down
Medium dark grey Flint	pinkish tan banded flint
Hills flint – fine grain	possibly from KAN/OKLA
	quarries or cobble. Very fine
	grain.

Quiet afternoon. Over ninety degrees. Sunburn.

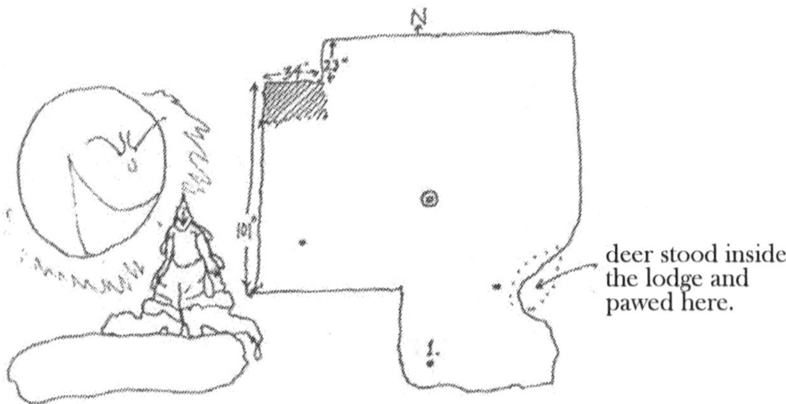

deer stood inside
the lodge and
pawed here.

BONE – Small quantity raw & white bone. Four or five small fragments
found *below* plow line.
One tooth fragment.

STONE – Handful sandstone nuggets, raw and burned. Soft yellow stone
bits. Two medium fragments of quartz cobbles, one pinkish-red with
white bands.

FLINT – 121 pieces. Small to medium, Flint Hills grey and cobble flint.
One beautiful cobble fragment – rose-red with dark yellow and brown,
brownish-grey skin. Four small chips were found below plow line.
Fossils: both in Flint Hills flint.

segmented curving
line fossil

crosshatch
pattern fossil 

Next: finish NW corner. Feeling like working on the area where the deer
pawed. Assuming posthole(?) no. 1, the furthest from the fire, to be the
outer lodge perimeter, the N, W, and East walls will have to be extended to
find further postholes. Should I follow the deer?

April 13
afternoon

Should I follow the deer? Nah. I stick with logic and square things away by working Area A and then Area B. In the NW corner of A, what appears to be a posthole mold, on further exploration, curves to the side and becomes an animal burrow. Of present "postholes," I suspect Number 3 of being an animal burrow. If they are all false I will have found the fireplace for all the wrong reasons. A pretty fair joke.

Windy. The iridescent beetles are back. One pair piggyback on the lodge floor. Putting my eye level with the floor, I rest and eventually they walk up to me. The male has the female around the waist with his mandibles, but is not riding piggyback after all. His back 4 legs walk synchronized with hers. They walk fast – stop – investigate – walk fast. The female finds a crumb of whole wheat bread from my lunch and eats it in the shadow of my nose, and they walk off fast, still together. Every so often they stop and vibrate rapidly, high-energy burst – then they walk off fast.

BONE – Normal quantity, same types as previously.

STONE – Few fragments sandstone, raw & burnt. One large quartz cobble, battered, two flakes knocked off.

FLINT – 121 pieces: 73 varied cobble flints, 48 Flint Hills greys. For the first time I note lack of matrix or limey deposit, on Flint Hills flint, suggesting it was rough-dressed at the quarry – blanks taken back to camp for refinement. One projectile point fragment – found below plow line with another flake beside it – but 2 different kinds of flint. Fragment #13 – rosy translucent cobble flint. Will continue to move North until nature of material changes, indicating edge of lodge.

23 inches S from N wall
12 inches E from W wall
10" from surface

Large Bullsnake
dead on the highway.
Red-Tail active
on site.
Fine day.
Many gnats

Worked Area A. Heavy rains have washed a layer of dirt over the entire lodge floor. Earth a bit reddish at east end of Area A. Looks like a burned area.

BONE – Handful small bits, all kinds. One fragment of sharp tooth.

STONE – Two medium flat sandstones in animal burrow.
One very small piece red paintstone.

FLINT – 104 pieces, both Flint Hills and cobble. Mostly small to medium flakes.

May 5
afternoon

On the road by the site, a large, dead Massasauga rattlesnake, est. 24+". As I drove on, I realized I'd forgotten to count the rattles (6 or 8 at a glance), but decided to count them on my way back at the end of the day. A voice in my head told me those rattles wouldn't be there to be counted at the end of the day. When I left the site I stopped for a look. They had been cut off and carried away.

A pit appears to be here

Urge to go west results in finding much fragmentary bone and flint – from plow line to, at one probe point, 26" deep. Seem to have come in on the edge of the pit. Much coloration in the soil as well as much burned rock grains and bone bits.

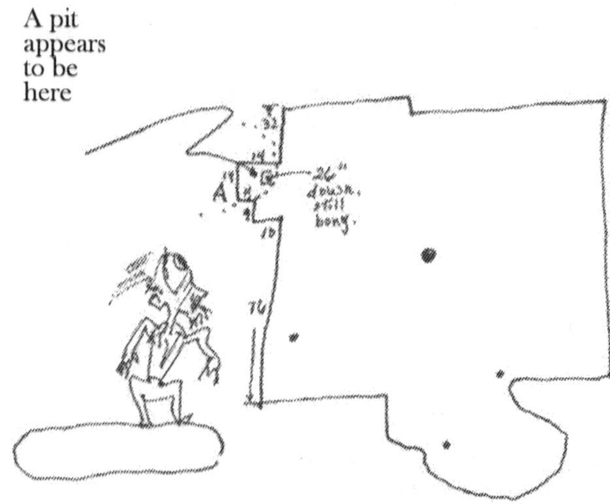

BONE – Three times as much as usual.
Calcified bone found at depth of 26". All fragments are medium to small and almost all are calcined or burned.

STONE – Handful small pieces of burned sandstone and limestone.
One small piece paintstone.

FLINT – 107 pieces, mostly medium to small flakes. Three large flakes, all cobble. One small piece is worked along 2 edges to form a worked corner, but the chip is too vague to call a broken artifact.

I will continue to work Area A – exposing the pit outline first by working down.

Stopped to pet the horses on the way out.

One of the sorrels asked me to remove a tick from his forehead, which I did.

May 12
half day

Continue to work in the area of the pit. Have not gone any deeper –
concentrating on defining the perimeter of the pit. There does appear a
wavy strong black line, within which the concentration of bone and rock
occurs. Sounds nice and scientific – appears so:

Next step will be to go down
to find the shape of the pit.
This appears to be a deeper
pit than the earlier one.

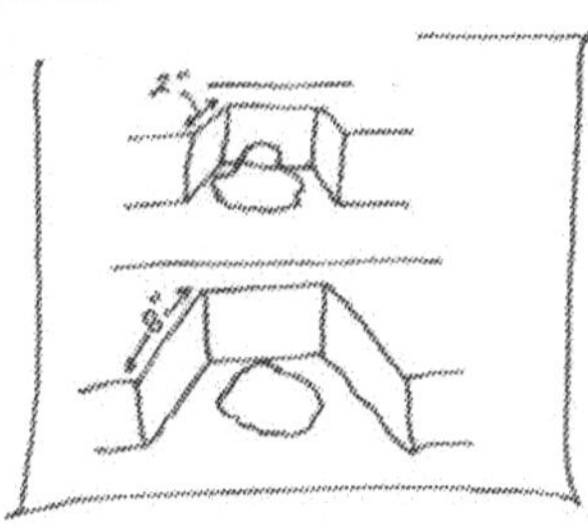

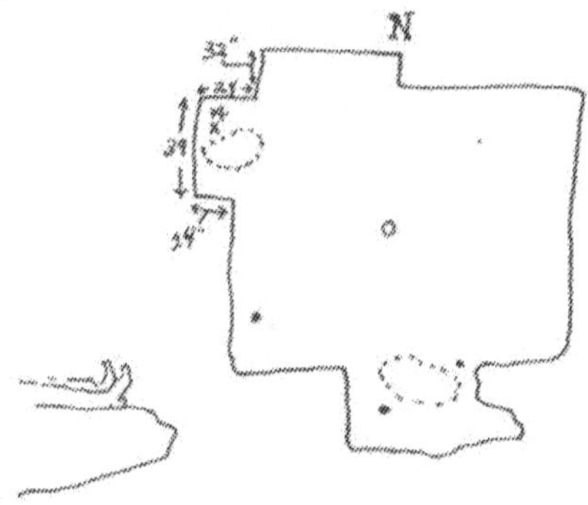

BONE – More than double
usual yield of bone.
Mostly calcined bone.
One large fragment raw
bone. Tooth fragments
of deer or buffalo.

STONE – One knuckle of pink quartz with white inclusions. Original surface looks like the product of glaciation. One medium fragment pink
quartz. One small piece dark grey sugar quartz. Bits of sandstone and
limestone, mostly burned.

CLAY – One fragment clay pot, size of a thumb joint, brown grading to
burned black. Shell tempered. Seams of coils visible. Found at 9 ½",
just below the plow line and covering a piece of bone – has not been
moved by the plow and was at the surface of the pit, first 2". This
makes for interesting speculation. More later.

FLINT – 115 pieces – mostly small and
medium –both varieties. Including
one projectile point, side-notched
and corner-notched. Neutral medium
grey flint from Flint Hills. Small specks
of white. Medium grain, finely worked.
8" from West wall, 10" from North,
9" down – has possibly been plowed.
North of the pit.

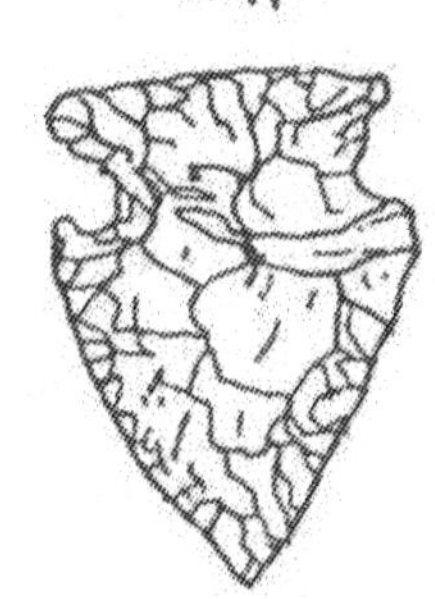

Completed excavation of trash pit and
I do mean trash – light on stone, heavy
on bone. At a depth of 36" a large pot
sherd, cord-roughened pattern, grit-
tempered.
Pair of Red-Tails hunting all day.
A Belted Kingfisher flew over
at lunch break.

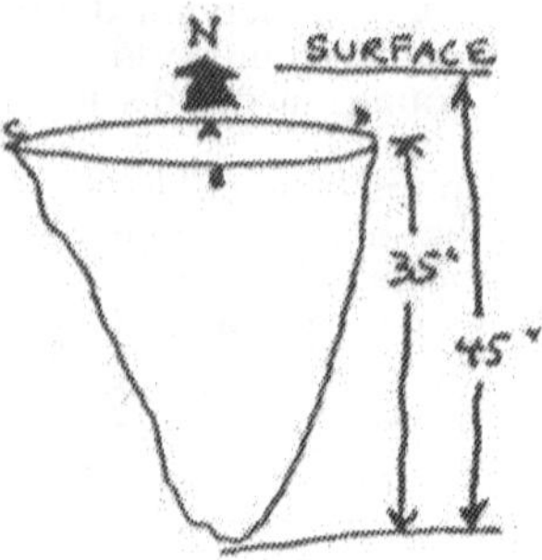

A to B = 15"
C to D = 17"
(original surface)

BONE – Many fragments in all stages.
    Larger pieces near bottom of pit, both raw bone and calcined white.
    Burned bone is plentiful throughout.

STONE – Very little amount of sandstone nuggets. One broken granite
    fragment.

FLINT – 84 pieces – 2 large cobble flakes, mostly small flakes. One of the
    cobble flakes has been nibble worked on two edges.

CLAY – One orangish pot fragment.

Surface walked also: in the vicinity of Rocking Deer, two fragments of
projectile points and a crude small thumb scraper. Two small fragments of
pottery – brown grading to black. Both grit-tempered. A fragment found on
a previous time was shell tempered. Intrusion? Or did these campers have
both shell and grit ceramics like the later, more southern Quivira people?
Sherd from the pit is fairly thin-walled and sophisticated, crisp surface
pattern. I expect it's because it's been well trash-pickled.

May 22
afternoon

Bindweed in the wheat,
not good for the farmer,
but the blossoms smell
fine. The 2 Red-Tails
hunt all afternoon.
Can sometimes hear
young ones screeching.
I presume these campers
to have been what's called
Plains Woodland. Usually
little evidence of houses –
(my post holes are
probably bogus). Pre-
sume pit B to have
been in later time,
although roughly
the same kind of
culture – the pot
sherd seems
more modern than
those found on
the original
surface. The
pit it was found
in extends c. 36" below the surface. AS YET – no shell, no worked bone,
no manos or grinding tools, no corn, no grain culture evidence.

BONE – Very little – small pieces, mostly white. 1 piece herbivore tooth.

STONE – More than usual amount of sandstone, mostly burned. 3 or 4
small nuggets of soft yellow stone. Two knuckles of white quartz, original surface areas crazed and reticulated by heat. Two small fine-
grained limestone cobble fragments.

FLINT – 104 pieces, mostly medium to very small flakes. No worked
pieces.

Most material came from Area A – heavy on sandstone.

Area B – bits of bone and sandstone – burned area – red-orange dirt.

Area C – least material here – some flint, little bone.

(A flake of very distinctive flint found on May 12 is obviously from a large
well-made scraper found on the surface here, in this immediate area, two
years ago.)

May 27
all day

The farmer and two of his helpers visited me today. The four of us surface hunted for a while. Mention was made of a man who found a complete buffalo skeleton in a creek near here, an arrowhead within the skeleton. Large or small point? The farmer didn't know. Need to find this man, who is said to have kept the skull of the buffalo and the point.

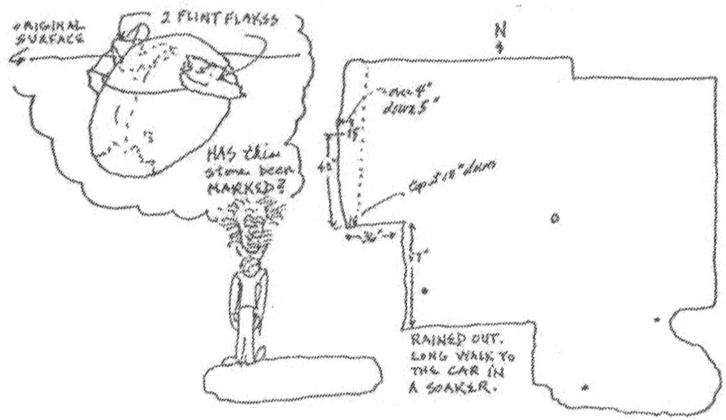

BONE – Large amount of bone throughout – small fragments. Original surface had bones lying about – not enough to consider a dump – but a throwing-aside place. Little bone found generally below plow line – 9".

STONE – Many sandstone fragments, some burned. One small bit of granite pebble. One brownish quartz hand-sized hammerstone for the making of tools. Good shape – top and both ends white with use-fractures.

CLAY – One small burned bit, grit-tempered. 5" down.

FLINT – 156 pieces, typical variety – one yellow flint cobble fragment found above plow line. One cutting/scraping tool, or fragment.

#15 – back side unworked. Yellow-brown mottled flint, greenish black covering. Seems to be large flake modified into a cutter. Fits right hand.

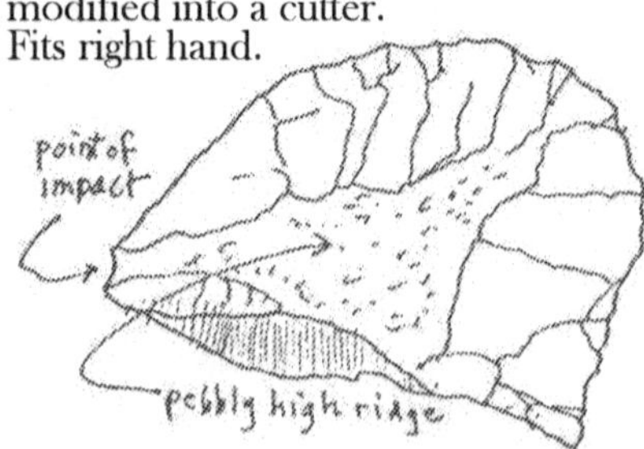

#16 – Hammerstone. Depth of placement and association of 2 flint flakes=? A seasonal hunter leaves the area & does not want to carry this hammerstone. He can throw it aside or ? The stone is a good one, seems to have sunk below original surface a bit, and had 2 flakes of cobble flint resting against it.

June 2/3
One full day

Only on site 45 minutes or so when rain was coming up fast in South. I picked up and beat it. Was there long enough to find out that the hammerstone from last time marked nothing. Went down 20" from old surface with no encounter. Soil did not seem disturbed. Back next day – very full hot day. Continued to work west.

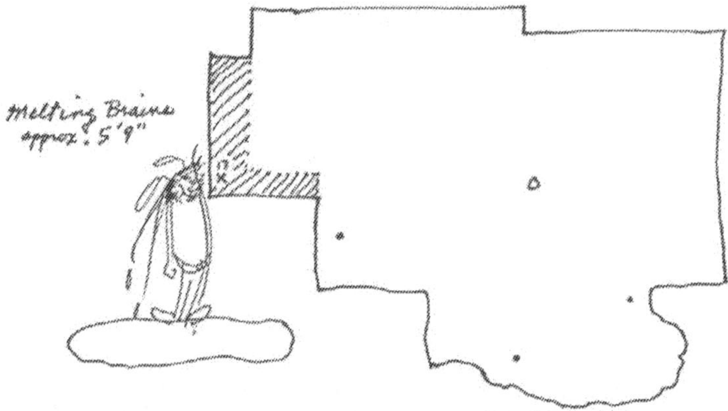

BONE – More bone than normal, probably refuse from the pit just east of the area. Indications throughout seem to show all material moved west of its original place. Very little burned bone.

STONE – Typical sandstone nuggets, one tiny fragment flat red stone. 3 limestone cobble fragments, all showing red fire coloration. 1 tiny limestone chip.

FLINT – 186 pieces; 2 are large cobble fragments – flakes mostly medium to small. One flake a rich maroon and butterscotch mottled. One fragment of a crude cutting/chopping tool. Coarse grain, yellowish-grey flint with mica intrusions. "Tacky" must have made this. Only one edge worked on each face, except around the curving edge. Somewhat similar to the tool found last time, but this seems to be edged for hacking and cutting – the earlier tool, worked on one surface only, seemed to be for scraping and cutting.

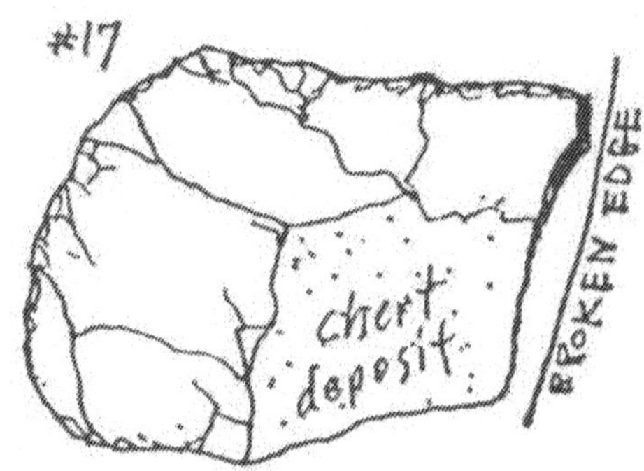

depth: 5" from surface.

June 8
half day

Standing water inhibits digging. Small amount of work in Areas A & B.

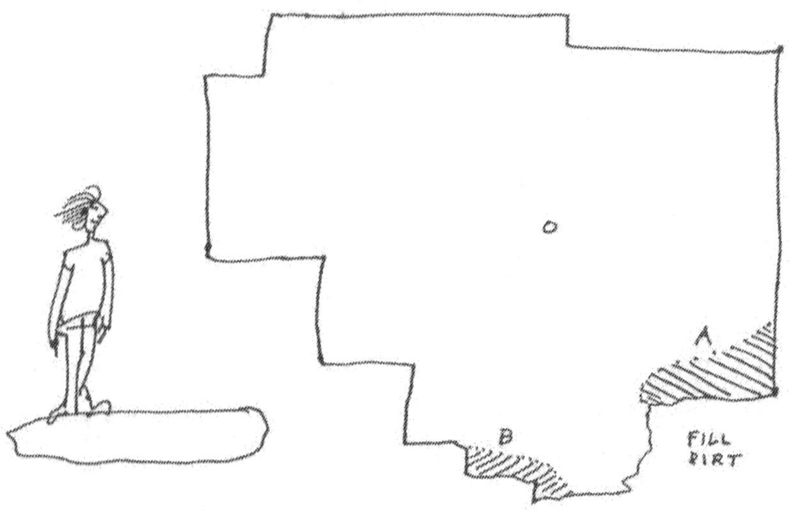

BONE – Bits, mostly white bone. Some raw bone.

STONE – Sandstone and soft yellow stone nuggets.
    One small piece flat hard brown stone.
    One small fragment limestone.

FLINT – 26 pieces – medium to tiny, assorted flint, all flakes.

Most of time spent surface hunting east of Rocking Deer. Found a broken hand knife, a broken projectile blank, base of a broken projectile, and a thumb scraper. Stone for the scraper is a fine-grained very dark bluish-grey with specks of white and blue-white. Many pottery fragments, grit-tempered.

June 21
half day

Son's first time at dig. We surface hunt east side, uneventfully, and cross creek. Earth has been baked hard – high clay content – many skinned knuckles. Son sees kingfisher.

BONE – Plentiful in Area B, including 3 teeth in a section, plus other bits of bison skull and jaw bone. The flat area of bone, dinner plate size, was all on original surface, did not continue below. In Area A, typical bits of bone. Earth is beginning to look streaky in NW corner of A.

STONE – Handful sandstone nuggets, some burned. One bit limestone, bits soft yellow stone.

FLINT – 79 pieces, mostly medium to small.

#18

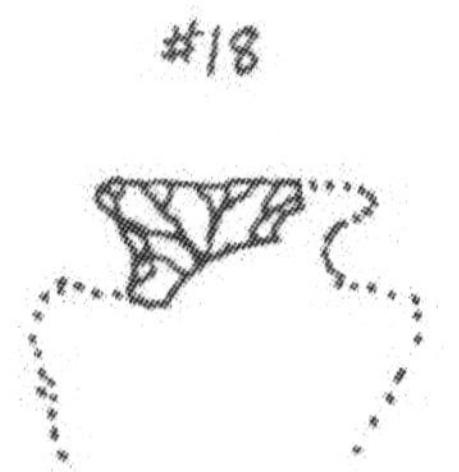

Med. grey flint speckled with white – fine grain – fine chipping. 6" down.

Ground very hard. Difficult to make headway. We haul buckets of water up from the creek and soak the face of the digging – helps some. I end up with many blisters.

BONE – Very little, raw and white, no burned bone.

STONE – Handful of sandstone nuggets, raw and burned. Bits of soft yellow stone.

Son finds 5" down, artifact #19, a flintworker's hammerstone – white percussion marks on one end.

FLINT – 63 pieces, typical mixture, 2 of which have been slightly worked on part of an edge. One flake of the beautiful maroon and golden yellow mottled.

Surface hunting the area, I find 3 fragments of projectile points – bit of a base in grey flint – midsection in pink banded – a base in white.

June 29
morning

Hot but breezy. We carry 12 lbs. of crushed ice out to the place and pack it on top of the area we want to work. Softens the earth somewhat – still large cracks, very dry.

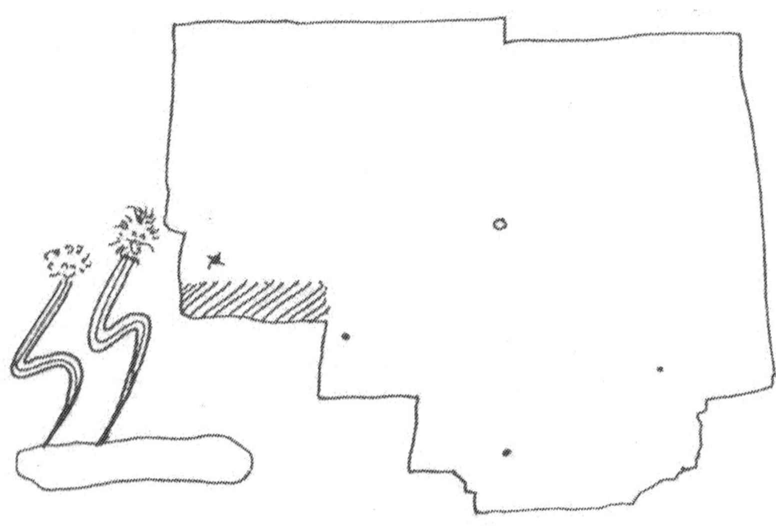

BONE – Typical scattered bits, not as much as usual.

STONE – Few nuggets sandstone, one small fragment pink quartz, 2 fragments brown quartz, one medium, one small. Small piece has high polish on original surface.

CLAY – 2 fragments – grey to black – grit tempered – rough surfaces.

FLINT – 38 pieces, mostly medium to small. Flint, as well as bone, seems more scarce as we progress west of fireplace.

Son finds a projectile point on the surface. Pink flint, fine grain, medium work. Medium size – slightly notched, barely any shoulders.

While digging, found 2 Lined Snakes, cooling themselves in a crack 10" down. Small-bodied – c. 10" long – pale clay tan with longitudinal deep yellow stripes.

July 2
half day

Sunny, some cloud cover, nice cool southern breeze. We work Areas A &
B, not finding as much evidence, but still in the area. On the way to the site
we see a Great Blue Heron flying low.

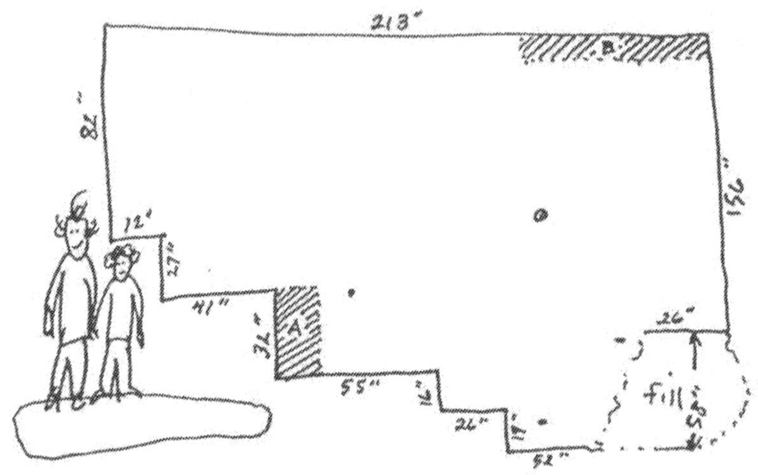

BONE – Small handful bone bits. One small bit burned bone in Area B.

STONE – ½ brown granite hammerstone –Area B, extreme NE corner, 5”
    down from surface. A few sandstone nuggets.

CLAY – One small bit clay pot – grit tempered, old, with worn edges. Area
    A – 3” down.

FLINT – 68 pieces, including one-half flint cobble, Area A, fine-grain
    yellowish-brown flint, grey-green skin. Unsuccessful attempt had been
    made to peel the rind from the cobble. Someone took a couple of
    cracks at it & tossed it aside? Larger % of large flakes.

Found scraper on surface – SW of area. ½ grey banded flint, ½ chert, grey-
white, divided diagonally. Fair workmanship – large. Limestone near tail
discolored where fingers wrap around it. Also on surface – W of area –
small bit of ceramic pot – grit tempered. Son finds, in crack under the
surface, a red-blonde jumping spider, size of an adult Phidipus Audax.
Don't know this kind.

July 9
long morning

Heavy rains 3 days previous. Much surface hunting. On the camp ¼ mile south, Son found a fine small corner-notched point (called a Palmer Corner-Notched by one source, Gordon Willey), dated as Archaic. Greyish-yellow flint with sparkling inclusion – this stone occurs on camps throughout the area. I found 2 broken blank bases – 1 rough Flint Hills med. grey, one greyish-yellow, grainy, and base fragment of medium size corner-notched point, fine-grain, pinkish. On Rocking Deer, Son finds one greyish-yellow grainy flake thumb scraper, 1 med. reworked, side-notched point, pink banded flint, 1 broken blank, greyish-yellow, grainy. I found 1 grey mottled thumb scraper, 1 grainy yellow side-scraper, 1 fragment (middle) grey knife, 1 fragment yellow-brown blank, 1 point reworked into a drill, fine-grained pinkish-grey flint. W. of Rocking Deer, Son finds a base of greyish-yellow grainy blank. East of RD he finds one side of a mottled grey corner-notched large point. 5 sherds of grit-tempered pottery on RD and E of it.

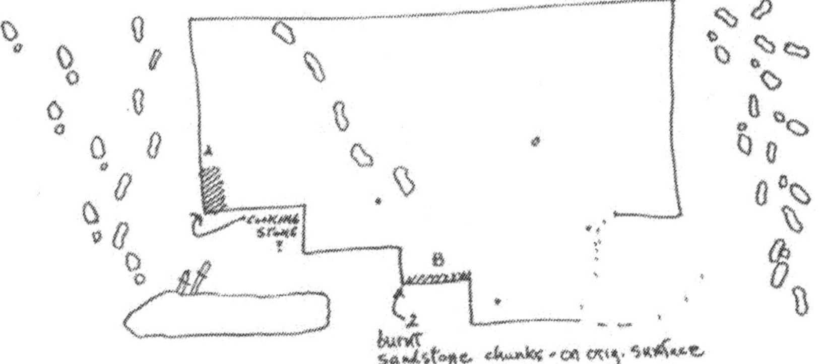

BONE – Slight amount, more presence of larger raw bits.

STONE – Increase of sandstone, some burned. One quartz pebble (cooking stone), dirty white. 1 small fragment white quartz pebble. 1 fragment grey quartz pebble.

FLINT – 41 pieces, including 4 cobble-end pieces. Suggestion is we are moving toward a fireplace and/or trash pit.

While digging, a large wasp hovers. Later comes walking between us dragging a Wolf Spider.

July 13
morning

Clear pleasant day – strong south wind.

On surface I find, about 10 or 20 steps SW of SW corner of dig, large scraper, grey-brown banded flint grading to grey-white chert diagonally. This area has yielded 3 scrapers since the last rain and is surely the "scraper area" I ran across walking 2 years ago – which I hoped to encounter with ditch 2, the westernmost one. A little off.

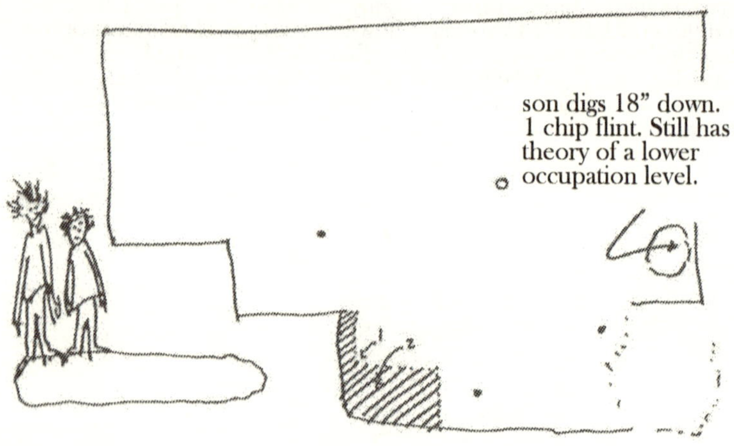

1 = 3 small slabs burned sandstone – continuation of feature found previous time.

2 = 2 large fragments broken long bone. All objects 9" down.

BONE – As above, + fragments raw and white bone. Some tooth frags.

STONE – As above, + small fragments sandstone. 1 small round fragment paintstone, 1 knuckle-sized fragment brownish granite cobble.

FLINT – 47 pieces, one with exploratory work along one edge. 1 primary core chip 9" down, in situ, fine grain and "greasy" luster of heat treatment. Rosy red – possibly the fine golden yellow flint found often at lowest level. Heated, it goes red. Supposition is that the *earliest* campers used this flint and used heat on it. Flint Hills flint, not noticeably found at lowest level (and resulting in larger pieces-tools) could have been brought in by later campers.

Before leaving, we take a 2-mile walk on the creekbank, but find nothing except 1 chip of flint.

August 6
half day

Dug small area
in east wall.
Dirt extremely
hard. Surface
hunting: one
large side-
notched point
with basal end
gone. One tip
large drill

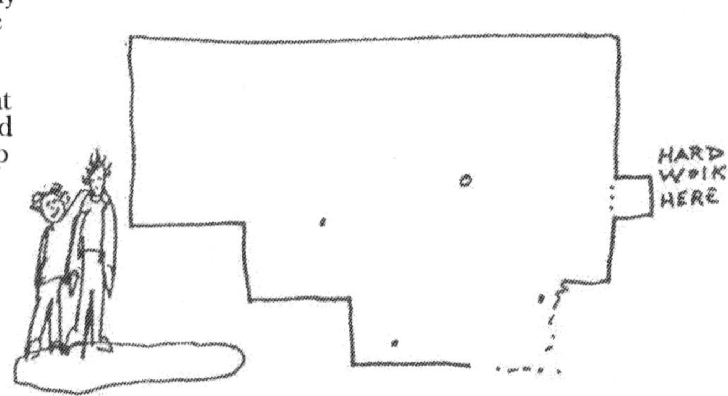

BONE – Small amount, small pieces. One medium piece raw bone.

STONE – Small handful small sandstone nuggets. One bit soft yellow
stone. One bit red paintstone.

FLINT – 29 pieces – 3 large cobble flakes, 2 of which show some edge-
work. 4 medium flakes – rest are small to tiny.

Through comparison with a point identification guide it seems that the
campfire and S and E portion of dig belongs to older campers (4000 –
1000 BC) and the trash pit of W edge belongs to later ones (100 – 500
AD). Earlier points are of a type called Williams, later points are Besant.
Pelican Lake points occur on surface SE of dig, as do Williams. Williams
occurs E of creek. ¼ mile south surface finds include Reed and Haskell –
1000 – 1400 AD, overlying older camp debris.

August 10
half day

Cool
cloudy
& Fine.

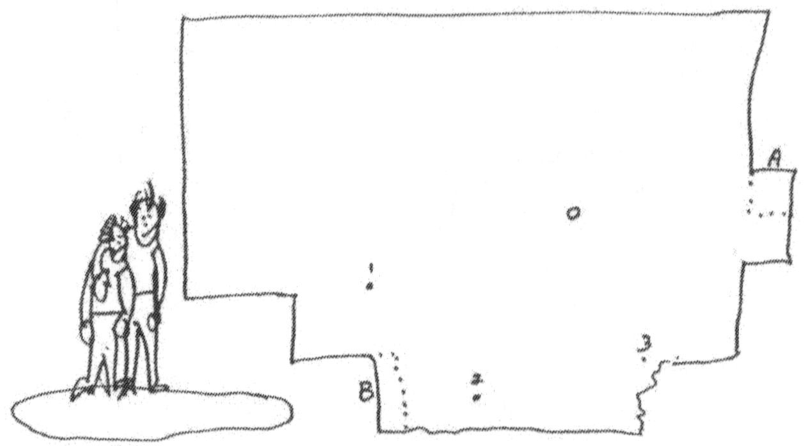

Began refill, breaking down walls with shovel and sifting dirt. Not a
satisfying way to work. Supposed postholes 1, 2, & 3 are animal burrows
(1, 2) and old tree root (3). So.

BONE – Small amount of bits. One medium piece raw bone from Area B.

STONE – Bits of sandstone – fragments of burned limestone from Area
   B. Two pieces soft yellow stone.

FLINT – 23 pieces, medium to small.

Surface: South of Rocking Deer—5 unidentifiable worked fragments.
               tip large sugar quartz point
               base small yellowish point
               mottled grey thumb scraper

               Rocking Deer—2 bits pottery - one coarse, one fine
               4 unidentifiable fragments

               East of Rocking Deer—2 unidentifiable fragments
               1 drill fragment

August 19
half day

Hot day – because
of rains, digging is
easier.
Worked East wall.

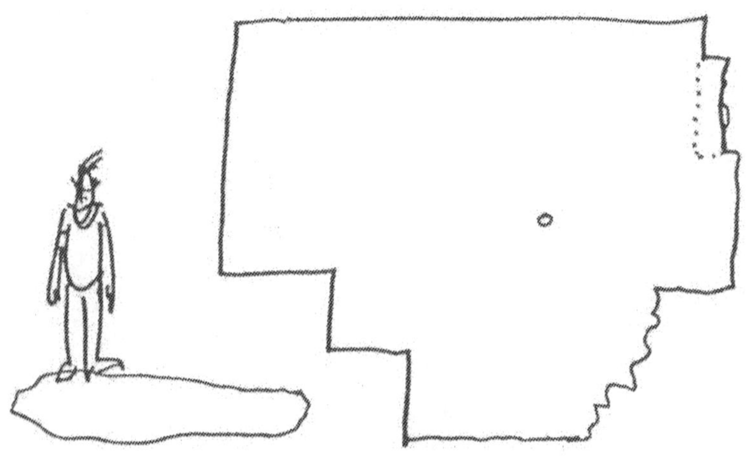

BONE – Small handful bits, raw and white, no burned. Some tooth
 fragments.

STONE – 3 medium pieces natural sandstone plus a few small nuggets.

FLINT – 38 pieces – medium to tiny – no worked pieces.

Surface finds: Rocking Deer south – One narrow Haskell point, missing
 base. One crude arrowpoint, one crude dart point. One
 crude drill, one modified flake scraper. Several broken
 items, mostly points.

 Rocking Deer – Base of a blank, tip half of dart point –
 both found N of the dig area.

Further plans call for concentration on S & W portion. Supposedly later
peoples, with possibility of polished stone implements?

August 30
six hours

Fine day. Black-Headed Vulture
coasting, sliding in the sky.
Giant Velvet Ant walking
through the dig.
Deer and
raccoon have
been checking
it out.
Lonely working
without my son.

BONE – Scattered raw bone at 12-14" level, large fragments bison or deer. No burned bone, two small bits white bone. 3 small legbones – size of rabbit.

STONE – Eight small fragments sandstone – none burned. Two small bits soft yellow stone. Some traces burnt sandstone and small bit of charcoal noticed in digging.

FLINT – 63 pieces – 3 large (1 of which is slightly worked) – rest medium to small. Some flakes show evidence of heating.

A sense while digging that flint is not plentiful here. More fragments raw bone than usual.

September 1
full day

Sounds of shotguns and 22's in the air all day. First day of
"dove season." Doves mighty flighty.

BONE – Less than usual – small bits, predominantly white, some raw,
   rarely burned.

STONE – Typical sandstone bits, usually not burned. One small soft
   yellow stone, two small bits paintstone. One medium & one small
   chunk pinkish-white quartz.

FLINT – 215 pieces – 3 large flakes, rest ½ medium, ½ small. Some show
   signs of fire. One small knife, found at x, 9" down, lying on edge.

#20 – Small knife – mottled light and medium grey flint grading to white
   chert at corner of wide end.

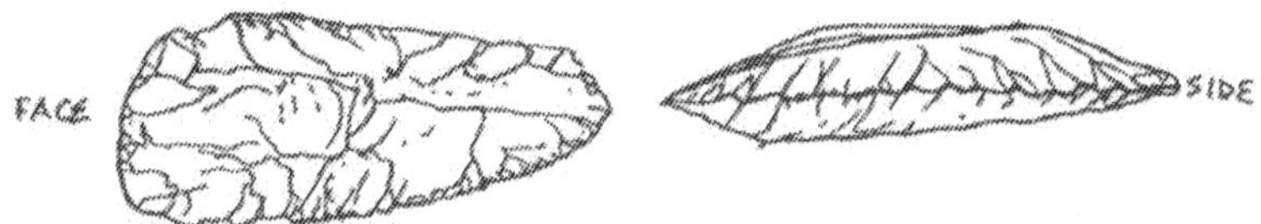

North is the way to go.

September 8
afternoon

Sunny & cool.

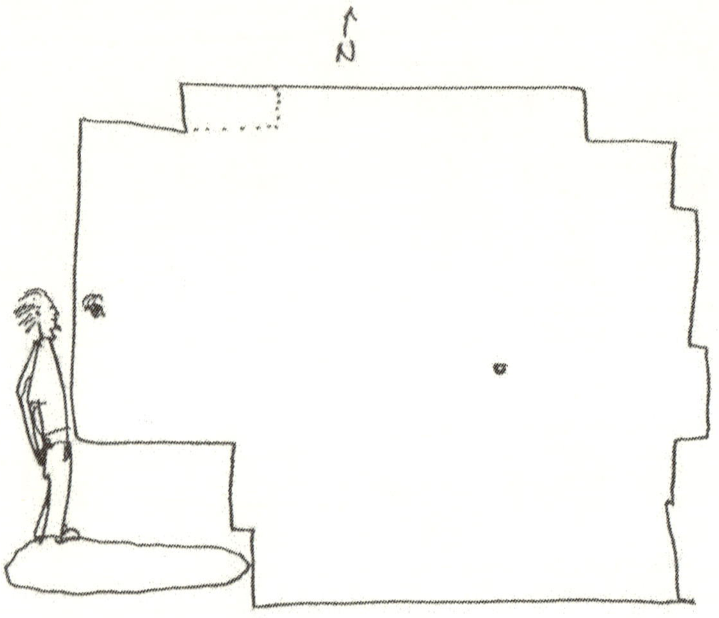

BONE – Small amount, raw or white. One fragment burnt.

STONE – Very small amount sandstone nuggets. A few bits of soft yellow stone. 1 small chunk limestone.

FLINT – 104 pieces, mostly medium. One large thick flake is worked tentatively along one edge. Nine fragments of long, thin blade flakes.

Concentration of flint along north wall – either a work area or, since the area slopes slightly down to the north, flint has washed more heavily in that direction over the years.

Flint concentration on North wall diminishes somewhat as I move to the west.

Buzzed three times by a bumblebee.

Sept. 12 & 15
c. 6 hours

Rain before.
Much surface
hunting

BONE – Very small amount, mostly raw, some burned, some white.

STONE – Usual sandstone nuggets, some burned maroon. One small bit white quartz, 2 bits limestone cobbles.

FLINT – 110 pieces, medium to small. At point x, front half of large well-made scraper, the broken end of which has been reworked! Light grey flint. At point +, front half of crude scraper, light grey flint. x = 2 inches down; + = 3 inches down.

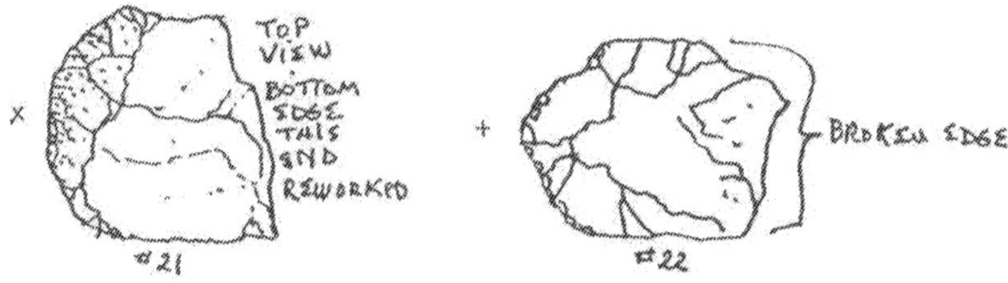

SURFACE – RD – 1 broken crude drill – yellow-grey coarse flint
1 broken point – coarse black flint
1 corner-notched point – grey banded flint, large, fine work, fine stone
1 medium grey mottled scraper
1 lip sherd rough pottery, identification to be pursued
1 strange medium drill, worked down from a point – pinkish-grey flint

RD South -   1 tip med. point – fine yellow-grey flint.
1 med. yellowish-cream notched point, missing part of base.
1 white quartz small flake thumb scraper.
1 small mottled blue-grey hand knife (led to by a fluttering owl feather).

November 15
full day

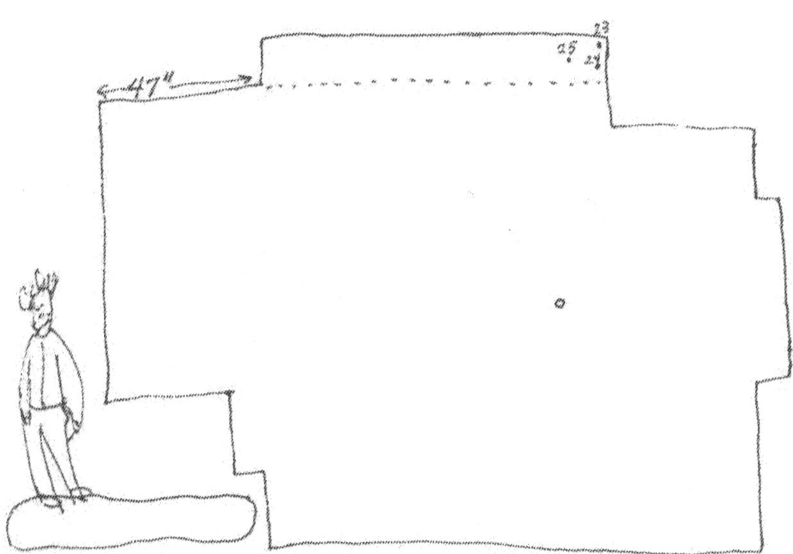

Long time away. Good long quiet day. Five Sparrowhawks along roads on the way.

BONE – Small amount, small fragments – raw, white, blue, burned.

STONE – Small nuggets sandstone, soft yellow stone – some burning
    evident. One small piece red paintstone. One tiny nugget clear crystal
    quartz.

FLINT – 98 pieces, mostly med. to small – typical variety.
    #23 – Yellowish-brown flint – fine grain – 1" down.
    #24 – Blue-grey flint – fine grain – 7" down.
    #25 – Light grey flint – med. grain – 5" down.

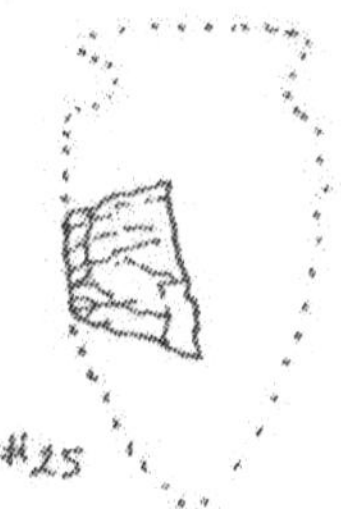

November 28
afternoon

Balmy. Quiet enough to hear squirrels hopping dead leaves on creekbank.

BONE – Increase in amount from last time. One medium fragment bison or deer legbone. Average size of bones somewhat larger than those from previous time.

STONE – Typical sandstone nuggets. One burned bright red.
Few pebble bits burned limestone.
One small piece smoky yellow quartz.
3 small fragments granitic or coarse quartz. ?

FLINT – 91 fragments, including one cobble half, yellow-grey flint. 1 slender flake pink mottled flint has been primary worked along one edge of one face. Not a fragment of a finished tool, but the flint is unique – this looks like a warm-up or "energy" work piece – or someone was taking the opportunity of exploring the properties of this rich pink spotted flint before starting to work on the blanks.

Deer season opens in December.

February 22
2 hours

Warm
and
Sunny

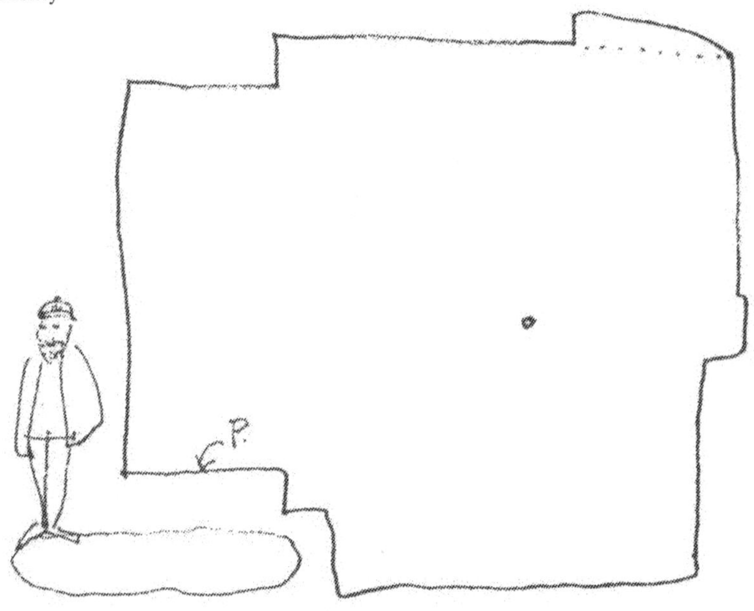

Worked NE corner. Finds are typical.

BONE – Few small bits white bone.

STONE – Small sandstone, yellow stone. 1 piece red paintstone.
   Small chunk grey granitic stone.
   1 flake dark grey sugar quartz.

FLINT – 26 pieces, mostly small flakes. No worked pieces.

Continued W, shaving N edge straight. Small piece of thick, coarse pottery,
   lightly grit-tempered, at point P.

Flock of seven prairie chickens on the way out.
A deer has visited the site.

Warm spring day. North wall. Evidence increases as I move to the west.

BONE – Typical mix of small fragments. Tooth bits.

STONE – Sandstone nuggets, 1 piece small paintstone, few bits soft yellow stone, 1 flake granitic stone. 2 flakes quartz, white & pink, latter has very smooth skin – glaciation?

FLINT – 100 pieces, including large black-skinned cobble with one flake off, yellow flint inside. 3 large flakes, one a coarse, granular pink. Others typical mix of med. and small flakes. 1 fragment of artifact.

#26 – fragment of projectile point. Streaked light and medium grey. Fine grained. 1" down from surface.

March 14
all day

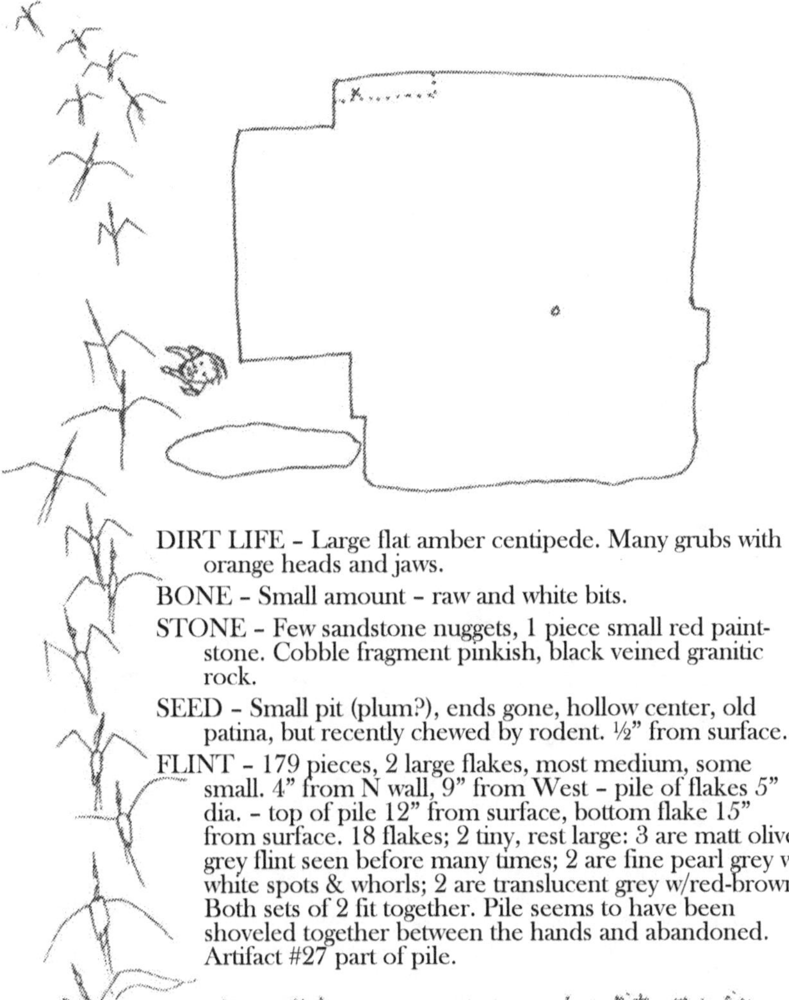

DIRT LIFE – Large flat amber centipede. Many grubs with orange heads and jaws.

BONE – Small amount – raw and white bits.

STONE – Few sandstone nuggets, 1 piece small red paint-stone. Cobble fragment pinkish, black veined granitic rock.

SEED – Small pit (plum?), ends gone, hollow center, old patina, but recently chewed by rodent. ½" from surface.

FLINT – 179 pieces, 2 large flakes, most medium, some small. 4" from N wall, 9" from West – pile of flakes 5" dia. – top of pile 12" from surface, bottom flake 15" from surface. 18 flakes; 2 tiny, rest large: 3 are matt olive grey flint seen before many times; 2 are fine pearl grey w/ white spots & whorls; 2 are translucent grey w/red-brown. Both sets of 2 fit together. Pile seems to have been shoveled together between the hands and abandoned. Artifact #27 part of pile.

April 4
all day

BONE – Typical bits, few in number, white or raw. One medium fragment raw legbone of large herbivore.

STONE – Small amount small sandstone nuggets, a few small pieces burned red or yellow. One knuckle-sized fragment Sioux quartz.

FLINT – 92 pieces – mostly small to medium – 7 larger flakes. One of the larger flakes, milky grey, along with 7 small flakes and capped with a large spall fragment of cobble flint, red-brown marbled,* was found as an undisturbed refuse heap at point 1. Another – only 5 small chips, at point 2. These piles of chips do not extend horizontally so much as vertically, suggesting a scooped hollow, chips brushed in, dirt scooped over the pile. These flint piles are stacked and compact in space no wider than a hand width. Makes sense in terms of common courtesy – otherwise many complaints about cut feet, hides, moccasins. This must represent the last step of the process of working flint – cover yer sharp mess.

*shows retouching

April 11
long afternoon

Fine day.
Shrikes,
Marsh Hawk,
Turkey Vulture,
Great Blue
Heron.

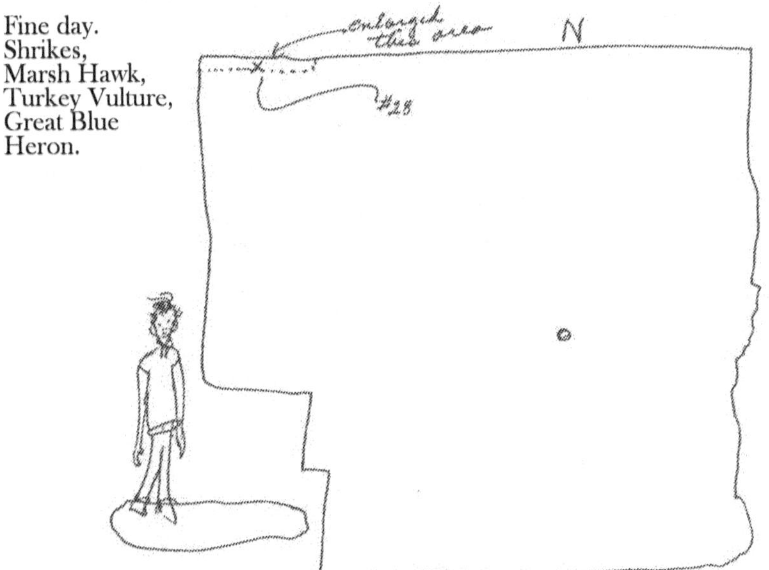

BONE – Very small amount – live and white bone.

STONE – 12 small nuggets sandstone – a few burned to soft yellow.

FLINT - 63 pieces, including 3 medium flakes; all other flakes small to
tiny. One fragment of a projectile point, found 9" from N wall, 27"
from W wall, 12" from surface – lying flat – appears just below plow
line. Base seems to be smoothed, indicating fracture in use instead
of fracture in the making of the piece.

A Besant-type point of medium
brown flint with yellowish cherty
deposits. This material is said to
come from creek deposits in the
Republican River drainage area –
NW Kansas. Found in abundant
use 60 miles south among the
Quivirans, c. 800 years ago, but
scarce on Rocking Deer. It is
called Niobrara Jasper. Problem
of source of other flint (cobbles) remains. Indications seem to point to a
Northern source but, if so, the people would surely have made blanks at
departure point rather than haul so much raw cobble with them. There
must be a closer source.

April 25
full day

Hot with a cool breeze. Deep double-note bird call in the air behind me. Looking back, I see a falcon pause rampant in the air and call the same two-note alarm, kee keee, wheels and flies to the southeast. I don't get my glasses on in time to get a detailed look, but much too large for a Sparrow-hawk – greyer and more banded. The call was too deep for a Sparrow-hawk. Not a Prairie Falcon. Pigeon Hawk very likely. Teal are using puddles in the fields – would a Peregrine pass through here? Whatever the make, I saw a fine falcon but failed to notice how hot the sun was, so didn't think to put my shirt on until an hour later. Very red. Also looked down on a Great Blue Heron as it flew just above the creek's path. Uncovered a small Lined Snake. THE TICKS ARE OUT.

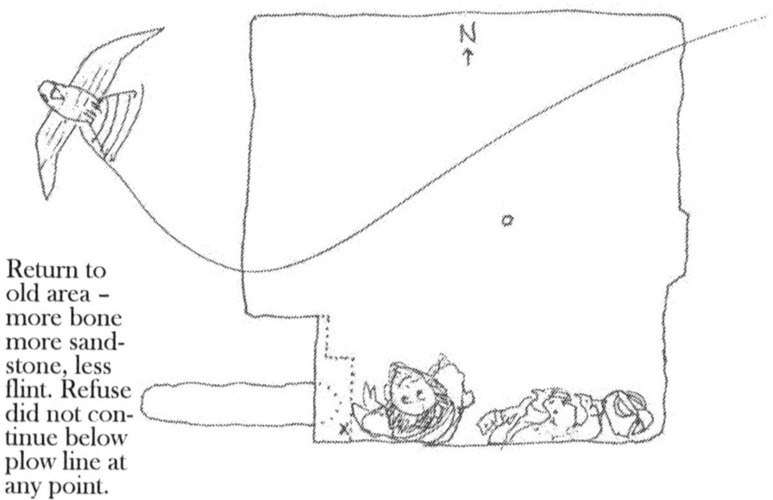

Return to old area – more bone more sand-stone, less flint. Refuse did not con-tinue below plow line at any point.

BONE – Mostly raw, largest piece knuckle-size. No concentration.

STONE – Sandstone nuggets, generally knuckle-size – 1 palm size frag-ment flat sandstone. Few small nuggets, burnt. One knuckle coarse crystalline white quartz, partly burned rind. One knuckle fine pinkish-brown quartz.

FLINT – 54 pieces – 1 cobble spall fine-grain mottled yellow/browns, looks like a fractured hammerstone given saw-like edge for rough cutting. Most chips are small. One blank?

– seems to be same material w/ traces of black rind flint and red marbling from heating. Could have been broken as maker began the first notch – or plow broken, though the fracture shows no metallic trace. The blank, 3" from surface, and spall, 9" from surface, both in plow zone. 4 feet apart.

At point X, 4" from S wall. Colorful stone – black-browns, reds, earth yellow. Reverse side flat. Rounded side thick – humped 2/3 way up from tip.

Interesting aspects about this broken blank.

Gives a clear picture of the "golden flint" encountered at lowest level. This cobble flint, at its center, in natural state is a fine-grained yellowish- brown with whitish spots or inclusions. Generally swirling forms. This blank was worked from a flake struck from a heat-treated cobble – natural coloration turns reddish and maroon where the heat has soaked into the cobble – immediately overlying this is a thin layer of the "golden" flint, then a thin layer of black flint, then the black rind. All colors within the cobble are lustrous, fine-grained. The piece, blank, is a very good indication of this type of flint and how heat transforms it. Details make more sense – e.g., every flake of "golden" flint found had black on one or more edges. Of artifacts, whole & broken, from 25 yrs. + of surface hunting Rocking Deer, only one fragment seems to be from this flint. So...a deep level flint – earliest campers? A tool of this flint would tell much.

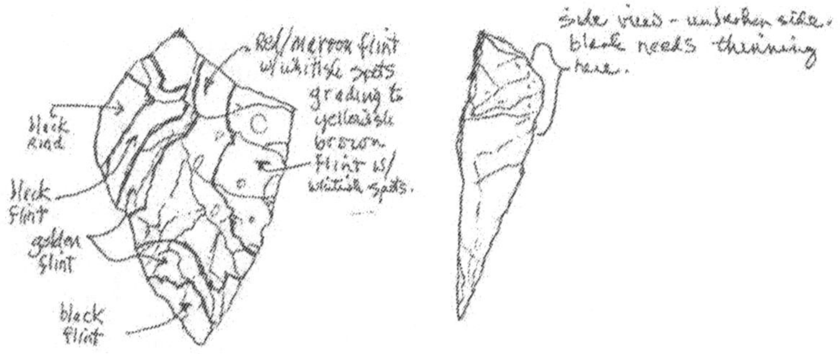

The ends of the fracture are at the top of the base and at "notchpoint" on the shoulder. Trying to follow the worker – both flat & curved surfaces rough-flaked. On curved side, secondary flaking all over and retouching up right side to point of fracture. Flat side retouched along its right side, to point of fracture at base middle. Whether the maker broke it attempting to thin the base, or starting a notch, or trying to remove tough cobble skin from the right shoulder of the blank – he was clearly intent on producing a fine point – and he would have had one, too – dramatic coloration and flowing forms. It's easy to visualize this blank as a thinned, notched projectile point of striking design. Here is one of the careful temperaments I have been looking for. In this case, he hurried or was unlucky in his pressure on the stone.

May 9
short day

A mother White-Footed Mouse pops out of a hole in the dirt in front of my face and runs across the dirt floor, up the opposite wall and into one of 4 holes there. She's followed hesitantly by 6 teenage mice - ready to go but

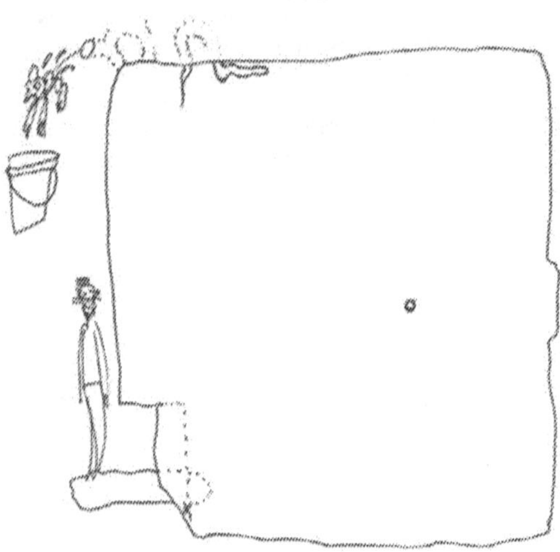

large heads and feet, short tails, uncertain, jerky leaps. They all make it into the same hole. Ten minutes later a large Bull Snake comes along the base of the wall, crawls up and into one of the holes. When it is half in, one of the young mice pops out of another hole and runs crazily back to my area, manages to stumble and fall into an empty green plastic bucket. Snake emerges from yet another hole. Dry run. He sees me and lifts up the wall, over, and off into the wheat. The adolescent mouse sits in the bottom of the bucket with a truly existential expression on its face. Tipped out, he makes it back to the hole the rest of the family is hiding in.

BONE - Abundant, mostly raw. One small piece burned bone. One raw knee joint (at X) - large, as buffalo. Bone seems to have been scattered on the surface here, does not go any deeper than that original surface. Also, tooth fragments.

CLAY - Very small worn piece coarse pottery - found in plow zone.

STONE - One double-knuckle white crystalline quartz. Craze lines from heat. 2 small fragments quartz. One flake purplish sugar quartz.

FLINT - 62 pieces; 3 medium cobble fragments - majority of flakes medium to small. The cobble used by the earliest inhabitants is plentiful in flakes, all but one of which show heat coloration.

One small angle left to do - then a shallow arc into the East wall, and the area will be ready to be recovered after harvest.

May 22
2 hours

Water Snake on
the road.

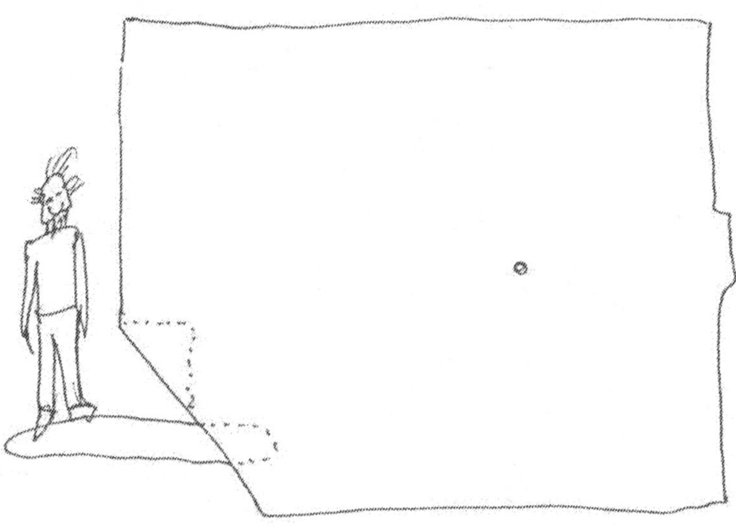

Finished last area. Ripe wheat around entire perimeter now. No more work
until after harvest.

BONE – Small fragments, mostly live.

STONE – 3 small pieces granular quartz.

FLINT – 20 pieces, small to tiny.

At this point, it's clear that the yellow-brown translucent cobble flint occurs
at the lowest level.

Only artifact so far of this flint is broken blank found April 25. They
brought this cobble flint from how far? which direction? Camped here,
made new projectile points, trashed the old, wornout ones, moved on.
Somewhere there is a campsite where the majority of wornout castoff
projectile points is this yellow-brown cobble flint.

July 14

Filled up, leveled out. Watched for flint in the fill dirt as I
loaded it back in the hole. Didn't see any.
These folks were travelers, camped here successive times.
They didn't work bone into shape, didn't make ground-and-pecked
tools, axes, celts, etc.
They didn't make beads. In fact, not one piece of shell was found.
I guess they didn't do clams. There were hammerstones but no evidence of grinding stones - no seeds, nuts, in the diet? The plum
pit does seem old and charred, but that could have happened during
a stubble burnoff anytime in the last fifty years.
The projectile points are all large – suggests throwing stick or
short throwing spear rather than bow and arrow.
The flint hide scrapers are generally large.
Pottery raises a lot of questions – all cord-roughened – one sample
shell-tempered. Different peoples, or different generations of the
same peoples?

The yellowish-grey cobble flint with the thin black rind is a puzzle.
I didn't think there was a source of such flint anywhere near here.
This isn't flint country – have walked creek and hills, gullies,
in the area, no flint. I've taken samples to geologists – they
didn't say much about it. One sent me to a bridge 30 miles west
of the site. There was rock below on the riverbank but no
flint cobbles.

What I think is glacial smoothing on some of the granite nuggets
suggests they passed through the country 100 miles NE of here;
brown Niobrara jasper suggests they passed through 100 miles NW
of here; Flint Hills blue-grey suggests they were 100 miles east
of here. If this same place has been camped on again and again
and extensive weapon repair gone into, which it has been for damn
sure, it would suggest that this was a good spot to camp *because*
these cobbles, a source of weapon points, were close at hand.
Can't believe it. Can't find it either. Something to look for.

Making Do in the Year One

When Walker had returned as an adult and begun to walk the old sites again, the irregular patch of ground on the Rocking Deer that had so absorbed his father's attention claimed his mind each time he walked upon it. The journal, its existence a revelation in itself, had surprised him in many ways. Walking hot, dust in his nose, he heard in the Kingfisher calling from the woody creek, not just a bird but the descendant of one his father heard call on a similar day. Deer still liked the site, and he saw them often, springing full bodied, white tails up and switching, the grown great-grandchildren of the doe that had danced in front of his father.

His old man had once seen two deer, the raised ears and sober appraisal, then bounding for the line of the creek trees. But the old man had gone back to watching the dirt and had forgotten about the deer by the time he reached the site proper. He'd wandered a bit, then went to piss off the edge of the field into the cheat grass and wild plum. If he'd been taking a piss here two thousand years ago, he'd have recognized it as a time to be very alert.

"Ever see a dog take a dump?"

"Well, yeah."

"Ever notice how worried he looked?"

But the old man was species master of the landscape in his own mind. Civilization had made it possible for him to piss in the wilds with a peaceful mind, so the old man had fallen to daydreaming, enjoying the sunshine and the clatter he was making on the dry, brown, oak leaves.

He said that when he zipped up and turned around, the doe was just there, behind him in the field, five strides away. She had come up out of the creek and walked across the field silently while he had idly concentrated on wetting as many leaves as possible.

He said she stood broadside, facing west, and regarded him from the corner of her eye, as if pretending she didn't know he was there and at the same time keeping an eye on his next move.

He said that when he just stared open-mouthed, she rolled her head slowly, stretched her neck, chewed once, turned her eyes directly on him and gave a little stabbing prance with her forelegs as if to say, "Pay attention, stranger because I do not do this often."

He said she danced, not an abandoned bucking but a stylized rocking and leaping in place. She danced on four legs, three, and two, arching her back, weaving her neck.

He said he felt no fear, was very pleased. She paused once and then danced again.

He said he recovered his wits then and, to show he was no threat, bent over slowly until he was looking at the dirt, whistled a soft rhythm and began a slow shuffle dance of his own, turning his back on the deer.

He said he never knew if he'd done the right thing, because he never got to see the expression on the doe's face. After watching the toes of his boots dance in three slow circles, and hearing nothing, he looked up. She'd gone just as quietly as she had appeared.

He said her dance was one of the sexiest things he'd ever seen, adding that he knew that was beside the point.

He said it was his choice and he'd decided it was a dance of welcome, not of warning.

And so the old man had dug during the day and worked on his journal of speculation at night. The wrongheadedness of some of that eager speculation became almost endearing to Walker as he lived with the journal down the years; the false nonchalance when the old man considered the possibility of unearthing a bannerstone, his dewy vision of a lodge based on what he thought were postholes, his benign neglect in not exploring and verifying the postholes until the end. He could imagine the old man's dismay when he discovered he'd been building lodges in the air. The old man was a pretty good list-maker but not much of an archaeologist; he hadn't even laid out a grid.

What Walker found to admire was the discovery that his father wasn't as much a slave to pretty objects as he'd supposed. If finding goods had been his goal, he could've used a shovel, bucket, and sifter and covered the area in two or three days. There would have been no need to measure, to shave the dirt carefully with a knife, to examine and record every boring chip and fragment. The bursitis he caused in his right shoulder, which encouraged him to move his right arm very slowly for eight months, never got mentioned in the journal, but Walker remembered, from the summer he'd helped at the dig, how the old man kept his right elbow tucked against his ribs as he sliced dirt with his knife, and the slow, grimacing ceremony of putting on or taking off a shirt.

From the objects he'd found on the Rocking Deer in the many years since the dig, Walker had revised and advanced his father's perceptions. The men who sat chipping flint around that old fire, the man who had leaned back and scooped a shallow pit to brush the scraps into, had come from Canada. A culture had existed in Saskatchewan around 300 BC, the Pelican Lake people, who made large points with broad U-shaped notches in the corners of the base. In the same area, around 300 BC, lived a culture archaeologists named Besant. Their projectile points were basically the same as those of Pelican Lake, but the notches had moved from the corners to the sides of the base. Many of these Besant points were intermediary: one notch coming in from the corner, the other coming in from the side. All three styles appeared on the Rocking Deer, and splitting the temporal difference, Walker dated the site at 1 AD.

Points similar to Pelican Lake and Besant had been found in Montana, both Dakotas, all the way down to Oklahoma. Those who had camped on the Rocking Deer had brought glaciated hammer-stones, molasses-colored chalcedony from Knife River, North Dakota, varied brown jaspers from northwest Kansas, gray and blue-gray flint from eastern Kansas. Had they followed bison south for the winter? Had the Rocking Deer camp been used only once or was it a traditional camping place? All the campers Walker knew, including himself, returned to the places that worked, and he assumed the same was true of this camp.

The creek came from the west like a snake, and the Rocking Deer was nestled in one of its northern loops, protected by creek timber from the west, east, and the cold north winds. A thin wrinkle meandering through the peninsula of land suggested that the creek had not always been in the same place, that it had shifted and the old bed healed over. Walker was not enough of a geologist to know how long the creek had been in its present bed, but if the camp had been on the earlier watercourse, it was still on the south side of the water. Knowing the bitterness of north wind in Kansas winter, Walker made a theory: there would be no camps found on the north side of the creek. He walked west along the creek one day, staying on the south side. An eighth of a mile west of the Rocking Deer he found another camp, a small one, four or five flint chips in an area not much larger than a bed. An eighth of a mile farther west, he found another; both of them, because of the scarcity of what was left behind, he saw as solitary camps, used only once.

Did these camps precede the accumulation on the Rocking Deer or were they the result of contemporaries who preferred to camp in private? An answer might be found by digging up the two isolated camps, but Walker was not a digger. All he could do was walk down and check the camps every year after plowing. The chips of flint were the same as those found on the Rocking Deer, and eventually he found a hide scraper and a Pelican Lake point with one shoulder broken, no longer capable of being hafted. It was made from a flint unknown to him, pearl gray grading into brownish-gray, shiny and heat-treated. He took it to be a cobble flint from somewhere to the north. Beyond the camp, he ran out of plowed ground.

That summer he and Young Walker drove to the farthest camp, crossed a bridge, and got out of the car on the north side of the creek. The entire area was plowed, with a smooth rain-skin in which stone would stand out. They walked east along the creek, exploring every curve, every slope, and found no flint, no bone, no pottery. The only sign of humans was a big crowbar, shaken off a tractor long enough ago to grow a skin of rust.

They drove home to cool baths empty-handed, but now they knew all camping had been done on the south side of the creek. There had probably been no lodges, at least not as the old man had thought of the term. These were hunting camps, seasonal and semi-permanent, and the living quarters probably fell somewhere between the words "lodge" and "shelter." Finding it difficult to believe Kansas winters were any less fierce two thousand years ago, Walker presumed these northerners went as far south as Oklahoma or Texas, stopping at the Rocking Deer on their way back, as winter slid into spring.

He had found dozens of broken and worn-out projectile points and only a handful of whole, undamaged ones. Points with damaged base corners and shoulders had been discarded as beyond repair, but the Pelican Lake people were frugal; when the tip was broken off a point, a new one was worked on, and the arrow went back into service with a shorter, but still effective point, and if that tip were broken, it would be reworked yet again. The worn-out points Walker had found were all the same, a notched base with a blade reworked so many times it was no more than a stubby triangle—less bulk, impact, and penetration power, but workable until the necessary flint and/or time was available. Success, a full belly, depended on many qualities, and one of them was the ability to make-do. The prairie encouraged a make-do philosophy. The people who lived here now, two thousand years later, drove tractors over the camps, and it was a good bet that somewhere in the guts of each tractor was at least one vital piece of baling wire that kept the machine going.

Since he was not a scientist, Walker could indulge romantic maundering with a clear conscience, and he thought often of the sense of renewal a hunter must have felt, having made four, five, or six new points, long, full-bladed and sharp, cutting free the blunt, battered points of the worst four, five, or six arrows in his arsenal. Undoubtedly, some of those old points were cast aside without a glance, but Walker imagined some of them must have gotten a moment's consideration and because these old people saw life in everything and weren't afraid to be heard speaking to inanimate objects, words might have been spoken.

I'm glad to see you go. You've been nothing but trouble, brittle and contrary from the beginning. Good riddance to a poor stone.

I'm leaving you here, remembering all the meat you've brought. Those were good times.

It was like the old man's junkers. Always strapped for money, his life had been a series of extensively used cars, each of which had ultimately died the final death, transported in a moment from a car into irrevocable junk. Some of these losses the old man had accepted without comment, but Walker had witnessed other occasions when, waiting for a friend to come help him push his heap of metal to the scrapyard, the old man had delivered a few words.

You worthless sow. You can't believe how glad I am it's come to this. So long, you whining, little bloodsucker, you had to be built by men with a grudge.

Well, hell, that's it. I'm gonna miss you.

Walker had been embarrassed then for his old man because other people had heard him speaking to a dead car, but the old man had been giving him an unexpected gift. He could trace to the old man not only his love of flint, his interest in Asian philosophy, passion for art, abuse of cigarettes, tolerance of solitude, disregard for money, recognition of the need to make-do, as he made-do with the old man's absence, but also an acceptance that everything had spirit, and the ability to speak to it comfortably, no matter who was listening, was a good thing to have. It kept him from falling into the trap of thinking that humans were the only thing worthy of communication.

Mystery and Gravy Cobbles

The point was the length of a middle finger. The base line was straight, notched at the corners, the notches curving into the stone quickly, forming sharp spurs at each corner of the base. The notches made wide curves and came out at a slant, so that the shoulders of the blade were not parallel to the base line, but slanted slightly away from it. The shoulders were sharp, equal in size and shape, and the lines of the blade were long curves converging into a sharp tip. A thread could be stretched from tip to center of base line, and each half of the point would exactly mirror the other. It had been used very little, or not at all, the edges crisp and thin. None of the broad shallow scars remained from the preliminary flaking; careful secondary flaking had replaced them with smaller, narrower channels, and over those, along the edges, were the marks of fine retouch flaking.

The flint was clear grayish-yellow near the tip, marbled as the blade widened with maroon and opaque butterscotch yellow, shifting again at the shoulders to a rich golden yellow, flecked with dark red. One corner of the base was a lustrous black. It was beautiful beyond use, the work of an artist, a tool loaded with magic, and it existed only in Walker's mind.

Long-dead Chinese poets had warned him not to set such wishful goals in his path, yet every time he approached the Rocking Deer, the image of this dartpoint, if only for one turn of a second, would enter his mind. He knew his desire for this Ideal would partially blind him to anything he might find. He accepted that dreaming of possibility was part of the process of walking, and he accepted equally that too much dreaming poisons the moment. Could he see, with this vision hovering in his head, anything the broken or worn-out or poorly made points had to teach him? And if he found a point perfectly shaped and crafted from ordinary uniform gray flint, would he only see it in comparison to his glorious Ideal? The shades of Chinese sages shook their wispy heads. On occasion, like the time he found himself staring at the plowed furrow and actually visually imagining the point, he had to speak out loud to himself.

"Shake it off, man."

He had chosen the cobble flint that had intrigued his old man as the material for his dream point, even knowing that had such a point been made on the Rocking Deer, it would move on when the people moved on and be broken or lost somewhere else. He would continue to walk the site and continue to struggle with desire. Though most of the old flintworkers who had sat there chipping away seemed concerned with nothing beyond function, he still hoped to find an artist among them. To an artist, rolling one of the old man's oval mystery cobbles out of the fire, positioning it a-cross an anvil stone, rapping the rounded ends off, standing it on one end, striking down at the edge to knock long flakes free, the bold color and swirl of the revealed stone would have been irresistible.

From his own walking and repeated readings of the journal, he knew three things the campers did: split and chopped bone told him they ate a lot of big game; flint hide scrapers told him they preserved the skins of those animals; flintknapping debris told him they made tools and weapons. There was no evidence of ceremony, ritual, or magic, no obvious stones or bones engraved for the purpose of petitioning chance, no projectile point that went beyond its purpose to use beauty and symmetry to gather force and accuracy to itself. Yet he continued, as he walked, to believe that the impulse toward magic had been with the campers and that one of them must have had the skill to give it form.

About an eighth of a mile of wheat field south of the Rocking Deer was another camp of the Pelican Lake people, and twenty miles north was another. Flint was scarce on the surface of the northern site, and almost all of it seemed to have come from the Flint Hills. Some hide scrapers had been found, some projectile point fragments, and three discarded points, each damaged slightly in the area of the notches. All were in the Pelican Lake style, all made of gray flint.

There were no fractured cobble shards, as at the Rocking Deer; if they were the same people, this northern camp may have been popular in the years before they'd expanded their flint sources. Conversely, the northern camp might have existed hundreds of years after the Rocking Deer camp if the people had abandoned, or been kept away from, all their flint sources but one. A single object picked up in the northern camp connected the two sites, a roughly fashioned oval chopping and cutting tool made from the mystery cobble flint prevalent on the Rocking Deer, an area of black rind still attached to one side. No special care had been taken in making the tool, but that was within the tradition of choppers. Meant to hack and cut at the same time, the edge needed to be coarse, a saw-like zig-zag created by knocking a large flake off one side of the edge, striking the second flake off the opposite side, back to the original side for flake three, and so on, alter-nating flakes the length of the edge. Walker had yet to find a chopper that could be called anything but crude, but this one was special for its implica-tions. If the Pelican Lake/Besant hunters left the Rocking Deer, headed back north with a newly made inventory of weapons, many of them fash-ioned from the mystery cobbles, and if one of those hunters was an ace flintworker who felt that making an object of beauty was an act of gratitude, then here, twenty miles north of the field strewn with cracked cobbles, might be the place where the perfect cobble flint dartpoint was mislaid or lost.

When he thought like this, Walker was beyond the help of generations of Chinese poets, worse than a fool, burdening another field with his expectations. Sometimes he was able to recognize the dream of perfection coming on and laugh himself into sobriety.

Ten minutes south of the Rocking Deer, the ghost of a creekbed curved into the middle of a field. The creek had once looped west here, and the tongue of land inside the loop had been camped on by the same people who'd camped on the Rocking Deer and used the same way; cracked and flaked mystery cobbles came up with the plow, along with Flint Hills grays and the various brown Smoky Hill jaspers. Before, after, or at the same time they'd camped on the Rocking Deer, the Pelican Lake/Besant people had camped here, but this site had an unexpected feature.

The old migrant hunters and gatherers had probably last camped on the southern creekbend no more recently than 300 AD. The old campfires sank slowly beneath the surface, weeds and bushes moved in, grew over, healed the trampled area, restored it to being just a bend in the creek, an identity it kept for roughly one thousand years, when a different people stopped, considered, settled in.

When Walker stood on that ground, he was in a plowed field. A broad shallow swale that swept around in a horseshoe showed where the old creek had been. It was plowed too. Some seven hundred years before Walker stood there, it had been thriving and lived on, but the creek, too, was a creature of change, and farther upcreek a shift of flow had choked off the bend. It was no longer a prime growing place for bushes and trees. The old timber died and made way for the younger trees, and as these grew into their maturity and died, the number of young trees coming up after them had diminished. And so on, until there were no more big trees, just a boggy bend choked with saplings, the long grasses moving in and taking over until the trees gave it up, the last of the big cottonwoods no more than log dust, saplings and seedlings fighting grass for water, sunlight, room. The creekbed became part of the tallgrass prairie, a curve where growth was particularly lush. In Walker's time, the old bed would still hold water after long rainy spells, and he'd once found tracks where a Great Blue Heron had inspected the curving, water-filled scar.

Sitting in the bare field, a bump under the sun, Walker could close his eyes and briefly conjure the old creekbed in full flower, the sound of cottonwood leaves and wind, the staccato Kingfisher, the way it had been around 1000-1300 AD, when the new people had chosen it as home.

Unlike the older people, they spent most of their energy tending instead of chasing. A small band of farmers who had tamed plants, they supplemented the produce with bison, deer, turkey. Hunting had not disappeared, it had been replaced as the primary passion by growth and harvest. Just as the hunt yielded to the garden, so a camp became a home, the shelters of hunters giving way to the lodges of farmers. Surely there were the outlines of lodges beneath this ground, no more than eight of them, Walker thought, considering the spit of land was no larger than half a football field, but not being a digger, he'd never test the proof. Their small green plots certainly held corn, probably beans, squash, gourds scattered in patches of rich soil along the creek. They had probably devised food cache pits for storage of surplus.

He could imagine the creek but not the settlement—it had gotten more complicated than a shelter and a fire, and he knew if he could be suddenly transported back, he would be amazed at his lack of imagination, in the same way a farmer of that time, spun forward seven hundred years, would be amazed at his inability to comprehend the orderly lines of cereal grass stretching away in all directions. To a digging-stick agriculture mentality, so many plants, so many seeds, so many holes, so many thrusts of the stick at the earth—cannot be! The sight of that enormous wheatfield would be enough in itself to freeze the poor shade into a shock of silence—its implications: cheeseburgers, gyroscopes, gourmet catfood, and genital deodorant, would have left him braindead, just as spending a day and night in the old creekbank world would have left Walker babbling with deprivation.

The farmers made pottery, used the bow and arrow, ground seeds between flat stones, and made tools clearly distinct from those of the earlier occupants. The migratory hunters had favored large, well-formed hide scrapers, topside humped, underside flat, with a broad, steep working edge, sides tapering back to end in a flat, mashed scar showing where the strike had been made that separated the flake from the mother stone. At least as long as a thumb and twice as wide at the scraping end, half of an enormous raindrop in stone, the best of the Pelican Lake/Besant hide scrapers showed an interest in symmetry and the careful flaking away of sharp irregularities on the humped surface. The people of the farming band showed no such concern, their hide scrapers were rudimentary flint chunks, worked mainly at the scraping end, a necessity to keep spurs and sharp edges from cutting the hide as fat is scraped from it. The farmers took no special care with the body of the scraper, knocking it into rough shape with the removal of large flakes. The same choppy work characterized several, thick crude gouge or chopper tools that didn't appear in the tool kits of the earlier migratory hunters. Some were as long as a thumb, some half that length; these hack-cutting tools were usually associated with butchering. The Rocking Deer bison hunters, doing more of it, had developed long, lance-like chopper knives that, gripped between thumb and all four fingers, presented a fine cutting edge the width of the hand.

By keeping what he found on each site separate, Walker could give his imagination certain handholds: there was no evidence on the Rocking Deer that it had ever been visited by the farm band who settled centuries later on the creekbend slightly to the south. The two little slopes in the same massive wheatfield told very different stories. Since both had been used by the bison hunters and only one by the farmers, it was fairly easy to suppose which group had made what object. The chunky little hackers belonged to the farmers, and the question it brought to Walker's mind was, what happened to these creekside farmers' hide-working industry? They made plenty of butchering tools, but he'd found only two hide scrapers, both made by working a scraping edge on the wide end of a thick flake, with no attempt to make it friendly to the hand that would use it. A lack of hide-dressing tools could be expected if skins had been replaced as the main clothing material by plant fiber, rolled, twisted, braided, or woven—or if the farmers traded produce for dressed hides.

Twenty miles to the east, at the same time, villages of farmers had dotted the banks of a river later called the Smoky Hill. These farmers clearly did have a hide-working tradition; they'd left behind hundreds of well-made scrapers. Differences in tools and flintwork pointed to different beginnings for the two cultures, but they may have been aware of each other in the same way a later community of struggling Scandinavian farmers would know of a nearby settlement of Russians or Germans. But you couldn't trade produce with people who already grew their own.

Once settled agricultural life was established, not everybody picked up the hoe. Bands of roving hunters were still a reality when the Europeans arrived, and there was no reason to think they hadn't been around in the days when the dead creek thrived. The wandering hunters would be rich in hides and vegetable-poor, but trade would be jittery; last year's traders could be next year's raiders. Trade seemed a slim answer to the riddle of the missing scrapers because two characteristics of what the small band of farmers south of the Rocking Deer left behind seemed to suggest they were a solitary band who did not range far from home and took part in no established trade system.

The first concerned the kind of arrowpoint they made. These points, no longer than a thumb joint, tended to long, narrow blades, sharp tips, and notches that bit in from the corner of the base, each striking at a deep diagonal toward the axis of the body. The wide notches created shoulders that swept back from the tip and were barbed, and a slender neck that flared outward on either side as it merged into the baseline. The edges of the blades were often worked into fine serrations, regular as the teeth of tiny fish.

This expanding base/skinny neck design allowed more room for binding so that it could be fixed more tightly than a point with shallow notches and a wide neck. Its drawback was in breaking, because of that skinny neck, more easily on impact. It was the preferred style of the little band of farmers—all the other ruined villages Walker had known, from the Smoky Valley river people to the complex society of the Quivira, preferred a different style of notching, and although one of the skinny-necked, corner-notched arrowpoints had shown up in a Smoky Valley village, it wasn't enough to suggest a mingling of styles.

In Walker's time, this narrow-necked arrowpoint was named Scallorn and was supposed to have been in use from around 700 to 1500 AD. A variation, in which the notches slid off the corner position and entered diagonally from the sides of the base, and the baseline changed from straight to concave, was named Haskell. It was dated at 1200 to 1350 AD. Both point styles were prevalent in Oklahoma, and the range of the Scallorn continued into Texas. This didn't mean much, since Scallorns and Haskells could be found, in varying densities, all throughout the Mississippi Valley, but it was armature enough to support a story about southern farmers moving north from misfortune, looking for a place both fertile and peaceful, or a clan or family group of incorrigibles, driven out like dogs. Whatever their origin, when they settled the creekbend, they brought a distinctive style of arrow-point with them that was not a part of the ruins of surrounding cultures.

This could be explained if the Scallorn/Haskell people were a tight group of malcontent farmers who kept to themselves and were left alone, but Walker suspected the truth was far less simple, something along the lines of the Great Plains populated with a wave of small farming groups gradually superceded by, and assimilated into, a larger wave of farming groups. The people of the first wave made Scallorn and Haskell points, and their settlements were small, few, and isolate in Walker's circle. The second wave expanded into villages all along major waterways, and the preferred hafting method called for thin, broad-bladed, little triangles with narrow notches coming in from the sides of the base. If the notches had been placed high on the sides, near the corners of the base, it was called the Reed style; if the notches were placed lower on the sides, causing a rectangular base, it was the Washita. In Walker's circle of footprints, the Scallorn/Haskell points and the Reed/Washita points were not found together, which seemed to him an indication of a slice of time between the first wave and the second that made the area not a good place for farmers. Whether the result of three hundred years of miserly rainfall, two hundred years of cannibals with wooden clubs and packs of trained dogs, or one hundred years of killer winter, the area had been abandoned as a bad place to raise food and youngsters. Generations later, when the area had shifted back to a more benign aspect, a new wave of settlers had trickled in.

The second characteristic that suggested the Scallorn/Haskell farmers were an insular group with little or no trade contact was the flint they used.

For every mile he walked of inhabited field, Walker had covered ten miles of ground that showed no signs of ever having been occupied. The fields were good rich loam, remarkably free of stones, but occasionally a strange rock would appear. These occasional rocks were always the same material and ranged from the size of walnuts to that of two fists held together. The material was silaceous shale, with a crystalline structure that would chip like flint. Though the appearance indicated extreme age, he had no idea which of the area's geologic shifts the isolated stones belonged to. They were not smooth, rounded cobbles, but irregular chunks seeming to have been tumbled, cracked, fractured, and healed over a very long span of time—about the time it would take to roll from the Rockies to the field where it was picked up, moving once a century. They were a dull, medium tan, the surfaces broken up with fracture scars of all sizes, the edges and cracks softened to wrinkles by weathering. Compared to the smooth pristine mystery cobbles, which appeared by contrast to have led sheltered lives, these randomly shaped, scarred and weathered ones made him think of wider loops of time where the land he stood on had been mountains more than once and more than once the bottom of a sea.

"Cold gravy skin," Young Walker had said about the way the cobbles looked, and the simile was so appropriate to color and form that the stones were stuck with the name. The soft, modulated rind was not thick, but tough and durable. Smoky Valley farmers, and later Quivirans, routinely picked up these singular stones when they happened upon them and carried them back to the village. They made good hammerstones.

If a flake were knocked free of an edge, the exposed flint, ranging from khaki-tan to sandy brown, showed a coarse crystalline texture, a matte finish. In the best flints, crystals are so microscopic that the texture of the flint seems creamy and has a luster. Neither the Smoky Valley farmers nor the Quivira farmers bothered to use gravy cobbles beyond the role of hammers. As a flint, it was stubborn and coarse, and they had access to much better raw material. But the Scallorn/Haskell farmers had made many of their tools from the occasional chunk of gravy cobble flint, to the degree that Walker and his son began to refer to the settlement as the Gravy site. Since there was not much about the tough flint that would make it a prefered material, its appearance in the form of arrowpoints, gouges, and small, modified-flake knives intimated a people who were either unaware of the Flint Hills and the jasper-lined creeks to the northwest, and other mass flint sources, or were physically or emotionally unable to go to them. The dartpoint hunters had made-do by refashioning broken tools; the creekbank farmers made-do with a lack of tool material. Neutral and drab in color, the granular, big-crystal gravy flint was not kind to the worker who placed the antler tip of a flaking tool against the edge of a blank and attempted through pressure and twist to wrench a narrow, shallow flake free of the surface. In fine-grained flint, the line of shock would travel far, a long strip of the surface would be removed. Gravy flint, with its big crystals and big spaces between them, let the shock escape from the stone early. The flakes were short and stubby, making removal of excess stone from the tool a frustrating job.

Over the course of a couple of decades, Walker had found seven complete Scallorn points at the remains of the settlement, and Young Walker had found one Haskell. Four of these points, including the more recent Haskell, were made of gravy flint.

Even with the toughest material, the Gravy site people, when it came to a matter of arrowpoints, were precise and particular workers. Though Walker, despite the fine-flaked promise of some fragments, had not found the work of an artist among the Pelican Lake/Besant leavings, he had found a masterpiece made by the Scallorn/Haskell farmers. The point was only half the length of most Scallorns, lying comfortably on the first joint of Walker's little finger. The expansive notches had removed the corners entirely, the narrow neck flared slightly at the base. The base corners, the shoulder barbs, and the tip of the blade were tiny and sharp. Minute serrations ran the full length of the edges of the blade. The flint was smooth, golden yellow-brown, and the body was slightly swollen. Walker's vision had been swinging from side to side, about five feet in front of his plodding tennis shoes that day, when the perfect point sucked his ranging thoughts into its vortex, fully exposed in the sunlight on top of a rainwashed clod. Walker had looked at the heat haze of distant trees and up through the vast sky, clearing his eyes, and looked at the point again. It lay in that landscape with unmistakable authority, a thought turned to stone. It was at once a symmetry of logic and will and an object of great passion, and it was clear that, to the maker, devotion made a difference. The point was a statement and a wish.

Walker had been alone when he'd discovered the point. His son had marveled at it the following summer. It became the pivot for their difference of opinion on the proper story of the site. Walker, because he wished it so, believed the perfect little point was made from a golden-yellow mystery cobble flake. He supposed further that the flake had originally been struck from the cobble by a bison hunter around the year one and thrown aside, too small. Thousands of these refused flakes of Flint Hills grays, Smoky Hill jaspers, and various cobble quartzites were on or just below the surface when the Scallorn-makers showed up to settle the bend. In Walker's vision, they were extremely flint-poor, and their discovery of this debris of what for them were large, usable flakes, would occur shortly after settlement, if it hadn't been the very reason for settlement. One half a cobble, fractured in an unusable way for a dartpoint maker, might yield enough blanks for a dozen Scallorn points. Because the refuse flakes were a finite source, they supplemented them with the gnarled brown cobbles occasionally found in the area. They used no other flint sources and didn't trade for it. They were too small a band to leave home for extended flint trips, too small to invite commerce with strangers.

Young Walker agreed that they'd made use of discard chips and gravy cobbles, but only for a generation or two, until they'd established contact with other settlements and found out where the good flint was. Then one or two men, with a dog hauling a pole sledge, would make the periodic trip for fresh material. The beautiful arrowpoint was made, according to Young Walker, from Smoky Hills jasper, brought in from creeks to the northwest. Over the summer they wrangled gently for their diverging stories. The site continued to give them fragments of tools and the infrequent whole one, but gave them nothing to support either version of the lives of the small band of farmers.

Where had the mystery cobbles come from? Where had the Scallorn-makers come from? Why didn't even a fragment of their stonework show up on the Rocking Deer, a short hike to the north? How could the old man have said in his journal that he'd picked up Reed and Harrell point fragments on the southern bend when they just weren't there? And what did the Scallorn-making farmers do for hide scrapers? The mysteries were thick. They were caught up in the search and the danger of the search. Looking so hard, they never thought to bring the stories full circle. Turned back on themselves, they never considered how much their stories came from the stones, how much from themselves, this cautious man and adventuresome boy.

"But, really, if there *were* cannibals with dogs, wouldn't we find their tools too?"

"Nah. All they needed was wooden clubs. Bop, splat, time to eat."

"Yeah, and when they'd eaten everybody they could find, they ate each other."

"Yeah, and their dogs too."

"Peace on earth."

"Well, sort of."

"Dad, if we did some digging, we could find out more."

"Digging's not a good idea, son. It just messes things up. Besides, we might disturb a grave. Bad news."

"But *your* father dug."

"Yes he did. I have to tell you, in many ways your grandfather was a fool."

"But you dug with him, didn't you?"

"Well, I have to tell you this too: in many ways your dad is a fool. I went digging with your granddad because he was my old man, and I assumed that what he did was right. Still, I have to give the old man the benefit of the doubt; I'm sure that if he found himself digging into a grave, he would have stopped right away and put back all the dirt. He was greedy for stones, but I don't think he was stupid about spirit."

2

"When you know a thing , to
recognize that you know it,
and when you do not, to know
that you do not know—that
is knowledge."

Confucius

Some Tramps

Some tramps like old
home places
just foundations
trees thick and wild

camping where others lived
the new fire stays calm
hard now to remember
the privileged

or those who dream
to dine on the throats
of the privileged
while these flames warm

once more the ghost
of a yard

Going After Flint

The sun had steamed white all day and now, settling into its own haze, cooled into a big, pink circle. Young Walker saw it as food.

"An egg, lightly basted."

"Pancakes and bacon," said the Guide's son.

"Don't get yourselves worked up boys," said the Guide. "It's gonna be..."

"We know, we know."

"Yeah, Dinty Moore's Beef Stew."

"There it is."

The sons were not the muddy little shoat-boys of past summers; beginning their teens, they were getting used to large elbows and knees, the sobriety of adulthood. They were less prone to the mindless frolic of thrown sticks and stones, loud wahoos of careless exuberance.

In past summers, camp for them had been a series of complainable events—too hot, too sweaty, too many chiggers, ticks, flies, hard sleeping ground, dust in the Dinty Moore's Beef Stew, and in the moments between fishing, canoeing, or hiking, nothing to do. They had been impervious then to the charm of sitting around camp, letting the body fall into the ease of sound, sight, smell, and idle thought, the sniff of fingers that had crushed a bud of sage, the musk of oaks against the tang of pasture weeds, the things that crossed the sky and where they seemed to go.

Now, bodies approaching the chemical purgatory of adolescence, they were champions of lassitude. Just as they no longer flailed and thrashed at canoeing, in a boyish effort to hydroplane, they no longer over-fed and tormented the evening fire, content, like their elders, to crouch in lawn chairs gobbling stew before the flies found it. Each camper cleaned his own tin plate at the big plastic container of utility water on the tailgate of the Guide's old station wagon and went back to slump with cookies and juice, a cup of evening coffee.

The Guide had a real coffeepot this time, with real coffee spooned into its guts. The Guide said he just couldn't live with himself drinking instant coffee in camp—that was the kind of thing he came out here to avoid. The adoption of a real coffeepot didn't make them noble savages by any means, but it did make them seem a little less like ignorant ones, since they had rejected an abstraction born of convenience for something a little closer to a coffee bean.

This third and last night in camp, they would all turn in early, ready in their bones to get a deep sleep against the return drive ahead. The first night's camp had been at the Old Home Place, the remains of a farm of the Guide's ancestors. He had played once under the big Tree of Heaven, which had survived the buildings. Part of the second night was spent there, too, until just after supper when the Guide got a familiar distracted look on his face. Before long, he'd begun to wonder out loud if it wasn't a good idea to move to the pasture camp, the bugs were fierce down here in the river trees, there would be breezes on the pasture hill. The others had already begun gathering their gear.

The last night deepened on the pasture camp. The promised breezes had come, but they hadn't kept flies from discovering them, flies which refused to disappear when the sun went down.

"We forgot to pack the most important thing again, Dad," sad the son of the Guide. "Fly swatters."

"Fly swatters?"

"Kill these dang flies."

"Uh-huh. You don't think you'd get a little tired, sitting in an open field swatting flies? As many as you swat, more show up? And keep showing up?"

"No, Dad, haven't you ever noticed? You swat some and pretty soon the rest stay away. Word gets around."

"Death vibes," said Young Walker.

"We're not talking a few flies in a room here, we're talking every fly in a radius of...however far away flies can sense beef stew and sweaty campers."

"I think he's onto something," said Walker. "All those flies squeaking out of existence might set up some kind of psychic distress field. But it wouldn't be worth it. Think of all those busted little corpses all over camp. Everywhere you look, dead flies, all bent..."

"It makes me queasy to think of it," said the Guide.

The son of the Guide was not amused by the men's squeamish skit, though he did smile to show that their stupidity had not offended him.

"All I know is next year I'm bringing a flyswatter."

It had been easier to bait the boys when they were younger. More guileless then, they'd enjoyed being teased, even tricked, but adolescent self-awareness had put a different spin on their desires; a little teasing would be okay, but mostly they wanted to be taken seriously. Walker and the Guide were proving themselves slow learners.

Walker could have recalled, if he'd tried, the vital need to be taken seriously in that shifting age between boy and man, but deep in his forties, he seldom thought of his own youth. The ache and bewilderment of his father's disappearance, withdrawal, abandonment, had grown an insulation of scar tissue over the years. His attempts at explaining the old man's disappearance had ranged from the fantasy of a seventeen year old of the old man being an agent of some kind, having to go undercover, to the thought, in his twenties, that the old man had found himself with a fatal disease and had not been able to deal with it, which made him a coward, or he'd gotten married to a woman with children and had felt he had to make some abstract choice between his first and second families, which also made him a coward. On his thirtieth birthday, Walker found the old postcard, soft with handling, of the ruminating Wyoming buffalo, and calmly flipped it into the trash.

Now he merely shrugged; the old man had gone off somewhere and died or had gotten killed, an isolated end of an isolated man. People of many cultures, some anonymous, most long dead, had encouraged Walker not to construct an obsession of grief or judgment. Regret, unpredictable as campfire smoke, would curl over him sometimes, but he called it by name and tried to let it go.

Since he had given the old man the benefit of a doubt, he could recall him with pleasure as he thought of flints, tools, the nature of their makers. He could think of the old man that was, but he had forgotten the subtleties of the boy he himself had been.

"What we need to do," he said, "is crucify one of these flies, make an example of him."

"You boys think you could put together a tiny little cross?" asked the Guide.

"Very funny, Dad."

"Even better," Walker continued, "a flamethrower. Hike that baby up to max nozzle..."

When younger, the boys would have seized on these goofy concepts and yarned them into mythical surrealities. Now, they were not altogether sure such behavior was proper for them anymore. They sometimes worried about their fathers. Did their fathers think they were idiots? Did their fathers know there was a limit to everything? Were their fathers, kind of, losing it? It seemed that the fathers actually enjoyed sitting around a fire in a hot, buggy pasture discussing existence at large. Both boys felt such discussions could be held as easily near a refrigerator.

As the night chill deepened, and the flies found someplace else to go, each camper inched a lawn chair closer to the fire. The son of the Guide laid a branch of hedge across it, and they slipped into jackets, balanced a fresh pot of coffee on the wire grill. The firelight was calming, the sense of being a group was strong, particularly on the last night of camp.

This year's camp, despite the chiggers (Walker had forgotten to bring the sliver of soap to rub on ankles, genitals, and waists), had been filled with good luck. After being skunked on the first day of fishing, the boys had hiked with the Guide down to a deep, narrow stretch of the Verdigris to fish from a gravel bar he remembered. The Guide laughed later, telling how Young Walker had ground his feet deep into the gravel and, holding the rod two-handed as far behind his head as possible, lunged forward with a grunt, casting as far down the river as he could. Reeling in, he'd set his feet and heaved again, as if he would beat the river into giving him a fish.

"It was like surf-casting on the Verdigris," said the Guide, "with a fly rod, mind you."

Walker had stayed above to investigate a cornfield for flint, but he'd finally followed their voices and stood on the river cliff peering far down through the leaves at the fishermen in the green light of the gravel bar. Unobserved, he'd smiled at his son's forceful yang approach to fishing, and at the quiet amusement of the other two fishermen. Consequently, the only one not surprised when the Bass struck was Young Walker. The Guide and his son recovered and began reeling in their own lines, shouting encouragement and advice.

"Well, I'll be damned," Walker said. His son had caught a fish through sheer force of will and energy. The boy had brought the fish in and landed it safely, a large White Bass. From his elevated spot on the river cliff, through a gap in the leaves, Walker had seen it all, and when the fish was strung and in hand, he applauded. Young Walker's face had swiveled up, scanning the high silhouettes of weeds and trees until he discovered, framed by walnut leaves, his father's shoulders, head, and hat stuck with feathers.

"Dad! Did you see that?"

"Are you kidding? You're the man."

The boys had naturally wanted to fish forever, certain they'd found the retreat of all the lunkers in the river, but the Guide had had enough of fighting mosquitoes, and lunch was long overdue. Through praise and promise he got the boys up off the river, both of them swollen like toads with excitement. The fish was admired, biceps squeezed. Thirty minutes later, they'd sat around camp over a late lunch of fried fish and bakery bread. For Young Walker, every morsel had meaning, and the others commented on the good flavor more than once.

Walker's luck came from wandering fields at the edge of the river. Luck had it that many fields had been plowed, and a good rain had tamped down their surfaces. He'd found two places where the old peoples had camped or lived.

On the crest of an old creek loop, he'd found a great many flint chips. He'd walked it thoroughly and found only the base of a projectile point blank, no pottery, no bone, no tools. People had stopped here more than once, Walker thought, to dress down the flint they'd gathered, make blanks. There was no way to tell who they were or how long ago they'd visited the creek.

The second field was high, plowed ground that tumbled in a gradual descent of sumac, oak, and cottonwood to the Verdigris River. An area no larger than ten lodges had many flint flakes, some small shards of pottery with a cordage pattern, much like that found on his home walking grounds, three fragments of small points, two tiny, banged-up notched points, a fat little triangle point of dirty white flint with pink bands, and a thick, roughly-flaked knife. The people had been there fairly recently. The notched points were battered examples of the style called Washita, popular from around 1100 AD to 1600 AD. One of these people had found a much earlier cast-off, a very large, fat projectile point of greenish-gray flint. The corners of the base had not only been removed, but the removal continued a quarter of the way down the sides, giving a blade with small shoulders and a stemmed base, rounded or squared away. The point, a Waubesa, had been made as long ago as 500 BC. One shoulder and part of the blade and stem had been sheared away. Viewed from one side, the line of fracture was straight, unworked, clearly a break. From the other side, it had been reworked, perhaps in order to become a knife, a tool broken and rejected long ago had been found by one of the recent river-dwellers and salvaged back into use. Such finds could bring stories of giants, but Walker felt the people had a general understanding and knew very well what they had found, a tool from the old spearthrower times.

As the flint grew sparse and disappeared, Walker had roughly determined the size of the settlement and covered it slowly and completely. Only when he'd begun to tread on his own footprints had he explored the rest of the field.

Fifty steps north, he'd begun to see flint again, large flakes and chunks, all Flint Hills gray. It hadn't occurred to him that he'd found the source of the damaged Waubesa—he was in the habit of following flint and was doing so automatically—until he saw, on its side in a furrow ahead of him, a complete Waubesa. A light gray blade with a squared stem, it had lost both shoulders and a stem corner. This smaller, older camp was still, for the most part, beyond the reach of the plow; the steel blades were bringing up the very top of the old surface.

There had been no pottery or bone showing on the old campsite. Taking fifty steps, Walker had strolled backward in time about fifteen centuries, give or take a few hundred years. He'd sat down then, out of the hot wind, and had a smoke, thinking that during fat times, there'd probably been as many camps in the Flint Hills river valleys as there were farms now.

It was not very likely that a small expedition of flint gatherers could just stroll into the Hills, make camp, and collect a supply of good flint. All settlements watched against the approach of strangers, observed numbers and behavior. If they clearly represented no threat, a flint-collecting group would probably be tolerated, allowed to finish its task and leave, but contacts between groups and, in the best of circumstances, resulting alliances, were inevitable and probably desirable. Cooperation with those who lived there would save the seekers from having to discover the exact locations of fine-grade flint on their own, and the settlers, if they invited the strangers to camp in the village, would have the advantage of keeping them close at hand, under observation against treachery and trouble. The locals wouldn't even have to give up their source; a couple of their own people could go out and bring back the desired quantity. Always assuming good will, the seekers could be encouraged to come directly to this village on their next expedition and certain things may have been suggested—salt, hides—that they could bring in exchange for flint. Such a trade relationship could last for generations.

That might be the way it would go, Walker thought, in the best of worlds. The history of the prairies was surely as rich in other worlds, other moods, in which strangers in a strange land were summarily surprised and killed.

Walker had stood, knocked the dust out of his pants, and begun the long trek back to camp, done with thinking in the hot sun, but simple-minded speculation caught up with him again around the last campfire.

In the old villages along the Smoky Hill River, where he lived, Flint Hills material prevailed. He was obsessed with how it had gotten there, and slumped drinking coffee with fire and stars, he came to believe a flintworker would leave the Smoky Hill River with his son or an apprentice, and possibly a large pack dog. He would have made this trip before, a necessary part of his occupation, and he would know where to camp along the way, which villages to visit, what to say and who to ask for. When the plains were at war, or filled with raiders, he would know the nearest and safest sources of flint. Many men like him had journeyed to the Hills, many campfires had been made, not much different from the one which heated Walker. Some of the individuals mined the flint matter-of-factly, some had special things to say and particular acts to perform. Some treated the Hills with the nonchalance of greed, others left offerings—herbs, tobacco, a well-made flint tool. Some journeys were expected to be great pleasures, others great dangers. A multitude of human experience had happened in the Hills; philosophy, invention, custom, ritual—all came down to the bare stones and what they might suggest.

While Walker sat, lost in this welter of suggestion, the boys had discussed the flavor of the White Bass versus Channel Cat, moments of sports glory, the cars they wanted, and when Walker tuned back in, spank-ings of their youth. Each could remember only two or three. They clearly had not been struck often as children, but each wanted to claim a high de-gree of intensity for the infrequent punishment.

"Whad your dad use?"

"Oh, my dad used his hand. My mom used a wooden spoon. Now,

that hurt.”

“Wooden spoon?”

“Solid wood.” You could almost call it a club, the one boy thought, but he didn’t want to sound boastful. “Whad your dad use?”

“Hand. He gave me an awesome whipping once.”

“Yeah. Mine too.”

“My mom used a real thick ruler. Like a club.”

“Yeah, I know what you mean. Wooden spoon.”

“I don’t know,” the Guide said slowly, “but compared to some, you guys might’ve had it pretty easy.”

“Did you get spanked a lot?” asked Young Walker.

“What? Granma and Granpa?” the Guide’s son protested. “No way.”

“Oh, no, no, no,” said the Guide. “I hardly ever got whipped, but, mmm....” he paused. “When I did...” He gazed into the fire and shook his head. His sober memory interested and puzzled the sons.

“Yeah,” the Guide mused, “those were some real spankings.”

“Gah,” said Young Walker, “whad they whip you with?”

The Guide looked over at him slowly, not quite smiling.

“Crowbar.”

The boys cursed gently; they’d been had again.

Tales of Fortune and Envy

"Oh, they're all around here. I come down here one day and one a these hogs, big old boar, he'd been plowin' mud and he'd got this big old spearpoint, just perfect, just perfect, stuck across his snout. The sun had dried that gumbo, now, and just glued that spearpoint on his nose. He could breathe all right and didn't seem to mind. Well, I got in there with some water to get it loose, but he felt that water on his nose and decided he was drowning and got jumpy, so I just pulled it free. He didn't like that too much, either. I've still got that spearpoint somewhere up at the house, but I haven't seen it in years."

* * * *

"Why, there's a gully up in the north pasture. We used to go up there as kids. Always find two or three arrowheads, big ones. I'm tryna think what happened to that cigar box they were in. Anytime you went up there you'd find a couple, no problem." (This story is repeated two hours later at the gully, where not even a chip of flint has been spotted.) "I just don't understand it, boys, my own damn gully has betrayed me. Now that hill over there, that one, we used to find some really good fossils over there."

* * * *

"So I said, 'Hey, fellow, what in the world are you doing digging a hole in my cornfield?' Well, I looked down and he had about three-quarters, or a half anyway, of a clay pot there, and some pieces. He had a pretty good foxhole dug between the rows with his hands and was digging around underneath the roots trying to find more pieces. He did find a couple more, too. I was kind of hoping he'd find the whole thing. I'd a like to've seen it."

* * * *

"I was walking down to the creek to do some fishing, leaned over to fingerblow my nose and blew a big wad of snot on a perfect little white arrowhead. Carried it with me for years."

* * * *

"During the Dust Bowl you could come out here, pick up a quart jar full of hide scrapers in a half hour, arrowheads, flint knives, all kinds of things. There was these guys then would come around. They'd drive up to your farm, get to talking, they paid a quarter for a jar full of those things. Many a jar full of scrapers and arrowheads was sold in those days, quarter a jar."

* * * *

"He was standing in this hole up to his shoulders. On the dirt beside the hole was this, he said it was a flint knife. Never seen anything like it, all kinds of colors mixed together. Tell you what, to look at it, it was too pretty, you wouldn't even think it was a rock."

* * * *

"I'd driven by that creek a hundred times, but there was nothing partic-ular about it, the field was kinda low, I never gave it any thought. Anyway, I was always on my way to, or coming back from, a field that I knew was good. So I drove by this little flat field by the creek for years, five or six years, and one day the place I was going to was in crop, couldn't be walked. I was driving back home and I went by that low place on the creek. It'd been plowed, rained on, and dried, so, what the heck, I really wanted to do some walking. I got out there and I thought I was going to have to carry my billfold and car keys in my hand, I was filling my pockets so fast. Scrapers, arrowheads, knives, drills, I found six complete drills! And this was like in just no time. I could hardly bend over, my pockets were so swollen, and I had a nice flint gouge in my back pocket. Yeah, that place was a dream, one of those places you dream about. And I'd gone by it a thousand times."

* * * *

"I was prowling down in the jack oaks with my .22. You know how boys are. I looked down beside the path, and there was this long, oval gray flint knife laying on top of the dead leaves like it had just been dropped there. I knew it for what it was the minute I saw it."

* * * *

"Yeah, I see them once in a while. I just keep plowing."

* * * *

"They say this guy was digging in that cedar windbreak and found a cache of pipestone pipes, eight or ten, all different kinds. There was some little elbow pipes, bigger council pipes. All kinds, all together."

* * * *

"One afternoon this archaeologist was walking down this creek. It was running low and the mud was hard enough to walk on. He was watching for exposed gravel bars in the creek, and he was checking the face of the creek-bank too, for things that might wash out. He'd noticed these footprints going down the creek the same direction he was, about the size of a kid, barefoot. The edges of the prints were drying out. He, the kid, had probably been down the creek sometime that morning. Ever so often, when he's swinging his eyes from the creek to the bank, this guy checks and the prints are still there, wandering out into the soft mud and back. So he's going on, looking, looking, and on a curve, just up the creek a little ways, he suddenly sees a place where three clay pots have washed out of the bank, and he sees the tracks where the kid has walked up and kicked all three of them to pieces."

* * * *

"These boys wanted permission to go in behind my place to get down on the river. They were planning to walk down the gravel bars on one side till they got tired, find a place to cross, walk back on the other side, looking for arrowheads. There was three of them and they each had one of those nail aprons on. They weren't carrying guns so it was okay with me and off they went. Close to sundown I was in the barn and I hear them coming back. Those boys were all mud and about worn out and, tell you what, every one of them had a nail apron almost full of arrowheads."

* * * *

"When I was a kid I was sitting on a rock shelf and I saw an ant go by carrying a little flat white bead. You know, when you're a kid you are not too surprised by things like that. But then here came another one with a bead, so I got interested, started looking around and off a ways comes another one, he's got a bead, and beyond him, another one. I followed the line backward on the rock shelf until I found there was this little crack in the rock they were coming from. I got down and tried to see in the crack. Couldn't see anything, but they kept coming out of that crack, each one carrying a little bead."

* * * *

"Arrowheads? I found a hell of an arrowhead when I was a boy in

Wisconsin, just a beautiful thing."

"What color was it?"

"Silver."

"Silver..."

"That's right, it was a pure silver arrowhead. I was offered a thousand dollars for it, and that was thirty years ago."

"Do you still have it?"

"It's back in Wisconsin, I know where. One of these days I'll cash that puppy in."

* * * *

"You know, my great-grandmother was a Cherokee princess."

* * * *

"You know, my grandmother was a Cherokee princess."

* * * *

"You know, my mother was a Cherokee princess."

Flow

Butterflies ignored him, followed him, flew in his face, landed on him. If one settled in the field, he would walk straight to it, eyes locked. None had ever led him to a discovery, yet he kept following their landings, fat Skippers and bright, lacy Monarchs. When the butterfly lifted off, he went and stood where it had stood. He found nothing except what it was like to stand in a butterfly's footprints.

The sudden metallic zeep of an insect would make him veer to the sound. He would trail his glance along the path of a Blister Beetle until it trundled out of sight. He took note of a passing tumbleweed, especially if it got hung up. The leaping grasshopper, the toad, the big black and orange Velvet Ant, tracks of deer and coyote, a bird on the ground, a blowing feather, a dust devil, the edge of a cloud shadow, a centipede, a clover breeze, he had turned and followed them all on a whim.

In summer, the hot south wind would cause the small feathers in the sweatband of his hat to vibrate a high, whistling tone. He would stay in this sound and study the furrows in front of him. If a wind had force and turbulence, he'd go where it pushed him, eyes open.

Through hours of walking, eyes crawling the ground, the universe shrinks, and events become clues. This idea, that a random circumstance could signal a centuries-old invention in flint, waiting for him to pick it up, seemed as reasonable as anything else to Walker. He didn't assume that one thing led to another, but he always followed the possibility. In this he was no different than the Etruscan, Ibo, Druid, or Chinese, but his peculiarly modern attitude showed itself those times he perceived the sign, thought about it, and walked the other way, the stubborn individual, the rational human being. It wasn't fear of being superstitious that caused him to ignore what might be omens—he already knew he was superstitious—it was a suspicion that he could just as easily become a slave to omens as to clocks, sex, compliments, or drudgery. Enough wise people, living and dead, had warned him about fixation that he made the effort to avoid it, sporadically to be sure, so that avoidance wouldn't become a fixation either.

Searching for flint tools in a plowed field was like searching for anything; the more demanding the searcher, the more elusive the gift. Walker couldn't urge arrowpoints from the ground, though to his dismay he sometimes found himself trying. He'd heard stories of people who charged and coursed across a field, a hound with a nose full of hot deer, cutting in front of other searchers, loping ahead, ranting when somebody else found something. Call it superstition, but these people's luck was bad. In the stories they never found anything and cursed the fields and their friends.

Life could be sweeter. All it took, in the case of walking a field, was surrender. Walker would have liked to have been able to fall into that dance of field, sky, and wind every time, but too often he lost touch and strode the dirt mechanically, his mind grinding away at some distant crisis of nonsense, the sun, the wind the Sweat Bees, all an irritation.

In fact, there was no evidence to show that any kind of behavior affected the probability of finding an object chipped from stone. Walker could bring resentment, preoccupation to the field, as he often did, or not; the finding of things was mostly chance. At the best of times walking the fields— no gas, no money, no water—he had felt like the happiest man alive, stumbling under a blazing blue sky. Going home empty-handed then meant nothing.

Half Asleep Near the Three Rivers

A sparrowhawk
eating in the
tree above

delicate grasshopper shells spiral down.

The red cottonwood flowers fall
like daggers on the river.

Saline

Solomon

Smoky Hill

Three long breaths
in the quiet-hearted afternoon.

The Bead Makers

The fields Walker knew best, the ones the old man had first taken him to, were along the Smoky Hill River where it curved from its gentle southeast flow across the state and ran twenty miles north to Walker's home. There it turned east again, eventually swallowing the Saline and the Solomon, becoming the Kansas River or, as the old people still called it, the Kaw. He followed the fortunes of seven fields along that north-flowing twenty mile stretch: the Bead, just south of town, the Celt, the Mano, the Bluff, the Spoon, the Little Cottonwood, and the Fungus the Dolly.

There were plenty of other old village remains along that twenty mile line of river, but these were the ones Walker had been introduced to by the old man, or had found himself, and he had stuck with them. Some of them were known to others—he often found their footprints—while some seemed to be his to roam alone. Some he visited rarely—they were too well known. Most he walked often, once a week in a season of deep plowing and heavy storms. He'd done so for thirty years.

During the first ten years, he got to know the first Smoky Valley bison-hunting farmers. The flint of choice on all sites was gray, many kinds of gray, from the Flint Hills. The preferred arrowpoint style was Reed, a thin worked triangle about the length of a fingertip joint, notched once on each side near the base. Almost as popular was the Madison, that same worked triangle, with no notches. The third recognizable style, Washita, had notches lower on the sides, making a rectangular base. Sometimes a worker would put a notch in the center of the base line, turning the rectangular base into two diamonds cocked at forty-five degree angles.

On all the Smoky Hill villages were pieces of the same kind of clay pots—coiled, shaped, textured on the outside with slaps from a wooden paddle wound with grass stalks or strips of hide. The pottery had a name, Cord-Roughened, and that name subdivided into many others. All villages used similar hide scrapers, some as long as a thumb, most about three-quarters that length.

During that first decade, he assumed all seven sites were being lived on at the same time. Sometime during the second decade, after a long day of walking site after site, Young Walker said, "Dad, how do you know they lived on all these places at the same time?" He began to look at the left-overs of the Smoky Valley civilizations with an eye toward differences. By the third decade of walking, he knew the differences between the sites were as many as the similarities.

All the sites but one were on old riverbanks. At the Bead, the present riverbed was a quarter mile east of the old one, but at the other sites, the river had moved a much shorter distance, and at the Bluff, it still flowed past the foot of the tall dirt cliff where the old people had made their village. All settlements except the Bead had been on the east side of the river, and the people of the Bead appeared to be the only ones who made shell beads. Walker had found shell on some of the other sites, but no indication that it had been worked in any way.

The Mano and the Fungus the Dolly and the Celt were home to others before the Smoky Valley farmers.

The people on the Spoon made heavy use of a dirty palomino flint with gray splotches that came from the southern part of the Flint Hills, near the Oklahoma border. It was on all the sites, but concentrated on the Spoon, and from it had been made, long, narrow, curved tools with tapered scraping noses worked on both ends. Were these strange tools made by a people or an individual? Who had lived where when? Were they interchangeable figures draped in anonymous brown skins, or was personal magic apparent in the way they dressed or looked? Was there among them a flintworker with an eye toward loading the stone?

The answers started beyond the south edge of Walker's town, just out of sight of neon and traffic, where a band of bison-hunting farmers had called the west bank of the river home, that river now a quarter of a mile away. There had been other villages to the north, but they were now neon, traffic, and suburban housing, as this place, where the people had made shell beads, would likely be someday.

Close to town, the Bead site had been visited for many years by many people. They left cans, shotgun shells, rubbers, broken glass and, because the field was on a dead end road, occasional worn-out sofas, chairs and mattresses. It was used as a place to change the oil in cars; the old oil and empty cans went into the ditch.

Developers had offered expanding dreams in the '70's and '80's, and the town, wanting to be a city, bought them. Housing tracts and industrial parks appeared, workers and managers arrived from urban hives, and among them were people who looked at the countryside and saw a playground. Each time Walker spoke with the landowner, he could sense the resentment and frustration of a man close to telling everyone to stay off his land. For all these reasons, Walker seldom went there. During the few times he'd visited the site, he'd found a crude Washita point, a small triangular flint drill, a hand-sized hide scraper, a slender antler pick the length of his little finger, fragments of scrapers and points, and eight shell beads in various stages of manufacture.

The living area was small. At the east end, on the gentle slope into the old riverbed, were thousands of bits of scattered shell, a few of them beads, almost beads, and barely started beads. The presence of these beads-in-progress, and the shell debris, convinced Walker it was a work area and not a plowed-through burial.

A person who preferred simple straight lines might think the presence of bead manufacture indicated a more recent people with a more complex philosophy, a social desire for adornment and greater leisure time to bring it about. That same person might think that refined flint chipping techniques accrued through time; the cruder a tool, the older it would be. Walker had thought all these things but had come to find there were no simple, straight lines in the histories of the peoples.

The distant elephant hunters made pristine lance points at times, and peoples could be found using pointed chips of flint, barely modified, as arrowpoints during the coming of the Europeans. Relatively recently, fairly comfortable people might go plain while, thousands of years ago, someone living on the edge of privation might invest much time and energy in the making of an ornament, a talisman, a thing, the only function of which was to exist.

Clamshell was scored and broken; one of the beads was a rough square drilled through the center with a flint drill, possibly the one Walker had found, a sharp tip that expanded quickly into a base that fit between forefinger and thumb. Twisted against soft shell, it pierced an opening and expanded it.

These beadmakers had favored a large opening relative to the body of the bead. The outer curve was formed by abrasion, probably supplied by the bits of sandstone still lying on the slope. One of the beads had been shaped into an irregular form, half-finished. The remaining six were rounded symmetrically to match the large center hole. All were thin, made from the outer edges of the shell.

The mystery was not so much how they were made, but why. If they had been made for everyday use, Walker would have expected to find sign of them up on the flat part of the slope where the lodges had been, but he'd found only flint and pot shards there. Were the beads buried elsewhere, with the dead? Were they manufactured for trade? The questions were further complicated by the fact that x number of people had been walking the place, picking up objects from the plowed ground, season after season, for around a hundred years. Many other people must have stood in the same field and wondered the same thoughts as Walker, and some of them had probably found and carried away clues to possible answers.

One late summer when his son was a young boy, they'd sat on the Bead site sipping at a canteen of tepid water, discussing the possibility that they were sitting on graves, that the beads were coming from eroded burials. They'd dismissed the idea quickly—burials wouldn't be at the river's edge, and they wouldn't be that close to camp.

"Yet, we might be wrong."

"Really?"

"Yeah. We just think it would be a bad place for graves because we think the way we do. I mean, people haven't always thought the way we think. Some cultures buried their dead right under the house."

This struck the boy as hilarious, and he fell back in the dirt. Perhaps the information had made death too personal and scary, and perhaps he was overreacting out of self-defense, for he sat up again.

"So, Dad, do you believe in God?" He rushed the question out all at once.

"Hmm." Walker moved the canteen into the shadow. "That's a tough one."

"Take your time, Dad."

"Almost everyone around you is at war with God, wanting to control their destiny, and others', and control the rivers, wind, rain, the universe, death. As for the great unnamable, we've forgotten all about that." That was the speech he was tempted to make, in all its pomposity, but he patted the ground between them.

"I think God is rhythm."

To his surprise, Young Walker didn't look puzzled or ask for an explanation. They sat and listened to a racketing call, predicting rain, from a tree by the road. It came from a bird officially known as a Yellow-Billed Cuckoo, but referred to by some of the country people as a rain crow. In Walker's experience, its predictions came true half the time.

"That covers even atoms" Young Walker said. "Rhythm covers everything." Walker kept his mouth shut.

Walker found an antler pick that day, as they made one last sweep of the shell area before walking to the car. He bent to pick up half of it, cursed whatever had broken it, raised his eyes, and saw the other half sticking out of the side of the next furrow. The pick had been broken by a farm tool just that season; both faces of the stair-step fracture were bright white. Reunited with a touch of wood glue, the pieces formed a tool roughly the diameter of a big wooden kitchen match, one end rounded, the other gently pointed. It had a heaviness, an unexpected weight, suggesting it was not bone but antler. Such objects were often called needles by the literature. Other authorities referred to them as picks, and this designation fit, for Walker, the function he derived from the object's form, the worn bluntness of the point, a flattened area of the shaft, the kind that could be caused by repeated friction with the ball of the thumb. It was a pick of a specific kind, a flaking pick, used in the final steps of the shaping of flint.

On the Gravy site, Walker had once picked up a tool used at the beginning of the flintworking process, a round, flattened cobble the size of a biscuit. Trapped by fingers against the heel of the hand, one rounded end protruding, the hammerstone was used to strike usable flakes free from a chunk of flint, and unlike other hammerstones he'd found, this one had been used so continuously and faithfully that the stone had taken on the shape of the hand that held it. The face that lay against the heel of the hand had been worn into a negative impression of that hand, a central ridge that fit into the lifeline, a sloping depression on either side, reflecting the pads of muscle at the base of the hand. How many years of use it would require to wear the granite to the shape of the hand, Walker had no idea, but the hammerstone had clearly been a favored one.

As the hammerstone represented the beginning of the tool-making process, the pick spoke of the last touch, the delicate flaking around the perimeter of the flint point, scraper, drill, or knife. Both the hammerstone and the pick carried the implicit presence of the flintworker in the impression of hand or thumb. The pick showed the ghost of the working hand; resulting flint tools, like scrapers, showed not only awareness of the hands that would use them but also the workings of the maker's mind as he sought to accommodate the tool to the grasp.

Ten years after he found the antler pick, Walker found a hand-sized scraper on the Bead site. Laying his thumb along the flat side of the scraper so that the scraping edge jutted just beyond his thumb, he curled his fingers over the curved side. His index finger slid naturally into a wide, shallow channel created by the removal of a single large flake.

The old man had said that any flint hand tool, handled for a while, would automatically fall into place in the hand, demonstrating how it was originally held. Walker had found this only partly true; any chunk of raw flint could be judged more or less comfortable to the hand, depending on the angles and facets of the stone. Flint was a friendly stone, offering many planes and edges for the hand to explore in search of a grip. Yet he had found enough large scrapers with that index finger channel purposefully worked to know that some flintworkers had tried to engineer a smoother and firmer fit for the woman who would be scraping the hides. Some were made for the right-handed, and a few were for the lefties. Held in the opposite hands, these tools were awkward, fingers curled across sharp edges. Switching it back to the correct hand felt like a homecoming.

Walker had found many scrapers to which the maker had given no thought of grasp, little more than raw flakes worked with a scraping edge at the wide end. He had even found sites where *all* the scrapers were crude, with no regard for the comfort of the hand, even though the small arrowpoints found there had been finely worked.

Arrowpoints had to align themselves to the nature of air, scrapers had to fit the ways of a hand. Arrowpoints were also the business of men, scrapers the business of women. The woman who used the large, gray scraper at the Bead site had had personal power, integrity within the group: the flintworker had cared enough to make a tool that saved her hand from cuts and bruises. On the crude scraper sites, the women, as far as hand tools went, took what they were given.

Making a hide scraper as an extension of the hand was not only a mark of the awareness of design, it also showed concern in the mind of the flintworker for the well-being of the hideworker and signaled abstract social awareness—that which eases the burden of an individual eases the burden of the group. This awareness was stronger in some groups than others, but it occurred at all points in time, among old peoples and more recent ones. In those groups women had the right to request or demand comfortable and effective tools. The magic resided in the removal of the single long flake that left a channel for the index finger; the woman was invited by the comfortable tool to invest the same care in the scraping of the hide. If she accepted, her people would wear better clothes. In these small things that they did, both the flintworker and the hideworker added to the group endeavor, whether pursuing the buffalo or trying to grow corn on the banks of the Smoky Hill. Some flintworkers would add beauty to utility—color, pattern, symmetry—and the stones left behind by some groups showed flintworkers vying with each other to make visually striking and absolutely effective scrapers for the women who worked the hides.

The marriage between stone and hand could become so subtle and essential that, one day in the land of the Quivira, Walker's son would take hold of a hide scraper and fall instantly and stupidly in love with a vision of a woman's slender fingers.

Gifts of Circumstance

In Missouri the old man had found fragments of celts, never a whole one. He'd shown Walker pictures: a tapering cylinder of hard, dense stone with a bit ground on the wide end. A combination wedge/chisel for the working of wood, there was no reason to expect one would be used in the grasslands, but on a field four miles south of the Bead site, Walker found one.

Though celts were sometimes a foot or more in length, this was only slightly over four inches long. Walker counted fifty-seven marks where a farm implement had scratched the celt. This was no clear indication of how long ago it had been turned up, how many years it had been churning in the plow zone; some years a field would be worked repeatedly—plowed, disced, harrowed—some years it would lie fallow. He was forty-five years old when he found the celt, and considering the number of scratches on it and the many smaller ones he hadn't bothered to count, it could easily have been turned up to the sunlight before he was born, tumbled repeatedly while his life lengthened and moved toward it.

The celt was not beautiful, the edge of the beveled bit was nicked and dulled with use, but it was unique because of the material. Typically, celts were pecked and ground from granitic hardstones; this one was made from dense, small-grained, brown sandstone.

Sandstone was native to Walker's area, and the little scarred celt was not the only instance where it had seemed to serve as a substitute for a traditional material that was rare in the Smoky Hills. Mauls—big round hammers with flat ends and a circling groove—were made elsewhere from granite, quartzite, tough stones to withstand the heavy pounding. Of the few mauls he'd seen found in the Smoky Hills, most had been made from dense sandstone, less resistant, but available. And the Scallorn point farmers of the Gravy site had, somewhere in their history, made large, flat, oval skinning knives of flint. Whatever the reasons for their resettlement, once they'd moved onto the Gravy site, they found no source of bedded veins of flint that would yield the large, flat pieces needed to make such knives. They did find seams of compact sandstone, and in this flat tabular material, they duplicated the knives, actually chipping the edges of sandstone as they would flint. Sandstone would never cut like flint, or cleave through wood like granite, but it was available. Newly settled immigrants might use it to make tools traditional to their previous environment, until they found the substitute unsatisfactory and devised a new tool, based on existing resources, to do the job, or until they realized that particular tool was no longer necessary in the new environment.

The little celt, a tool of woods dwellers, would find sparse timber on this prairie, except along the rivers. The battered, scalloped bit told Walker it had been well used; where it was found told him it was not part of the later farming hunters who left small arrowpoints and thumb-size scrapers, but had been used by an earlier people who came from the woodlands to the east.

He had walked the small village area thoroughly, and then, because there was a breeze, because the sun was gentle, and he was neither tired nor thirsty, he'd kept walking, beyond the boundaries of the village, finding only a rare, lone chip of flint and then none at all.

Usually when Walker searched beyond a village area he found nothing, but there had been three or four instances, wandering where no one was supposed to have lived, when he had a surprise meeting with a solitary object. Each time, the tool was older than those used in the nearby village; each time it seemed far from home, more typical of the woods of Missouri and points east.

It had been fifty paces since he'd seen a chip of flint, his eyes had gotten used to the pattern of bare ground when, in the shadow of a hedgerow at the edge of the field, he'd discovered the sandstone celt. Belief, disbelief, belief. He picked it up, and that particular section of plowed riverbank, which had known other names, automatically became the Celt site.

The celt could have been lost there, or discarded, by an eastern people passing through, and since there were no associated flint chips or other signs of residence, this seemed the obvious interpretation. Equally possible, eastern people on the move may have camped or even lived there long enough before the farming bison hunters that the evidence lay slightly lower in the earth, with only relatively substantial stones, like the celt, being nicked and nudged to the surface.

He could drop to his knees and dig with his hands, down below the plow line. Maybe he would unearth chips of flint, more likely he would not. Even if the easterners had lived on the field, it would take more extensive excavation to find out; uncovering a space the size of a coffee can would tell him nothing. For two reasons, he wouldn't be the one to undertake more elaborate excavation: he didn't know enough to do it properly; and he had only asked permission to walk upon the field, not to dig into it.

He walked to the area once more, saw nothing , and returned to his car. He would consider the celt a gift of circumstance, and if he lived twenty more years and walked the field regularly, a determined old man, maybe plowing and erosion would bring more answers to the surface. But the questions posed by the Celt site were no more and no less important than those posed by other sites along the Smoky Hill, and because it was close to town, visited often by hunters, fishermen, other searchers, he went less and less frequently, giving his attention to sites farther south on the river.

He hadn't visited the place in years when he heard the land was sold to a corporation in Texas and posted with bright black and yellow KEEP OUT signs. That was fine with Walker; in this tumbling world fetched up in pieces by the wind, he'd long ago stopped assuming all his questions would be answered.

Norski Tao

The sky a delicate blue, mare's tail clouds, summer gone balmy and thin filaments of winter wheat poking up in rows, a green fuzz on the fields. They were squatting, man and boy, near the top of a long hill, facing each other, wrists on their knees, backs of their resting hands almost touching. They were looking down into the rough diamond shape formed by their planted feet.

If a driver on the highway had looked to one side across the sweep of plowed ground, he would have momentarily seen two figures on the distant hillside, crouching in the dirt. A strange glimpse providing speculation to fight the hypnosis of the highway—had they shot something, were they having sex, taking drugs, were they reading a map, had they found something?

"So Dad, what do you think?" Near the bottom of a furrow, the base of a small, notched arrowpoint protruded at an angle. The point was a Washita, the notches narrow, deep, and even. Just past the shoulders, the blade of the point, if there was a blade, disappeared into the earth. The base was light gray, shifting to ashy pink near the shoulders. It had the shiny luster of a stone that had been subjected to heat before being worked. The base suggested an exceptional arrowpoint, made with care and precision.

"Well, son, I know what I'd like..." Walker let the thought trail off.

It had happened before that Young Walker's father had called him in a field, and he arrived to find his father crouched, staring at a scraper or point half buried, which when finally grasped and drawn from the dirt would be either complete or broken. It was hard for him to understand why his father would hunker and stare at a buried object. He himself saw no fascination in not knowing—he would simply pluck it up and find out if it were whole or broken. But he also understood it was impolite to reach over and pick up what another's eyes had found. So he waited and prompted his father with comment.

"It's gonna be a beauty, Dad."

"Man...I don't know..." Walker was thinking of a theory he'd heard concerning a cat closed in a box with a decaying isotope that would, at some point release a fatal gas. The gist was that, with the box closed, the cat was equally alive and dead; once the box was opened, it was one or the other. The metaphysical gist was that the *other* continued to exist after the opening of the box as well.

Walker had done okay with the theory, up to the opening of the box. He preferred to find a living cat, as he preferred to find a whole arrowpoint, but his brain was stuck in a one-or-the-other reality. If the arrowpoint turned out to be broken, the idea that it nevertheless existed complete in a reality that didn't coincide with his, ran like quicksilver when he tried to grasp it. It was said to be good metaphysics and good Zen, but it was also, for Walker, too much. The arrowpoint that could only be broken or could only be whole, still lay at the end of his gaze.

They had been staring at the half-revealed object for no more than a minute, but a minute, especially to the boy, seemed a long time to stare. He had none of his father's wish to savor not knowing, or his father's need to see what the object would tell him before he touched it; because once he did touch it, the way he saw the object would change.

"I'm betting it's whole," said Young Walker.

"I think it's broken."

"Oh Dad, come on."

Walker took the base of the point between thumb and forefinger and gently tugged. There was no resistance, the piece of flint came free. They saw the shoulders emerge, the beginning of the blade, the clean line where it had been broken straight across. Walker let it drop into his palm. Following the exquisite flintwork of the base and shoulders, he could imagine the missing blade, narrow, crisp, deepening pink with the signature of fire.

"Aw..." Young Walker searched for an acceptable word. "...crap."

Walker saw himself peering into a box at a dead cat. A Siamese, one of his favorite kinds. He knew the blade was lying beside a stone it had struck, overgrown in the bark of a tree, under the earth where the deer or bison had fallen and been butchered. Or it was here in the field, separated from the base by a ringing strike from plow, disc, springtooth harrow, or in a cigar box in a stranger's house, or surrounded by cotton in the basement of a museum. He didn't think it went on, reunited with the base in some ineluctable space and time. But then, he also thought that the tree in the isolate forest fell with a hell of a noise.

"Dang. Bummer, Dad."

"Double bummer."

He stood and slipped the fragment into his pocket. When he was younger, he'd taken such disappointments intensely personally, and for that matter, so had his old man. The old man could lay out some rich curses when he'd uncovered a heartbreaker. But to do so soured the moment and spawned a victim of regret. Walker had dragged resentment of the world with him on walks before. It was a habit he was trying to avoid.

They walked together after the finding of the well-made, broken point, one or the other of them dipping down to flick at a piece of flint. The boy was thinking he wanted to find a piece as nicely made as the broken base, *but all there.* Walker was thinking he'd found out something new about the long hump of hill.

On the Bead and Celt sites, he'd found stones that hinted at artistry, the creative channeling of a finger over a hide scraper, but no evidence of a masterpiece, the ultimate product of that creative thought. Here, five miles farther south, where the river had once curved over to wash away one end of a long hill, he looked on a fragment of such a masterpiece. He'd walked on the hill since he was a boy, and it was the first sign he'd found that an artist had lived there.

The hill was only a mile north of the Bluff site, and the old man had referred to it as the North Bluff until the day he picked up the mano stone, a long, well-formed oval of sandstone used for the grinding of seeds. He began calling it the Mano site then. The old man had gone there often, but it was visited only rarely by Walker. There never seemed to be as much flint showing there as on the sites farther south, and the objects he found there were roughly made. Thumb scrapers, long and short, were carefully worked on the scraping edge, but modification of the body was usually haphazard. Walker had found four well-made scrapers, the rest were rough adaptations. Arrowpoints were basic, functional. The site was also visible from the highway, a circumstance that hadn't bothered the old man. Walker found it intrusive. There were times when he walked the Mano when he forgot the highway was there, but usually he was aware of the distant whisper of traffic, and though he knew most drivers focused on the highway, the suspicion of being under observation nagged at him. Of all the sites he knew, he felt most uncomfortable on the Mano, like an ant in a classroom ant farm, a dummy in a diorama. He conceded the irony that it was his own fault, a flaw in his spirit that assumed he was a center of attention, even passing attention. He hoped someday to be able to go on about his business with the world in suspension. But hope was cheap and he was lazy.

They walked the spine of the hill and both flanks, finding only infrequent flint. It seemed to Walker there had been more flint on the site when he was a boy. He assumed people had taken flint away to put in flower beds and aquariums or, as he himself had done, to stare at. They walked across where a European house had stood, bits of foundation rock tumbled and scarred by the plow. He had once found a small porcelain bird there, severed at the legs and stamped JAPAN, and he had found a 1944 penny, corroded pale green. They walked the slope where the old river had curved into the end of the hill, where large hand scrapers had been found, chunky tools made of strange rust–tinged flint that seemed to belong to another people than the Smoky Hill farming hunters.

There were times, on any site, when hours of walking, searching, yielded nothing. This day they had found half of a masterpiece. Neither of them had said much until the drive home, when Young Walker spoke with a casualness that showed he had been in the grip of hard thought.

"Dad?"

Walker cocked an ear out of the wind.

"You know when you found that butt of a point we didn't know was whole or not?"

Walker nodded, keeping a watch on the car behind an approaching semi.

"Well, you bet it was broken."

"Yeah. Man, I hated to be right on that one."

"Well, Dad, you *always* bet they're broken."

"I do? Yeah, I guess I do. So...what, you think I'm a pessimist?"

"Well..."

"Bad outlook on life?"

"Kind of."

The semi went by in a sheet of wind, the car behind a tail-gating glimpse of frustrated hurry.

"You got me son. It's my Norski Tao."

To Young Walker, the phrase sounded like nor-skid-ow.

"This Tao, it stands for the Way, with a capital W, like the way to exist. Like not wasting your life trying to make the world come to you—you know, fit you? It's like you don't waste time *supposing*, you just get on with it, and whatever it is, you do it well. Ha ha. No problem, right?

"But , you know, I come from Norwegians and Danes, and the Scandinavians are real gloomers." He thought of Ibsen, Kierkegaard, Rolvaag, Munch, Bergman, all heavy hitters in the Great Northern Doomfest.

"Maybe it's living with all that cold and darkness."

"But Dad, you joke a lot."

"Oh sure, Norskis can joke, but we're bent to the dismal. That's why I always think the hidden stuff is broken."

"Or that it won't rain."

"Or, if it does, it won't rain enough."

"The farmer hasn't worked the field anyway."

"Yeah, or I'll be looking the wrong way and walk right over the good stuff."

"Or they'll build a mall on the site. And the stuff they sell will fall apart!"

"You got the idea." They had reached the monolithic factories on the edge of town. "Anyway, about the time the people on the Mano were growing their little ears of corn, Europe was in a mess of wars, plagues, starvation, you name it. Just before that time, the Greeks and Romans did a lot of crowing about how special human beings were, and after the plagues and all, that attitude came around again, another celebration of ourselves.

"The middle-ages thinking, between those times, was just the opposite, life's a bastard nodd and then you die. They didn't have much to look forward to on a daily basis—bubonic plague, getting your head bashed for a crust of bread. And even if you were rich and sheltered, your brain was probably oozing out your ears from some disease."

"Gah, Dad!"

"Sorry, son, Norski Tao. Just trying to give you the picture. Out of this misery came great art and literature and music, and most of it was about faith and worship and the idea that human beings are nothing at all really. They could be snuffed out like...*that*!" He grabbed the boy's knee and was rewarded with a yelp.

"Dad, you jerk!" Young Walker struck him on the elbow.

"Sorry, son, I thought you were drifting. So. When things got better, humans started to see themselves as pretty smart again. That kind of thinking usually came from the southern half of the world, Greece, Italy, but the northerners..." Walker shook his head. "They tried to buy the glory program, but their hearts weren't in it, you know. They hung onto that middle-ages attitude."

"Bummer."

"Most of the time. It's probably a genetic imprint by now. You know that story about a half a glass of water—it's sitting on the table, and do you see it as half full or half empty?"

"Is this a trick?"

"No. The way you see it is supposed to tell you something about how you see life in general. Well, the first words out of a Scandinavian's mouth would be that somebody better move that glass, it was going to get tipped over."

"That's dumb."

"A-yup." Walker knew he thought too long, too much, too often in useless ways, and melancholy indulged was a miserable trap. He had done it, and even enjoyed it, shaking his head at himself later. The answer for him was not to streak above existence, his world, but soak into it. In his good moments, he could soak clear through to the other side of melancholy. There he found that the philosophies of the Svenskis, Norskis, and Danzkis were not much different than aspects of some Asian philosophies or the dancing, serenading skeletons of the Mexican Day of the Dead—give death a capital D, kiss its wormy lips with a laugh, and get on with a finite life. The cat sprang out of the box, the arrowpoint rushed full in the air. Walker would not be surprised if the code of the Viking and the bushido of the Samurai were similar, or if the people who'd scratched for corn on the Mano had held Medieval views, down to earth and, beyond that, part of it.

"But, Dad, *I'm* not like that."

"Well, sure, you're different, you're only half Scandinavian. You've got your mom's Peruvian, Spanish influence to even things out."

"You know the Incas worshipped the sun."

"There you go, what could be brighter? Seems like that strikes a perfect balance for you."

They were back in their own civilization, part of intimate traffic, offerings of automobiles, food, service of all kinds.

"Was your dad, you know, was he like that too?" Young Walker never used the word "grandpa"; he didn't have the memory to support it.

"Like what?"

"You know, gloomy?"

"Well, he was a dang Scandi. What can I say?" Walker saw a sign that told him how many billion had been sold. "How about supper here?"

"Sure." The voice should have been excited—Young Walker loved grease—but it was not, and because Walker wasn't thinking when he glanced at his son, he saw through the face to the connections being made. From the beginning, the boy had been told the truth about the blank his grandfather had become. All his questions about Old Man Walker had been dealt with, and the blank remained. Walker pulled into the parking lot.

"As far as my old man goes, he was one person, but that isn't me. You know that, don't you, son? You might have a distant father, but you won't have a disappearing one."

The boy looked at him sharply, surprised.

That night, as Walker sat in bed reading a popcorn thriller, he heard a loud roll of thunder.

"Dad? You awake?"

"Yo." The voice had surprised him. He'd thought his son had gone to sleep long ago.

"Did you hear that?"

"Sure did." He kept reading. The hero was getting his ass kicked.

"Dad. If it rains tonight, can we go back to the Mano tomorrow?"

The thunder clamored again. Walker paused.

"*Ohhhh*, what's the *use?*" he said, with an exaggerated whine. His son's wild laughter was a comfort.

Prairie Wind Talks Big

What are you
doing out here dustbait?

You want to avoid something
avoid me.
Don't even think
while I grab your hair
and whip your face with it

of romancing me stranger.
More clever tongues than yours
are quiet now.

Get down or get ready.
I go around
nothing out here.

River Charm

Everything the Mano was not—private, rich in flint, home to many craftsmen—the Bluff, a mile to the south, was. It was also the only place Walker knew of on the Smoky Hill where the river still flowed where it had when the Old People had been there. It was the place Walker had found his first arrowpoint and the place where he had seen his only ghost.

Memories of walking in gray cold, blowing sleet, the pitiless, sapping heat of high summer—those memories belonged to other sites; what he remembered of the Bluff was springtime, new leaves uncurling strong, green odor, a vast sky made of breeze. He knew it was romantic twaddle; there had been times he'd walked the Bluff with feet frozen cold, picking up flint with numb fingers. He also knew he must have slogged there gasping the hot, wet air of July. In the abstract, he could imagine it, but he remembered nothing but pleasure.

The charm was the river. Walking west across the field to the edge of the plowed area, three steps onto the grassy verge, Walker had stood, man and boy, at the edge of a sixty-foot cliff overlooking the fast brown river. Gazing down at the trees of the opposite bank, listening to the water, he could sense the thump and wind-snatched chatter of long-vanished life, a dogfight breaking out, a shout, a length of wood thrown, a yelp. The river, by being there, and having been there, encouraged thoughts of life. Walker allowed himself these delusions remorselessly. As a boy it had been easy— he looked over the river and let his boyhood do the rest. He could smell grease and hear kids yelling in a game. But age had its way with that dreamy ease. The river that could never be wholly described, wholly caught when he was a boy, took on dimensions, attributes, familiarity, as Walker grew through his twenties. The word "river" had clouded the thing itself; he was no longer so easily seduced. Then, a warp in the equilibrium, the Bluff gave him a ghost.

That day he had turned off the dirt road and driven slowly west up the rutted access road to its dead end. In front of the car, a shaggy pasture, scattered with Osage orange saplings, lay between his car and the river. Ten steps to his right, a barbed-wire fence marked the north end of the pasture, and on the other side of the fence, lay a plowed field that rose quickly from the low lands to the east and ended at the river cliff to the west. To the north, the plowed area curved around a thicket of wild plum and swooped down another slope to the flood plain. The chips and shards of the old village were on the high ground, bordered by the river cliff on the west, low land to the north and east, high pasture to the south. The area was large enough that he could walk it for five or six hours before feeling he'd given it a thorough search.

As he'd quietly closed the car door and stepped onto the site that afternoon, he had every reason to anticipate great fortune: an early spring day full of cool sunshine; the tiny winter wheat plants had not grown enough yet to obscure the ground; the surface of the furrows was smooth, dry skin; he saw no other footprints entering the field; and he had not yet encountered the holistic philosophies that would warn him of the folly of expectation. Life was good. In one pocket of his light denim jacket were cigarettes and matches, in the other a small box of raisins. His brown cowboy hat was stuck full of found feathers, mourning dove, prairie chicken, horned owl. Young, dumb, and privileged, he scooped the coins from his right side pants pocket and slid them into his left with his keys, making room for all of the objects he would find.

In later years, Walker could not remember if he'd found anything that day. He must have noticed the increasing chill of the breeze, he might have registered the tall, solid, flat-bottomed clouds drifting in, but the sun still shone, and he walked on. He may have seen that the ground darkened with cloud shadow more and more frequently and felt the almost illusory twinge of one or two microscopic sprinkles of water on his hands, but he had searched through spring showers before, so he walked on. He certainly saw and heard the scattering of large, dark spots appearing on the dirt. He looked up and saw the sky closed and dark, sensed the fall of great water at an unknown distance above him.

From the north end of the Bluff, he glanced back at his car, too far, and at the plum thicket just ahead, made up his mind as the pattering of big drops increased. It would be hell getting out the access road once it was muddy, but did he want to try it during the storm or after? The drops became less scattered. It looked like rain, it would rain, and then, as he began to sprint for the plum bushes, it rained, a drilling, roaring rain that caught him as he reached the bushes and scrambled for entrance. The dense, prickly branches resisted parting twice, until he crabbed around to the east and found a gap and floundered in on all fours, trampling his hat.

The cavity in the heart of the bushes had been made by coyote, deer, dog. Walker didn't know which. He was just relieved to find it empty. There was room for him to sit cross-legged and bent over once he'd jammed his hat back on and flipped his jacket collar up to keep water from running down his neck. The crown of twigs and foliage above was thick, breaking the force of the rain, fracturing it into spray that ran, twig to branch, down to the ground. There were drip areas, and he adjusted to all but one, a steady, inescapable staccato on his jacketed left shoulder blade.

"Oh, man!" That for the intensity of the rain.

"Damn." That for being wet.

He wallowed in a brief spate of misery—the muddy road to come, the rain mashing his afternoon into a space the size of a shopping bag, the lively stutter of drops on his shoulder, but he grew quickly resigned, sighed, used three matches lighting a cigarette.

In fact he was lucky: the thicket had been there, and in it a dry hollow that made it as good as a cave, and blind headlong choice had led him to it. He was in the storm and out of its effect at the same time, surrounded by the hiss of speeding water, the loud clatter of its striking. He turned his gaze over his right shoulder, through a gap in the leaves. The verticals of rain had turned the world a shifting gray. Within that gray, a long stone's throw from where Walker sat, a man on a horse, both darker gray, moving slowly and casually in the downpour at an angle away from Walker, had started down the far side of the slope to the low ground. The walk of the horse was easy, the posture of the man relaxed.

Several things happened at once. Walker's brain micro-flashed explanations involving a real man on a real horse, and shorted out; his scalp and the nape of his neck puckered cold; he wrenched his gaze forward and focused on the twigs in front of his nose. Then he looked over his shoulder again. The man's torso and the neck and head of the horse were still visible, sinking a little more with each step behind the crest of the slope. A few more steps, the man's back, shoulders, and then his head sank below the crest. Walker had swallowed an urge to yell out at the departing figure; now he rejected a similar urge to crawl out of the bush and stand searching in the rain. Figuring the angle of the horse's direction, he shifted his gaze between the dripping leaves. Through the drops falling from his hat brim, he should have been able to see horse and rider reappear on the low land once they'd moved beyond the bottom of the slope. The rain continued hammering. When he'd waited longer than it should have taken for the distance to be covered, and still not seen anything, he widened his scanning area.

The base of the thicket had gotten saturated; water pooled under his left thigh. He was still watching for the horse and rider when the slash of rain lessened, the noise subsided. The storm faltered, hushed itself, and was over. Walker had no idea how long he'd sat in the bush. He waited, listened to the breeze shaking water off the leaves, until he was sure the calm wasn't just a lull in the action. The drops on his shoulder were slow and single. He tipped his head, drained his hat, and clambered out of the thicket and stood, hands thick with mud. The field gleamed dark brown. There was no horse and rider.

His mind had already carried on a lengthy discussion about Newtonian physics and mysticism, wish fulfillment and delusion. He'd accused himself of manufacturing a vision from a romantic desire to see one of the people of the Bluff. He knew that was a poor explanation because he knew enough about the people to manufacture a better vision than the one he'd seen. Science told him the Bluff people had moved on before the Spanish brought horses onto the plains; they had never seen one. He would have more probably invented a woman with an armload of branches, a man walking with a digging stick.

He considered the memory: a man on a horse, all dark gray, a shape, detail blurred in the rain. He had no sense of whether the man's hair was short or long, or if the man even had hair. He remembered the contours of shoulders and back and believed the man wore no shirt. He had seen no saddle, bridle, or rope on the horse. The man's hands had been down, as if he gripped the base of the mane in his fingers. He had looked away and back again, and the apparition had continued moving through space and time without his attention.

Rubbing the mud from his hands, he began to walk the crest, stepping between rows of wheat. There were no tracks anywhere on the crest, above it, or below it. He stood there long enough to chew and swallow a handful of raisins, looking around, and around again.

He made it out of the slippery access road, gunning and braking, weeds streaking his elbow with water.

In the years that followed, indulging his human love of reason, he cobbled together makeshift explanations—the Eureka Principle of exotic context, a thicket in a downpour, refractive qualities of a waterlogged atmosphere—all of which may have secured his mind about why or how he had seen. The question of *what* he had seen was not susceptible to the world of equation and formula. The crawling of his skin at the time told him it was spirit, ghost, apparition, and words like that stood alone, untrapped by explanation. He often wondered, if it hadn't rained and he'd continued walking, would the horse have plodded across the field at the same place and time? And would he not have seen it because he was busy doing what, to him, was normal?

For a less private person, it was the perfect campfire story: a man charmed, first by the river and then the falling water, into seeing past belief—but he only told it once, the day his son saw for the first time the civilized Bluff, the house, redwood deck, metal barn, scattered machines, gray pit bull, and asked him what it had been like when it was just a bluff that hung over the river. He told the story as if it were a story the river had told him.

Sojourners

The impulse to magic ran high among the flintworkers of the Bluff. Of the eighty-five relatively complete objects Walker had found in the field before it was homesteaded, forty-seven were arrowpoints, and more than half were notched two, three, four, five times, and half of those had been refined further for thinness, mindful of the space between a bison's ribs, and symmetry. The urge to excellence extended to hide scrapers as well: of the thirty-one Walker had found, seventeen showed great concern for harmony of use and appearance, with random ridges worked off the full length of the curved back, giving a firm, smooth grip between the ball of the thumb and the curl of the forefinger. Although most fell one or two steps short of being that statement of intent in stone, six of them, though they could not be called exquisite, like those best scrapers made by the Quivirans forty miles to the southwest, came close. Generally, the length of a thumb or longer, they were carefully worked, not only on the flared scraping end, but down the tapering sides and completely around the narrow end as well, a triumph of will over material, since the narrow end was where the strike had been made to knock the long flake free of the block of flint, and the grain there was compacted and tough.

Scrapers from earlier peoples, like those of the Rocking Deer, were usually large, heavy-bodied, and broad across the scraping end. Those on the Bluff and all along the Smoky Hill showed a preference for a narrower scraping end and a slight, gradual taper toward the tail. They were made from long strips of flint rather than flaring chunks.

Most of the hide scrapers, and virtually all of the fine ones, had been made from the palomino tan flint with gray splotches, and a dramatic gray dark-and-light banded flint. The first was a characteristic of the southern Flint Hills near the Oklahoma border; the banded was more plentiful in the northern Hills. Shorter, and usually cruder, scrapers were chipped from a variety of gray Flint Hills stones, scattered sources of which could be found as close as twenty miles to the east.

The flint preference was reversed for projectile points; almost two thirds of them were Flint Hills grays, including all but five of the twenty-four notched points. The blotched tan flint was used to make seven points, and two were made of the banded gray. As a group, the notched points referred to the Hills of the east; the triangular, unnotched points represented a greater variety of flint sources, cobbles, southeastern Hills and, in the case of two coarse pinkish-white stones, parts unknown. Yet nowhere in eighty-five tools, or the hundreds of broken tools, did the multi-colored browns of Smoky Hill jasper appear.

From these observations, Walker's shaky history of the Bluff people began, but suggestions given by the stones arranged on a table or rug were of limited use without the considerations of context. Similar tools made of the same stone and all found in a certain area of the old village would give another dimension to those suggestions. The most obvious example had occurred just south of the Bluff proper.

Past the south edge of the plowed area, across a fence and scrub pasture, was another plowed field, sloping down from an eastern rise to end in weeds at the low area. The cliff had diminished here to a bank and curved to the west, so that the village had been set back from the river's edge. On the toe of the hill and up a third of its gradual slope, were found the same flints, the same tools, as on the Bluff. The old man had never called this field by a separate name, referring to it as "the low end," and so neither did Walker until, many years into his own adulthood, he realized that a certain kind of tool was coming out of the slope, halfway up, in an area no larger than his living room.

The tools were clearly a kind of scraper, but with four modifications: they were long, so long that any one of them, laid across Walker's palm, would jut beyond both sides of his hand; instead of having a flat or slightly curved bottom surface to lay along the thumb, these described a radical arc from end to end so that viewed from the side, they were shaped like a crescent; while the nose, the working end, of a traditional scraper was typically wider than the body, these tools had narrowed heads, the widest part of the flake was at the top of the arc; both ends were developed equally. There was no tail.

After finding the first of them, Walker suspected it was a specialized scraper of some kind. The second, third, and fourth finds resulted in curiosity, suspicion, baffled wonder. By the time he picked up the sixth, twenty years after the first, they were beginning to give him ideas.

All were made of palomino flint. The name was Walker's own and was highly relative, since color ranged from a pale yellowish-tan to an earthier yellow that could as easily be called buckskin as palomino. In addition, it could be threaded or splotched with a dark gray or banded with thin lines of dark yellow-brown, spaced progressively closer together until they abruptly met the point where flint turned into the dull white limey excrescence that signaled the weathered rind or the top or bottom of a seam of flint. Walker had found four of the long, humped, narrow-headed tools in that room-sized area, another on the main part of the Bluff, and one on the Mano site, a mile north. He found them nowhere else.

Most of the body of a traditional hide scraper was hidden in the hand, only the broad scraping edge protruding beyond the end of the thumb. The long crescent tool fell into the hand differently. Walker learned to grasp it at midpoint, ball of his thumb against the inner arc, and wrap his fingers around half its length. This left the other half curving out past his thumb like a tapered finger. Reckoning a use for that finger of stone while the world dropped snow, grew flowers, beamed bright, turned brown, every so often in those cycles he'd grip one of the palomino crescents with hand and eye. He thought eventually of pumpkins and marrow.

Each symbolic of a different path, they were specific things that could have called for the invention of long, curved tools. Long before the time of the Bluff people, hunters, both men and women, discovered the value of marrow. As cooks, they couldn't have resisted trying it, and it naturally followed that they soon made a practice of splitting the long bones of their prey to get at the marrow in the center channel. Walker thought of himself picking up split long bones with his left hand, right hand inserting the tapered finger of flint in the top of the channel, and—zip!—scooping down marrow into the pot. The scraper nose had been narrowed to reach forward and inward, and the length of the half-crescent kept the right hand away from the surface of the bone during the gesture. Split bone creates splinters, so the tool not only fit the job, it also had a reason to be invented.

Walker's assumption of marrow removal started with bone-pricked fingers, went on to sticks, narrow stones, long flakes of flint. It envisioned the invention of a specialized, rounded nose on that flake, the further invention of putting an identical nose on the other end, and consequent refinements of form, balance, and visual pleasure. Because it had no "right" end, the tool could be picked up and used instantly. Excess stone had been worked off the back to give it symmetrical balance. The hand no longer needed to struggle with an object, the object had come to it, belonged to the hand.

Such a tool would be made by a good technician and a thoughtful designer with a strong streak of the tinkerer. Tinkering was the art of invention, as practiced by those who reached out and jiggled something or decided to twist and press at the same time, to see what would happen. The tinkerer was the protagonist of Walker's assumption, though he represented generations of his kind who altered the equation of function and form.

Walker also found that the tool lent itself well to a scooping motion, the clenched hand turning down and inward. When he sought the other end of this practical gesture, he dismissed the hides, the way the worked edge curved through the air suggested that it would slice and cut as well as scrape. He lingered over wood, scraping the bark off arrowshafts seemed a warm idea, but the way the tool was built to the hand meant the strokes would be directed toward the individual, which, not being a woodworker, he failed to recognize as desirable. Walker finally saw himself stripping the meat from big shards of pumpkin. The tool probably had many uses, the natural result of tinkering, and Walker thought they were tasks of going-in-and-getting rather than scraping-off or boring-through; marrow spoons, pumpkin scoops.

The function of the humped flint spoons was a small question. Spreading from it like rings in water were questions of occurrence—what did their concentration on one hill slope imply?—and sequence—were the people who made the flint scoops contemporaries of those who lived on the high part of the Bluff and, farther north, on the Mano?

South an eighth of a mile from where the marrow spoons were found, were more flint chips on a modest rise of the old riverbed. Though the river had swung west at this point, the old channel hadn't fully died but was a capillary that went nowhere, a creek on its way to extinction but, for now, supporting short, twisted oak, sumac, and cottonwood saplings. Called Little Cottonwood by the old man, the rise represented a smaller group of people than either the Spoon site or the Bluff site. Flint was not plentiful in this small area, artifacts were seldom found. Walker had picked up only two small, irregularly-notched arrowpoints. The first, squat and pinkish-orange, seemed to be mostly base, salvaged from a break that had left just enough of the blade to be worked into a nub of a point, eventually replaced and discarded. The other, a curved triangle with sketchy notches, was a deep russet pink. The colors suggested the original flint, cobble or chunk, had been heated before being fractured. Of the scattered chips Walker had picked up and rubbed between his fingers on the Little Cottonwood, most were palominos and grays, and most had come from heat-treated stone.

All these qualities of Little Cottonwood, Spoon, and Bluff suggested a logical, though potentially simple-minded story. In this dream history, a people from the southern Flint Hills began a journey to the northwest or perhaps, using the Hills as a metaphorical road, due north. Since journeys of relocation are no respecters of geometry, they may have even traveled to the northern Hills, doubling back once they'd turned their steps to the west. With them the voyagers carried tools from home, material from the Hills. Such a journey could take months, or generations. At the Little Cottonwood they stopped, camped, and planted. Visitors to the original homeland returned with flint, news, and fresh adventurers who had liked what they heard about plentiful game, few enemies, good growing dirt. The Little Cottonwood had probably deteriorated some in the thousand years or so between its first dwellers and Walker's tennis shoes, but it couldn't have been much of a rise to begin with, especially when the village began to grow. Situated on the first gentle rise of land beside the river, the camp would be at the mercy of a prolonged rainy season. Perhaps over generations, perhaps in one concerted move, the village migrated to higher ground to the north, the Spoon site, spreading north along the riverbank to the top of the Bluff. The place they left would come to be known as the Old Place.

Almost every time they'd walked across the pasture separating the

Bluff and Spoon sites, the old man would remind Walker that someday this pasture might get plowed, and if Walker would remember and have a look at it, he would find things. The old man would likely never have dreamed a farm would be built on the Bluff site, but he was right about the pasture.

Three years after Walker had discovered with great dismay the earth-bermed double-wide, the metal barn, and the gray pit bull, he'd puttered down the dead end road again, planning to see how the Spoon site was doing. The shock of finding a farm on the Bluff had kept him away, but he remembered the Spoon was there, a sloping hillside to the south, and curiosity eventually pulled him back. Before he reached the end of the weedy lane, he saw that the pasture was gone, the skinny, twisted hedge trees that had dotted it were gone. To his right, the homestead, the dog barking on the deck; rolling away to his left, the slope leading to the Spoon site; in front of him, the transformed pasture, freshly plowed, and the river beyond. The Spoon site was freshly plowed too—dark, crumbly, and granular. Whatever stones there were on the Spoon, and on the turned-over pasture, needed rain to become visible.

In the days that followed, days in which he anticipated rain, courted and cajoled it, Walker's imagination crammed the turned pasture with objects and information; arrowpoints by the handful, a hat brimming with hide scrapers, a cache of flint knives, a marrow spoon with its nose still wedged tight in the groove of a split long bone. Such excesses were not to be. The rain did come, flint was revealed in the plowed pastureland, the village was shown to be more or less continuous from the Bluff down to the Spoon. As Walker, joined later by his son, continued to visit and walk there, always keeping his eyes loose in case the pit bull decided to expand his territory, he began to find the occasional base of a snapped arrowpoint, a gray or tan hide scraper. The plow bit deeper annually.

One day he knelt beside a notched arrowpoint, picked it up, and noticed another one an arm's length away. As he leaned toward the second one, he saw a third beside it and knew he was kneeling on the floor of a lodge. Someone had fresh arrowpoints, homemade or traded for, which had been laid by, and then unclaimed. One of mottled gray, one gray burned pink, one of the handsome Flint Hills bluish stone. On hands and knees in the invisible lodge, he could look down the slope to the Spoon site, and south to the modest rise of the Little Cottonwood. The three arrowpoints could have been made generations after the initial settlement of the Little Cottonwood; they could have been made centuries later.

Walker preferred the latter timeline, simply because of topography. Once the population outgrew the first small site and moved north to the nearest suitable area, the high ground Walker knew as the Bluff, the safe ground, would be settled first. As the band prospered and grew, and was perhaps still joined by immigrants from the original homeland, new lodges grew on the southern end of the Bluff, the tilled pasture where Walker knelt, and down the slope to the Spoon site. Once this less-desirable lower ground was fully claimed, the village area had been developed to its maximum. This would place the marrow/pumpkin tools during the later development of the area, rather than during early times. Perhaps they had been brought from the southeast by a later band of settlers or perhaps developed to accommodate the growing success of vegetable gardening. Surplus population would follow the river north to the Mano site, or closer places Walker hadn't found.

Such a view of history, built largely on a foundation of intuition and omen, would likely not stand up in academic court, but settlement, saturation, and expansion had been an effective way to traverse time and space for everything from strawberries to fungi. A forward edge of magpies had been moving into Walker's circle from the west and north for at least twenty years, and more recently, roadrunners and armadillos had begun to appear from the south.

The linear thinker had to remind himself often that the Bluff dwellers had not arrived and developed in a vacuum. The remains of similar growth sequences could be found in any direction from the Bluff. Conventional wisdom held that, by the time Europeans arrived, the Smoky Hill farmers had gone north, settled in Nebraska and, in European history, become the Pawnee.

Had Walker been in love with clay instead of flint, he could have gotten more answers; the development of pot construction and decoration had been thoroughly defined and dated by science. He would discover this later when he began walking twenty-five miles to the north in the company of a potter who pointed out the varieties of shape and decoration indicated by the shards of fired clay. On the Smoky Hill sites, the shards were uniformly thick and cord-roughened, from pots that were flare-necked or had no neck at all. Little interest had been shown in rim decoration, other than to smooth the lip all the way around. At the northern sites, cord-roughening remained, but many shards were smoother, and lip fragments showed pinching, poking, engraving, impression—attributes that echoed Woodland cultures moving in from the east.

Walker's mind, streaking erratically like a water-strider on the time-line, saw alliances, meldings of need and solution, cultures moving into or around each other. But these were just ideas. Walker might be able to say that all the bone and shell he had seen on the Smoky Hill had been trash, with nothing modified for use, with the exception of the Bead site, which he conveniently thought of as an earlier, unrelated group of people, long gone when the gardening hunters arrived from the southern Flint Hills—but what did any of it mean? From any idea, possibilities expanded in a frazzle of lines. Walker had no laboratory, but like any citizen, he could tap into the literature and find what those who did have laboratories had to say. Such accounts were fascinating, but in the end, his mind always strayed to detail, circling, hovering, landing on the stones themselves, stones that would not always tell him what had happened but could possibly relate what had been thought and felt by one individual.

Many of these individuals had clearly gotten satisfaction from making objects in which visual and tactile presence went beyond obvious use. In most cases the desire had been tempered by difficult flint, impatience, a miscalculated angle. The maker of a little, pinkish, five-notched point had worked one side of the blade more heavily than the other so that the blade seemed slightly askew to the axis of the base. A well-made point of palomino flint, sides notched near the base, maintained symmetry all the way to just before the tip where it took a micro-veer to the side. The long, five-notched gray point Walker had slid from the Bluff mud as a young man had complete symmetry, the bravura fragility of exaggerated length, the skill of five notches, yet the stone had resisted the flintworker's moves at two places in the center of the blade, leaving two small, angular warts that would not be removed. The deal the flintworker had struck with the stone—accepting what insisted on staying—could only be seen as failure if the goal was absolute control, unless being an artist sometimes meant recognizing the spirit of material and letting it stand.

Someone had thoroughly worked a neutral gray point, interrupted low on the sides of the base with equal notches sloping slightly toward the blade. Flakes had been removed from the entire surface of the thin arrow-point, yet down one side of the blade, the flakes had popped free with an inconsistency of thickness, as if there were hidden "easy" spots in the stone. Everything had been controlled except the waver in the line from tip to one shoulder.

The one arrowpoint loaded most successfully with beauty and balance was an unnotched triangle of light gray with an area of dirty white, a blotch of darker gray. The stone was not exotic in color or pattern, there was no added attraction of notches. The elegance of the work was its simplicity and precision, a dead level baseline, sharp corners, sides falling in equal grace to a needle tip, as if the mind behind the hands had decided to keep it simple and, beyond that, perfectly simple.

Walker continued visiting the Spoon, the pit bull finally content to merely lift its gaze from crossed paws on the redwood deck, check that Walker was not coming to the house, and drop its head again. The man, who had grown predictable to the dog, walked south watching the ground, but even as he walked away from it, he often thought of the Bluff.

It was the site of his first arrowpoint, the place where questions had baffled his reason. His mother was brought there by his courting father, and certain opaque statements the old man had made led him to think he might even have been conceived there. Because he never saw people at the pit bull's house, it grew to have no substance for him, so sometimes, walking, he forgot himself, thought that when the buildings had been abandoned, fallen-in, dismantled, plowed under, he would still be there to walk the Bluff.

Fungus Goes to the Country

When Young Walker's big sister was three, before Young Walker was born, she grabbed an armload of dolls to join her mother and father for a couple of afternoon hours in a field. They drove eighteen miles south, followed a meandering dirt road, a rough, jarring lane, and parked in a grove of trees. They walked through the trees and onto a sunny, plowed field.

"See that long rise facing us? That's where we're going." The old river-bed was only a couple of minutes away, adult walking time; to the little girl it was far, the clods were enormous, her legs were small, she was balancing a load of floppy dolls—but her father had promised a shade-giving tree at the edge of the field where she could play, and so she struggled on.

The tree was small, the dirt was soft, the shade cool. She sat and began to arrange her companions. That afternoon Walker looked up often from his search to see her talking earnestly or wagging a finger at a doll who'd given sass.

Walker had no memory of what was found that day, for after the dusty search, the trudge back to the car, the half-hour drive, the key in the lock, the familiar house, just when he was contemplating a bath, his daughter dropped the bomb. She'd taken her dolls to her room and come rushing immediately back with word that she'd forgotten her favorite in the field—a small, nubbly blue doll with a rubber face, named Fungus. Fungus, a simple handful of doll and the first she'd taken to, was her number one doll. A pink cloth rabbit she called Carotin was number two. She'd brought Carotin back in her arms but not Fungus, and the little doll wasn't in her room with the dolls who'd stayed behind. The anguish in his daughter's face was real, but what touched Walker was the realization that she knew he was tired and she was hesitant to ask that he go back.

Walker looked at his wife, who calmly gazed back, saying nothing. Both mother and daughter knew Walker could be churlish in defense of his laziness. It was his call. In this case the conclusion was foregone—he couldn't leave his daughter's soulmate sitting out there after sundown. He saw the doll smiling dumbly into the night at the edge of the field, at the mercy of sniffing and tasting raccoon, possum, skunk, coyote, dog, excavated by enterprising deer mouse for the stuffing. He would be a hero. When he announced he would go get Fungus, his daughter threw herself against him and embraced his leg. He was already a hero.

He half-expected to see the little doll lying in the driveway, and when that wasn't the case, he searched the car thoroughly. Fungus wasn't there.

With forty-five minutes of remaining light in which to complete his mission, he started the engine. It seemed impossible that the doll could have fallen from a window without his daughter's knowledge, yet as he backtracked out of town and onto the highway, he watched for a mound of pale blue. He tried to recall their departure from the site. They hadn't hurried. The family had sat together under the tree, relaxing with small talk, while she gathered her dolls. Had Fungus gotten pushed back into the weeds along the fence, or had she misbehaved and been made to sit apart from the others, forgotten in her isolation? Walker knew this was unlikely—Fungus was the bright, obedient one. It was Carotin who had a mulish streak, was prone to tantrums at the tea party and momentary banishment, yet Carotin had returned from the field, and Fungus, that supremely good doll, had not.

Once he had negotiated the rutted lane and parked in the trees at the same spot they'd left earlier, Walker ran a visual search of the weeds around and under the car. The doll wasn't there, and he didn't see the hoped-for spot of blue as he walked across the furrows to the tree. His vision of himself as returning hero began to sour as he reached the tree and saw no doll, scoured the weeds and saw no doll. He patrolled the fenceline both east and west of the tree, no doll and no tracks of an animal he could turn into a culprit. He wandered the site and retraced their steps to the car, watching for blue as the sun gave up in the west. Fungus was a victim of mystery.

Driving away in the dusk, his view of himself as champion laid low, he began to consider how to deal with his daughter's sorrow at the loss of her first and most constant companion.

He entered the house with the dread of one who brings bad news, only to be greeted with his daughter's rush of ecstasy and apology, the resurrected doll clutched in her hand. She had found Fungus in her mother's sewing room, where she must have played with her the day before. Beneath his daughter's joy he sensed a shift of apprehension: she'd caused him to drive to the field and back for nothing. Would he take the opportunity to break out in irritation?

It would be years before Confucius would insinuate to him the vital need to reciprocate, *I Ching* remind him that action must not anticipate reward, or the Yoruba trickster Eshu needle his vanity, but it took the mere face of his daughter's relief for him to know that among all the failed moments gone and to come, he had gotten one right.

As she lay in bed that night, Fungus and Carotin cuddled on either side, his daughter admitted to a powerful confusion; she remembered clearly playing with Fungus in the field.

"What are you doing, Daddy?"

"I'm feeling her foot. If she ran home faster than we drove, her feet should be smoking."

"Oh, Daddy, quit." She felt the other foot.

Walker had a vision of stumpy cloth tubular legs whizzing over hills, leaping barbed wire, transcending rivers and creeks.

"Could she fly?"

"Hmm." Walker lifted one of the cloth arms and let it fall. A spitcurl had been formed in the rubber dome of Fungus' forehead. His daughter saw the doll flailing sausage arms in the air.

"No, not fly," she said. Her brows lowered into her stormy look of thought. "I'm *sure* I took Fungus."

"Fungus did a mystery."

"Daddy, that's no answer."

"It isn't?"

When his daughter was a young woman living in a big city and working in the world of books, she would still believe she'd played with the blue doll in the field that afternoon. She'd been the one who told him the vexing story of the cat in the isotope box, and the one as well who explained it once a year. They'd survived departure, divorce, and distance, relieved only by faithful letters and visits. Throughout that time, whenever he spoke of the Fungus the Dolly site, his daughter came to him.

The field itself, the journey to it, the thought of going there, no matter when they occurred in Walker's life, belonged to her. It was the spot along the Smoky Hill river he went to ahead of all others, even when he knew the ground hadn't been worked, the rain hadn't come, there would be nothing to find.

A Call to Attention

When one of Old Man Walker's two Missouri friends pointed out the distant field at the end of the turnoff lane, the old man slowed the car, but tried to drive on. He admitted later he was looking for home, disgusted with the hot afternoon. He'd driven his visitors along the river from the Bead to the Bluff without finding a field in walking shape. They'd drifted south then, determined to discover something new and had already walked two slopes that looked like good village sites, but weren't. The old man was disinclined to tramp another field.

"Looks too low-lying."

"You think? You don't think that's a pretty good place?"

In the end, the condition of the field made the decision; old-plowed, a smooth rain-skin, light brown, it invited walking.

"Ooo-kay," the old man said with Nordic weariness. They found the landowner in the first house down the road, and so began the old man's crowfest as the round, red-faced farmer not only gave them permission to walk but assured them there were arrowheads to be found there. He ate a bit more when the woman from Missouri, ten steps ahead of her husband and himself as they walked to the plowed rise, said she was seeing flint everywhere. By the end of the afternoon, his beard was thick with black, downy feathers. It was a crow he ate gladly. The three of them had found points, scrapers, signs of heavy and prolonged living.

The old man had referred to it as the South site, since it was the southernmost place he walked on the Smoky, and Walker had gone there with him a dozen times in his growing years. The place had not been particularly special to Walker until he returned as an adult to set foot to it again, and his daughter claimed it with her phantom doll.

His son, too, became part of the field the afternoon he found his first arrowpoint. And Walker, over the years, had discovered a story of a fifteen hundred year old spot of bad luck, had found the ultimate arrowpoint, and got stared down by a badger, or thought he did, all of which made the field he called Fungus the Dolly a pleasure, particularly since the Bluff had grown a farm.

The origins of flint on the Fungus, and the kinds of tools made from it, suggested that the villages were part of the same wave of migration that settled the Bluff and, according to Walker's reading of the stones, an earlier wave. Elaborate multiple notching of arrowpoints was not strongly developed, the banded gray flint characteristic of the northern Flint Hills had not been used to make any of the tools he'd found, and the long, crescent scoops, a specialized tool in response to specialized food preparation, was not among the tool kits of the Fungus the Dolly. Both settlements shared similar hide scrapers and heated their flint before working it, but the ability to work flint was more developed on the Bluff. Yet the most beautiful arrowpoint to come to Walker's hand from the Smoky Hill river people had come from the Fungus.

It was so perfect that Walker sometimes doubted it had ever been bound to a shaft, used as an ordinary arrow. If he had been the flintworker, it would have been kept aside, a pattern, a talisman, a source of support and inspiration. Historic peoples tell of traditions of treating certain tools that way, reserving an arrowpoint meant to function not as a bringer of meat but a bridge to spirituality, wrapped in a bundle, kept in a pouch, revealed only at specific times and accompanied by ceremony. But what Walker would do didn't count. It hadn't been his mind crouched over the heated piece of deep, red-orange flint a thousand years ago. If that mind made it to be hafted and fired, then surely the sight of it, fitted to the bow, reminded the hunter of his breathing, his grip, his stance, his target, the state of being true.

Thin and sleek, the length of a thumb joint, the point was notched low in the Washita style. The notches were narrow and deep, parallel with the straight baseline. Equality of dimension and precision flaking gave it a sense of being alert, ready. The rich, red-orange was draped by a line of white that streaked from one notch diagonally across the blade like a narrow sash. This dramatic coloration, translated by Young Walker as tomato soup with milk, was a visual call to attention. To see it was to remember the importance of doing things well, the most mundane action performed intently, the nocking of arrow to bowstring, the pull, the tension, the breath. Walker might question what any of this meant to the deer about to die, but the maker of the arrowpoint had perhaps not seen the deer as separate from the hunter, the arrowpoint, the moment of release; all were fluid currents of his own moment as he shaped the flint. The deer, a gift standing before the bow, was a debt that called for excellence.

Walker couldn't remember when he'd last acknowledged the food he'd put in his mouth, Thanksgiving, Christmas, a singular meal so satisfying it bypassed all his preoccupations and rendered him truly thankful. He'd forgotten the ritual of thanking life. The arrowpoint, commanding presence of poise and alertness, hunting magic or spirituality, made to fly with both, reminded him.

Badger Logic

Not just African spirits and Asian sages took a swipe at Walker's psyche now and then, altering it forever with each blow. Other teachers stayed his hand or moved it, leaped to his mind when emergency created a void. Marcel Duchamp, Elmore James, and Modigliani had saved him more than once. Richard Wright, John Cage, Henry Miller and Kenji Miyazawa. Garcia Lorca and Garcia Marquez. Tolkien, Kerouac, Stafford, Marley, Caravaggio and every shadow painted by Caravaggio. Berry, Raitt, Hendrix, and Young. And people who had been created but never born, like Reverend Jim Ignatowski. All these and yet more, anonymous waitresses who advised on the run, strangers on buses who instructed his life by relating their own.

One among this horde struck with clarity becalmed, showed Walker to himself, about to let his hanging hand swing forward and toss the chip of flint into the badger hole. He saw himself clearly, a man about to engage in some dangerous meddling. If the flint went through an illusionary trick of mind, a face of not-badger, he might have been a fool, but a vindicated fool. If the flint touched black lips, nose, grizzled gray muzzle, he would be instantly presented with a vindicated badger, boiling out of his hole in a fury of dirt, and him staggering backward, having gotten his answer and registering the prospect of flight across the choppy field, knowing that to fall in the path of a mad badger made a bad day for the vitals.

The badger had moved onto the site in Walker's fortieth year, a sudden hole at the toes of his shoes. He took a step back. The throwdirt was raw, dug out since the last rain. He looked cautiously into the angled hole, scanned for tracks, found none, and went on. Growing wheat kept Walker off the site, but after harvest and plowing he was back. The hole had been plowed over and a new one opened in the same vicinity, and scattered around it were little search pits where the animal—skunk, badger, coyote, there were still no tracks—had dug for mice and grubs. When his son came to stay that summer, and they went to walk on the Fungus, Walker warned him.

"There's some kind of animal denned up down by the second flint area, so don't go down there without me."

The Fungus the Dolly had an established walking route, starting at the fenced north end, following the long curve of the old riverbank as it swung southwest, but a six-year-old boy had been thrown a negative and immediately began petitioning for the opposite. Walker had resisted.

"We'll get there soon enough. Let's start here where it's happening."

He had his rituals in walking, and though he might have profitably asked himself what distinguished ritual from habit, he didn't. Field licked smooth by rain, flint at hand, he took fever with the search and was off, his son grumbling behind. Years later, when they walked the same field together stride for stride, he would remember the trail of the kid, falling behind, running to catch up, falling behind, and remember further that it was a trail he'd traveled himself.

The flint was high, clean, and bright against the dirt, and Walker found fragments of arrowpoints, a gray hide scraper. Each time the boy caught up, they sorted his handful of flint; each time it was unworked flakes, until Walker said, "Okay, the hole's right up ahead. We'll have a look at it, but we're not going to hang around."

"We're not? Why not?"

"Well, how about because I don't want to take a bath in tomato juice tonight. This might be a skunk den, and he might be having a bad day."

"Tomato juice?"

"You get sprayed, that's supposed to be the only thing that takes the smell out. But it might be a coyote or badger den, and if they feel threatened, we might wish we'd just been pissed on."

They started walking. They passed through an area where no flint showed and stopped a few steps away from the hole. New rain had smoothed the throwdirt. Each stood wary, imagining beyond the entrance, the darkness and what might be there listening, alerted by the rustle of their sweat on the wind, their breath and whisper.

"Are coyotes mean?"

"No, you couldn't say that. They just know the things people are liable to do."

They left the silent hole, looked at a few pieces of flint, continued southwest through another patch bare of stones. The old riverbed crossed the access road, sinking as it did, and they searched there, where another small group of lodges had stood, before turning back. They passed through the sterile area again, and Walker lengthened his stride, eager to reach flint, until his son was far behind. He heard the boy running to catch up, the sudden gasp of breath and shout. His son ran up, red-faced, sweaty, one fist clenched.

He had found a small point, short and wide, lightly notched—his first. The stone was not characteristic of the site; light gray, a white spot on the edge, it let the light through when held to the sun. Young Walker told the story, how he'd been in mid-leap and seen it between his feet, staring up like an eye, how he didn't believe it until he'd picked it up. The intensity of the find had made him, uncharacteristically, a babbler. Walker admired the point, praised the eye, congratulated good fortune, since it was found in an area where they never saw flint. He remembered his reaction to his own first arrowpoint, sullen disappointment that it wasn't absolutely perfect.

Walking, stopping to feast on the arrowpoint occasionally, they passed the animal hole without a thought and may not have remembered it until after supper if they hadn't found a shallow dig north of the hole, and a single track in the soft valley of a furrow.

"It's a badger."

"Wow." Young Walker looked at his arrowpoint. "Can we go back and look for him?"

"No-o-o-o, we'll be leaving that gentleman alone."

The only badgers Walker had seen had been distant ones, chugging for cover. Like some strange composite of animals, badgers were to animals as purple was to color. A small, hairy, fully-armed carpet with a bad temper, strong cousin of skunk, weasel, mink, the fighter, long claws, Dog Bear, the badger had a bad reputation only because it had no choice. Though it had a signature musk, it didn't have the chemical accuracy of the skunk; though it could move fast, it didn't have the quicksilver escape of the weasel. In the face of encounter, it had only the ability and willingness to fight, and Walker had heard more than one story of an astonished human bolting across a pasture, gun on the ground behind him, while the badger tore the heels off his boots or worse. It was hard not to admire such a warrior, and wise to cut him plenty of slack.

When they returned next summer, the badger hole was located slightly east of the old plowed-over one. Each season the badger came back, dug a new den.

"This badger is stupid," Walker said at one point, "digging den after den in this ground that's constantly being worked. He could den up in a pasture and save himself a lot of trouble."

He was only able to give this unsolicited advice because he could think of the badger but not like the badger. If that were possible, he might have seen the virtue in an agitated field, waiting until the vibrations of the machinery stopped, digging out the plow-ruined doorway and lifting a long nose to the moonlit field, newly turned and rich in possibility. With that vision, Walker would know that each time he walked the place he called Fungus the Dolly, it had already been searched by another, sliding past arrowpoints with no concern but a feast of disturbed eggs, insects, earthworms, mice.

Seven years Walker stopped and scanned ahead as he reached the scattered edge of the first group of lodges on the old riverbank. Each time, the den was there, location shifted slightly. Each time he and his son passed close enough to crane a peek, indulging their human nature to look into any hole found in the earth. Each time they passed on, wondering if the chamber beneath them had been empty or occupied.

Checking out the badger became one more point along the route, and

Walker passed and peered into the den in all seasons, whether the field was fresh-plowed or old and flat with overwintering stubble, until the fall of that seventh year, when wind and water pounded rows of shorn milo stalks, thwarting the eye, turning the shoe, scraping the shin. He paused a few steps shy of the hole, stretched frame and neck, arched one eyebrow, and looked in to see the badger looking back.

Walker felt immediately like a bad imitation of a rooster. The face was not at the portal in three-dimensional black, gray, and white, rounded ears laid back on the skull, but down in the shadowy curve of the hole where Walker's eye had slid into it and recognized it as pattern. Shadow on shadow, the dark smear of the eye mask, gray saddle of chops, black nose, all foreshortened and overlaid with shadow. Very slowly, Walker squinted. The face he saw didn't change, the pattern static in the weak autumn light. If there were eyes in the mask, they didn't shine, which made them all the more implacable. Walker hadn't moved, not even to the extent of uncraning his neck, and that, more than anything else, told him his body believed the face of the badger was real and not a story his eyes had constructed.

Crepe blades of milo leaf had been drifted by wind against the low mound of throwdirt, and a stripped wire of cheat grass hung over the top lip of the hole, springing in the chilly gusts of air. The mask was unwavering. It did not emit ferocity or even discomfort, but was relentlessly neutral, ready, a fixed expression of controlled waiting. Yet Walker could still, with an effort of logic, turn it into a harmless, understandable patch of gloom, eye-mask the darkness of the tunnel, lighter muzzle a rise in the tunnel floor, trickle dirt that had been tamped down.

In his right hand, hanging at his side, he carried a thin flake of flint, no bigger than a nickel, and it occurred to him that, to know the truth, there was no need to leap forward with a challenging woof; all he had to do was lazily swing his arm forward, as a branch in the wind, and send the chip of flint in a slow arc down the hole. This he could do to test the proposition, face or illusion, in the name of science and his own ego.

It was then that an anonymous one among the many who had given him a way to live washed through his mind. Fortunately it was not the Trapper, who'd sat around the campfires of Walker's youth, and whose favored expression was, "When in doubt, floorboard it," but some gentler flash of memory that reversed him suddenly so that, as if he were in the hole, he saw a ring of gray sky circling the head of a potential fool debating whether or not to meddle. He even saw the face of the fool changing as it balked to a decision. For no longer than the firing of a neuron, he lived that view, then settled slowly back onto his heels, swung one foot behind the other once, twice, turning his gaze aside, and walked way to the north end of the field, the flint in his hand unthrown.

When Walker told the story at a campfire, he reached between his shoes, selected and held up a small rock.

"And this is the actual piece of flint I was thinking of throwing at the time."

"Sure it is, Dad."

"Hmm. You're smarter than you used to be."

For two more years, the badger made a lodge in the worked field, but the next year and all those following, it didn't return, though Walker never stopped watching for the hole.

More years would pass before Walker, while crossing the area the badger had favored, shaking his head at all the work the badger had gone to, patiently re-digging its lodge each time the field was worked, would stumble into an answer to a question that had plagued him for years.

The sites he walked on the Smoky Hill River had been lived on heavily, and some of them—the Celt, the Mano, the Fungus—yielded tools that told they had been favored campsites of other peoples who preceded the gardening bison hunters by hundreds of years. Yet other places along the river, places equally well-endowed in terms of water availability, flood elevation, and vantage point, had been ignored. Walker had logged puzzling hours searching such likely places and found them barren of flint, pottery, shell, and bone. Why certain spots had been chosen repeatedly for settlement while others, apparently just as attractive, had drawn no one, was a question that had long tumbled cloudy in his mind.

He was thinking of the badger when he saw an earthworm in the newly plowed field one afternoon. When he saw another, he stopped and began to make sense of the badger's persistent re-digging of dens and why certain places drew campfires and villages when others did not.

He had forgotten to consider food, particularly the buffalo, a creature of herd and habit who would have established watering and crossing places along the river, a tradition that could have lasted through generations of both bison and humans and attracted settlement for the same reason a badger favored well-scrubbed field.

It was a basic oversight, decades old, that demonstrated why he was not a scientist. Progress preferred to spend little time with the question and much with the answer. Walker's misapplied thoughts had assured the question a long life until the badger suggested an answer as clearly as if it had stood before him and spoken: *I hunt for my food. I make my lodge where the action is.*

The Master Pauses

The two bits of granite were found two years and twenty steps a-part. Crawling between rows of cornstalk stubble under a stream of autumn blackbirds, a gaze threading around stalks, long, withered blades of corn leaves left in tangles by the wind, shattered stalk chaff, Walker picked out the piece of granite. When he rubbed the dirt off, he found himself holding a corner of an ax blade, no longer than the first joint of his thumb, dark tan striped with brown. The broken surface was rough, the other three sides had been ground and polished smooth.

An ax begins with an oval granitic cobble, flat on both faces. A third of the way from one end, a groove the width of a finger is made around the stone. Depending on the extent of its circuit, it will be a half-grooved, three-quarter-grooved, or full-grooved ax. To the short side of that groove, the end of the cobble has become the poll of an ax. The long portion of cobble on the other side of the groove is ground down on both faces until they meet as the bit of the ax. The narrow sides of the cobble may also be ground flat, so that clean, angular lines are formed between flat top, blade, flat bottom. In zealous cases, the poll will be ground too, into an angular shape. The hardness of granite guarantees that any shape alteration will be a slow, tedious process of pecking and grinding, knocking against the cobble with a stone equally hard, pulverizing and diminishing the granite bit by laborious bit until the form appears, groove, poll, and blade. As onerous as this process is, grinding the surfaces of the new ax smooth is even more time-consuming, and some are ground and polished so intensively that the finished object has a smooth sheen, more like skin than stone.

The piece Walker found had such a surface. The ax it had come from, instead of lying under the earth on its side, appeared to have been sitting up, cutting edge vertical. For a long time it had probably been just below the curving edge of the plow, but the season came when the steel plow blade, slicing diagonally, met the vertical stone blade of the ax. Since most of the body of the ax was still held tightly in the earth, the granite yielded, the upper corner of the blade was sheared, snapped free, lifted to the light on the new black dirt thrown up and aside behind the tractor. It could have been tumbling in the plow zone, now on the surface, now beneath, since before Walker was born; it could have been struck free the season he found it.

An early spring morning two years later, light drizzle brushing his arms and the back of his neck, he bent down in the same area for a piece of stone and recognized it even before his fingers plucked it up. When the two blades had met earlier, the stone ax must have been jarred back and upward by the sudden contact before the corner broke free, making it more accessible to the plow next time, but another indeterminate number of years could have passed before the stone ax lay again directly in the path of the steel blade. Eventually the alignment arrived; they met head on, plow striking ax just to one side of the leading edge, knocking off a wide flake that included a portion of the bit.

The two pieces did not match up exactly, but the pattern of dark brown lines indicated they were originally close together. Taken together, they comprised most of the ax bit. Since the plow in that area of the field ran west to east, Walker imagined the blade of the ax facing west. The collision would have to come again, so each time Walker neared the area, he watched for the ax, scraped and tumbled free of the hard grip of dirt at last, or another fragment, perhaps the other corner of the blade.

The remains of the thousand year old village of the Smoky Valley hunter/farmers that Walker called Fungus the Dolly stretched down the east side of the old riverbed, but there was isolated evidence that earlier peoples had been there. In the same flint-sterile area of the plow-contoured bank where his son had found his first arrowpoint, Walker discovered a dartpoint. The stone was thick, the flintwork adequate, the corner notches broad and round so that the shoulders were wider than the base. It could have sailed right out of the old man's collection of Missouri artifacts, and the pinkish-white flint would have been at home in a Missouri field. On the Fungus, it was an obvious stranger.

Such points were contemporary with axes, and the loser of the point could be the loser of the ax, even though they were found in separate parts of the field, the dartpoint on the southern end of the old riverbank, the ax at the northernmost end.

As Walker stepped out of the trees each time and headed east on the plowed field, he crossed the old bed of the river and began to see flint as he ascended the long, modest slope of the riverbank, softened and broken down by generations of farm machines. Flint was most plentiful at the crest of the slope, sparser on top. Traditionally, Walker turned right and followed the bank south, searching through three separate areas of settlement before the old bank hit low land and showed no stones. He would then walk back, searching again, to the north end, and only then wander east fifty steps, occasionally finding flint, to what had been the west bank of the small creek feeding the river.

The old creekbed was now plowed field, the creek was another hundred steps to the east. A scattering of flint chips showed on a small area of the old west bank, and Walker had routinely checked it, finding not even a fragment of a tool until he'd crawled upon the amputated corner of the ax. From then on, he walked directly to that area before turning his attention to the southern route. He found only chips of flint until the day, two years later, when he picked up the second flake struck from the blade of the ax. Season after season he returned without guarantee; the ax could still be gripped in the earth, or wallowing out of sight in the plow zone, or found long ago by another searcher who might study it on winter nights and mourn its missing parts. Finding nothing more, he began to expect nothing more, though once or twice he lapsed into talking to the ax as he walked. Then the field threw him a surprise.

Having walked the ax area, the southern route and back, he slogged east once more, avoiding his old footprints. The ground had been plowed too wet, clods the size of small pumpkins baked in hot sun. When the rains came, they put a skin on the clods but couldn't break them down. Stumbling through the dog days heat, Walker glanced up and saw, five steps ahead, a large clod of dirt holding up a lancepoint by one edge.

He looked away, looked again, dropped to his knees and gawked. The large point was an unfamiliar style, basal corners removed, leaving straight shoulders and a short, narrow stem of a base that flared slightly. Over the point he placed his hat, anchoring it against the wind with a clod of dirt, and began to search the area, circling outward. He anticipated the possibility of other lancepoints, but foremost in his mind was the battered ax. He had no doubt the point and ax were related, had been carried by the same individual or band of individuals. Apart from sporadic chips of flint, he found nothing. He returned and lifted his hat, admired the point for a long moment before he reached to take it from the clod. He lifted it free and was surprised again.

In the clod, the point had appeared perfect, elegant base with finely tipped corners, even flake scars one after the other down the length of the exposed edge of the blade, a centered tip, but the edge that came free of the clod was not a twin to the exposed edge. Halfway down the blade, the line bulged outward, a strong irregularity in the silhouette of the point. Since Walker had assumed he'd found a perfect object, the incongruity brought a momentary disappointment, but it was disappointment that couldn't last in the face of his complex good fortune—that the point had been unearthed, that the plow hadn't snapped it, that his last-minute wandering had encountered it.

He would have many evenings to speculate on why such an obvious craftsman had not removed the four or five flakes that would have eliminated the bulging contour line. The answer was in the stone itself, and the finding of it brought the mind of the flintworker close to his own.

The flint was an unfamiliar deep gray, the color of wet clay. In Walker's hand, the point reached from the tips of his fingers to the hollow of his palm, and he could follow the knapper's journey down the edge of the blade as he twisted the long, thin flakes free. The flint had a dense, creamy consistency, accommodating to the worker's intentions, but on one edge of the blade was a semi-circular area where the flint changed. The color went abruptly from dark gray to dark brown, and the grain became less compact. Flaking down that edge, in the heart of the brown area, the maker pressure-levered a flake free that did not lift thin and clean. The shock wave had traveled just under the surface but, unlike all the others, encountered a void or density of mineral or air, a knot in the grain that pulled the wave down into the stone and kicked it up and out again at a right angle. The flake flew away with a spur on its nether end, and on the blade, the scar ended in an angular hole.

At that point, fifteen hundred or more years ago, the maker surely paused. The crazed flake had bitten deeply into the blade and put the entire point in jeopardy; pressure in the wrong direction or applied too heavily could cater to that weak divot and crack the stone. The next three flakes, all in the brown area, were very shallow, lightly removed. The worker was in the gray, stable area of the stone then, and four more flakes down the edge carried him to the tip. The point was formed, but while the gray edge dropped in a smooth, gentle arc from shoulder to tip, the side with the brown spot swelled outward. Symmetry could be achieved by trimming, but the flaking would have to be done in the brown area with its mark of unpredictability, the deep fracture gouge. The maker considered desire, considered risk.

The point was made from fifteen hundred to thirty-five hundred years ago, somewhere in an area extending from eastern Oklahoma to the Great Lakes and east to Illinois, Iowa, Ohio, Indiana, Arkansas. The maker had chosen caution, utility over art; the point would remain whole with a lump in its contour. It had tipped a spear carried by a man who camped on a creek rise at least a hundred miles west of his usual range. There he must have found bad luck; the lance and a brown granite ax never left the campsite.

Earth grew over the abandoned point. Clasped in dirt, it lay through the span of many lives, the fortunes and tragedies of individuals, groups, nations, wanderers, villagers, raiders, the coming of the horse, the plow, the homestead, the corporate farm. Whole cultures waxed and disappeared. Rivers changed their courses, moved alive from place to place like snakes. The thundering blankets of bison turned to bone. There were hundreds of wars, and twice they ruled the earth. Magic was eaten by knowledge, human beings flew through the air, created exploding suns, leaped up and touched the moon. Gods received new forms, new faces and pronouncements. Great monuments were raised and some torn down. Children whispered dreams into the ears of dolls. Through all that could be imagined in the fates of women and men, the spearpoint lay buried, dark, its shaft and bindings reclaimed, molecule by molecule, until they were again the earth itself, until the chance convergence of stone and plow returned the point to light and shadow and further chance, on a day among multitudes of days, brought a human hand to close upon it again.

The point became a lodestone to Walker, connecting him not only to the man who'd carried it but to all that had occurred in the long interval between the brief flicker each of them called life.

But the history of the world at large that stretched between that ancient hand and his own overflowed his grasp, so that his focus fell on what he could reach and examine, the prairie under his feet, a microcosm of the human struggle between hope and sorrow.

In the dream he stood at the railing of a very tall highway overpass, looking down at the patchwork land, a geometry of greens and browns, in the distance smoky blue hills and the river named after them. A stranger stood beside him on the elevated highway.

"What are you doing?"

"Looking," Walker said.

"What are you looking for?"

"Roads." And as he said it, the civilized design below began to shimmer, the surface of crops, weeds, pasture keeping their colors but becoming translucent to reveal a developing network of lines, wide, narrow, straight and curved, trails and paths, so many they could not be counted, of all the creatures that had crossed the valleys of the Smoky Hill long before the illusion of orderly fences and fields.

If You Had a River

If you had a river
would you pull it straight
give it something
strange to carry
and how long?

If you had a bird
would you decide to operate
paint the sky
and take whatever color comes
teach it to sing?

If you had the time
the moment   the place
how much would
you take?

If you had a river
would you have an outlaw?
If you had a breath
another breath
another breath
would you live?

LOADING THE STONE

3

"Their power to hold things,
called attraction, is one very
important property of rocks."

The Rock Book

Invisible

The frogs were nervous, the heron impatient. The frogs were experienced, the heron clumsy. The frogs were alert, the heron starving. All these theories were offered after the large blue heron had walked the entire perimeter of the small Flint Hills pond without catching a frog. More elusive of explanation was the fact that the heron had slowly passed within spitting distance of the two men and two fourteen-year-old boys without alarm or even acknowledgment.

The four of them had retired to the top of the pond dike to sit in plastic chairs and take what little there was of the hot, late afternoon breeze. A long hike through gullies and jack oaks had depleted both energy and interest. The white hot center of July had sapped the charm from crinoid fossils and ornately camouflaged whippoorwills nestled in leaves. With each step, jeans had dragged at their legs like wet tents. On returning to the pasture camp, they had sipped at the plastic water jug and hauled chairs onto the dike in the spare shade of a willow. As soon as they'd settled into a line facing the pond, Walker began grousing about the heat, the insects, the unavailability of a cold glass of cola.

"What the *hell* are we doing here in the middle of July?" he carped, aware as he said it that he was caught up in the disease of complaint and needed the appearance of a master to smack him between the eyebrows with his walking stick to restore a sense of proportion. Young Walker had soaked a bandana in water from the wash-up jug and he draped it around his father's neck, which made Walker feel like a mad expatriate.

So this is old age, he thought, one year shy of fifty. He was spared further cheap philosophy when the Great Blue Heron coasted in and landed at the upper end of the pond. All four campers abandoned their thoughts, focusing on the thin vertical as it stood briefly and then began walking slowly along the margin of the pond. At that distance it was merely a silhouette, and Walker wished for binoculars, certain the bird would approach no closer than half the length of the pond. As a point of attention, the heron was gradually taking his mind away from the merciless sun and his chigger-bitten crotch and ankles.

Born in the hills, the Guide had inherited a contempt for bellyaching. He was grateful to the heron for shutting his friend's mouth. Young Walker and the son of the Guide were thinking identical teenage thoughts: a bird with a neck that skinny and long could probably be killed with one blow of an invincible young hand.

The heron came on, head elevated slightly forward, preceded by the squeak alarm of tiny frogs disappearing in a plip of water just ahead of that long blade designed to tweak them from the mud. After each escape, the heron paused. When stillness returned, it took another angular step.

As it came steadily closer, silhouette gave way to solid form, shadow to silvery gray. Dark edge appeared where wing met body. It passed the halfway point and came on at their left side, stalking around the curve of the pond, so close that the four campers had slid their eyes far left to keep it in sight.

Walker's concentration on the bird had canceled his earlier preoccupations; he no longer itched with old sweat, insistent prickle of chigger bites, the ache of over-walked muscles. All his attention gathered in his eyes, and the heron at the end of his gaze. The rest of his body became numb, sliding into weightless lassitude.

The heron hunted, a step, a pause, a step. It was going to pass directly in front of the line of chairs where the four sat. Frogs continued to squirt into the water ahead of it. With each step, the long toes of the lifted foot folded, hung down dripping, then the skinny leg swung forward, toes beginning to spread as they slid quietly underwater. Then it was before them. Walker soaked in the details of the heron's form and motion, the dusty blue-gray color, the narrow, lank feathers warm breeze lifted along its neck, curled whiskers at the base of the tapered beak, and the pale eye with centered iris, round and direct as the eye of a fish.

As it walked in front of them, it gave no sign that the watchers existed, no twitch or quick glance, no spooky prelude to flight, but continued in the motions of its search for the one slow-witted frog in the pond. Its slow hunting dance of stride and pause passed the four sets of eyes. It rounded the curve of the pond on their right, and they watched its long, oval back moving away in the same unhurried rhythm. The heron never looked back.

Along the right side of the pond, the frogs proved to be no more stupid than those along the left side. Chins up, the little mud-colored peepers sensed the shift in the water, shadow, and presence and bailed out well ahead of it. The heron became a dark shape in the distance again and stopped where it had begun, at the far end, where the pond died in a shallow of hoof-churned mud. There it stood, evaluating the unsuccessful circuit just completed, fixing the route to the next pond it would try, or just standing. Then long legs flexed, wings opened, and with a casual leap it rowed itself up into the air and moved away, watched by the four immobile campers until its flight took it from them, curving below the edge of a hill.

They looked at the pond, which was different now and, for them, always would be, a pond with a line drawn around it by the walk of the heron. Then all four chairs emptied at once, the men standing on one leg, stamping the other to reclaim a sleeping foot, boys, leaping up to stretch, casting the spell aside. All along the base of the dike, frogs plopped once more for deep water.

Because they had been trained to assign reason to events, because the heron had confounded logic, discussion of this strange bird occupied them as they carried chairs off the dike and into the short weeds by the tents, the car, the banked ashy coals of the campfire. The sons pursued explanation at length—they were at an age when control in a confusing world had great personal value. Walker and the Guide revived the fire and made supper in the pink light of sundown, content to leave philosophy to youth for the moment. Beef stew and rest came first.

Between spoons of gravy, the son of the Guide fervently invented a chickhood for the heron, hatched far back in the Hills. Haunting only skinny backwaters, it had never seen a human until this day.

"So he just assumed we were cattle."

Young Walker's theory, no less baroque, posited a recent trauma, the heron's mate blown out of the sky with a load of buckshot as she flew beside him, for example. The heron's mind had snapped and he was one hundred percent insane.

"Maybe only temporarily," Young Walker amended with a finger in the air, "but so crazy he just doesn't care."

This was too ridiculous for the Guide's son. "If he was crazy, he wouldn't remember how to hunt frogs."

"He didn't catch any, did he?"

"That's because you were throwing rocks at them yesterday and made them goosy."

"So were you."

"So?"

"So...I guess you didn't look at his eye. It was crazy, completely white."

"Fried heron," observed the Guide. Both boys ignored him.

"It wasn't white," said the Guide's son.

"It was more white than yellow. He could've come, he looked like he *might've* come charging up the dike and wiped us out."

The sudden violence of this idea silenced both boys, plunging them into cinematic fantasies of a killer heron, the old dudes slashed out of their lawn chairs with a beak like a saber, each boy the grappling solitary hero of his own dream, a welter of flaring wings and flapping severed arteries as he dealt justice to a heron run amok.

Walker hadn't noticed that bickering had turned to reverie. He was thinking of wild plums.

He'd spent most of the previous day on a high ridge in a rangy part of the Hills. Scattered over an area the size of a city block, flint chips indicated a workplace, and after hours of letting his eyes wander through the short curly grasses, he'd found four bases of broken blanks. He'd assumed the flint had been taken from the lip of the ridge, where chunks of it were available in the eroding limestone. The question was: why carry the chunks as far as a city block from the bluff edge before sitting down and hammering it into flakes? It had taken three hours of walking to determine the boundaries of the work area, and he walked it another hour, considering the question, before he made himself stop and sit down. He ate sunflower seeds and a small apple while he looked again at the ridge on which he sat. There was an electrical pylon on the edge, one in a long line, carrying power across the Hills like tall human figures, spraddle-legged, arms out and bent down at the elbows, each hanging fist holding a cluster of cables that swooped away in a low arc, sagging and separating, until they rose to be gathered in the grip of the next pylon. On the highest crossbeam of the one on his ridge, two vultures stood. There had been five at one time, but three had moved on. He dismissed both the power road and the vultures—neither had anything to do with the Old People who had gathered flint. He ran his eyes around the ridge for some time before he paid attention to the plum thickets. There were four of them, each about the size of a car, and he had noticed them before but had called them silently by their name, wild plums, and passed them by. Seeing the names of things instead of the things themselves was one cause of his frequent confusion. Another was his tendency to forget things he already knew. The plum thickets were about to remind him of one of them.

Over the edge, where the talus slope provided root support, plum bushes flourished, but along the rocky ridge with its thin soil, the only plum thickets were the four within the work area. He got up and walked to the nearest. It was growing in a circular depression. At each thicket he pushed through the sharp branches and found the same condition. Then he re-membered, with embarrassing clarity, the dry, skeletal nature of weathered flint like that eroding from the edge of the ridge, and knew he had found four mining pits where the old flint-seekers had dug after the living flint, sleek and tractable. In the hundreds of years following, the depressions had filled with blowdirt, becoming rich plant beds. Of all the plum pits scattered by birds and animals upon the ridge in that span of time, any one left in those four bowls of soil would grow and multiply.

Now Walker sat by the fire wondering if the same blindness that kept him from seeing the plum thickets for what they were was at work in the encounter with the bird. Because he knew enough to call it by the name Great Blue Heron, had he not seen it clearly or freely?

"Maybe it wasn't the heron," the Guide said. "Maybe it was us."

Walker shifted his thoughts. Each of the boys threw his bloody private scenario into fast forward, victory over the homicidal bird, the saving of the wounded, mass public acclaim, all telescoped into a few concluding sec-onds.

"What I mean is, we may have been invisible."

Both boys snorted at this theory, one which clearly deprived them of personal glory.

Walker was more accepting, since he'd tried many times to become invisible, usually to the eyes of other animals. He knew it could be done. A deer hunter had told him of sitting in dawn light beside a bush, rifle across his legs, while a white-tailed buck had browsed its way right into his face. Knowing he would lose both trophy and meat, but unable to resist, he'd slapped the deer on the nose. His reward was a thundering fart, instant flight, nothing he could hang on the wall, the satisfaction of a different kind of mastery. Walker had not been as successful, though he'd learned certain things. An animal allowed greater approach to a person with empty hands. Anticipation, like a radiating odor, engendered flight. The human voice was equal to alarm and threat.

"I can see you guys don't buy it," said the Guide, "so let me ask you, while the heron walked around the pond, were there any clouds in the sky?"

"No fair," said Young Walker, "if we moved our heads to look up, he'da freaked."

"I see. How about the sky in the west, then, where we were facing—any clouds?"

"I don't remember any," said one boy turning to the other for support.

"Did any cattle come down to drink at the far end of the pond?"

"Well...do you know the answer?"

The Guide laughed. "I was sitting right beside you. I know what you know. But let's pass on the cattle. How many airplanes did you hear go over while we sat there?"

The boys thought. Walker thought. So far he hadn't been able to answer any of the questions.

"You see what I'm saying?" asked the Guide. "If any of us were asked about the heron we could answer in great detail, but for the time it took him to circle the pond, everything else was invisible, not just to our eyes, but our ears, our noses, our skins."

"It's true," said Walker. "I don't remember a damn thing."

The boys weren't so sure. "You mean he was so locked in on looking for frogs that he didn't see us?"

"Oh, he saw us all right, the same way we saw the sky, the hills, the cattle. He saw us, but we didn't count. If we'd moved or made a noise..."

"He'da been outta here."

"Like that. But since we didn't, we might as well have been tree stumps. Or invisible. It doesn't always work, but now you know how to do it. I was impressed at how still you guys were."

"It was hard at first. I had itches on top of my itches."

"I had to cough really bad."

"My leg went to sleep."

"My whole butt went to sleep."

"You did good," said the Guide. "I guess you're not boys anymore."

After summers of being told they were too fast, too little, too loud, this compliment was more valuable than money. They accepted it with sober, manly nods.

"Invisible," mused one of the sons, so quietly he might have been talking to himself. "Yeah. We were just like the Old People."

Walker and the Guide exchanged a glance across the fire. Neither of them offered a correction, but both knew none of them was anything like the Old People, and it would take much more than being ignored by a heron to make it so.

Campfire Smoke

Campfire smoke survives
washing of the hair
clothes and body
finds a home in the sweat.

In this burnoff pasture
green grows from black
as the eight herons on their
black meander through the sky
have all been named Green.

Fallen light turns green
grass red and black to blue.
The companion of campfire smoke
sees black Green Herons
shadow purple.
It is all the same

to campfire smoke
going as it will it remains
Always to remember...
Never to know...
so is the traveler
going along with campfire smoke.

Tales of Privilege

"My wife was doing dishes when she heard the bullet hit the house. She didn't know what it was at the time, so she thought about it a little and went about her business. I'd have damn well known what it was, but I was in town trying to run down a tractor part.

"At supper she mentioned it. She'd about convinced herself it was a walnut blown off the tree east of the house. I didn't think too much about it at first, old house like that is always making sounds, but I got to thinking about it, about how sharp she said the sound was, so after supper I went out and had a look at the east side.

"I painted that house just last summer, so I know it pretty well, board for board. I saw the hole right away, about shoulder high, that'd make it about belly-level in the house. I knew what it was. I took my pocketknife and dug it out, what was left of a hunting rifle slug. It'd hit a two-by stud— that kept it from passing into the house.

"Now that was the day before I went to town, bought the signs and posted every damn bit of my land."

* * * *

"It's not like these pipes were laying in the weeds. They were laid out right on the edge of the plowed ground, forty-foot irrigation pipes, three of them, about three hundred dollars worth. Big mistake, leaving them out where they could be seen.

"From the tracks I'm pretty sure it was a jeep. I don't know how many times they ran over them pipes. Just smashed the heck out of them. They had one heck of a good time with my three hundred dollars. I say 'they' because I can't imagine a man alone in a jeep doing such a thing, can you? But you get two or more...there's a lot of liquored-up kids driving around the country at night, a lot of them. You get some, they got this idea that out here it's no law, no restraint, no code. Don't get me wrong, I'm not much of a Christian; if I find the guys that did this, I'll kick their asses up between their shoulder blades."

* * * *

"Let me tell you about these so-called hunters, not real hunters, but the majority who think they are. First, they don't like to walk, they ride in a truck. Now they have to walk eventually, to get the pheasant, quail, dove, turkey, deer—but if the field they want to walk is across another field, why,

197

they just drive over there, doesn't matter if the field they're driving across has a crop on it or not, it's just distance.

"Second, they don't like to jump out and close a fence after they've gone through. Many times the phone would wake me up. It'd be my neighbor telling me some of my cattle just passed by his place. I spent many nights rounding up my stock.

"There's four hunters have permission to be on my land. They're all honorable men. For the rest I have these NO TRESPASSING signs. For some of them, still, it's just too big a word."

* * * *

"I kicked out a load of fishermen once. They'd parked two pickups on the drive to the milo field and walked into my pond from there.

"There ain't much in it, bunch a little bullheads and some sunfish, but there's three or four pretty good size bass I've been nursing along. I don't fish, but my grandson has been trying for one of them big bass. Eight years old, getting to be a decent fisherman.

"So these guys, there were five of them, were a little upset when I walked over the berm of the pond and told them they were on private land. I believe in being polite if people will let you. The way they all looked over at one guy, I knew he was the one who'd brought them. I could tell he knew better, the way he kept his head down and didn't try to argue. They left and I sat by the pond until I heard both trucks pull out. I didn't think anymore about it.

"Next day I was driving by and, God's sake, my milo crop was torn all to pieces, mature plants, all headed out. There was a swath about ten rows wide, commencing at the fence and going all through the field, where the plants were broken off or knocked down. It didn't take long to figure out what they'd done was hook one end of a tow chain to the tail of each pickup, lined those trucks up and driven all over the field with that chain stretched between them. They didn't just drive into the plants and back out, either—they made a pretty good tour of the field and that chain took the milo down slick as a blade. I hadn't made note of their license plates, either. Such a thing would've never occurred to me then."

* * * *

"Pheasant season, I saw two campers pulled off the road by the north windbreak. I got out and waited and presently I seen them walking back along the hedgerow, all fanned out. Jesus Christ on a crutch, there was a whole convention, eight of them, all wearing orange and pink glo vests and hats. I believe they saw me then because they bunched up. Pretty soon a couple of them turned into the hedgerow, the others watching; they were fixing to cut through the hedgerow and head away from me at an angle across Anderson's alfalfa field.

"Well I could've just waited, they'd have to come back to their trucks sometime, but I had a lot to do that day, so I shouted, 'Hey!' and started walking up the hedgerow.

"A couple of them looked up and I saw they said something to the others. There was a lot of milling around and then the three who'd gone through the windbreak crossed back, and the group stood there tugging their vests, looking at their bootlaces. Then they went into a pose, only two of them let their shotguns hang over the crook of their arms, four were at port arms, and two had them braced on their hips, barrels to the sky.

"As I got closer, I could see they were all well-fed men, and you didn't have to be the Secretary of Agriculture to see they were well-oiled too, if you know what I mean. Most of them had let their eyes roam across me once in a while, but this one big old Texas Ranger type boy, who had a fancy mustache, just watched me come, his rifle up on his hip. You know, some people just have a bad attitude. He yelled at me, 'Guess you don't mind us checking this treeline for birds, do ya?' I just kept on walking until I was close enough for civilized conversation.

"'Is that what you fellows are doing here?' I said. I slowed down but kept walking until I was on the other side of them. One of them shook his head and snorted through his lips. He put my fur backward a little bit, but I stayed calm.

"'There's a NO HUNTING sign on the fence back there,' I said. 'You fellows are gonna have to leave.' My wife and I had decided long ago that our place would be a refuge for everything, even coyotes, but that was none of their business.

"'That sign was on the other side of the row of trees,' said the big guy, 'That means no hunting over there.'

"'I put it there. I guess I know what it means.'

"A couple of them raised their eyebrows at each other and pursed their lips. They were tickled as hell with the idea of someone telling them they couldn't do something. I'm sure they were all middlemen of some kind, used to working it out when things got in their way. They just stood there in the cold looking at me, so I said it again.

"'There's no hunting on this land. You all will have to leave now.'

"'Now look,' he said in a softer voice, 'will a little permission fee clear this up for you?'

"'It's clear to me already,' I told him. 'You're trespassing on private property, you got caught, you're leaving.'

"He shifted his shotgun to port arms. 'Seems to me you're in the minority here,' he said. I think the rest of them might have been ready to let it go, but for this guy. He was getting red in the face.

"'I'm backed by the law,' I said. I took a step forward, hoping to start herding them toward their trucks.

"'Shit,' he said. 'I don't see no law.' He slipped his finger inside the trigger guard.

"Well, you see me, I'm an old man. I used to scrap some, but I've pretty much let those days go. I didn't much fancy the idea of wrestling this guy for his shotgun. He let the barrel drift down until it was pointing just to one side of me, just far enough to the side not to be direct, but close enough to make my skin itch. I just stared at him—I wasn't about to waste my breath anymore. He wasn't talking either, just standing there with this grin like he'd won my farm in a card game.

"I won't lie to you—that floating gun barrel scared me. He was too drunk to be cutting things that fine. One of the others said, 'Aw hell, Randy, let it go,' and started back to the trucks. Then the rest kind of grumbled and started shuffling off too. This Randy kind of nodded at me once and give me a look. Then he turned too.

"They took their time walking back to the truck, and I could hear them talking. A couple of times somebody laughed. I stayed where I was until they pulled out. In all that time not one of them had unloaded his gun, not even when they got in the trucks.

"Now, let me tell you, I've chased off a lot of trespassers, and a lot of them would sulk, you know, because they'd been caught and they knew they were in the wrong. But the last eight, ten years I've heard all kinds of backtalk. They don't see they're doing anything wrong at all—they see me as a guy with a problem, a guy who refuses to cooperate. I come close to getting killed on my own land.

"Anymore I don't fool with it. I notice a vehicle parked by my fields, I call the county sheriff. We've got an understanding. If they're just walking or taking pictures he sends them on their way; if they've got firearms he puts them under arrest. I press charges every time, no exceptions. It costs me a little, but it costs them more.

"It's different than it was. Money's all they understand now."

* * * *

"I hate to say it, because I wasn't raised that way, but people are basically hogs. Something they don't want, they'll drive out to the country and dump it, everything from animals to refrigerators. If they can find an access road to a creek or river, they'll dump it there, where they can't be seen from the road.

"You and I both know some farmers will use their own riverbanks for a dumping ground, and that's the worst, fouling your own nest. Some of them will tell you it's erosion control. I just laugh in their faces, but I'm a pretty large man, so I get away with it. It's too bad when someone doesn't respect his own damn land, but arguing isn't gonna change his philosophy a bit, where, with a stranger dumping on *your* riverbank, why, you've got some leverage.

"There's a road goes down along the creek on my south forty, it puts you right down in the timber, out of sight. There's one open spot where the bank slopes to the creek. Folks have probably been sneaking in and dumping stuff there for over fifty years. Fishermen are pretty good about keeping things clean, hunters are pretty bad, but the worst by far are city people stuck with something they don't want. I've been meaning to set a couple days aside and wench that stuff out of there and haul it to the dump, no matter what it costs, but there never seems to be the time.

"I had driven down there to check the weeds in my beans, and here was this brand new pickup backed up to the bank and these guys in the back just at that moment tipping an old oven off the tailgate.

"Well, they weren't too happy to see me. I pulled right across the front of their pickup, blocking it off.

"'Good afternoon,' yells one of them. Shit.

"Make a long story short, they soon understood they weren't leaving there until that stove was back in their truck. They were in their late twenties, early thirties, and I'd bet money they were hotshot investment landlords, teachers, lawyers, whatall, getting into the rentals game. Too cheap to pay some poor bastard to haul the broke stuff away, too cheap to take it to the dump themselves. You know, they never argued one word, just looked at each other and slowly crawled out of the truck bed, like they'd been raised to do the right thing but had forgotten.

"They got lucky, the stove had only rolled halfway to the creek. I never said one word to them while they rassled that old range up the bank. They were wearing nice slacks and those knitted sport shirts. I don't know if you've ever tried to carry a stove, just you and another man, but you can imagine trying to hump it up a muddy slope. The top had sprung off, so they had it in two parts, but it was still an ugly piece of work. It took forty-five minutes, and by the time they got that thing back in the truck, they were both a mess. One of them had torn the knee out of his pants. I didn't know whatall they might have unloaded before I showed up, so I made them go down and get a couple of them old tires down there to take with them too.

" 'Consider it interest,' I said."

* * * *

"I slept in the trees beside this field once, four nights running, with my twelve-gauge and a box of double-ought shells. I didn't sleep much because

I was so mad. I'd just got my wheat in the ground—we'd had a good long gentle rain—and I drove by two days later and about fell out of the truck.

"There'd been a four-wheeler rally all over my field. Somebody'd seen that big muddy field and got the rest of the boys together, and there it was. Down in the bottomland like this, nearest place is four miles away. If they kept their lights off—hell, if there was any kind of wind up—it'd cover the sound. That field looked like those pictures you see of a rough ocean, ruts everywhere, and big smooth scars where they'd lock the wheels and slide. It wasn't just rutted, it was scrambled. And wasn't just a couple of crazy laps around a muddy field. No, it'd had to have gone on most of the night. Naturally, there were beer cans sticking up here and there in the mud and probably three times as many churned underneath. Every year I plow up a couple more of those damn cans, squashed flat. Smart thing that morning would have probably been to collect those cans carefully and see if I could get the law to find prints on them. Maybe they would've done that for me and maybe not, but I was too mad to think about it. I picked up two armloads of cans before I quit. I could see more, glinting in the field, but every time I picked up a can I cussed, and each cuss got louder. By the second armload I was ready for a hanging. I drove to the landfill and kicked them out.

"Well, I can smile about it now, but not much even now, and I'm not proud of how I ranted and raved all day and made life miserable for Mary, shouting at the walls. Oh, I was pitiful.

"Just before sundown I took my sleeping bag and shotgun shells and bullied Mary into driving down there and dropping me off. She really didn't want to. She was sure I was going to kill somebody, or maybe myself, out of frustration. That first night was a real bastard. I'd forgotten bug dope and I paid for it. It's a good thing I couldn't see the mosquitoes, the shape I was in, or I might have actually shotgunned one or two. How would I ever live that down?

"Mind you, I wasn't after blood, but I did plan to blow the tires off as many of those vehicles as I could. Naturally, they didn't come back. They weren't stupid. I'm embarrassed to say that around three o'clock I was yelling a lot of challenges into the night. After four nights I come back to my senses, but for months afterward, when we got rain, I'd drive by there on random nights, and every time I find one of those flattened cans when I'm working the field, I get off the machine and pick it up. Every time I plow I hate the thought of turning up another one of those cans."

* * * *

"I've lost two, both Herefords, prime meat. One was probably killed accidentally by a deer hunter who hightailed it out of there when he saw what he shot, but the other was killed with a shotgun. Right. You explain to me how a cow is like a pheasant.

"Somebody's been killing and mutilating cattle in these parts for years, but this wasn't that. Someone just felt like murdering a heifer."

* * * *

"Didn't I ever tell you about Checkpoint Coyote? Pretty damn weird. We'd been out fixing fence and were heading home, about an hour before sundown. We came over Big Hill, and down at the bottom, right in the middle of the road, here's a guy, standing wide-legged, got his rifle across his chest, wearing those camouflage pants and khaki tee-shirt, grinning away. Just beyond him there's a pickup pulled over to the side. We're rolling down the grade. The guy just stands there grinning. I says to Phil—my oldest boy Phil was driving—he was about thirty years old then—I says, 'What the hell do you make of that?' Phil just grunted, started tapping the brakes. 'If he swings that rifle our way,' I said, 'mash it.'

"Well sir, he kept the rifle slanted across his chest while we rolled up and stopped in front of him. I don't know guns—Phil could tell you what kind it was if he was here—but it looked plenty heavy-duty, had a scope on it. He was smiling away, this bird. He kind of snaps his legs together and walks up to the driver window, still got his rifle up like he's gonna pass it over for inspection.

"'Howdy,' he says. It was the damn grin that was getting to me. It must have gotten to Phil too, 'cause he just sat there, one hand on top of the steering wheel, staring at the guy. That made me even more nervous, so I leaned forward and said 'Howdy.'

"'Hotanuff for ya?'

"'Pretty hot.'

"'A couple of 'em won't be bothering you no more.'

" He must've seen I was having trouble figuring that one out 'cause he swings his chin back toward his truck.

"'Have a look,' he says. Phil let us roll forward and he walked even with us. I lean out my window to look in the bed of his truck.

"'Two dead coyotes,' I said, loud enough for Phil to hear me. I look back across him, and the guy's still by the window, smiling, smiling, that guy never did stop smiling. I seen what he wanted, plain old praise, but I just said, 'They sure are dead.'"

"It was enough. 'Deader'n hell,' he said, like I'd just give him a medal.

"'Yep, deader'n hell,' I said. I could always take coyotes or leave 'em. But I wasn't gonna argue the fine points with this guy. There'll always be people who kill coyotes, but this was the first one I'd seen stop traffic to point it out. I looked up the road and back at him and smiled like a coonhound and said, 'Good luck,' and Phil eased us on down the road. I tell you I was real aware of the back of my head. I reached up and tapped the mirror and saw him growing smaller. He was back in the middle of the road, legs wide, rifle slanted, his back to us, waiting. I watched him until he was lost in the dust. That was Checkpoint Coyote.

"We were rolling down the far side of the next hill when Phil finally said something. I remember it clear, just like I can smell the dust and alfalfa and hear the rattles our old Ford made on the gravel road.

"'Well Daddy,' he said, 'it's sad isn't it, some of the things that gives a man big balls?'"

* * * *

"Living as close to town as I do, I've got to work for my privacy. People do take advantage. When I saw a camper pulled over by my field, I reckoned I was going to have to kick some fishermen off my pond, but I saw it was a big picnic instead, about halfway to the pond under the double cottonwood out there.

"There must have been seven or eight, not counting babies. One guy was sitting on a plastic cooler playing a guitar. People on blankets. Couple of young kids running loose, but there's nothing to hurt out there but weeds. I decided not to chase them off; you don't see many people have picnics anymore—maybe its too primitive for people these days. Anyway, they didn't have guns or fishing poles and I drove on by, but force of habit, I copied their license plate with my finger in the dust on the dashboard.

"Turned out to be a good thing. I passed by there a couple hours later. The camper was gone but even from the road you could see a heck of a mess under that cottonwood. First I got mad and then I got an idea.

"You might find it hard to believe—I did—but I filled a big plastic leaf bag with garbage, not just full, but stuffed and bulging full. There was plastic plates and forks, plastic pop bottles, beer cans, chip bags, wrappers, a peach can—oh, I can't begin to tell you—baggies, watermelon rinds. There was three wadded up diapers, them plastic ones, all full. I picked up every bit of garbage, down to the pop tabs. I tied that leaf bag and put it in my pick-up and went to town. Saw my nephew Dave. He's a county deputy.

"It's all computerized now and they've got a cross-reference system. You can use a tag number and get who it was issued to, description of the vehicle, and an address, which is what I was looking for. It wasn't a street I'd heard of, so Dave had to access a city map. Actually, it wasn't too far from my place, part of the new housing on the south edge of town.

"I buzzed out that way, made sure I could find the place. It was a two-pattern, four color housing development. I'd carpentered layouts just like it in Omaha. Curving streets, deluxe models on the *cul de sacs*, sharp lawns, a sapling in each lawn, maple and sycamore. The sycamores had all been hit with virus and weren't going to make it. My man had a maple. The camper was in the driveway and the curtains were drawn. I went home and had supper.

"It was a little past midnight when I returned the man's garbage. I took my time, too, and spread it out evenly on the lawn. It looked pretty horrible.

"They say revenge is no good unless you witness it, but no reality could do justice to the many versions I've imagined of that guy standing on his front porch the next morning. I didn't want to haul that garbage up to his front door and get in a shouting match. I didn't want to confront him at all. I just wanted him to see a lawn full of garbage and get instantly boiling mad. Then I wanted him to recognize it."

For Farmers

Surrounded by broken
pots and arrowheads
you walk the space where
earth dome houses stood.

The kingdom of Quivira
neolithic farmers
tattooed arms beneath the stars
and a sight named Coronado
winding through the smoky hills

in a dazzle of crosses
and weapons on animals
with stone hard feet.
Gold squash and pumpkins shudder.

The man of metal speaks
of seven cities made of gold
streets and temples
gold clothing and shoes
coffins plates the very
gutters made of gold.

The farmers stare
off at the sky
a high-pitched blue above
where wind and stone remain.

"We hear you stranger.
Sit down
drink   eat.

That which you
desire is just
a little farther on."

Naming Many Colored Stones

Among the peoples who mined the Flint Hills, or traded with those who did, was a large farming culture, called Quivira by the Spanish who encountered them. Later Europeans called them Wichita, a name that was probably closer to what they'd called themselves, but Old Man Walker had always used the Spanish designation, and liking the sound of it, Walker followed suit. And when he had a son, the boy called the people Quivira for the same reason.

So things are named sometimes by a regard for the beauty of language. Both names were honorable and ripe with intrigue—Wichita, which Walker had also seen rendered Quichita, depending upon how it might have been spoken by the people, could also be expressed H-U-I-C-H-I-T-A, Hwee'-chee-tah. Which suggested the HU word beginnings of the Aztec, Maya, Inca, and other peoples south of what is now called Texas. On howling winter nights when he had nothing better to do, Walker supposed a people pushed northward through many lifetimes. But this was only an exercise against the solitude of winter, and ultimately, Wichita was a city one hundred miles down the road, and the name suggested cattle drives, the hogleg pistols of what was referred to, without irony, as the Old West, while Quivira, free of familiarity, seemed to belong less to his world and more to that of the people whose abandoned villages he walked.

Each of the three fields Walker searched had held fifty lodges or more, and the extended villages were plentiful in the lower half of central Kansas. Walker drove fifty miles southwest of his house to the three fields he knew; the Quivira tradition stretched another seventy miles southwest, and he'd found a Quivira site seventy miles due east. This line represented a front of population spreading from the south. Or this line was the path of a few large villages that used a place for a few generations, until game was scarce and soil overworked, and moved on. Or the line was just a paper reality straining to express a truth too complex and too shadowed.

Wichita or Quivira, they were many; the Knife site, the Hummingbird, the Jasper were thick with flint, bone, and pottery shards. Walked after a deep plowing and a heavy rain, any of them yielded flint tools and fragments, and always questions about the stones, the tools, the uses, the thousands of minds who walked the same piece of ground when it was something else. Leaders, humanitarians, visionaries, losers, jerks, and liars—Walker was interested in them all, but the stones gave little in those directions. They indicated the degree to which an individual would, or could, do something well, but artistry was no guarantee of character nobility, and a poorly made piece was not automatically the work of a deadbeat. When he was tempted to think that a particularly fine object must necessarily come from a great person, Walker had to remind himself that history was speckled with excellent artists who were violent personal failures, and it would be a disservice to the makers and users of Quivira to rob them of their humanity. All the women would not be beautiful and demure; all the men would not be sober and fair. Some of the hands that had made and used the tools would belong to schemers, cheats, and ordinary fools.

"Now don't go Hollywood on me," Walker or his son would say when the other tended to wax poetically on the person behind a particularly attractive work. Walker had his own way of combating such romantic notions. He imagined the person, man or woman, stepping from a lodge into the morning, taking pleasure in the loosing of a great fart and laughing at the surprised look on the face of a dog. There was a kind of romance to this view too, but it was a coarse variety, smelly and human, and Walker preferred it to the more stoic stereotypes his imagination might seduce him with.

Apart from his imagination, history, science, and the debris he walked upon were the only sources of clues to the people of Quivira. Spanish chronicles recorded that the people were tattooed and met the threat of strangers with diplomacy. Archaeologists told him their great mystery—after almost a hundred years of digging into the remains of the large Quivira population, they had yet to find a graveyard. But Walker spent more time with flint than with historians or archaeologists, and it was the stones that told him the most, though not always clearly and never fully.

Sometimes the stones of the Knife, Hummingbird, and Jasper said the same thing—not only were the Quivira populous, they were well known. Stones had been procured or traded from all four directions.

At other times the stones related differences. The highest percentage of flint on the Knife site was gray, from the Flint Hills to the east. On the Jasper, seven miles west, brown jasper from the northwest was the preferred stone, and the Hummingbird, between them, had an equal mix of both. Present on all three fields were bacon flint from Texas and pipestone from Minnesota, obsidian, petrified wood, and swirling, colorful agatized jaspers, all from the south and west. All these exotic stones were most abundant on the Jasper, lowest at the Knife, suggesting to Walker that the two villages had existed apart in time. It seemed a more realistic thought than believing the villages were contemporary with each other, one filled with expert flintworkers and one with poor cousins. If it was considered an earlier site, the Knife would indicate a general movement to the west with increased development of trade resources and flintworking skills. If later, the Knife represented the down side of the culture, a harder life, erosion of both trade and skills. Early or late, the village on the Jasper indicated a culture more developed than that on the Knife, more extensive trade, more variety of material, better workmanship, and a fuller inventory of tools, particularly those made from bone—bison shoulder blade hoes, needles and awls from long bone fragments.

By the time Quivira had reached that stage of development, the Smoky Hill River villages Walker knew had already been abandoned, the people gone north, becoming part of another cultural flowering called the Pawnee. Quivira called them the Harahey when the Spanish asked what lay to the north. The two village complexes, Quivira to the south, Harahey north, were surely aware of each other through trade, hunting boundaries, and the circumstance of getting their primary flint from the same source, the bluffs and creek banks of north-central Kansas and southern Nebraska.

Walker would have liked to know the names Quivira had for the rich flint found there in cobbles and seams. The people of his own time were engaged in polite taxonomic skirmishes over the material. Graham jasper, Smoky Hill jasper, Niobrara jasper, Niobrarite. Though the flint did not occur naturally on the part of the Smoky Hill river he walked, it was available in the western stretches of the same water, so Walker used the name that honored the river.

Almost all of the stone material left by the Quivira would come to have more than one name in Walker's time. Alibates was to bacon flint as obsidian was to volcanic glass, as pipestone was to catlinite, as agate was to jasper. Some of Walker's choices of names were governed by signs, most by pure prejudice. He was a big fan of the Smoky Hill, Alibates sounded too much like an anti-anxiety pill, obsidian was the perfect sound for the black glittering depth of the stone it described, and he decided not to call a stone long prized by the old pipemakers by the name of a great dead white man.

The tangling of names was compounded by names that had risen between Walker and his son. They called a particularly plentiful variety of Smoky Hill jasper Butterscotch because its color and smooth texture resembled that pudding. Even within such a specific name there were variations, from flat neutral tan to rich golden brown, and it served only to identify the most common variety of Smoky Hill jasper, the yellow-based browns. There were also solid browns, dark and light, and reddish-browns, dark burnt orange, oxblood red, and all the combinations in between. There was a green variety, spinach green at its darkest, the color of celery leaves at its lightest. Translucent bands of chalcedony could occur within any of the varieties, sometimes a weak milk white, more often pale amber.

All varieties were usually uniform in color or, if from bedded seams, like petrified shallow pools, banded in various shades. Mottling of color, so common in Flint Hills grays, was more rare in Smoky Hill jasper, and though both occurred in rough forms, the jasper at its best was more vitreous, finer-grained, quicker and more accurate flaking material than most of the gray flint from the east. The jasper was a rarity on Walker's sites along the Smoky Hill, but in the Quivira lands it overwhelmed the Flint Hills stone on the Jasper site, on the Hummingbird it struck an equal balance, and on the Knife, only seven miles east, it was in a clear minority. That Walker identified the people of Quivira so strongly with this stone was a result of his own inexperience. If he'd gone north to Nebraska and walked a Harahey village, he'd have found the same stone, fashioned into the same kinds of tools as those he picked up in Quivira, and he would have found it in use as well in South Dakota, Colorado, and Wyoming. Even the migrating bison hunters whose trail he'd crossed on the Rocking Deer had brought some Smoky Hill jasper into camp. Still, to Walker, it was the signature stone of Quivira.

The bluffs and outcrops of northern Texas provided bacon flint, white streaked with a dark, purplish red. Bacon flint was one of a variety of alibates. Two other varieties, a deep maroon, swirled together with vivid red, and a muted purple and pink one with white spots were also used, all valued not only for dramatic color design but for the uniformly fine grain that made them easier to predict and friendlier to work with. Occasionally Walker would keep a chip of bacon flint he'd picked up, simply for its beauty, but there were four kinds of stone he picked up every chip or bit of and kept for their rarity and intrigue.

Seeing a chip of obsidian on the ground was an exotic event, sudden black glass, the easiest of all stones to flake, quick to cut and quick to break. Walker had accumulated a double handful of these chips. Petrified wood was always saved, though he'd only found a dozen chips. He picked up every piece of a pink, easily carved stone from Minnesota and had a dozen small rough bits and four times as many thin shards, large and small, of polished pipe bowls.

The fourth stone he saved was the green jasper, because it showed up so rarely in the three fields, and he was entranced by its vegetal color. When Young Walker was a man, he would write his father, "You were right about that green flint. It grows on you."

Of the other occasional flints used by the peoples of Quivira, Walker recognized most—varicolored jasper like those he'd found in New Mexico, banded flint, both pink and buff, from the southern Flint Hills, and the tough cobbles of gravy flint which, because Quivira was not flint poor, were not flaked but used as hammerstones.

There were also the strangers he couldn't identify, white with asterisks of black, salmon colored with parallel rippling lines, a coarse-grained earthy pink. All these stones he had found but one—turquoise. The diggers of science had uncovered bits of it in Quivira, but it had not shown up for Walker. All the years he'd walked Quivira he'd carried a wish list in his mind in spite of his best efforts to free himself from wanting. He wanted a flint knife, an obsidian arrowpoint, a tool from green jasper, a pipe, and any little bit of turquoise.

Some of these things he would find, but turquoise, the one he'd chosen for his favored stone, was not among them. If he still hadn't found a piece by the time his legs gave out and forced him to embrace an old age away from the fields, there would be no bitterness. What he had not found would be laughable compared to memories of Quivira and the many steps he had taken in the richness of its stones.

Levels of Use

"**E**ven without horses," Old Man Walker said, "they still found ways to kill plenty buffalo. You'll know that by all the hide scrapers you're gonna see today."

Walker remembered none of the details of his first trip to Quivira—the feel of the day, the make of the old man's junker, or even what objects he might have found. What stayed with him through the years was the anticipation, keyed by the objects the old man had already found there and then remarks he made as he drove. Later, when he'd found the Jasper and the Hummingbird, Walker would say some of the same things to his own son as he drove him to his first Quivira visit. By then the old man was a cloud of electrons on an unknown horizon, but he'd been right about the hide scrapers—the fields of Quivira were thick with them, thousands of lost and abandoned scrapers, a thriving industry in the cleaning and preservation of hides, the legacy of good hunters who walked out and killed, day after day, the buffalo and deer, so many that it was clear that Quivira, as sophisticated and large as its agricultural nature was, still maintained a strong hunting tradition.

Amost all of Walker's memories of Quivira centered around scrapers. In part it was because he was lucky with them. The old man had luck at finding knives, Young Walker happened onto flint drills, and Walker was a scraper boy, a scraper man. One afternoon in his fourteenth year, under a sun so hot the meadowlarks and horned larks only flew when they had to and didn't sing at all, he stumbled off the Knife site with twelve hide scrapers in his jeans. He lined them up on the dull hood of the car while he waited for the old man to wear himself out. Walker had been pleased to discover he had a way of finding scrapers; they didn't have the adventuresome, almost aristocratic identity of arrowpoints—they were grunt tools, domestic, meant to scrape the fat off fresh, staked-out skins, nose down to the grease. Yet he liked the way they settled naturally into his grip. An arrowpoint was meant for the air, and holding one was like holding a butterfly, but a hide scraper, once picked up, made itself at home in the hand. He liked the simple shape; flat side down on the car hood, the scrapers looked like whales on a dull, green sea, tall foreheads and sloping backs.

Quivira had made adjustments in technology, shortening scrapers generally to half the length of a thumb, often less, and most seemed to be made to be held between the thumb and the tips of the first and second fingers, or pinched between thumb and curled side of the index finger. The old large scrapers, over the backs of which fingers once curved, had shrunk, taking the tool out of the hand and giving it to the fingertips. Less area could be scraped per stroke with these smaller models and they couldn't gouge as much fat as the large ones.

His pudding of a mind, as he draped his shirt on the hot car fender and leaned on it to stare at the scrapers, didn't see that as an indication of a desire for better hides, better performance, and a strong work force. He didn't know the hide scraper was traditionally a tool of women making clothing, so he didn't wonder yet if women knew the process as honorable work, worth as much as the killing of the buffalo, or whether power turned weird and the women who had it saw that the hide-scraping was done by the ugly sisters, the weak, the maimed, and the old. At fourteen, with no thought of the hands beyond the scrapers, he wasn't ready to ask himself those questions.

Sweat dripped from his nose to his forearm. His mind was blank as the sky, roaming over color, size, and form of the twelve pieces of stone. Two of them, without his knowing it, were leading him to the eye of the maker.

Some among the twelve were crude and irregular, most showed an attempt at symmetry and flaking that ran up the sides and across the back. The only part of these sculpted stones left unmodified was the flat bottom, already smooth for a thumb. His attention circled back to two. One had a very high brow, a quickly sloping back. When he squinted, it looked like the front half of a nose rising through the car hood. It was made from glossy, dark, blue-gray flint and a wide blaze of white ran down the spine. The other was low-profile and the same flint, made so that the flat bottom was dark gray, but seen from above, the object was mantled in ivory white surrounded by a dark gray line. Both the skunktail and the cameo effects called attention to themselves. Walker did not consider that afternoon whether the color and contrast of the two scrapers had been placed rather than settled for. He knew that he liked them and that two, three, even ten years later, when he thought of this moment, they would be the scrapers he'd remember. Only years later, would he realize how important they were to him, his first examples of Quivira flintworkers manipulating the stone for visual effect. Many miles later, one foot in front of the other, he would glimpse the desire for artistry in Quivira, how very many artists there were, and how often that impulse found expression in scrapers.

The journey would be slow because when Walker went rational he started like a good hyena, at the ass, and worked forward. By the time the old man showed up that afternoon, boots barely clearing the clods, the boy had stared up a theory about the manufacture of scrapers, the scraper being chipped into shape on a chunk of flint and then, pah!—a sharp tap on the narrow end, popping it free of the stone.

He would look next for chunks of flint that bore the imprints of those released scrapers or, better yet, a chunk with a fully formed scraper still in place. Wisely, he kept this theory to himself and when he got to know flint better, he could laugh at the ignorance of starting at the wrong end of the process, putting the scraper before the flake.

Bedded seams of Smoky Hill jasper were plentiful north and west of Quivira, some very thin, some as much as three fingers thick. As opposed to cobbles, seams yielded flat sections of stone of varying lengths. These were perfect blanks: long, flat bars of flint were knives-in-waiting, a small section, no larger than a deck of miniature playing cards, could be stood on end and fractured diagonally, providing blanks for two scrapers, and many potential arrowpoints, drills, and scrapers could be harvested from a large tablet three fingers thick and relatively flat on top and bottom. Such a tablet could be reduced to flakes quickly, laying it flat, striking it down at the corners, striking next at the new angles created by the departing flake, diminishing the stone inward. It could also be done slowly, a moment of study between blows, in order to compare possibility with desire regarding the flake to be released. A secure society would allow the worker time to approach the process critically from the beginning, and when there was a touch of Hollywood in the air, Walker could conjure a noble workman noticing, as he scans the tablet he is fracturing, the possibility of obtaining a blank that will make a symmetrical and ornate scraper and striking the rim in just the place that knocks the flake free. In his more Norwegian moments, he saw the worker hammering the hell out of the edges of the tablet, symmetrically and accurately, but intent on getting the job done. Once the flakes had been sorted into piles of what was possible and what was useless, this worker might notice a particularly well-proportioned shape with dramatic coloring.

"Hmm. Not bad."

In either case, the artistic eye was at work, but some of the scrapers Walker found convinced him some eyes were open from the beginning, choosing the stone, trying for the desired flake, loading the scraper with beauty, a contrasting streak accenting the spine, alternate bands of dark and light draping the back, striking spots or lines of color.

Why they bothered at all was not a question asked by the boy who walked the Knife; when he returned as a young man and began to learn the big, expansive field again, he was open to questions of motive. One afternoon he picked up a tiny, curved gray chip and saw that he had found a miniature hide scraper, proportional in every way but able to sit in the center of his thumbnail. He would find another of these on the Knife, less, well-made, four on the Hummingbird, three on the Jasper. He'd referred to them at first, with a smile, as mouse hide scrapers. Only when he found more did he begin to consider that the skins of birds, weasels, and mice might have a use, ornamental or ritual, and that such skins might be too small and thin to be scraped by regular tools. Possibly they were a matter of education. Just as small boys were given a little bow and arrows so that they might begin learning to stalk, surprise, and kill the food and clothing they would provide, so small girls learned beside mothers and aunts the work they would grow into—butchering, fire-making, the preparation of food and the dressing of skins. The miniature scrapers, part toy, part text, could be made for those fingers. Walker accepted both theories equally though, skins and fingers long gone, they were beyond proof. He was initially less accepting of a third possibility—that the tiny scrapers had been made *as* miniatures, a variation on a theme by curious artists because the small flake had suggested it, and the maker had accepted the challenge to his skill to make objects of curiosity and charm.

He would grow to learn it was not an altogether frivolous idea. On all the sites he walked, regardless of culture, he would eventually find that objects had been brought into camp whose qualities transcended function: a long, angular quartz crystal, smooth river pebbles, too small to be used in burnishing clay pots.

It took a force of will for him to see the value in these objects. Even into the shaky wisdom of maturity, he usually thought he was standing in a crop field, part of a pattern of farms, roads, and telephone lines. He had to force his recall of worlds where wind and stone had spirit, where an object might have importance and power, no explanation needed. Walker was no stranger to the phenomenon of picking things up for no earthly reason; his house was cluttered with bits of wood, stone, feather that had attracted eye and hand. Most of it had no real meaning. Once a week, a month, a year, he would pluck one of them up from the shelf or table and handle it. But in the fields he got too easily lost in the search, forgot about spirit, magic, implication. The smooth pebbles and knuckles of lump quartz would remind, jar him into remembering what things could be alive in the stones that were shaped into tools. With magic on his mind, it was easy to believe that an arrowpoint could be made that was never intended to fly, a scraper created that would never be used.

The Twisted Blade

The Knife site had been named for Old Man Walker's luck. Seven knives had appeared to him there—four irregular ovals and three finely chipped bevel-edge daggers. Quivira made knives with the blade edges worked equally on both sides into a lance-like form. With others they took long chips from only one edge the length of the blade, turned the blade over and flaked along the same edge on the opposite side. A broken beveled blade, which Walker had many of, was diamond-shaped in cross-section.

A neck would be worked above the expanding dagger, and the head, worked to fit into a socket of bone or wood, usually resembled a rounded playing card spade.

Though there were other designs—flake knives large and small, straight-backed and oval hand knives, diamond hand knives with a point at each end—the bevel-edged daggers were most numerous. Size varied from the length of a middle finger to the length of a hand from fingertip to heel. Some had been broken in use, others by decades of steel tools preparing the ground for wheat, corn, alfalfa, milo. Walker had a cigar box full of bevel-edged knife tips, heads, and blade sections. He had two complete knives.

They were both small, one made from a dark brown jasper, one a white-banded pink flint that turned abruptly gray at the tip. Neither had been found on the Knife site.

Young Walker had found a small, freckled lavender diamond knife there, but the field that had given up its knives easily to the old man never showed Walker a complete one.

When the Knife was the only village Walker knew about, he sometimes drove fifty miles to find it unplowed, or not rained on, or covered in crop. On one of those days, unwilling to give up the afternoon, he had driven slowly west on dirt roads. He used two hours getting permission and walking on a likely plowed hill without finding a chip of flint. It was a hill he wouldn't have to wonder about any more.

Wandering farther west, he drove slowly, trying to calculate which land forms would attract settlement and which of those might be in condition to make a walk worthwhile. Driving past a windbreak of cedars, his eyes snagged on a spill of charcoal and bone fragments from the graded ditch.

He turned in at the nearest drive and spoke with a stout man with a red face and white forehead.

"Oh, that stuff is out there all right."

"I was wondering if I could get your permission to walk out there and have a look?"

"Well, I can't see it would do any harm."

Ten minutes later Walker was picking up flint, and soon after he picked up what he thought was a fragment and found himself holding the dark brown knife.

That was his introduction to the Jasper site, and from then on, when he went to Quivira, he went there first. After years of five-minute conversations, he came to appreciate the farmer's easy smile and, in spite of the seeming lack of interest in the flint tools on his farm, his politeness about other people's obsessions. Sometimes a year or more would go by between Walker's visits.

"Hi. I don't know if you remember me, but..."

"Oh heck yes, down to do some walking?"

The Jasper was the field he chose when he introduced Quivira to Young Walker. It had been good to both of them. They picked up arrow-points, drills, many scrapers and, after Walker had filled another cigar box with fragments, his second knife.

The pink knife with the gray tip was more precisely formed than the brown one, but Walker had fragments of elegant bacon flint knives that would make them both look ordinary. When the thrill of *whole* knives wore off, and when Walker and his son decided to become statisticians one summer night, it was the fragments they turned to. Curiosity about the beveling caused them to unpack the cigar boxes and arrange all the knife pieces with the blade tips pointing away.

They counted seventy-four pieces of bevel-edged knives, and all but one were beveled on the left edge. Unlike the flat, thin lance and oval blade, the bevel-edged was narrow and thick, the form of a tapered spike. A flat-bladed knife would pierce and cut, but twisting would risk snapping the blade. Young Walker picked up a broken beveled blade and held it out in his right hand, rotated his hand to the left and watched the beveled edge turn under, the bevel of the opposite side rolling over to take its place.

"That's like a drill. You could drill a hole in wood with it. But then, why would you want to drill a hole in wood?"

"A hole in wood... A hole in wood..."

"Maybe it's not a skinning tool at all. Man! You know what you could do with this?"

"What"

"Trim wood."

"Trim, like in...?"

"Cutting away the branches and knots, you know, smoothing the wood, like..."

"Like making a..."

"Making a bow."

"Yeah, twisting and scraping..."

"Can you see doing that with one of those lance knives?"

"Bad dynamics."

"No kidding."

"This would work for wood."

"Yeah, why not? Or for boring holes in hides... Hey! Boring holes in hides!"

"Uh..."

"Lacing them together... You know, clothes, robes..."

"Yeah, I got it now. I guess it depends on whether they were just going around wrapped in a hide or whether they had daily robes and party robes, jobs with holes around the edge for a border of feathers or fur."

"I'm thinking buffalo hide is really tough too."

"Yeah, I think they're hide borers."

"You know what, they could be used to drill bowls on those big pipes."

"Right. But we hardly ever find a piece of a big pipe."

"Oh yeah, there should be, well, a lot, with all these knives."

"But they *could* be used for that, even if they were mainly meant for something else. Maybe there weren't a lot of holes made in pipes, but a lot in hides."

"An all-around hole maker."

"An all-around hole maker."

"Yeah, but these things... We've got three, six, nine..."

"Twenty-one."

"Twenty-one flat diamond knives."

"Busted."

"Yeah. Too bad. But these are a whole different thing, worked to a blade on each end. These are hand tools."

"Got the bevel. It's like halfway between, flat, wide, but beveled. They've got the beveled edge down, but it's still a lance blade..."

"Still break easy."

"Yeah."

"But I'm saying it's a whole different tool. Point on both ends here. Just pick it up and go to work."

"Oh. You don't think oval knife evolved to diamond knife to bevel knife? You think they were all in use at the same time."

"Well, I'm not sure I really *think* that. Well, yeah, different knives for different jobs."

"I think it was a development—first the flat, oval knives..."

"That's because you like things logical."

"I do?"

"Sure. First this, then that, then the other."

"Fat lot of good it's doing now."

"Really. We need a portable carbon fourteen dating lab."

"A portable atom sorter."

"An electron scanner."

"No, you know what we really need?"

"Brains?"

"No, a time machine."

"What do you think they'd do when we showed up?"

"Kill our butts."

"Yeah, guess so."

"What would be the first thing you'd do to show them, you know, you came in peace?"

"Fill my pants."

"Right, right, but after that?"

"I'd find the baddest looking guy and give him a plastic lighter, real nice, and I'd look for the wisest one there and give him...my pocketknife."

"Mhm."

"What would you do?"

"Sing every song I know."

Lost in Quivira

You forgot your life. The weather was sweetly seductive or so fierce it squeezed everything down to footsteps and eyes. A pink and orange sky might eat your past, thunderheads float the future, darkness breathe over your shoulder. A mantra by an insect, coming stars, the shifting of owls, one hard mud footprint of a coyote's thought, the fragmentary echo of all that came before, and you were lost in Quivira.

Walker had been there, his son had been there, the old man had surely been there. It was not an event to be courted; it came along, like the call of the Take-it-easy bird. *Tiki-deé-zee, si si.* It was to hear this and remain thoughtless, when the Old West was more than white boys ripped on cheap grunt whiskey, and also less. When dirt was no more than dirt and the footsteps meandering beyond choice. When you didn't know you were lost, and only then, you were. Later you'd feel hunger, want to make love, electronically view men chasing a ball, but none of these things came to mind lost in Quivira.

It wasn't a matter of walking the village of the Old People back into existence—that was all still there. But it was now the dust of mothers, hunters, fllintworkers, fools, dust of dogs and robes, digging sticks, fly whisks. The shouts and murmurs long downwind, the rub of life remaining was held in stone. Seeing the arrowpoint suddenly eye-to-eye and falling into the old world, slapped in the chops, a flash of distant hands, a piece of work, a stone with the orderly scars of thought. But those were only dreams, the fall brief, the rebound quick. Walker thrown back into his shoes, the small obsidian triangle flat in his hand. Young Walker sitting lost in the dust where no one ever found anything. His rolling gaze runs into the long red-and-white flint drill, and he bounces back into himself.

You didn't have to be lost to find things, but finding them sometimes anchored the moment so deeply that you realized you had been lost in walking for an unknown span of time, without opinion, history, or want. No job, no car, no bed, goals, fears. A rabbit, a weed, something the wind moved over and around in a time without glory or regret.

Stepping in ignorance out of your own place and not yet into another, you could take no pleasure in simply being. The moment you recognized that the clutches of identity had fallen away, that you were free in mindless circumstance, you had revoked the condition. Though you might pretend you still floated like smoke, the mind was roused and gathering context, naming the weather, the time, the barking of a dog three farms away, and you were back in the smell of your clothes, charted by calendars, clocks, the turn of a key, no longer lost in Quivira.

So there were times, when Walker and his son found tools, that they found themselves as well, blinking confused, a chicken one of them had hypnotized by drawing the symbol for eternity in the dust, startling awake and looking around at the dirt, the others, the roost.

On the Hummingbird

The long hump of a hill had taken his eye more than once as he drove between the Jasper and the Knife. One season he turned off the route and drove to it. Most of its length was being used to grow wheat. A fence near the south end marked the pasture with tall grass that tapered down into elm, cottonwood, hackberry, white flashes of a tall house.

The driveway was skinny, curved, not graveled enough to prevent rain gullies and potholes. The house only showed patches at a time through the trees until the crooked, rising drive reached a clearing, swinging into a wide turnaround. A walk made of slabs of sandstone the size of dinner plates, a wicket-topped wire fence, a gate with a double scroll of flat metal bands opened onto a shadowed lawn, civilized grass a color between green and blue. A white tractor tire lay on its side, a clutch of red tulips in the center. There were peony and iris beds and, around the house, head-high trumpet-flower bushes merged into one curved line.

Walker was not tall, but the white-haired woman who opened the inner door barely came to his chest. He began to explain himself, but she smiled, held up a hand and, turning, walked away. A white-haired man, no taller than the woman, came slowly through the parlor.

"Yes?"

Walker introduced himself, stated his business, told how he'd noticed the long, cultivated hill, and requested permission to go up on it and wander.

"Well, you're right," said the little man. "They were up there. Just a minute here." He disappeared to one side of the doorway and returned with a small wooden case held in front of his chest. With one foot he pushed the screen door open, inviting Walker forward a step.

He took the step and leaned further, peering at the points, scrapers, drills held to the wood with thin wire loops. In the center of the case was an oval knife of butterscotch flint as large as his hand.

It was a schizophrenic moment for Walker; he was pleased and excited at seeing the tools, but disappointed that the little white-haired farmer shared his interest. Walker, had the situation been reversed, would have had no inclination to let others walk on his land, his field, his village. But he was given a lesson in charity.

"Go on up and have a look if you want. You can drive toward the barn. Turn right, it'll take you through the pasture, right up to the fence. Now, I walked it last week, but we've had a fair rain. You might do all right."

"That's really nice of you."

"Ah." The old farmer waved a hand in front of his face, as if dispersing gnats. "One thing. If you don't mind stopping by the house on your way out, I'd like to see what you find."

He caught the wary look on Walker's face and smiled. "Just like to see what I missed."

The first time on the Hummingbird was not the best, the tendrils of winter wheat were large enough to obscure much of the ground, but from the moment he climbed over the barbed wire, Walker saw that the field was loaded with flint. He walked for three hours on the spine and sides of the long hump. The old farmer's footprints, softened by rain, were scarce, and he'd walked by many chips without investigating them. Walker super-stitiously picked up every flake; there had been times when what looked like a chip turned out to be a tool buried enough to fool the eye.

He found one whole arrowpoint, six broken, eight broken scrapers and four complete. Only one of the objects was remarkable, a well-propor-tioned hide scraper made from bacon flint. When he drove out of the pasture at the end of the afternoon, he dutifully stopped and rapped on the door.

"That's a big village up there," he said, holding out the stones in the palm of his hand.

"Oh sure, one of the biggest around. Now there's a fine looking gentle-man." The little farmer wagged his finger at the maroon and white scraper. Walker held it out and he took it, holding it in its working position. "Dandy." He placed it back in Walker's hand.

Walker had tendered his thanks and taken one step aside from the door when he saw one, two, three brilliant green and red flashes darting through the porch, one almost touching the brim of his hat. They curved to the bushes, zipping from one speckled orange trumpet flower to another. He had seen few enough hummingbirds in his life to stand with his mouth open.

"The missus and me they know, but I guess they had to get a closer look at you."

Each time Walker searched there he stopped at the porch on his way out, even if he'd only found fragments. In spring there were hummingbirds, and in the fall, when bushes had no flowers and few leaves, he thought of them as he walked the high field.

Scrapers came to him, drills, arrowpoints. Some stood apart from the others; two more finely made bacon flint scrapers, a shiny double-ended drill like a miniature flat cigar, half green jasper, half brown.

One day when no one answered the knock, he stood by his car gazing at the driveway, with its thin scatter of river gravel, and saw chips of flint working through the ground. Before long he'd found a clear, dust colored arrowpoint with its tip missing. He went to his knees and found the tip two hand-spans away. He knew then that the village had continued through the pasture, through where the house stood, and down the slope of the hill.

In good seasons he went to Quivira every weekend, stood on the porch with the farmer.

"Now they say the lodges were these beehive dome affairs covered with mats of grass," said the farmer.

"There must have been nearly a hundred of them here alone."

"No doubt about it. They were all over this part of the country." The farmer waved a hand. "Had to be thousands all told."

Once Walker was invited inside the dim parlor, with its dark, gleaming furniture and shown more cases of the tools.

"I can't get over those big ovals."

"Skinning knives. But these were all picked up years ago. I don't see one these days."

"Were you here during the Dust Bowl?"

"We were."

" What was it like?"

"We raised what little we could, just vegetables, you understand, and ate it ourselves. Hard to get money, but we ate.

"Right now I hire out the crop work. I'm too darn old to do it. He gets most of the crop, but we're pretty well set. Fact, the missus says I just keep that hill farmed so I can go up and walk it."

"I saw somebody plowing up there a couple times."

"Didn't pay you any mind, I bet."

"No."

"That's him. Young man, got a family, hungry for acres right now. Brings in a good crop."

"He interested in flint?"

"Not hardly. When I was farmin' and happened to see something nice, why you just know I had to stop everything and get down and get it. But him, once he's on that tractor, he don't get off until he's done or the sun goes down. Sometimes not even then, when he's racing the weather."

"Did it rain here Thursday?"

"Sprinkled. I went up and walked a bit. Didn't see much. Have a go at it."

Three dry seasons came, one after another. Rain, when it fell at all, was capricious and brief. Even the winters, relied upon for heavy snows to put moisture back in the ground, were miserly. Fields were worked and planted, but without rain the stones didn't show, and Walker's trips to the country were rare. When he did go, it was only for the sake of a walk, and he stayed close to home, reluctant to drive fifty miles to scuff through Quivira's dry dirt. He found very little and joined farmers, merchants, even children, in cursing the hot wind and the dry, pale sky.

After the third thin harvest, rains came: night thunder, a strong clean wind that woke him, the clattering hiss of rain coming down full. It was still hammering when he drifted back into sleep. That weekend he drove to Quivira.

The Jasper was in wheat stubble, ground cluttered and confusing to the eye, but he walked anyway, once across the field and back, before he returned to the car, hoping the Hummingbird or Knife had been plowed before the rain.

He was disappointed when he turned onto the road that paralleled the Hummingbird and saw the green tractor crawling the familiar long hill, the stubble just then being plowed. It wouldn't be worth looking at until another rain had tamped the fresh ground. As he neared the southern slope of the hill, thoughts of fields and rain were swept from his head so abruptly that he stopped the car. There were no trees. There was no house.

Driving on, up the curving, weedy driveway, he stopped at the turn-around, motor running, and stared at the square hole filled with gnarled fragments of bushes and trees. Off to one side a tangle of branches had been dozed onto the upturned roots of cottonwoods. The old lawn was scarred with gouges, weeds and long grasses beginning to take it back. He turned the car and drove around the side, up into the pasture.

When he crawled through the fence and stood on the strip of black, plowed earth, the tractor was a small square turning at the far end of the field. He didn't wander into the stubble searching for flint, but stood watching the tractor slowly enlarge. When it reached him, the man stopped, left the motor running, sat looking down from the cab, face neutral under a stained feed cap. Walker pulled himself up the metal step and shouted an introduction over the sound of the machine.

The old couple had died over a year ago, first the woman, then the man. The estate and machinery had been auctioned off, the house sold and moved off its foundation. Someone in Wichita owned the land. The sharecropper gunned his engine and yelled that he guessed Walker could keep coming to the field.

That was the last time he used the driveway. When Young Walker grew old enough to walk with him, they parked on the road and walked directly up to the field. Walker told him about the house, trumpetflowers, hummingbirds, the little white-haired couple, but to the boy, who knew only the field of many colored stones and exquisite tools, it could be no more than a charming story, the yard in the shade and darting hummingbirds, equal to the lodges of earth and grass, village dogs and children under the hot blue sky, all soaked equally into the past.

Different Smoke

People so distant their dust had turned to dust threw herbs on campfires, leaned in to drink the smoke through their noses. Smoke went from
earth to sky, a messenger. Inevitably people would see it as a path for
praises and entreaties, taking it in, sending it out and up. Experiment found
the smoke of leaf, flower, or bark that would bring contemplation,
celebration, communication, and fire was moved from the ground into a
small, portable bed. Straight pipes of bone, wood, and stone were used by
the early hunters and gatherers of Walker's country, evolving eventually
into the right-angle pipe. Baked clay was used, but more permanent pipes
were carved from fine-grained limestone, sandstone, and steatite, a talc
stone, usually gray, that took a handsome polish, but the final stone of
choice was pipestone, a reddish clay compacted by time.

Pipestone invited carving. Dense but yielding, it could be scraped and
sanded into shape, bowl and smokehole bored with long flint drills. It had
been carved into pipes in the shape of creatures, birds, frogs, bears, humans, and flat or cylindrical pipes with the bowl at midpoint so that, fitted
with a long, wooden mouthpiece, the tip of stone projecting past the bowl
could be propped on the ground in front of the seated smoker. These elaborate versions were clearly ceremonial; a simpler kind was a squat, rounded
bowl very much like that of a modern pipe with a short arm at the base to
receive the mouthpiece. Both of these styles had been found at Quivira,
but the culture was noted for a third innovation, the small L-pipe, a slightly
swollen tubular bowl half as long as the little finger and about the same circumference as that finger, short arm at the bottom drilled to hold a stem of
wood or reed. Loaded and touched with the tip of a glowing twig, the little
pipe would provide six or seven draws of smoke. The majority of tiny pipe
fragments Walker had picked up over the years had come from these small
L-pipes; in Quivira smoking had expanded from a ceremonial activity to a
domestic one.

More fragile than flint, a hollowed pipe struck by plunging plow steel
was easily shattered. Each fragment found hinted at the possibility of a pipe
unearthed and unbroken, and even unworked bits of pipestone were saved
by Walker because, like obsidian, it had traveled a long way to end in his
hand.

The only major source was a region in southern Minnesota. Its red-
ness signified the blood of the people or, in some legends, the blood of the
Creator. Traditionally it was a spiritual gift to the peoples, given with the
commandment that all weapons would be put aside at the quarry, all ani-
mosity suspended. The stone was sacred. Fighting among those who came

to quarry it would dishonor the spirit, the stone, the intended pipe, and the smoking prayer it would carry. Another in a long line of character tests, the rule may have actually worked for generations, but by the time Europeans arrived and began documenting tribes and activities, stronger groups among the peoples had apparently taken control of the quarry and the distribution of the stone.

In Walker's time, the place had become an attraction and he'd gone there, a willing tourist, to see for himself the home of the stone declared holy, a place people had died for in spite of the Creator's wish.

Walker parked beside a building of varnished logs, and a Lakota in a plaid shirt and feed cap walked him to the quarry site, a flat area of short, tough grasses, pitted with shrunken, overgrown depressions where the stone had been dug, reminiscent of the collapsed flint pits he'd seen in the Flint Hills. They stopped near a pile of rock and a hole not much bigger than a chair.

"This is the one we're working on now," said the Lakota. "You can see the pipestone down on the bottom edge." The pit went down about four feet; it had been dug, not through easy dirt, but through a solid mantle of tough Sioux quartzite. Flint miners had had to dig through stone too, but that was limestone, porous and brittle; dense, hard quartzite was the stuff of boulders. Walker would want a sledgehammer and crowbar to go through four feet of it, but the old quarriers had done it with stone hammers and wedges of wood and bone. Along the bottom of the pit he could see the red layer, no thicker than his wrist, a jagged edge where pieces had been broken loose and handed up.

Inside the pine visitors' lodge were displays explaining the legend, the quarry, the way stone was extracted in early times. On the wall behind a long glass case of books and souvenirs hung seven long pipes of the ceremonial form, tall cylindrical bowls, groundrest and neck projecting from opposite sides of the bowl base, long elaborately carved wooden mouthpieces hung with feathers and price tags. Some of the pipestone was inlaid with silver.

"These come from our modern pipemakers," said the woman behind the counter.

"Beautiful work," Walker said. It was, and for forty dollars he could have carried one of the pipes away, but his interest was only visual.

On the counter a flat basket held raw rectangular pipestone chunks, each about half the size of a cigarette pack. A cardboard sign propped among the dusty pink blocks said 25 cents. Walker handled them all. Some had whitish flecks and veins. He chose one that was uniformly pink and paid his quarter.

In the parking lot he remembered his manners, stripped a cigarette, and scattered tobacco to the quarry. He had decided to carve a pipe to remind him of this land of red granite, red pipestone, pink Sioux quartzite, a place where even the highways had a pink cast.

Walker's desire to carve a pipe had grown from the desire to find one. As a boy he'd found enough fragments to assume that that was going to be the rule; no pipe would survive the plow. But he had been there the day the old man found one on the Knife site, an L-pipe lying on the field as if it had been dropped there a moment before.

"Christ, looky here," the old man had said. "It's still got the dottle." The bowl had been half-full of burned plant. The pathos of that half-smoked bowl had struck the boy, as if he'd encountered a half-eaten apple in an empty room, or a book laid open on a sidewalk, pages turning in the wind, and in ensuing years he thought of the smoker more than the pipe, and the turn of fate that had interrupted the smoke. According to the old man, life in Quivira hadn't always been placid; roving bands of people would try to take what they wanted from the settled ones, particularly after Spanish horses had been captured and bred and raiders became mounted forces with names like Comanche.

When the old man disappeared the pipe went too, and Walker would never know if the dottle had been sent away for analysis, or if the old man had finished the smoke himself, or if, in a circling act of completion, he'd returned to the Knife for a last walk, scattering as he went all the things he had found. Sometimes on that field Walker would think of the pipe and imagine himself re-finding it and answering at least one of the many questions about his father. But the mystery of that pipe, half-smoked, uncleaned, would remain as impenetrable as the mystery of the old man, and when chance led him to his own discovery of a pipe, it would speak of impatience instead of interruption.

He had driven to the Jasper on an early December day. Walking season, comfortable walking season, was over, but snow hadn't fallen and the sun was lighting up a chilly wind. He and Young Walker had been to Quivira twice that summer but not on the Jasper; that field had been covered in shoulder-high milo.

There would be lines of stalk stubs in December, a puzzle of withered leaves and chaff. At best, wind would have cleared the rows, exposing flat earth between the lines of stubble. The farmer with the white forehead had given permission with some amusement.

"Not gonna be much to see out there."

"Well, you know, I felt like taking a walk." Walker shrugged.

The wind had done its job. He found just enough flint in the bare lanes between the stubble rows to keep him interested, to justify the fifty-mile drive. He would walk a row the length of the field, move over two rows, and walk back, thinking as he did each December, about Christmas with his son and daughter. Would his car make the trip to Denver? Would he take the midnight bus? Would he have the money? Slapped and swatted by the wind, he found the tip of a broken drill, the base of a brown, triangular point. The car was a joke. He would have to take the bus. He would need seventy-five dollars. Were there bills he could postpone? He stopped, hunching his back to the wind to light a cigarette. Wind snuffed the match. He went to his knees, struck another in cupped hands. It went out. Curled around his hands, he tried three more before frustration put him on his belly, stretched out in a row, forming a cave with his hat brim and the folds of his coat. He got the cigarette lit.

It was a quieter world on the ground, wind broken by the milo stubs on either side of him, and the dirt was warm. The difficulty of striking a light had cleared his mind of cars, buses, and money. He jammed his hat tight on his ears and laid his chin on folded hands, watching smoke snatched away as it rose. Blank as a snake, he listened to the rattling stalks, gaze crawling aimlessly up the converging row and back, dried scrawls of long milo leaf speckled with rust, flat valley of pale, scoured dirt. Just beyond his chin, a flush of ashy pink. He brushed his finger over it, shifting fine dust, and uncovered a curve of pink stone. Suddenly he was on his knees and then his feet and the small L-shaped pipe was in his hand.

When he made his own pipe, Walker was instructed by the example of the man who'd made the pipe from the Jasper. That man, seeing his pipe take shape, had pushed for completion, forcing the process, and in doing so, cancelled his work.

The tall, narrow bowl had been carefully carved and bored and the maker had incised a decorative line around it a third of the way down from the lip, but in boring the short neck of the L, the last step, his anticipation had overtaken concern, and he had failed to keep the flint drill straight as he twisted it. The force and bad leverage had cracked a piece off the lip of the neck. The worker had trimmed the fractured neck until it once more had a clean, circular rim, shortening it considerably, and resumed boring the smokehole. His patience should have improved, but his attention moved ahead again, away from his fingers pushing and twisting the drill, toward the moment when the smokehole would join the one bored through the bowl. Hands hurried to catch up with vision, each twist of the drill growing in force and wobbling in accuracy: he broke another piece off the rim of the hole. This time the flaw was irreparable; the base of the L had already been trimmed down until it barely existed. The pipe would remain unfinished, the holes unconnected. Years later, Walker would find another instance of untimely force, one half of an L-shaped pipe that had split along its entire length just before the two drill holes had met, and Young Walker would find half a large-bowled pipe on the Knife that told the same story.

The dismay and anger of these pipemakers hung close to Walker when he set about carving a pipe from the chunk he'd bought at the quarry.

He used a pocketknife to form the pipe, scrape by scrape, and to hollow the bowl, and a small Phillip's screwdriver to bore the smokehole and, through the process, began to understand how a person could be lulled into thinking the stone would forgive anything, accommodate speed and force. It absorbed the sweat of his hands as he worked, deepening the warm earth red, and the warmer, darker, smoother it became, the more it seemed to invite the knife. More than once he caught himself scraping too hard, as if he could carve it like soap, and then the memory of that other pipemaker would cause him to lay the knife down beside the growing pile of pink dust and regard the stone as if it were a child who had charmed him into forgetting discipline, or the most pliant of lovers who, yielding, drew him deeper until nothing mattered but his own implacable will.

Eventually he learned, his concentration centering less on the destination, more on the journey. The vision of the pipe-to-be was replaced, night after night, by the careful draw of the knife, the slow turn of the screwdriver down the center of the stem. In this way he avoided the seduction of the stone and kept the pipe out of his mind until it was complete.

He rinsed it in warm water the night he finished it, a modern bowl, a thick stem that stretched far enough away from the bowl not to require a mouthpiece. A bird lay along the stem, face disappearing into the side of the bowl so that only the back of its head was visible.

He smoked the pipe that night, loaded with shaggy tobacco, blowing smoke in all directions. It was different smoke than the assembly line of cigarettes he ran through his system in trivial habit. With the pipe he inhaled, held, released the quarry, the carving, the smoking stone.

He didn't smoke the pipe often; months, sometimes years, went by between smokes. A moment would come when he discovered himself tangled in his life. The smoke, the pipe, brought the hypnotic comfort of detail, the vitality of every choice in random existence. It brought to his mind, too, the impatient among the pipemakers of Quivira, staring at the pipe suddenly split in the hand. If you can't laugh, said the smoke, at least in passing, smile at this useless quacking you make of your life. Empty the ashes. Gather your time.

Slim Fingers

They were six feet tall and over, very dark, with tattooed chins and cheeks. The Spanish had heard rumors that they were cannibals, and scientists had found crushed human skulls in their trash pits. They had been driven away to the south by nomadic raiders in the early 1700's. These bits of Quivira knowledge and rumor from his father passed through Young Walker's mind as he searched the field called the Jasper. He had a ten-year history of walking, dozens of objects to study for clues to what a people had done and how they thought, and because he was sixteen, tender and confused, he was susceptible to the romance of personality.

Given the nature of his information, the personalities he came up with were not comforting. He could imagine kindness and humor for all people of the Rocking Deer and Smoky Hill because they were untouched by rumor, but "tall, dark, tattooed cannibals" created a narrow and menacing portrait. Each time he tried to think of a woman and child engaged in an ordinary activity, his teenage love of the bizarre would bring a looming killer on the scene, chewing a suspect piece of gristle. In this way his imagination denied Quivira humanity until the day a hide scraper caught him unaware, threw a personality at him so quickly that the gossip of centuries was useless.

They had started that abundant summer afternoon of flint walking together, assuring each other that many objects lay waiting to be discovered, but as each followed his intuition, they'd drifted apart. Twice their paths had crossed and they'd examined each other's finds—a small, white, triangular point and a chip of obsidian for Young Walker; two brown scrapers for his father—before wandering again.

When Young Walker saw the blunt tip of dark red flint sticking out of a furrow, he thought he'd found a larger than usual arrowpoint. He picked it up and continued walking, keeping his eyes on the ground while his fingers crumbled the dirt clinging to the stone. From his father he had picked up the habit of letting his hand discover the form of the stone before he looked at it. It felt fairly thin, curved, smooth on one side. He ran his thumb over the wide end and felt the worked edge. He had found a hide scraper. Just as he brought it in front of his eyes he shifted it into the working position in his hand. As his fingers curled over the back of the scraper he felt a sudden rush of weakness. The bones of his knees dissolved.

"Oh, man."

It had happened instantly. There was no time to rationalize or chide himself for romantic befuddlement of fact: he had fallen in love centuries too late. He knew the feeling; at sixteen he had fallen in love twice and twice been wounded by indifference. He sat down. The feeling was receding, a scrap on the wind. He let the scraper fall into his palm and stared at it.

Many times he had held a flint tool and tried to imagine the person who had held it before, but these experiments in curiosity had been purely mental, a large hide scraper calling up a picture of a big woman with heavy hands, an arrowpoint suggesting a generic successful hunter. But these were only thoughts of people, silent, odorless, breathless. What he had just experienced was the full impression of a personality that had run through him like a current. There was no picture in his mind, yet he felt he had just made the acquaintance of a smiling and graceful young woman and been stunned with the intensity of her happiness. Twice before he had noticed a girl and his blood had gone quicksilver, every pore on his body had startled, his mind had turned to a pudding of confusion, longing, desperation.

"Oh, man."

He took hold of the scraper again between thumb and first two fingers. She was still there, not a shock this time, but an echo.

"Don't be a dope," he said out loud, but it changed nothing. He returned the scraper to his palm, as if to grasp it too much was the equivalent of staring.

It was maroon, heavily flecked with cream yellow spots, back only slightly domed, sides tapering gracefully back from the scraping edge. Maybe I'm just freaking out because it's a good-looking scraper, he thought, and gripped it again. When he felt her this time he realized it was coming from his own hand, that just beneath his two fingers shallow channels ran across the scraper back, and because his overflowed those narrow channels, he was sensing her slim fingers beneath his own. Yet, if he could say he'd been arrested by the scraper's suggestion of a delicate hand, he still could not explain how the rush of admiration and desire had arrived before thought, without thought, or why he was filled with regret not to have known her.

At the north end of the field his father wandered, hands behind, head down. Young Walker whistled. His father looked up, nodded, began to walk his way.

"Find something, Son?"

"A real nice scraper."

"Oh yeah. It is."

"Take it."

"I can see it okay."

"No, Dad, pick it up and hold it."

"Oh. Hmm. Yeah."

"Feel it?"

"It feels real good to hold, doesn't it? Hmm. Imagine this woman."

"Exactly, Dad."

"No, it really feels like it gives me a buzz."

"That's just what it did to me. A big buzz. I don't know what she looks like but she's just...well, Dad, I think I'm in love."

"Wow. Really?"

"Well, I got a grip on that scraper and just something about the way it felt, I got this feeling. I, like, just found myself liking this girl. Don't ask me how."

"Yeah. I see what you mean. It's almost like holding hands."

"Give it back now, Dad."

"Oh, yeah, here."

"A girl really dug this scraper. She liked using it, and she had this slim little hand. Have you ever noticed how beautiful girls' hands are, Dad?"

"Well, yeah."

"She was probably right where we are now. Man. What's the matter with me, Dad—is it a hormone warp? Has this ever happened to you?"

"No. Not like that. Was there any..."

"All I know is I feel a girl in this stone. Jeez, Dad, I'm getting feelings for a dead cannibal."

"Hey, it could've been worse...like a live cannibal. And maybe those were just nasty rumors."

"Well what about all those skulls?"

"Oh."

"Yeah."

"Those skulls. But so what? A young woman in love with life, they always exist, regardless of other labels."

Young Walker found another point and two more scrapers that afternoon, but he hardly considered them. He kept fetching what he thought of as "her scraper" out of his pants pocket, holding it as he walked, stopping to examine it. The Jasper site had been transformed; it was now her home. Anything he found there became an object used by someone who might have known her. He returned twice to the place where he'd picked up her scraper and stood thinking: here was her lodge where she slept, ate, dreamed and thought.

That night while his father struggled to make spaghetti, Young Walker got all the scrapers he'd found in Quivira and laid them out on the rug. It had occurred to him, after studying her elegant maroon-and-cream hide scraper, that he had a rival. The scraper had been made beautiful by a man, and though he could have made it for his own satisfaction, Young Walker knew that if *he* had been alive when she was, and as stricken with her as he was now, he would have made her just such a scraper to delight her eye and hand. If the gift and gesture made her happy, the stone would be a question, an answer, an invitation, a memory between them. Someone had made that gift, and someone had used it; the scraping edge had been polished and worn. Young Walker thought he had fallen in love with a feeling.

"She was in love, Dad." If she hadn't been, he never would have felt her.

"What's that? The water's boiling."

"You know that scraper I found? What I felt was her happiness."

"Her happiness?" Walker appeared in the living room with a wet wooden spoon. "Hey, these all Quivira scrapers?"

"Thirty-two. And these three are really, really fine."

"Yeah, the one you found today."

"And this little pink one, and this highbacked butterscotch one."

"So let me get this straight. You're gonna feel all the real pretty scrapers?"

"And after supper can you get out all your Quivira scrapers?"

"And then are we going to separate the really fine ones and feel them too?"

"Yeah."

"Like, beautiful scrapers belonged to beautiful women? Are you expecting to feel the same thing you felt today?"

"Well, maybe."

"Mmm. I've heard of going to great lengths to pick up chicks, Son, but man..."

"So lets do it."

"Absolutely. But first you need to come out to the kitchen and throw a spaghetti against the refrigerator."

Walker had many Quivira scrapers, but it took little time to pick out those of superior work and attractive material. Thirty minutes after supper they had added twenty-five scrapers to Young Walker's three exceptional ones. All were symmetrical and carefully worked, all were made from stones that were colorful or had a striking banded or mottled pattern. The eleven larger ones, each almost as long as a thumb, tended to be humpbacked rather than flat, and the material included a dark, mottled purple, terra cotta red with a yellow lightning line, rhubarb pink looped with darker bands, a shiny cream white, a milky white, a blotch pattern of pale pink and blue-gray, a marbled lavender and white, three mottled with red maroon and nougat yellow, and a speckled red and pink with a blaze of white crystals.

Eight smaller scrapers, half a thumb length, were chipped from a light purple mottled with red, a two-tone pink, a dark blood red, marbled yellowish gray, shiny pink, lavender with dark purple stripes and a large white spot, a gray with a cream-colored mantle, and a gray with a long white blaze down its back.

Six very short scrapers made for the tips of the fingers and thumb were bacon flint, white splashed, banded, and streaked with maroon.

The twenty-five scrapers represented the best of the flintworker's efforts. Young Walker held them all, one by one, and felt nothing.

"I'm not surprised, Dad."

"No?"

"Really. I'm not even disappointed."

Walker nodded. "If there had been anything like that with these...well, I remember picking them up, every one of them."

"Nothing happened?"

"Oh, I felt good that such a thing had been made, but not like you felt today."

"I didn't imagine it, Dad."

"No, I don't suppose you did." Walker turned one of the scrapers in his hand. "I dig your idea. I don't know why I never thought of it before. If I could make scrapers and there was a woman I was crazy about, you bet I'd make her the most gorgeous scraper I could—hell, three or four. I'd get them to her somehow, and I'd make real sure she knew they came from me."

Young Walker had begun making two separate groups of the scrapers, placing some next to the one he'd found that day and others to one side.

"If she liked you, Dad, what would she do with it?"

"If she liked me? Use it all the time. It'd be her main scraper."

"Like these here." Young Walker indicated the six scrapers he'd grouped with the one he'd found. "But these nineteen over here, they look sharp, fresh, like they were just made."

"Let me see those." Walker looked carefully at each of the nineteen, ran his thumb across the edges.

"Be damned." He was thinking that he should have noticed the crisp new quality of so many of the exotic scrapers. He would have once, he thought. Young Walker, noticing his father's frustration, allowed himself only an abstract murmur.

"Strange."

"Very. Always strange to find a scraper that doesn't look used. I must have noticed that on each of these when I picked them up, but I've never looked at them together like this."

"Then if all these beautiful ones were gifts, some of them never even got used."

"Uh-huh. Not all women are the same, Son, I know that much. It looks like most of these young women tucked certain ones away. Like they were too special to use. They'd be taking these out in the evenings, looking at them, handling them, thinking about the guy."

"You're onto something, Dad."

Walker would always believe he had walked point in the search for the meaning of the perfect, unused scrapers leading his son to understanding and discovery. Young Walker allowed the fiction. His father needed to see himself as a solver, a man who sniffed clues into a trail, a trail into a road, road into destination.

Young Walker accepted that an arrowpoint, a scraper, a knife, could be made poorly or well, that the way the maker felt at the moment could affect the way the tool turned out, and even that the maker believed the way it looked would influence its efficiency. He had no argument with this, what his father called magic, though he thought the word clumsy, smelling of trickery and illusion. He believed in that link between process and function: he'd made his own walking stick, carving Osage Orange to bring out the golden yellow, smoothing the poll to fit his palm, sanding the stick until it gleamed. Proud of the work he'd done, fond of the product, when he walked with the stick he had absolute faith it would support him if he slipped. It levered him up Flint Hill inclines, parted weeds and overhanging branches in his path, tested muddy ground. At rest, it pleased him with the way the bright grain took light.

But the notion that young men might make beautiful tools as tokens of persuasion, a currency of the heart, hadn't entered his life until the afternoon he'd picked up the freckled maroon scraper and felt the rush of slim fingers.

Essentials of Care

He lay sleepingbagged in the dry limestone creek bed, head on the slope of one bank, feet on the other, staring at stars, bone-tired, trying to think himself past a jammed sleep mechanism.

There was an abundance of causes for Walker's wakefulness. If the Guide hadn't burned down one of his two tents a month earlier, they wouldn't have been forced to sleep four to a tent. The Guide had not volunteered an explanation for having only one tent, but his son had been glad to, the moment Walker and Young Walker stepped into the car for the drive to the Hills.

"We've only got one tent. Dad burned the other one down."

The Guide sighed. He'd decided to spend a couple of hours pulling thistles at the far end of the pasture and didn't think it was fair to have to restart the campfire when he returned. It had been a quiet afternoon, so he laid the wood on, in what he would later think of as an excess of competence. With plenty of insurance on the fire, he was almost to the thistles when he felt the wind come up.

"Oh, shit," he'd said, but went ahead and actually pulled up two thistle plants before he glanced back and saw the greasy black smoke. The only thing he was able to save was a purple towel, which he used to beat out the creeping grass fire; tent, cot, bedroll, and clothes were ash. That night, the Guide slept in the car.

This year the four sleepers had pitched the surviving tent in jack oaks at the base of a hill by a dry, step-across creek; the Old Home Place was too buggy, and the Guide preferred to avoid the pasture with the pond, which still bore the burned patch of his embarrassing canniness.

Sleep still might've been possible, four to a tent, if the two boys had still been fat little cubs, but they were seventeen, taller, thicker, with long arms and feet like great loaves of bread. One was a bodybuilder, one was a skier. They no longer giggled or ran up a sweat in mindless play, and when it was time to chop firewood from the countryside, a task they'd long coveted, it was the sons who took the big ax and sheared the hard deadwood to campfire length.

When he'd left the campfire that night, the last to do so, and crawled into the tent, into the narrow space along one side, before he'd struggled into his bed, causing the other three to shift and grumble in their sleep, he'd already judged the tent an insufficient space for so many shoulders, elbows, and feet. He lay pushed against the canvas by the body of his son, waiting for his thoughts to tumble and unravel. But his mind was stuck wide open; he could hear the sighing of the embers outside as they settled, and he could hear the Guide shift in his sleep at the other side of the tent, and he knew the son of the Guide would also soon shift and then, a few seconds later, his own son. After the first sequence, when he caught a sudden elbow in the chest, he was keyed to the sound of a moving body. His thoughts might pile up and overlap, nearing the nonsense of sleep, but one motion would bring him instantly alert for the flung arm, the flexing knee. The sleep of the others was restless, but the fact that they could sleep at all intensified Walker's irritation.

"This is hell," he said, and repeated it louder. No one answered, but the Guide turned and Walker braced against the wave of motion he knew would be coming his way.

He almost slept once, but was revived by his son's shoulder rolling onto his face. He pushed himself free, managed to get out of his sleeping bag, crawled, avoiding shins, and unzipped the tent, climbing into darkness, a pink blush where the campfire still breathed. He saw that he had forgotten to fold up his lawn chair, so come morning, the seat would be thick with dew. He pulled his sleeping bag out after him and zipped the tent closed. From the bottom of the bag he unrolled his jeans and tee-shirt and put them on, slipped his denim jacket over his shoulders and began to consider what to do in that world of darkness.

He thought of bringing the campfire back, using a concentrated bout of flame-staring to knock himself out, but he would have to wait until the fire burned down before he could sleep, and it was too much trouble to drag the wood over there, and he didn't want to sleep sitting in a lawn chair. He'd done that already. Bunching the bag under his arm, he took a step and discovered he'd left his shoes in the tent.

The dark held thorns, sharp twigs, and shards of rock, so the ball of Walker's foot explored first and, slowly, the toes, the heel, and arch, to grip, monkey-like, a solid footing. He had chosen to walk a dozen steps to the creek bed, and it was just as well the journey was slowed by vulnerable feet; the methodical care he took with each step allowed him to finally sort out bushes, small trees, and the creek bed itself before he reached them. He had no desire to add pain to the list of things keeping him awake.

He found a gentle spot in the creek bed, flat slabs of limestone, earth slopes for shoulders and feet, rolled the bag out and crawled in. He smoked a cigarette and then, collar up against trickling dirt, hat pulled down, folded his arms and bowed his head to sleep, meaning to hold that posture until his mind tired of comment.

But his mind had some thoughts it wished to review, the most urgent concerning the fact that he was lying crosswise in a dark creek bed. Didn't animals use a dry creek bed like a road? Was he not lying across a potential highway for coyote, skunk, bobcat, or farm hound out for the night with a bad attitude? Would not a snake travel the creek because the bare limestone held sun heat? The small sounds of night began to take on form. He raised his head and scanned left and right. The creek met his gaze with dark ambiguity. He shifted shoulders and tried to drop out of the night. Head back on the bank, throat bare to phantom packs of weasels or dogs, he looked at the stars.

They were strangers; he'd spent most of his life looking at the ground.

He might look for the Dippers, the Polestar, the belt of Orion, the litle blur called the Pleiades, The Seven Sisters, The Blue Flint Boys. These had been pointed out to him on midnight lawns, pastures, parking lots. Because he was lying among hills of blue flint, he searched for The Blue Flint Boys but didn't find them, and with few reference points in the massy throw of lights, he was soon lost. Jack oak branches and twigs broke the glittering pattern like black matrix, irregular angled shapes fractured into smaler shapes by crossing twigs, some sections full with stars and others sparse. High up near the twigs a soft flow of air caused the smaller star-filled shapes to wriggle and twist.

Prolonged stargazing inevitably caused Walker to consider his infinitesimal place. He'd thought to numb himself to sleep, but this shifting mandala of dark void and glittering dust soon made him very much aware of himself, a man over fifty, sacked out in a creek bed, stark staring awake.

He saw anger and irritation bringing him there. The tent, elbows and knees, had not kept others awake. He had been the last to leave the fire and would be the last by far to sleep, as if by staying awake he could deny the future.

This might be the last summer they would all four camp in the Hills. The sons had other lives and other claims upon their time. Walker briefly felt old as the shell fossils on which he was propped.

The sleeping hulk in the tent, the son he'd fathered to through letters for most of the year, waiting for summer, who had innocently gouged his ribs and shins, was charting a natural course away.

Christ, thought Walker, all these years of joking about it, and now I am old. His daughter had already turned onto her own path; his son stood at the crossroads, ready in strength and patience, but Walker had no money, no goods, to give him for his journey, no security other than a bed in Walker's house, and a rented house at that. You have failed to administer your life, said the stars.

"Piss off and put me to sleep," Walker answered, unwilling to let his Scandinavian genes throw a doomer on him. He would grow old and he would die. Admitting that was Norski enough. Had it been human nonsense like that, a deep and irreversible curdling of hope that had overtaken his old man? He had surely cursed his last junker years ago.

The old man had introduced him to the world of campfires and riverbanks, advised him to measure himself only against himself, and then slipped into the stars. Walker had had to learn that venom, manufactured from that experience, though it might let him live long, would never let him live wholly, not with part of every passing moment blunted by resentment. Through the long sweep of anger and sadness he found slowly the way to freedom, to be able to give himself absolutely to the moment and at the same time to let each moment go. He would find that the old man had already given him a method and started him on his way: flint tools and the invisible lives they evoked.

The longer he looked at the intent of past minds, moments of crudity or exactness caught on the edges of stones, the clearer the necessity for excellence in his own life became. Like the ones who worked the stones, he would become brittle in the stalks and eventually fall, but unlike them, he hadn't left marks of his mind and spirit on stone to survive beyond all caring.

The magic of caring, anyway, of making the stone a celebration in spite of the limit to life, inevitable dust, was the gift Walker plucked from that dust. He had only his son to give it to, one short summer at a time.

Such magic might take over a stone completely. Both Walker and his son had seen and held the double-handful of a long, notched obsidian blade made by a Karok of northern California, to be held in dances as a symbol of wealth and prestige. Both had seen pictures of the long, elaborate flints excavated from the base of a Maya temple in Honduras, objects made by an individual Walker thought of as the master flintworker of all time.

Nine objects had been found: a blade was at one end of each object, but it was insignificant compared to the remaining three-quarters of length, which blossomed out to either side of the blade into sickle-shaped angles, corners and curves. The worker had known a way to chip into a piece of flint and keep going, leaving a trail of space like a worm feeding its way across a leaf. To chip a notch into the edge of flint required technical savvy; to continue into the body of the flint in a path both meandering and geometrical required artistry beyond Walker's imagination.

The worker had chipped into the sides of the path in places, opening islands of space surrounded by delicate curving and angular peninsulas of flint, barbed tails, bent arms, chin, lips, nose and sweeping forehead of a man, a large headdress of intricate shape. Complex portraits of rulers and gods, the large, eccentric flint scepters were created for a purely symbolic use; they were magic and nothing else. Walker, a child of place, would not find these among the Rocking Deer campers, the dwellers of Smoky Hill or Quivira. Even Quivira, for all its sophistication of design, was still a massive collection of grass huts. He would find the work of people who had not yet gained the time and technique needed to work flint into a glyph of pure thought. The Karok and Maya made metaphors of stone, spiritual tools, the use of which was solely to convey meaning. The meaning of the stones chipped by the people of Walker's circle was determined by use, hide scraper, arrowpoint, and the expression of spirit was limited to the making of common tools in an uncommonly beautiful way. In some of them Walker thought he had seen hope, desire, respect, even worship.

I made it for the dignity of the buffalo.

I made it for the success of the hunter.

I made it for the pleasure of the woman.

I made it for the sake of the spirit.

His son had read these thoughts as well. There would be times he would need them, Walker thought, to help embrace joy or sorrow when it came, and to help let it go, for time would not wait for long answers. One moment you were young and stupid, driving to Denver to see your children, and back again, without a spare tire, without the thought of a spare tire, and the next you're knocking on a farmhouse door and it's answered not by the man who's let you walk his fields many years, same corpulence, same red face and white forehead, but a stranger, and when you ask about the man you knew, the big new farmer tells you he's retired and moved to town.

"Oh, and you're his son?"

"Grandson."

The stars were changing and would continue to change. It was the time of night when lovers struggle for balance. Dawn was a long time to come and the campfire was down to luminous ashes. Across the flow of dark, the tent breathed an even rhythm.

The Cottonwood Line

Flat on his back at the edge of a plowed field, a clattering cottonwood day, a fitful breeze on the Hummingbird, the Rocking Deer, the Little Owl, Two Wings, Jasper, the orange light of his eyelids could be anywhere. The warm ripples of wind take their time rolling over him. The sky he has stopped looking at is a seamless pale blue, or a deep ringing turquoise, or filled with thunderheads coasting, or a nearly white blue sketched with thin cloud ribs.

All skies were just beyond his closed eyes and the random clash of swaying leaves was a time line in each ear. He had walked out of himself, around the corrugated field, until he found his own wandering tracks every few steps. Swinging his eyes on the rain-smooth skin of the furrows, he did not find, or did not see, the flint arrowpoint, hide scraper, or knife he searched for, and having lost anticipation, he simply roamed, coasting his eyes, thinking less of tomorrow's meatloaf, the legs of women, the canteen of water he should have brought, water still in the kitchen faucet of his house. Thinking less and finally not at all of the insects that cross his vision, wrestling their way up and over monumental clods, and less, certainly, of the fumbles of his life. Not even the victories remain. His name falls out of his head and sticks in the dirt. Left behind, surrendered of thought, jettison, jettison, he knows no one, no thing, but the rhythm of meaningless walk, and so falls, empty, dead to purpose. Ready to be anywhere, he is everywhere cottonwood leaves have rattled above his closed eyes, free of praise or blame, to feel the place beyond the collection of creatures and beyond the names of the creatures.

He knew the names of most animals, birds, and reptiles he encountered, and some of the names of insects and plants. At one time he had burned to know those names; at one time he had known even the Latin names of all the hawks and owls of his country, and a few of the snakes as well. A bird seldom gives more than a dozen wingbeats or song notes before it is named. He knows if he is looking at a Diamondback Rattlesnake (Crotalus Adamanteus) or a Prairie Rattlesnake (he has forgotten the Latin name). But he soon found that names, medicine for the intellect, were dangerous to vision. The tendency to mask creature with label led to a tendency to perceive the abstraction instead of the thing, which led to blindness. The strange bird, once identified as Red-Headed Woodpecker, became all Red-Headed Woodpeckers. In making the name important, he saw only Red-Headed Woodpeckers, but did not see the one that was a joker, or the pensive one, the bewildered, the fierce. And never mind all the other traits they could be named for; their drumming, penetrating call, swimming flight, stark black-and-white pattern; they are all Red-Headed Woodpeckers now. And so, having artfully tangled himself in names, he had to learn to see and hear the thing itself new each time.

He could not stop using names, like the name of the tall plant whose jingling leaves carry him along in his rest, but he could stop focusing on them. Then the world filled with many spectacular things, some of which pecked on wood.

Sometimes a creature would come near him where he lay; he could hear the nervous sounds. At some perimeter of their own choosing, they would retreat or lose interest. Sometimes they approached. He had once opened his eyes to find himself crawling with tiny black and red dots, covered with ladybugs.

In all the times he had listened in on the cottonwood line, he had heard nothing of the people who once walked, hunted, lived in these fields before they were fields. Traces of human spirit always remained, but riding through the world on his ears was good only for feeling the spirit of the place, without human echo. The Jasper, the Rocking Deer, orange and blue riffing through his eyelids, he got no sound of water boiling in a clay pot, no feedback of prehistoric squabble; just the wind and the leaves defining it, a song to lift a body by its ears and fling it in any direction.

He was a speck, lying at the edge of a field named for hummingbirds, a long hill of raw plowed dirt with nothing to interest a hummingbird. Floating, he renewed the grove of trees that used to be, the two-storey white house circled by trumpetflower vines, the gnarled man and woman with white hair, the sudden, vibrant hummingbirds circling the porch. The story had been plowed under, along with stories of those who'd come before. To renew this by dying to civilization in the remembered shade of cottonwoods was one of the purposes of walking. Under phantom cottonwoods and impartial wind, his muscles pushed against the earth.

Summer Morning

Unplanted fields steam
pink vine flowers
a memory of breath

the print of bare feet
going nowhere